Collective Mind

by V. Klyukin

2016

Turning from the bottom.

Part 1. Collective Mind

1

One of the packages went flying into the center of the hall, another one over the reception desk. A moment later there was a loud explosion, then a second, and a third. Smoke quickly filled the space of the Agency.

Isaac instinctively covered his head. He didn't feel any pain, only his eyes hurt and his throat was sore from the pungent smoke. Nobody seemed to scream or whimper, but people were beginning to cough everywhere. Isaac saw the terrified face of the reception clerk in front of him. She was in shock but seemed okay. Suddenly, she let out a cry and right away several other women began to scream.

The fire-extinguishing system went off and water ran down from the ceiling. A nasty loud wail of a siren filled the space. Another explosion – or rather a thud – was heard. There was no fire or shrapnel, no shock wave either, just the smoke. However, after the next thud Isaac felt a wave of panic and irrational, hideous fear. He realized it wasn't over yet and anything could still happen, that after the thud a real explosion can come. Fear made him crawl towards the door, seeing nothing, blinded by the acrid gas, tears streaming out of his eyes. Thinking calmly was something he couldn't do at the moment, he functioned only on instincts.

"Where's the main computer? Where do you keep this devil's heart?" the terrorist screamed in a booming voice, lifting the respirator away from his face.

His voice brought Isaac back to reality, forcing him to focus. Since the terrorist breathed the air without the respirator, it was not poisonous. This wasn't a chemical attack. What Isaac had to do was cautiously crawl towards the door, trying not to attract attention.

"Move it, or I'll kill'er!" shouted the attacker.

A woman squealed again. The old man nearby was breathing heavily and coughing. The water had settled down the gas a bit, and the air was gradually clearing, so Isaac had to move quickly.

"Askin' ya for the last time! And don't anybody move! You! The doomed one!" Through the smoke Isaac could see the gun firmly pointed at him.

At that moment Isaac couldn't think rationally, but he registered one disappointing thought: he had just destroyed not only his own life, but his sister Vicky's as well. That morning he was sure that it couldn't be worse, but he was wrong, and his recklessness would cost them both their future.

Well, yes, his future turned out to be not what he had thought. He was an excellent student in high school and easily got into a prestigious university. At that time, his future seemed totally clear. But we can't predict what will happen in the world in a year, or five, or ten. Neither can we predict the lives of those around us, or our own. A war or an epidemic, or even such a seemingly positive thing as progress, can change the world in just a few months! So here you are, studying, working your tail off, taking out educational loans, passing exams, not sleeping nights, looking forward to becoming a specialist in demand, and – poof! – suddenly the damn Agency appears, and all your knowledge gets outdated in just one moment, and you are totally screwed.

As a teenager, Isaac craved adventures and discoveries. He envied the young professor from the film *Godzilla* and the cool nerve of Jean Reno's character. He saw himself in the future, traveling and making appearances at scientific exhibitions and congresses. At first, everything went smoothly – he was a graduate of a highly prestigious university, a young engineer. But after being presented with a beautiful diploma with the name Isaac Leroy embossed in gold, the future bartender hadn't come across any more gold anywhere. Living in glamorous Monaco, the European paradise, one would think life is cool and glorious. But that's not the case when you have absolutely no money. The sun and sea are free, but you have to pay for the rest. The way reality turned out was a bit different from Isaac's dreams. He had been dreaming of America, and he got it – "America" was the name of the bar where he worked. As a matter of fact, the owner looked a little like Jean Reno and had a temperament every bit as ferocious as Godzilla's. As for the real

America – the best place of all for the brilliant and talented minds – he never got to go there. Now there was no sense in traveling: if you have your creative energy, just go ahead and sell it to the Agency, no need to fly anywhere. Who could have thought before, that instead of oil, uranium or palladium the most valuable resource in the world would be human creativity?

The most ironic thing of all is that his beloved science was to blame!

A few years ago, Jeremy Link, a Professor at the University of London and Doctor of bioenergetics, identified human energy, which was responsible for an individual's originality, fantasy and imagination. He called it "orange energy", or simply OE. Skeptics made fun of him, but the professor calmly continued studying the phenomenon called "creativity". Five years later, Link successfully downloaded creativity for the first time. Two years after that, he learned how to store and use it.

Having obtained the OE of four old scientists and a couple dozen volunteers, the professor summoned a press conference and introduced a new type of a computer that he called *Collective Mind* – a bio hard drive computer that worked off human creativity.

Jeremy Link picked a random person from the audience who turned out to be a third-year student, put some sort of a semi-transparent helmet on his head, connected the student to his strange creation, and squinting slyly gave the guy a task from quantum physics. The audience began to whisper in disbelief, somebody giggled, but however impossible the task was to solve, the student easily did so!

Having found out that the young man was a medical student, Link gave him another task – to think about the cure for cancer.

The audience froze. It took the young man a couple of minutes to do his calculations, and then he passed his solution to Link. The professor displayed the sheet with the calculations and the thickly underlined final solution on the big screen and uttered contentedly:

"Ladies and gentlemen! This is the new generation cancer treatment – the most effective one in existence!"

For a few seconds there was dead silence, and then everyone heard a gasp – the dean of the department of medicine duly appreciated the solution.

The professor was about to continue his lecture, but at that moment the hall exploded with applause. After savoring the moment of triumph, Link carried on:

"Energy is just energy. It is similar for people of different races and religions, it doesn't have language barriers; it can't contract viruses, has no tastes and preferences, no emotions; can't have a violent temper. What matters for *Collective Mind* is the power of the human cerebral battery. It can unite specialists of different professions – chemists and physicists, musicians and artists, astronomers and restaurant chefs. All of them together, to be precise. Having received the OE of several ordinary students, it will outclass Albert Einstein."

That day everyone who wished was welcomed to measure their own level of creativity. A long line formed quickly and the professor himself used the meter, that looked like a simple thermometer, to report approximate results. If anyone wanted to get a more precise level of their OE, they could put on the helmet that was connected to *Collective Mind*.

That very night the scientific world, the press and the Internet literally went crazy. There were hopes, doubts and excitement, but in the end, everyone agreed that *Collective Mind* can be called the first artificial intellect in the world. It was very useful, but the most important thing is that it was safe! Disconnected from an operator it could do no harm, since it cannot create tasks and make decisions on its own.

It was not just a scientific breakthrough, but the beginning of a new evolutionary leap. Each new portion of OE increased the power of the bio-processor, with thoughts stored automatically in it. A lab-assistant connected to *Collective Mind* temporarily acquired the pooled creativity of all the people whose individual OE had been downloaded before. An idea that was previously abstract immediately became concrete, proper and meaningful. Virtually any problem was processed by the computer like a simple jigsaw puzzle. Missing pieces became as clear as if they were traced out on paper; gaps were analyzed, and the idea itself was finalized, with tasks growing more and more complex.

Human beings aren't computers, they can't concentrate intensely enough to visualize a picture in its finest details. They don't possess absolute memory, often missing important parts. Link's eliminated such a problem. Activated by an operator, it remembered everything up to the smallest detail.

The world press was competing in exalted headlines: "World's First Artificial Mind", "Safe Artificial Intellect Created", "Everyone Can Become Part of the Mega Brain", and even "First Step to Immortality". People were talking about and recalling how many scientists had wrestled with a problem, solving it just partly. Some brilliant ideas seemed impossible to implement, even utopian, but the answer was really within easy reach. How many scientists died without ever bringing their research to conclusion, taking their ideas with them. What would have happened had such a computer appeared earlier? How many lives would have been saved!

Three days after the news was announced, Professor Link – the most brilliant inventor in human history – disappeared without a trace.

Having handed over the technology to a friend of his, Anthony Blake – UN Deputy Secretary-General, the professor vanished. Temporarily, as people thought at the time. Everyone was sure that the new "Person of the Year" and Nobel laureate was going to reappear soon, but they thought wrong. And now, after seven years have passed, no one still had any idea about the professor's whereabouts. Most thought he was dead.

Very likely the decision to transfer the technology to the unbiased UN saved the world from someone's domination, and possibly even from World War III. The United Nations International Collective Mind Agency, COMUNA, was set up and in one year it not only presented hundreds of extremely useful technologies, but also made creativity the most expensive resource on the planet.

Three years after *Collective Mind* was presented, the Agency completely vanquished such diseases as cancer, AIDS and diabetes. Even smoking became a thing of the past. Mankind finally stopped abusing natural resources: oil, gas and minerals consumption dropped dramatically, and most cars ran on non-polluting hydrogen. Plastic became soluble; metals, coated with a new compound, didn't rust; problems of Freon, CO_2, and other harmful emissions have been forgotten. COMUNA became a very successful commercial institution as well, priding itself as a host of inventions and achievements. The Agency earned fantastic profits from the sale of patents, at the same time paying extremely generous fees to those who uploaded their creativity. Four *Collective Mind* servers were installed in different countries, along with a considerable network of OE downloading centers.

2

Slowly getting ready in the morning, Isaac had a cup of bad coffee and went into the shower, which he loathed. It was just like his life, dysfunctional – either scalding him with heat or dousing with ice-cold water.

As he was taking a shower he felt the familiar rising anger. He had some great ideas, but the world had changed way too fast and just spat him and his ideas out. He lived in extreme poverty, vaguely imagining what he'd be doing the day after tomorrow. Someone might call it freedom, not having a strict schedule and planned holidays. Maybe it is so, but in a couple of months of such "freedom" one can go completely nuts. There's much more comfort in the clarity of life. Although, not the kind of clarity he was about to obtain. Today was his last day being poor. Tomorrow the agency will make him rich.

He wanted to drag out the time, think about anything, just to avoid getting dressed and going to the download center. He wanted to drag things out since thinking was also work, and his typical excuse for not doing something.

As soon as Isaac went outside it started to pour. He didn't get wet, though – the device he invented turned on automatically. Finished just the other day, the first prototype was unique. A generator collected the energy of falling raindrops, creating a magnetic field, which didn't let the water through. One could stand there in the rain and remain completely dry. The patent could have solved all Isaac's problems, but as usual, he was out of time.

Deep in thought, he didn't notice how he reached the Agency. He didn't feel like going in at all, but there was no other way: the bank gave him the final warning and his apartment had to be auctioned off, because he had no way to pay for it. Most importantly, his sister Vicky – his most loved person in the world – needed another surgery. So the only thing he really could do was to sell his OE. He knew what was going to happen to him after, what happened to those who sold their creativity. His best friend, Pascal, had fallen in love and sold his OE two years ago.

At the very center where Isaac was about to sell his. He threw a last glance at the sea and pushed the front door.

It was cozy inside, with soft music coming from somewhere under the ceiling and Agency officers briskly filling in the necessary forms. As for donors, there were four of them: a well-groomed older gentleman; a tired-looking, chubby woman of about fifty; a young man, lacking any expression on his face; and a hippy-looking hobo, who, luckily, though strangely, did not smell. Five portions of creativity ready to replenish the power of the artificial brain.

On the wall, there was a poster showing a smiling man sitting by a swimming pool. The caption on the poster read: "I'm happy to have gifted people what was granted to me from above!" Former donors did look happy, indeed. The Agency made a lifelong support contract with and took care of its newly acquired "Happies".

Isaac had already seen this and other colorful posters when he came to the Agency for an interview, and to measure his OE. Everyone had a different amount of creativity, so one could have it calculated for free prior to the procedure, and find out how much money they can count on. When he came in the first time, he thought that this was just a safety net, that he would surely have enough time to get the money. However, it turned out that selling the rights for his rain protection device, which he called *V-Rain*, was a much more difficult task than it could seem. The patent office was now sort of a vestigial relic. These days, everyone bought their technologies only from COMUNA. In the end he ran out of time, his sister got worse and her surgery was quickly scheduled. Even though there was still no money, or any prospect of getting any.

That was when Isaac made his decision. He knew that his creativity level was high and having sold his OE, he'd have enough money for surgery, for buying his own house, and for many other things. He definitely would never forgive himself if his sister died. He wouldn't want any money then. Better to be a Happy with a zero creative index, than a smart guy whose wealth cost the life of the only person he really cared for.

So yes, this was the other side of professor Link's *Collective Mind* – thousands of gifted people turned into meaningless ruck. But was this a price too high? After all, wars and diseases that had taken millions of lives every year were now a thing of the past.

The cold tip of the creativity meter touched Isaac's temple and stopped the flow of recollections. One of the Agency's clerks glimpsed at the meter readings, wrote down something and turned to another donor. Isaac felt like hypothesizing about the other donors, about who they were, and where they came from. The old man clearly decided to supplement his pension plan, or maybe was just a patriot. Straight-backed, despite his age, he was not slouching at all. He was probably not from the area, since many people came from other places to upload their OE and then stay in this paradise. The hobo, most likely, was also looking for money, tired of living on the street. Even with a climate as beautiful as that of Monaco, living on the street is not the best thing. The plain-looking, goofily dressed young man was trifling a photo of some girl, so probably his reason was the same as Pascal's – love.

Isaac never had time to finish his thought. The hobo leaned away from the creativity meter, and suddenly jumped up, grabbing everyone's attention. He pulled out a large crucifix and screamed:

"May the Lord be with us!" As he began throwing the explosives.

That was when Isaac made his unsuccessful attempt to flee...

"The doomed one!"

These words tolled in Isaac's head like an alarm bell. Scared and full of adrenaline, he froze, not moving a finger. His eyes saw nothing. He hated himself for this pathetic attempt to flee. It was not him he worried about, it was Vicky. If he got killed now, she would inevitably die too. How could he have acted so stupid, without even knowing if the terrorist had accomplices or if the door was unlocked? How could he risk Vicky's life so recklessly?

"Please, don't kill me!" He mumbled huskily, closing his eyes tight.

There was no answer and Isaac slowly opened his eyes. The smoke was clearing and his eyes no longer watered. When he cautiously looked at the terrorist, he couldn't help but laugh: the thing pointing at him was not a gun, it was the crucifix! Water, smoke and fear portrayed the big black thing in the terrorist's hand as a pistol.

The terrorist beckoned him to get on his feet and suddenly gripped the receptionist by her throat. With his other hand he held something to her back and shouted:

"Where is it? Where's *Collective Mind*?"

The girl gasped and fainted. She didn't fall to the floor, because the terrorist was holding her tight. The security guard, still on his feet, looked as if he had no idea what to do, too scared to move.

"Let her go," the old man, who was among the donors, suddenly said in a firm, but calm voice. "She's just an office worker, not likely to know anything. My name is Colonel Joyce. Tell me what is it you want?"

"What I want is to destroy this devil's machine. I want to tear its devil's heart out!"

"Hmmm," thought Isaac. "Yet another religious fanatic, and it looks like he's genuinely insane."

He stood there obediently, gradually recovering his wits. His panic was receding. The news sometimes reported terrorist attacks on the Agency. But these were rare, and besides, when you watch something on TV it doesn't occur to you that the same thing could actually happen in real life, your life.

The colonel got up off his chair and asked the guard in a commanding voice:

"Where's your central computer?"

The guard shrugged in uncertainty and the old man addressed his question to one of the employees.

"Over th-th-there," one woman gasped out, stammering through her tears, and waving her hand in the direction of a big futuristic-looking silver computer. It was located in the room separated from the reception hall by a glass wall.

The terrorist pushed the woman aside. In two rapid strides he reached the back office door and kicked it open. He lifted the computer above his head and slammed it down hard onto the floor. Ripping the wires, he furiously raised it again and again above his head and slammed

12

it onto the stone floor until it fell to pieces. As if trying to reduce them to dust, he began to stomp those pieces with his foot.

The security guard was still standing on the same spot, glued to the ground.

"Everyone down on the floor, cover your heads! Don't do anything!" roared the colonel, getting down himself.

The ferocious power in his order sent everyone tumbling unquestioningly to the floor. Even the security guard obeyed. Isaac was the only one left standing. He didn't want to piss off the terrorist again.

The hobo carried on smashing the computer in the office, frenziedly ripping out wires and various attachments. Isaac could hear plastic splintering, and through this racket came the wailing of a siren. The police! He remembered that the police station was just a block away. He heard the sound of shattering glass and then a monstrous blow to the head knocked him off his feet. He lost consciousness.

3

It took a while before Isaac could think clearly, his head was buzzing and spinning, and he felt slightly nauseous. They were dragging him somewhere, with his arms in handcuffs, painfully twisted behind his back. A van, a police station, iron bars slamming loudly... He fully recovered his consciousness only when he was in the cell.

"Never mind, they'll figure things out," he thought wearily, sitting down on the metal bed. Still feeling a bit sick, he closed his eyes and instantly passed out.

He dreamt of a war, a big war. He didn't know who was fighting whom or why, but he saw a nuclear explosion and a plane falling. Entire neighborhoods were set on fire. He saw many different cities that had no names, and all he knew was that one of them was Paris. Isaac observed the immense, towering conflagration from a hill about thirty kilometers away. He couldn't make anything out clearly, but he knew for certain that it was Paris. He was looking, spellbound, at the appalling spectacle, when suddenly soldiers drove up, six or maybe eight of them.

There was no fear, he calmly emptied his clip into the first two soldiers, grabbed his rifle and killed the others. There was no emotions, he killed quickly and without a single hitch, feeling slightly frustrated that the bullets – he could see that they were bright blue – flew through the air too slowly. Then there was darkness. The picture had disappeared. Isaac was somewhere between sleep and waking. He even started trying to analyze his dream, while still being in it.

"In real life I am not capable of murdering someone, but this wasn't the first time I killed in a dream. What can you say about the life of a man, who dreams about cities burning, planes crashing and wars being waged?"

Someone was prodding Isaac insistently in the side, and he finally woke up. He just wanted to be left alone. All he wanted was to sleep. His head was filled with some kind of soft goo. Weariness had eaten its way into his thoughts and settled there. But his annoying neighbor would not stop prodding. The drowsiness in Isaac's eyes gradually dispersed and he recognized the man next to him. He was in the prison cell with the terrorist! Isaac knew there must have been some sort of a mistake.

After waking up Isaac, the hobo persisted on staring into his eyes.

"Hey, how are you doing?" He inquired.

"Fine," Isaac answered.

"That's good, good. You sure?"

"Fine," Isaac repeated angrily.

The stranger gave him another searching look.

"What's your name, lad?"

"Fine," hissed Isaac again and closed his eyes.

"My name's Mr. Elvis. I'm the Messiah, I fight the devil. I saved you. We've got to…"

Isaac heard the stranger speaking on and on. He opened and closed his eyes repeatedly, without attempting to understand what this madman was driveling about. His head hurt badly enough already.

Suddenly he felt something on his palm, something hard and prickly. He tried to turn away, but Elvis jerked him rather sharply by the shoulder.

"Hey, you? Don't you understand? I've been talking to you for half an hour and you still don't understand?"

"What? Yes, I understand, I do," Isaac gasped out. He could say anything to get this guy off his back.

"What does he want from me? Hell, I'm in here because of him. Someone clubbed me over the head because of this asshole. I wish those knuckleheads would get on with figuring this all out. Maybe I need to go to the hospital," Isaac's thoughts flowed sluggishly through his head.

He closed his eyes, but soon felt someone shaking him by the shoulder with crude determination.

Elvis continued spitting his words:

"Hell spawn! Heart of the devil! Cursed machine! This devil will bring misery upon all of us! I saw the light, the determination in your eyes. They will take this away from me…"

It was some kind of a hideous dream. A waking nightmare. Isaac tried to stand up and call a guard, but there was such sharp pain in his head that he groaned loudly and fell back on his cot.

"God has no need for soulless bodies. The end will come soon..." Elvis went on raving, as if nothing had happened. "Are you listening to me?"

The hobo didn't look like he was going to give up. He seemed blinded by his own insanity.

"Orange energy is people's souls, don't you understand? They're taking away our souls. That is what makes us human."

"Gibberish. Roaring. Roaring in my head. Everything's strange. I'm so thirsty," Isaac thought.

"Well then?" Mr. Elvis was certain that what he was yelling out was convincing, even though Isaac didn't say a single word.

A sharp pain in Isaac's shoulder woke him up completely and he concentrated.

"And only by tearing out the devil's heart and destroying it, can I complete my mission. What you have in your hands is absolute evil! Destroy it! Burn it!"

Only now did Isaac finally realize that everything that was happening was real, and that he was holding an object that looked like a piece of a microcircuit. Of course! It was from that computer, a piece of the motherboard with some kind of circuits and microchips on it.

"Henri Cavalier, get out here."

"My name's Mr. Elvis!" the crazy messiah growled, then he turned to Isaac and added in a whisper: "Remember what I told you. Burn the heart of the devil. Promise me. And then we will be victorious!"

Isaac nodded, and his thoughts immediately turned to Vicky.

"Oh, God! The surgery... The money for the surgery. Oh, God! I'll be too late. Where am I? Oh, God! Vicky!"

It was a nightmare: the jail cell, the policemen running around, Elvis. Isaac hammered desperately on the bars several times with his hands, but no one took any notice of him. Only once did a doctor come, examined Isaac's head, shined a little torch into his eyes and said indifferently that it was no big deal, that Isaac would live. He left, leaving behind some kind of a prescription. This was a nightmare. Only it wasn't a dream.

"Isaac Leroy!"

Isaac opened his eyes and stared at the policeman who was shining a flashlight in his face. Isaac took an instant dislike to him. First, because there was a bright light shining in his eyes; and second, because shining a flashlight in someone's eyes was quite abusive. Especially since he was innocent.

"Out you come!"

The attempt to stand up gave him a dull, aching pain. Isaac sat back down again. Something pricked his hand. The motherboard! He put the hand holding the piece of the computer into his pocket. "What a fool I am," he thought. "What did I take it for? If they find it, I'll never beat the rap." The words of Mr. Elvis came to his mind.

"Come on, move it, you little shit," Isaac heard the same malicious voice say. "I'm not going to hang out here all night because of you."

The policeman walked into the cell and put handcuffs on Isaac. They walked down a long corridor, turned the corner and went into an office.

"Patrice, take the handcuffs off him and bring him something to drink," the officer sitting in the office told the policeman who had woken up Isaac so crudely.

"Good evening," Isaac heard the dry voice say, this time speaking to him.

"Evening," Isaac mumbled. His hands had turned numb from being in his pockets for too long.

Feeling the piece of the motherboard in his hand and realizing in how much danger he was, Isaac clutched it tightly and pushed it deeper into his pocket.

The pocket was strangely empty. Although, why was that strange? They'd probably taken everything he had as a safety measure. His belt was missing too. Now he understood why his trousers kept slipping down during the short walk. He wondered where Mr. Elvis had been hiding the motherboard. They must have searched him. But that was a fanatic for you – he would give his life for the cause, so hiding a microcircuit was no big deal.

The policeman was confident.

"I've already gotten to the bottom of everything, but we need to run through a few formalities, so let's get started quickly and then you can go home."

Isaac nodded again. He didn't understand what these formalities could be. He wanted to find out as soon as possible how Vicky was, and dump the dangerous object that was in his pocket.

"First name?"

"Isaac."

"Last name?"

"Leroy."

"Age and date of birth."

"Twenty-nine, December 28."

"Parents' names?"

"Alexander Leroy and Anna Kramer."

Isaac kept on and on, answering questions as precisely as he could. The interrogation wasn't bad, but he wanted to sit down. He kept shifting from one foot to the other.

The officer looked up from the report.

"I'm sorry, have a seat! I'm not usually very courteous during an interrogation. A habit. Pardon me. Take a seat on the chair."

Altogether the questioning and drawing up the report took about twenty minutes. Isaac explained why he was standing; he didn't know the police was going to storm the Agency.

The officer's name was Captain Robert. He explained to Isaac that he had been stunned when the Agency was stormed, because only two people were standing – the terrorist and Isaac. The security guard in the Agency had switched on his walkie-talkie, so when they stormed the place, the assault team knew that all the hostages were lying down. That was why they had taken Isaac for an accomplice.

However, the testimony of the other victims had completely convinced Captain Robert that Isaac wasn't involved in the terrorist attack. The captain checked that Isaac was there to download his OE, having first drawn up a provisional contract. The captain read it and discovered that Isaac's only relative, Victoria Frank, was in the hospital, waiting for surgery, and the contract stipulated that the cost of the surgery should be paid out of the COMUNA money. Thus, his final doubts about Isaac were gone.

"You can collect your things now," Robert added calmly. "By the way, what's this gismo?" he asked, holding out the *V-Rain*. "I can tell you quite frankly that I deleted it from the inventory list of your things. Otherwise, we would have to hold you for another week, until we figured out that this little thing wasn't connected to the attack in any way. I'm really sorry, we dealt with Cavalier first and sent him to Marseilles, and then a whole horde of people descended on us: our bosses, prosecutors, the deputy prefect, journalists. It took us a long time to get around to you. And then, your sister's surname isn't the same as yours. I didn't know she was your stepsister. But I checked all the information on you today, so that you could get back home, even if it is late. Off you go, it's already ten o'clock."

"It's my invention. Harmless. It's just to keep the rain off."

Isaac picked up his things from the captain's desk, and the *V-Rain* squeaked plaintively. Captain Robert's friendly demeanor made him feel uneasy

"Isaac, I'm very sorry," the captain suddenly added in a quiet, fatherly voice. "The news I have from the hospital isn't too cheerful. Your sister has been in a coma since this afternoon."

The ground suddenly crumbled under Isaac's feet. He started crying. His mouth still felt dry, but tears the size of large hailstones rolled down his cheeks. He couldn't say a single word. Change scattered onto the floor and his hands, full of his possessions, shook so badly that he simply couldn't find his pocket.

It wasn't fair! Bastards! Nobody specifically. Everybody. Isaac hated them all.

"I spoke to the doctor and he says there's much hope. Of course, it's bad, but her life isn't in any danger. You'll definitely find the money for the surgery. And you should also see a doctor yourself, our medic said you have a slight concussion."

No one was waiting for Isaac in the dark street. There was nothing for him in the future, either. Rage against the whole world and his own helplessness filled him. He picked up a stone and threw it into a shop window. The siren wailed and Isaac ran into an alleyway. He got home at dawn.

It was already lunchtime and Isaac was just barely waking up. His body was aching from everything that happened the day before – the explosion, the concussion and the visit to the police station didn't go unnoticed. Yet, his heart was aching even more –Vicky being in a coma didn't let him rest for a minute. When he went to bed the night before, he couldn't even undress, and Elvis's present was painfully prickling his leg, as a reminder of his promise.

Isaac pulled out the piece of the motherboard from his pocket and looked at it closer. This was just a piece of an electronics device, nothing special. Some parts of it were still intact. Elvis will spend a lot of time behind bars, not even knowing that he didn't really destroy anything, but Isaac's plans. Actually, it was the other way around, and in reality, he did Isaac a favor. If not for Elvis, Isaac would have been a Happy or a Vegie, as opponents of OE upload call it, by now. Now he unexpectedly won some time and gained new hope. He didn't want to feel doomed.

Isaac undressed and plodded into the bathroom. Looking at himself in the mirror, he opened his eyes wide and raised his eyebrows. Then he squeezed his eyes shut and opened them again.

"I look no better than a homeless man," thought he.

Gazing out at him from the mirror was a thin young man with dark hair and piercing grey-green eyes. His nose was a bit on the large side, so were his ears, and his cheeks were slightly sunken. You couldn't really say that he was handsome, but girls always saw something in him and they probably knew better. Even the small scar on his chin didn't spoil his looks. Instead, it added a feel of the brutality that was lacking in his character. Isaac made an attempt to tidy up his hair, but it still stuck out rebelliously. He glanced at the uneven stubble on his face.

"Unshaved as always, and I'll remain that way. Women like stubble for some reason," was the first good thought that came to him that day. "Although they complain that it's prickly all the time."

He tried to imagine what it would be like if he stood by the mirror first thing in the morning, and a girl would walk up to him and run her hand over his unshaven cheek like he's seen in commercials. But that was all television. That sort of thing didn't happen in real life. In real life he would take a quick shower and run off to work. The few girls Isaac has dated before never did anything like that.

He thought that for something like that to happen, one needed a real girlfriend. One who would love him, not just some casual hookup. There hasn't been a genuine girlfriend in Isaac's life since his sister got sick, but he never really thought about it. There was no place for a girlfriend in his life right now.

No one needs a boyfriend with problems, especially one who's nearly homeless. Everyone has enough headaches of their own, they can do without someone else's. After discovering that Vicky was ill, Isaac didn't have the time or the money or, more importantly, the desire to have a real relationship.

He had to make do with the drunk girls who came his way at the bar. They often hinted at, or told him straight out, that he was cute, tall and well built. In fact, he wasn't that tall, but that didn't bother Isaac. It wasn't a problem in his life. No one needed to explain to Isaac what female tourists had in mind when they said that sort of thing to the first young guy they met. Take what is given, as they say. He was always short on stamina after a long shift, and those short-term lady friends simply highlighted that nobody needed him for anything else. But what he wanted was to be genuinely loved. Isaac could really be very dedicated to a woman. It's just that he had no chance of showing it. He was ready to sacrifice himself even for his sister. When she fell ill, Isaac got deprived of the only source of genuine love that was given to him.

Isaac came out of his thoughts next to his computer, with a cup of coffee in his hand.

"Oh, coffee! When did I manage to make that? Some things get done on autopilot, as if you have your own bartender sitting inside you,"

Isaac chuckled to himself, but he wasn't feeling cheerful. "Stop. Why go straight to the computer? That's a habit. I have to call the hospital and find out about Vicky."

"Grace Kelly Hospital, how can I help you?" the phone said in the familiar rapid manner.

"My name is Isaac Leroy..." Isaac cleared his throat, his voice was hoarse. "I'm calling to find out about the condition of my sister, Victoria Frank."

"One moment."

He was connected to a different line, introduced himself again and was reconnected again. Finally, he heard the nurse on duty in the right department rummaging through her papers. Clatter of a keyboard and then a considerate voice chirped in his ear.

"Monsieur Leroy," Isaac could never get used to that ceremonial form of address, and winced every time. "Monsieur Leroy, your sister's condition is stable, the worst has passed."

"But I was told she's in a coma! I want to speak to her doctor."

The stupid, pathetic hope that was born out of the medical term "stable condition" was a mistake. The doctor confirmed that Vicky was in a coma, but only yesterday her condition was much worse. She could have died. It was all over now, the doctors were monitoring her progress, and it would soon be clear when the surgery could be performed.

"There's no need to hurry with the money, Monsieur Leroy. Nonetheless, we have to be ready to carry out the surgery at any moment," the doctor concluded, said goodbye and hung up.

Isaac was trembling. He instantly pictured Vicky pale and fragile, seeking help and sustained by only hope. Something inside of him broke and Isaac burst out crying. It was painful to realize that he was the one that delayed the surgery. He felt sorry for Vicky and for himself.

"She could have died, because I didn't even consider selling my creativity till the very end," thought he in frustration. "The intrusion of the dumb-ass terrorist could have taken the lives of both of us. Why did I not come at least a day before? What a fool I was! Worse than any Veggie. The damned Agency! They have everything they need to cure people: the technologies, methodologies, high-class specialists. All of that thanks to sucking creativity out of people like me and Pascal. But no one benefits from it all because the treatment has to be paid for. Until we go to that freaking Agency to sell our OE, those dearest to us just keep getting worse!"

What was going on in the world?! The media praised COMUNA. The whole world was rejoicing at the rosy forecasts of a happy future for mankind. Problems were being solved, scientists have been given answers to their questions, and solutions have been found for many technical puzzles. Even the people who became total Veggies after uploading their creativity were happy and looked content. What about those who didn't want to upload their OE? They had two choices: either *Collective Mind* or the abyss.

No one paid any special attention any longer to terrorist attacks, like the one Isaac got involved in yesterday. Even the police ignored the feeble street protests. Solitary messiahs, protest graffiti – there were always plenty of mental cases and petty hooligans around. These troublemakers claimed we should be afraid of the power held by COMUNA. Some opposition scientists claimed that pooled creativity was only useful to make progress on the kind of projects that had some prior work already done. Not even a billion donors, they said, could be helpful to start novel ventures of the future, such as conquering the Universe or curing viruses not yet in existence. Thanks to COMUNA, people could accelerate research and bring it to a conclusion more quickly, but without prior inventions, pooled creativity was useless. Teleportation might seem like science fiction, but in the middle of the last century, smartphones were pure science fiction, too. Not to mention the Internet. No sci-fi writer could picture its importance in today's world.

Last week, the Agency announced that it was going to double the payout for those who study quantum physics. It's as if the Agency was saying: "Alright, you guys think, create, and then we'll buy you out, because in quantum physics we have serious gaps and a great deficit of ideas!"

Extracted Orange Energy would never be able to do what its original owners could do. It wasn't capable of asking questions, having a dream, inventing a new fantasy. Only human beings could do that.

"Nonetheless," objected the experts from the UN, "there's no guarantee that a man who holds on his creativity would make rational use of it by himself. We still have to reap the full benefits of the revolutionary leap forward that the world has made. We have to readjust. Let's harvest the scores of new inventions that COMUNA creates and deal with the problems later. We're studying them, but their number is miniscule in comparison with the thousands of supremely important successful new developments that we have."

The success of COMUNA was well protected by the number of useful technologies.

"Supremely important," Isaac spat out angrily. His hand reached out for a cigarette. "But I don't smoke!" In stressful moments, Isaac's old reflex of reaching his hand for a pack of cigarettes sometimes came back.

He tried to pull himself together.

"The invention could still work out, there's still time. You can earn the money you need to pay for your sister's surgery by selling the idea for *V-Rain*. Then there'll be enough for a decent human life, too. Use the chance you've got! The doctors still don't have a full picture. Just get on with the work like a grown-up while there is still time. And don't forget: long comas may cause permanent damage."

His rage and the pain inside his head made it hard to focus on his work.

"What the hell was going on here?!" Isaac slammed his hand down on the computer mouse. The plastic cracked, but thankfully, the mouse still worked.

One thing the terrorist was right about was that the people who run the Agency and sit on all these inventions have too much power. In all of the futuristic films, there always has to be an omnipotent corporation or empire. Essentially, that is the model of the future world. Of course, no one ever thought the dragon would emerge from the UN. The more Veggies there are, the more docile the world is. Total elimination of crime has weeded out a whole mass of freedom-loving individuals who were beyond the government's control. Tomorrow, they will call anyone opposed to COMUNA a criminal.

All that was left from the rebel Elvis was the small prickly piece of a motherboard and a half sane promise to burn it.

As Isaac tried to focus his mind on work, he played with the piece, intending to throw it out as he had promised himself to do. After his reflections about COMUNA, Isaac felt a certain respect for Elvis's audacity. To keep his karma clean, one had to follow through with his promises, especially if those promises aren't that easy to fulfill. Isaac looked at the piece of the motherboard again – it had a couple of microchips and a mini-memory card on it. A mini-card, but with big memory, and it wasn't a fragment at all, it was complete and undamaged. Happy to do anything but work, Isaac decided to take a look at what was on it.

He plugged the card into his own computer and saw a mass of folders with files and tables. He opened the first one and froze, dumbfounded. His intuition or maybe it was that same karma didn't let him down. He was looking at a table of people who had been tested, but have not yet uploaded their creativity. First names, surnames, IQ's, creativity ratings, and other data. Isaac leaned closer to the monitor and quickly ran his eyes over the highly confidential information.

"Holy shit! Didn't that crazy hobo say: 'Destroy the heart of the devil'? He wasn't all that far from the truth, that Elvis."

The memory card contained a whole heap of incomprehensible information, but the most interesting things on it were the various ratings. This wasn't the devil's heart, it was his database! Isaac's fatigue instantly evaporated. His fingers flew over the keyboard as he avidly devoured the content.

"Lord, what do you want me to do with his?" he thought to himself.

4

Isaac's hands hovered motionless above the keys. Destroying something was easy, if you knew for sure what needed to be destroyed. Isaac had come into possession of a database, but what was the right way to deal with this sudden knowledge?

"What if I search the table for names I know?" thought Isaac, in earnest excitement.

He opened the file named Human Imagination Tone. First, he decided to try his own name, typed it in and launched the search.

"I'm not in the top hundred, but I made the top thousand, labeled number 996," he grinned to himself.

His next search was for "Jeremy Link". There were many rumors available on the Internet about the professor, but no real open information.

 The search engine quickly found the inventor. Wow! His name was in a separate table with the striking title "Top 50 geniuses". The top list of the smartest people in the world, no less! And these were people who have not uploaded their OE!

Isaac ran through the list eagerly: Europeans, Australians, Americans, Asians – talents could be born anywhere. The first two were unfamiliar to him; number three was a well-known Russian mathematician, who worked at MIT. Isaac and Pascal were taught by his textbooks at the university. What had pushed him to want to sell his creativity? Isaac found the answer to that question in the "Remarks" section, where it said that the mathematician needed to raise money for medical treatment for his child who had a rare brain disease.

Isaac winced at this coincidence. Vicky, dear little sister. Isaac's resentment of COMUNA overwhelmed him. The feeling would never release him now and will forever live in his heart.

Vicky was Isaac's stepsister, but she was the closest person he had. No matter how hard Isaac tried, he couldn't clearly recall the moment when he first met her. He remembered being introduced to a frightened little girl in a blue dress. And that it was a good day, because he was given a radio-controlled car. And a bit later Vicky's dad – his mother's friend, as he was introduced at the time – bought Isaac a really great bike. Then he started coming around more and more often, bringing Vicky with him. For Isaac, playing with someone, even if it was a girl, was better than playing on his own. On the weekends, Vicky's dad drove them to the amusement park and bought them ice cream, and there was no reason to be afraid of someone like him. Isaac quickly got used to him, and was glad when he came, always with a present, even if it was something small. Isaac was delighted when he and his mother moved in with Vicky and her dad, where the children had their own room.

They grew up like that together, spent summers at camp together, always went to the amusement park together. Then to school, to parties at school, and then to bars and clubs. He told her about his inventions and the problems he had with their development, and she listened closely and encouraged her brother, not letting him give up. She used to laugh and say that he was her very best girlfriend, who wouldn't ever look at the same boy as she.

Isaac drove away the memories and concentrated on the table again.

He saw another famous name, the founder of the unique search engine "Piquet". Johnson Pike lived in Beverly Hills and was a very successful man. He got rich after launching his search engine, which was based on a totally new data analysis approach.

Before Piquet, search engines focused on the amount of website traffic – a lot of traffic automatically made a site rank high in the ratings and drove it to the top of the search list. Users saw the most popular sites first, but not the reference that they actually needed. The information they were looking for was either hidden somewhere in the last pages of the search, or was never found at all.

Piquet was better and faster at finding results for specific given search parameters. The results analysis algorithm was complex and, of course, wasn't made public. Specialists in the field assumed that the search engine analyzed all of the words on each site found. Piquet assigned credibility to sites based on the frequency of the search words relative to the total number and the presence of specific, strictly professional terms and phrases. At least, that was what the description claimed. Paranoiacs hypothesized that the search engine also analyzed the files on the user's computer, in order to figure out what he did and rank the results more accurately.

Apart from everything else, Pike was a superb PR man. In his numerous interviews about the search engine specifically and his company in general, the inventor frequently toyed with the journalists, only talking about what he wanted and cracking jokes, including dirty ones. At one press conference, he put eight penguins in the front row, and he arrived to another wearing an astronaut's suit. In the first case, he announced that he wanted to see a decently dressed audience, and in the second, that he had been searching for an answer to a very difficult question out in space, and found it. The journalists loved him and hated him at the same time. On one hand, he was rude, but Pike only attacked people in response to an attack on himself, never crossing the boundary of decency. On the other, he threw fantastic parties, at which he was always very hospitable and generous. In any case, he was a newsmaker, and no one quarreled with him openly. Everyone understood that tomorrow Pike can block their names in his search engine, and they would instantly find themselves in journalistic oblivion.

Late last year, the extravagant Pike had put on yet another show, in which he jumped off the roof of a skyscraper in Los Angeles, flying a yellow hang-glider into the sunset with "Search in Piquet" written on it.

The journalists outdid each other in inventing catchy headlines. A superb banquet was laid out for them on the roof. The next day, the wings of the bright-yellow hang-glider appeared on the front pages of all major newspapers and news-sites.

The world was shocked when Johnson Pike announced he had decided to upnload his creativity. At the test session, to which he invited the press, he said that his creativity level was off the chart, and declared that from now on his imagination would serve for the good of the society.

However, before offloading his OE, he was required to hand over the Piquet algorithm to his company's board of directors and finish all of the activities that required intellectual capacity. In the table that Isaac was looking at, it said that the uploading of Pike's creativity had been postponed once again. Probably, it was just another of his PR moves, a way to announce to the press how high his creativity is.

Isaac clicked around other tables in the database. He went into the top 100 of those who had already uploaded their OE. Among them he recognized the name of a celebrated artist Andrei Sharov. He was a Veggie now. Although he didn't make art any more, those pictures he had created prior to uploading became internationally famous.

Isaac recalled that story, which was all over the media. The artist, solitary and anti-social, never left his studio, scraping by on occasional sales of his pictures, which were not especially popular. Not a single serious art gallery wanted to take him on and exhibit his works. After all, he hadn't invented anything conceptually new, they said. Frustrated, the artist burned down his garage containing all his unsold works and was one of the first to sell his OE. His creativity index turned out to be astronomical. Of course, they wrote about it in all the newspapers. The artist's works were noticed, and everyone suddenly wanted one. His few remaining works were declared masterpieces, and not a single critic dared to say anything derisive about them anymore. The owner of a tiny local restaurant, who took pity on the artist and fed him in return for his paintings, got a lot of money for his collection. The six works hanging in the dark little restaurant were moved to the National Gallery and the artist was invited to the opening. Only he didn't care any longer about the fame that had suddenly descended on him.

Isaac went back to the table that included Link. Where was he now, this professor? Isaac wanted to meet Link face to face and tell him what he thought about him. He wanted to tell him about *Collective Mind*, and the Veggies, and people like Isaac, who were stuck on the sidelines of life. Link probably read the avalanche of ecstatic articles about himself, so it would be great to let him hear a different opinion for a change. Isaac wondered why Link disappeared and why he was hiding. He ought to be held accountable for what he's done, and for what was happening now, and for what it would all lead to in the future. Isaac wondered what the professor thought now that his invention has been at work for seven years?

It would be ideal to make him fix the shortcomings of the machine or destroy it all together. If the professor knew how. He would have to be convinced, of course, pressured or even threatened. The world was turning into a new goddamn Matrix, only this wasn't the movies. Isaac recalled the old film with Keanu Reeves, in which people seemed to be alive, but they were asleep. They lived in cocoons, in illusions, believing that their world was real. What point was there in being born, living a quiet life, always being proper, staying in line, and then dying? Was the point in erasing human individuality?

If Link has managed to build his machine, he would surely be able to destroy it. Destroying is easier than building if one knows what to destroy. The technology was classified and hard to get to, but Link must surely know how to do so.

Isaac went back to the previous file that mentioned his own name and scrolled up and down, then up again. The names of creativity-carriers who, like him, had their levels measured, but haven't yet uploaded their OE. There were quite a lot of them.

Isaac winced at the title 'Creativity Carriers'.

"Creativity Carriers! What am I saying?! They're just normal people who haven't sacrificed their individuality."

Eventually, they had to understand the same thing that Isaac realized about *Collective Mind*. Maybe, they already understand it? Maybe, they have known it for a long time, and Isaac was the only one who has taken so long to see the light? Today, they download creativity, tomorrow people's sense of humor, memory, emotions? It was the dismemberment of human individuality. The Agency is obviously evil, Jack the Ripper of the human consciousness!

Again, Isaac found his name in the list of yesterday's donors. The manager's report contained data about his debt to the bank, about his apartment, about his sister's illness and the conclusion: "of no value to the society".

"I have no value to the society?! We'll see about that!" Isaac exclaimed angrily.

This insolent note stung him painfully.

"Bastards! *You* will soon be of no value to the society yourselves!" Isaac repeated, using the mouse to select a random name from the local list. He stopped at the name Eric Delangle. Just as he thought, there was a page on a social network and a blog registered to that name.

A biologist, Delangle has written in the very first lines of his resume on a business social network: "I'm not selling my identity, and advise you not to." He moved to Marrakesh.

"It's a shame that Morocco's quite a long way from here," Isaac thought. "This guy would have been perfect."

Catching himself thinking that thought, Isaac realized why he was looking at the list in the first place. He was looking for allies and needed people like himself, who were dissatisfied with the present state of affairs. Isaac knew he wasn't a born leader. But he had no choice, he could only begin with himself.

If there were other dissidents somewhere in the world, Isaac hadn't heard about them. But he did have quite a lot of experience in solving complex problems, and knew where to begin. In principle, he had to approach this like any complex problem. Logically.

Isaac arranged the table of locals by their education and age. He thought that it would be easier to start with people who were approximately the same age as he. He ran quickly through the names. In a three hours' time he had a list of candidates lying printed in front of him. The next step was finding their whereabouts. Unfortunately, neither phone numbers nor email addresses were given. By evening, Isaac found one or the other for ten of them. Social networks, company or personal web sites – all this information was available on the Internet, and anyone with enough perseverance could find it.

The part that was still not clear to him was how he would actually approach those people. How to make an appointment or start a conversation? He didn't even get through the reception of the first two candidates, whose offices he called before the end of work day. Two others asked that he call back tomorrow. He managed to get through to just to one. Ralf Bongardt, a lawyer, forty-seven years old, well off, a good clean website, nice smile, two kids. Isaac liked him at once. However, the talk itself didn't come out so well – Isaac realized too late that he should have prepared his speech in advance. The conversation was rushed, he mumbled a lot and couldn't present his thoughts clearly.

Finally, he blurted out that they had to meet and talk about COMUNA. When Ralf realized that Isaac was not calling to hire him as a lawyer, he lost interest completely. Trying to be more specific, Isaac decided to risk and explain that his goal was not his own protection, but the salvation of all the mankind; that it was necessary to study all the consequences of *Collective Mind*'s work, and that he was present during the terroristic attack the day before. After these words the lawyer went silent, listened to the rest of Isaac's speech without saying a word and promised to think.

Isaac was angry with himself. He was lucky enough to speak with a potential accomplice, but possibly blew his only chance by not being properly prepared. It was clear that he wouldn't get any results over the telephone. He had to meet these people personally and present his ideas eye-to-eye.

The word 'accomplice' sounded scary.

"What am I doing?" Isaac thought. "I have more than enough of my own problems." But something told him that he would never forgive himself if he didn't follow this through. Someone needed to start this fight, and he was the only who 'got lucky' with the classified information.

Isaac concentrated and wrote emails to other candidates, trying to find a personalized approach to each one. To the owner of an IT-company he introduced himself as a research associate; to a deputy bank manager – a rich client. Speaking to another lawyer, he asked for legal advice concerning the concussion he received during the attack and his illegal imprisonment. He sent eight letters in total. All candidates he picked possessed both high creativity ratings and a considerable fortune.

"Good thing my folks brought me to Monaco. There are plenty of rich people here, and everything is much easier with money," he thought. Feeling content, he went to bed early, looking forward to the replies.

His morning started with a surprise, an unpleasant one, as it proved to be. Captain Robert called from the station and asked him to stop by. Isaac cautiously inquired what was the matter. It turned out that Ralf Bongardt had reported him to the police.

Now, he certainly could have done without that! Lying that he had a bad headache, Isaac promised to come over after lunch. Knowing that his neighbor has gone away for a long time, he hid the motherboard in his mailbox. He knew that he would have to clean his computer from everything he did yesterday, leaving no trace. And there was still not one reply to his emails.

If the police sees who the letters were sent to, they will realize what Isaac is up to. He didn't know if they had the technology to find history on temporary or hidden files. Anything could give him away. He definitely had to get rid of the computer. But what if someone sees him throwing the thing away? He couldn't be sure he wasn't being watched? What could have this Bongardt guy told them?!

Isaac tried to recall every single detail of the conversation, looking for a possible way to explain it as an innocent chat.

He had to erase everything suspicious, defragment and format the hard drive, download as much junk as he could and format it again. Done! Defragmentation over, now formatting. While the computer was performing the task, Isaac wanted to have breakfast, but it turned out that there was nothing to eat. He didn't plan to come back home after the Agency. Once he offloaded his OE, he was supposed to go directly to a temporary boarding house. The only thing available in his house was coffee.

After the disk formatting was over, Isaac created a new mailbox, forwarded all potential replies there and started downloading various data from the Internet. Now he had at least an hour and a half of free time – enough to take a walk, look around and think things over.

There was no sign that anyone was following him, so Isaac calmed down a little. Why would anyone watch, anyway? He didn't say anything suspicious on the phone, they really had nothing on him. Feeling a surge of courage, he headed straight to the police.

Catching the captain on his way to lunch, Isaac told him he had an appointment later on and asked if they could talk at once. Robert glanced at his watch and agreed, saying it wouldn't take long.

"We got a statement that you threatened Mr. Bongardt, Isaac."

"Excuse me?" Isaac sounded genuinely surprised.

"Well, you called him and introducing yourself as participant of the terrorist attack, he says. Was it so?"

Isaac could remember that this was, in fact, what he said.

"Well, I meant to say, I was a witness, you know. Or rather a victim! He's a lawyer and I have trouble with my sister now. I wanted to know what I could count on. I had a bad headache, so I might have been a little incoherent. However, I definitely didn't say that I was a member of a terrorist group or anything of the kind. No, sir."

"Right. That's what I thought. I calmed him down all I could, but still, you'll have to write an explanatory note. A short one," he added, throwing another glance at his watch.

It took Isaac three minutes to give a short version of the conversation, adding in the end that he didn't mean anything illegal, blaming the slight concussion he had for any misunderstandings.

The captain seemed satisfied. He put the paper into a file and set off to lunch, letting Isaac go.

Isaac felt quite calm, but admitted to himself that he had to be much more careful. He checked his email on the phone and saw two letters.

The first one was from the bank, quite predictably. The letter stated that he had an appointment; however, not with the person he needed but some other manager. That didn't work. The other reply was from the lawyer and Isaac also had to brush it aside. No more trusting lawyers. No one else replied.

"I have to change my tactics," Isaac said to himself. He decided to take a closer look at those who, like him, had nothing to lose, and the people who were closer to his age.

At home, Isaac picked up the motherboard from his neighbor's mailbox and copied the data to a thumb-drive. After that he threw the piece away, making sure that no one was watching him.

When he came back inside, he sat down at his computer and began to analyze the list again. The first name he picked out was a young man with a computer science degree, a local programmer named Laurent-Marie Affre, who also worked as a bartender. This lad wasn't the only one with talent who had been dumped overboard, or behind a bar counter, rather. Coincidentally, Isaac had a technical degree, as well. Isaac hoped that he could find something on Affre on the Internet.

The candidate called himself Bikie on social media and was crazy about motorbikes. Isaac found his blog, in which Bikie was scathingly abusive about COMUNA, *Collective Mind*, and Link, and mocked everyone who offloaded their creativity. He posted various photographs including his own and of his Harley's. Looking out at Isaac was an awkward, longhaired clodhopper with big round eyes. Plumpish and ungainly, Bikie's build was frighteningly heavy-caliber. He looked like he was rather good-natured, which could not be said of his posts.

"I hope he really is good-natured," Isaac chuckled.

Bikie's last entry was fairly old and very short: "No one reads me here, what a Down-steiner!"

Isaac clicked on a different link and found Bikie's blog, which consisted of many very short messages. All of the words were R-rated, except "down with", "Veggies", "people in coma" and prepositions, like "up" and "off".

A plan was finally coming together in Isaac's mind: summon a team of people like this Bikie, and find Jeremy Link, since he seems to be alive. And then see what happens. What mattered most was getting together a good group of people and finding money.

"Damn it, money! Forgive me Vicky, I really will earn the money for your surgery, just hang on a little bit longer. Right now I have to do this. Let's ask the database a question. My dear ladies and gentlemen, potential accomplices, preferably, young heirs, which of you has money?" Isaac thought as he searched through the lists and through social media before he finally found what he was looking for. Half of them were eliminated immediately – some turned out to be in America, some in Hong Kong and other places. Three candidates remained.

The first was Peter Wolanski – a German who has lived in Monaco since he was a child. A member of a prestigious scientific society, the same one that Isaac had once belonged to. There weren't any photos of Peter on the Internet and Isaac decided to look for them later. Peter's blog consisted of beautifully laid out scientific articles. A couple of them were devoted to discussing why no one should offload their OE. He was an ideal candidate and Isaac thought that it was best to start with him.

In one of his latest articles, Peter told the story of his father's life and his achievements as a successful entrepreneur. He talked about his grief and boundless sense of loss since his father's death.

"This guy definitely has money," thought Isaac and wrote Peter's details into his notepad. "Lord, I'm like a gold-digger looking for a sponsor! It's disgusting, but there is no choice. Money is the lubricant of any operation."

The second candidate was a girl and what a beauty she was! And with a name as if it came right out of a song: Michelle Blanche. Long, shapely legs, a beautiful face, a great figure, and a mischievous twinkle in her eyes.

"A beautiful girl! And to judge from her rating, very intelligent too. I'll never be able to handle a girl like that: beautiful and rich. How do you come on to someone like that?"

Isaac started to daydream, but had to admit that it was impossible. He wouldn't have the nerve to come up to her.

"She'd tell me where to get off before I could even start saying anything. Or she would think that I was a psycho. I'd love to screw a girl like that, only they don't come by our bar," Isaac chuckled despondently.

But he wrote down the address anyway, just in case. The idea of giving up without even trying made him despise himself. Isaac fantasized for a little while longer and closed Michelle's blog.

The third candidate was somewhat dubious. His father was a military man who offloaded his OE amongst the first. It was obvious that the son wanted to follow in his father's steps and was proud of him. There was a risk that the guy would turn out too righteous and give Isaac up to the police. So he should be set aside as a worst-case scenario option.

"If I think like a character from a movie," Isaac thought, still fantasizing. "Getting together a strong team means finding people who think alike, who have the same goal as you. It's a thousand times harder being a lone-ranger. Let's go that route. For now, I have enough candidates with the tech guy and the one who has money. Maybe they have friends who have similar ideas and would want to join the team. That's less risky than chasing after strangers and enticing them to commit a crime. And it would be best to keep my mouth shut about the database."

5

Isaac found himself unable to resist the urge to meet Michelle Blanche. He got the idea that he ought to start with her. That night he dreamt about the long-legged brunette. Isaac almost completely forgot the dream, but he thought he remembered them getting together, and Michelle smiling at him and kissing him. Then they were in some beautiful room, she was wearing a bathrobe, and Isaac spotted black lacy underwear lying in the corner. He tried to kiss her, but she beckoned him towards the bed. After that, unfortunately, there was a gap, but Isaac woke up aroused.

He was in a great mood and tried to recall if they'd had sex or not. No matter how hard he tried, though, he couldn't reconstruct the dream in his memory, but he decided it was a good sign. Deep down inside Isaac realized that with his creativity level and imagination he could find a good sign in anything. Living was easier when you saw the good in things, it was an additional reason for optimism.

Pinning down Michelle proved to be difficult. She had moved to Monaco a year and a half ago. Before that, from the look of things, she had lived in London. The address given in the database turned out to be valid only for correspondence, and her English mobile number was disconnected. Michelle didn't use geo-location in social media, and she didn't reveal where exactly she lived. She often posted her photographs the day after she was at an event, a party or a get-together. In the photos she was either posing alone, or always with the same young man who also didn't look local. Isaac kept looking at her Instagram, hoping his eyes would spot some familiar place. In some of the photographs Michelle was flaunting herself in a swimsuit on a yacht with the same name. After his erotic dream, Isaac looked at Michelle as if she were his girlfriend. He imagined her naked, next to him.

"If only I could see that dream again, I'd definitely see things through," he thought.

Before going to sleep, he reviewed her most explicit photos. That made him feel horny, but he couldn't summon any more erotic dreams.

The good thing was that Michelle didn't sit at home every night. But on the other hand, Isaac couldn't afford to go around the most expensive spots in Monaco, hoping she would show up. In any way, the effectiveness of that approach was quite doubtful, to say the least. She could be anywhere on any given evening. It might seem like he could just show up and drink coffee every night at Sass Café or Cipriani, but at places like that, if you didn't order anything on the third day, they would politely ask you not to come back there again. Isaac couldn't afford more than two dinners at a fancy place like that. Nevertheless, it finally seemed he managed to get a real address for her.

In anticipation of meeting Michelle, Isaac shaved, abandoning his beautiful stubble, and put on a t-shirt with a deep V-neck. A vintage diver's watch – not expensive, but very stylish – was on his wrist. He even changed the ringtone on his phone to a melody by INXS. Isaac liked himself like this. He didn't know whether Michelle would like him, but after his dream, he believed in some kind of a sexual connection. If creative energy existed, then why shouldn't there be some other kind of energy, responsible for dreams and attraction? Isaac dismissed all his thoughts about the fact that Michelle has never seen him before. What if she had seen him some time ago, and even taken notice, but he simply hadn't spotted it?

Having arrived at the upscale condominium where he thought Michelle lived, Isaac first tried to strike up a conversation with the concierge. The man examined him suspiciously and asked if Isaac could stop pestering him with questions about the residents. If Isaac wanted, the polite concierge said, he would be glad to pass on a note. Taking pity on Isaac after all, he hinted that Michelle rarely spent the night in her apartment. Privacy had always been highly valued in Monaco, but the concierge saw Isaac as just a young man desperately in love, and thawed out a bit. Only what could Isaac write in the note? "Please contact me in connection with…" or "I'm not an admirer, that is, you are beautiful, but I know what high level of creativity you have"?

No, leaving a note with the concierge was not an option. Isaac had to come up with something else.

He went to Sass Café and had a word with the manager there. Monaco wasn't New York, thank God, and all the locals more or less knew each other. The manager promised to text Isaac if he saw her. Isaac visited a few more restaurants and snazzy bars and left his request at five of them.

In the evening, he ran through list of potential donors who had money one more time, and picked another couple of candidates just in case. Since they might not live at the address given, it would be best to find out where they really lived or worked. He would start with the first on the list and go down it.

He then copied the details of another four people with various skills that he thought might be useful, but no obvious money sources. Among them an artist and a photographer. Artists were often extremely independent and free-minded, regardless of how much money they had. Good allies.

"If I were an artist, I'd ask Michelle to pose for me," Isaac fantasized.

Yes, artists were often outsiders. Only Isaac couldn't imagine what use their knowledge could be for his plans.

"But it can't hurt," he decided, writing out a couple of addresses.

On the third day he got lucky. A huge fireworks display was taking place in Monaco, and Michelle posted two beautiful photos. Isaac didn't spot them immediately, but figured out roughly where they were taken. The girl was photographed on the roof of the Fairmont Hotel.

It was only a ten minute walk from Isaac's house to Fairmont, and he thought that he would arrive in time. He did. Michelle and a girlfriend of hers were sitting there, surrounded by a group of respectably dressed men.

"My God, how sexy she is," Isaac thought. Pascal would have come on to someone like that without a problem. He wouldn't care about the competition. Isaac couldn't do that. In his mind, he visualized his friend's manners and tried to set his mind to being similar.

There wasn't a single free table anywhere nearby, with fireworks like these, everything was booked in advance. Isaac hesitated for a moment and stopped not far away from the restroom. It was a hot evening and there were several bottles of water and champagne standing on Michelle's table. Sooner or later she'd need to visit the restroom, and since the restaurant's exit was right there as well, she couldn't just disappear.

She wore an elegant beige cocktail dress, not too revealing, but short enough. Isaac's imagination immediately shortened it even more and he thought of what might be hiding underneath. There was no jewelry on her already lovely wrists. Her legs were so beautiful that Isaac had to stop thinking about them, because he was short of breath. Skyscraper legs, with small, sexy knees. This girl was the real deal, for sure. How lucky she was to be born like this, and not to a poor family, too. Isaac noticed that she drank water, while the men kept competing with each other to top off her half-empty glass of champagne.

Eventually, after slightly adjusting her dress, Michelle set off, arm-in-arm with her girlfriend, in the required direction. Sipping on his cocktail, Isaac tried to stand more naturally but felt too nervous and fidgety. Uncertainty in himself made pretending that he belonged there almost impossible. He awkwardly tried to find a better pose and as he was moving around one spot, disaster happened. In his last and most desperate effort to make himself look as interesting as possible, he leaned against a door with his elbow, but the door turned out to be unlocked and swung away from under him. Managing to trip over his own foot, he dropped his treacherous glass from his hands. It shattered with a loud crash, with the contents of the glass flying right to the feet of Michelle and her girlfriend, covering their light-colored shoes with the dark cocktail. Isaac felt like finding a hole and crawling into it, and must have looked really frightened, because Michelle gave him an enchanting smile, put her hand on his shoulder and said in a gentle voice:

"Don't worry about it, we're fine. Just get yourself another cocktail and the staff will clean this up."

Thunderstruck, Isaac broke out in a cold sweat. Meanwhile, Michelle walked away imperturbably and headed out of the restaurant. Her admirers, who had immediately darted across the hall and to the scene of the incident, cast glances of contempt at Isaac.

"I've offended their queen!" Isaac thought spitefully.

When the entire group almost passed him, he managed to put a look of almost uncontrollable rage on his face, which scared the last of the royal retinue.

"There you go," Isaac told them with his eyes. "You're not lounging about on your yachts now. Unlike you, I have experience of being in real fights!"

The last one of the posse realized that if Isaac was pushed just a tiny bit further, he was ready to attack, despite the consequences. Smartly, he chose to look away as he walked by.

Michelle's party left to go somewhere else, but ten minutes later Isaac got a text message from his friend at Sass: "Michelle's here!"

Fortunately, not the entire group had moved to Sass, only Michelle, her girlfriend, and one young man. Isaac sat in a place where the girl would surely see him, and noticed that she looked in his direction several times, but seemed to look straight through him, without noticing him at all. He obviously didn't fall within the range of her interests. If she did recognize him as the young man who dropped his cocktail and broke the glass, she didn't give any sign of it. No matter how hard Isaac stared at her, hoping she'd pay attention, nothing happened.

"Wrong choice," Isaac thought sadly. "But okay, there are still other candidates on my list."

Even though he had failed to attract any interest at all, Isaac decided to try to get acquainted with Michelle anyway.

"After all, this is business," he thought, psyching himself up. Concentrating as hard as he could, he convinced himself that not to approach her would be cowardice and he had nothing to lose.

"I'll finish my cocktail and walk up to her," he thought, finding with a way to put things off for five minutes. Eventually, after gathering all his courage, he put his glass on the table and set off towards where Michelle was sitting.

"Excuse me, Michelle, but could I have a couple of words with you?" Isaac said, with his most adorable smile. "I hope you're not upset that it was only my cocktail that fell at your feet, and not me. Are you?"

The girl failed to appreciate his humor and looked at him without any particular curiosity. It was obvious that she had absolutely no interest in meeting strangers in public places.

"What do you want? Do you two know each other?" Michelle's friend asked, coming to her aid.

"No, we don't know each other. My name's Isaac and there's something very important that I need to say."

Michelle shook her head very slightly and the young man continued:

"Isaac, please have the courtesy to leave us alone. We want to relax; we don't want to make any new friends. No one's angry with you because of the broken glass."

"But it's very important," said Isaac, trying to insist.

"If it's so important, tell us. I have no secrets from my friends," Michelle intervened.

"Well you see, Michelle, you have a very high creativity level, and so do I. And there are other people like us. People who don't like COMUNA," Isaac rattled off. "And we can't just sit back and do nothing. We can do a lot. And you can help!"

Unfortunately, Michelle and her companions saw Isaac as nothing more than an overexcited weirdo, who should be given as wide a berth as possible. Michelle's reflex response was to lean back on her chair with her arms crossed.

"Please," Isaac continued quickly. "Let me finish. You're intelligent, rich and very beautiful. I can't go into this fight on my own, I need your help. I'm not a psycho, I'm an absolutely normal young guy, an inventor, and I have a very high OE level."

"And you broke that cocktail glass very inventively, didn't you?" Michelle's friend persisted. This was his great chance to protect the beautiful model from an obnoxious gadfly, and he wanted to milk the opportunity dry.

He got up off his chair and stood between Isaac and Michelle.

"Please leave. I'm asking nicely."

"And what if I don't?" Isaac asked, starting to get angry and immediately regretted it. His aggression only made Michelle more frightened. A good half of the restaurant was already watching their table, including the irate manager – the acquaintance who had sent Isaac the text.

"All right, I'm sorry. I'm leaving." Isaac looked at Michelle one last time. She was so beautiful and so indifferent.

He realized that she would never be his ally. She lived a life of luxury and admirers, and people like that never risk disrupting their own comfortable stability. Michelle didn't even seem so beautiful anymore. The uneasiness of the situation made her worried, which turned her skin pale, almost gray. Her eyes peered out spitefully from under her brows. Isaac suddenly smiled. He realized that he was stronger than many brilliant and rich people. Even in his present condition, he was capable of far more than many of the people around him.

"See you later, Michelle," Isaac said with a wave of his hand and walked away with a confident stride. Maybe his mission has failed, but he felt an incredible rush of energy at having moved from theory to action.

Isaac's legs carried him home without any thought. He wanted to run, not walk and get back to his computer as soon as possible. He didn't really know what had happened, but his head was absolutely clear and working at a maximum capacity.

It was time to search among the ones who had nothing to lose, those who attacked the Agency openly. He had to look at all of their social media pages again, focusing on the marginal types. To hell with any celebrities. To hell with the rich ones. First, he had to create the backbone of the operation.

Isaac carried on working and analyzing until morning. It appeared that the most suitable candidate was Laurent-Marie, AKA Bikie, after all, with his obvious hatred of *Collective Mind*. Some of Bikie's posts reeked of disillusionment and rage – everything that Isaac himself felt yesterday. A conversation with him would go differently than with Michelle, for sure. One of Bikie's strong points was his profession as a systems administrator and programmer. On the other hand, he worked as a bartender, was as strong as an ox, and. Had all the makings of an anarchist. If things worked out with him, physical security would come as part of the deal. It wouldn't take much to find Bikie. He definitely didn't have a concierge for correspondence, so tracking him down would be easy.

Thinking about physical protection, Isaac spotted another candidate – a husky young professional athlete. "With such high creativity rating, what could have attracted him to sports," Isaac wondered. Although, if one had enough natural talent both for sports and intellectual work, then why not?

Abdul Djebali, age twenty-three, a member of the national track and field team. French father and Algerian mother. A Muslim. Training, training, more training.

"Aha, I know that gym!" Isaac exclaimed, examining Abdul's Instagram. "That's where I'll find him."

Feeling relaxed, Isaac poked around another file that he hadn't seen before. "Creativity statistics on children born to Happies". Notional zero, notional zero, zero again, zero for almost all of them. Not even COMUNA could bring itself to call these figures a rating.

Isaac went to bed, but tossed and turned restlessly even though it was already morning. He fell asleep around eight, maybe later, and then woke up at least twice, with the clock showing 8:40 and 9:30. He had to force himself to sleep a bit longer: he had two candidates for today, and the second one worked until three in the morning. Isaac closed the curtains tightly, plunging the room into total darkness, and fell sound sleep.

The administrator at the gym said that the afternoon training session would finish at four o'clock. Isaac went to grab a pizza and came back a little earlier than that. When he spotted Abdul, he introduced himself and asked what he was doing after the gym. They agreed to sit and talk in a café in the marina at six. The athlete turned out to be a very amiable guy. That was the pattern – the less money people had, the more accessible they were.

With nothing else to do, Isaac went straight to the café. He sat behind a table on the terrace and looked out at the yachts. Some were empty, some had jolly groups of people on them, music playing. Sailing into Monaco was always an event, and people were usually in an excellent mood about the fact.

"I live here," thought Isaac, "but I don't see the beauty of this place. My eyes stopped registering it ages ago. I can't even remember the last time I looked at the sea. I don't value what I have. But people are willing to cross the ocean to be here for just one day." Abdul found Isaac engrossed in these thoughts.

Isaac called over a waiter and ordered a large bottle of water. There was an awkward pause.

"Abdul, I'd like to ask you a couple of questions and make you a proposal. A week ago I almost became a Happy, but I was lucky, God spared me, or maybe I was just fortunate, but I decided it wasn't a coincidence. I don't like the present system and the uploading craze. My gut feeling tells me it's all wrong. And if you dig under the surface, some facts that are very unpleasant for the Agency will come creeping out."

Isaac made sure that Abdul was still paying attention and continued.

"I know you have a very high creativity level. You had it measured two years ago at the local branch. Why didn't you upload?"

"Well, apart from my creativity, I have a couple of other things I can use to pull through. I can always upload if I wish. Meanwhile, I am in training and getting excellent results. In just a little while, I'll make the national team."

"I also want to ask you to join a team, a team of people who will sort all of this out independently. And maybe put an end to all of this."

"All of what?"

"*Collective Mind* and offloading creativity. It all looks just too smooth."

"And what do you want from me?"

"To take part. I want you to help."

"But how?"

"Abdul, can I trust you?"

"Sure. No matter what, this conversation is just between you and me."

"Great. I'm looking for partners, those with high intellect and a lot of creativity to work together, to stop this trend of turning people into stupid amoebae. You see, Happies say that they're happy. But a drugged-up junkie is happy too, as long as the drug is still in his blood. A junkie is just a sick person. What if Happies are sick, as well? Like being high. No Happy has ever returned to a normal state."

"That's just paranoia. Of course, they're happy, you can see it, and you can cast doubt on any achievement that way."

"Well, maybe it is paranoia," Isaac retorted. "But maybe not."

"Anything is possible, but why do you need me?"

"You're strong."

"Are we planning to beat someone up then?" Abdul chuckled.

"No, we're not, and I hope we won't have to. I read that you're a hot-shot mathematician and that's important for my plan."

"But just what is your plan, I don't get it yet."

"Find Professor Link."

"And more specifically?"

"There's nothing specific as of yet. We'll create the specifics together. First, we're going to figure out where Link is."

"You know Isaac, maybe I'll regret this later, but I'm going to pass. I won't tell anyone about our conversation, but as for joining, it's not for me. No hard feelings?"

Isaac wanted to object, but Abdul stopped him, raising his hand.

"Until you say something you might regret later, I'll interrupt you. I'm not interested. Don't give me any more details."

Another candidate was waiting for Isaac in the evening.

6

The door of the bar swung open and out spilled a colorful pair, both pretty loaded: a husky guy in a bandana and a bearded lanky man. They were talking so loud that Isaac could hear from twenty-feet away.

"Now that's what I call a real bike," said the hunk.

"You bet…. none of your modern garbage. This is a classic!"

"Is that a Harley Sportster?"

"Yup! And not just a Sportster... This is my bro! Even born the same year as me!"

"Okay, cheers, Bikie. See you in a week or two. Going to Trieste tomorrow and from there to Prague, but the Friday after that I'll be back here."

"Ciao, buddy! Smooth riding and no stones on the road."

Isaac already knew that Bikie's shift in the bar was due to end shortly. He had read a lot about this guy and didn't want trouble, so he addressed him in a familiar tone.

"Bikie the Biker… that does sound funny."

Bikie swung around and looked Isaac up and down.

"Is there a problem, boy?" Bikie asked menacingly. "A problem with that pretty face of yours, maybe?" And, after a pause, added: "We can fix that right now. Now what were you saying?"

He leaned down bringing his ear close to Isaac's face. His stubble almost touched Isaac's nose, the reek of alcohol was abominable. Isaac recoiled, realizing he had clearly overdone it with his sassy approach. Getting a punch in the face wasn't quite what he was looking for.

"No, chill dude, it was just a bad joke."

"A joke? There's a trauma wing for jokers in the hospital."

"Sorry. Why don't we just forget about it, and I'll buy you a beer?"

"Not one of those queers, are you?"

"Hey-hey, don't you forget about that trauma unit for jokers."

"Ha-ha-ha!" Bikie guffawed. "Attaboy, I like you. Just don't forget that the last guy who joked with me went broke from his dentist's bill. Okay, let's have a beer, as long as you are paying."

Isaac and Bikie walked into the bar. Everyone here knew Bikie, and many of the customers came over to hug him, or slap him on the shoulder.

The shaggy gaunt bartender chuckled behind the counter.

"Back to work? Who's this with you?"

"My beer. A special import, from the land of fools," Bikie replied.

"Please don't," Isaac grinned.

"Hey, since you want something from me, you'll have to put up with it," Bikie snapped and plumped down on a chair. Compared with Bikie's beefy frame, Isaac looked really small.

Although they weren't off to a great start, Isaac gritted his teeth, said nothing, and sat down beside Bikie. No one promised this was going to be easy, but Isaac's enthusiasm for the idea of telling Bikie about his plan slowly melted away. The biker seemed too drunk and offensive to deal with. It took all Isaac had not to leave.

Seeing Isaac's sour face, Bikie slapped him on the shoulder and added good-naturedly:

"Okay, won't do it again. You started it, so I got wound up and enjoyed it. I like pissing off smart-asses and drunken superheroes. When all's said and done, everyone's afraid of fucking with me, anyway. In real life, I'm the kindest and sweetest bouncer in this hemisphere," said Bikie, pointing to the right side of his head and cracking up again. "I've never given anyone a genuine mauling, though. By the way, this is my private table," he added, casting a proud glance at his companion.

The private table was small and was located in the very center. There was a large brass plaque embossed with "Elvis and Steve Tyler can sit here without Bikie's permission."

Elvis again.

"Well now," thought Isaac. "Sometimes you don't remember a word or a name for years, and suddenly it invades your daily life like a virus."

"I see you're well-respected here," said he to the biker.

"You bet. I can do more than just make good use of my hands, if need be. I once crashed the bar's website for seating a pair of freakin' tourist suits at this table," Bikie stopped short and gave Isaac a cunning

49

glance. "I'll listen carefully to what you have to say, just as soon as you bring that beer you promised, fella."

"I brought a bottle of twenty-five-year-old whisky instead of the beer. I hope you don't mind that? Your friend," Isaac nodded in the direction of the other barman, "won't object to us drinking our own liquor?"

"What the fuck's going on here?" Bikie exclaimed. "I'll be damned! Now you're talking! How could anyone object? What are you, a member of the Good Old Rock'n'Rollers Support Society?"

"Almost," Isaac replied, pouring the whiskey into glasses. "I used to work as a bartender too. I quit my job last week. They gave me this in lieu of severance pay."

Closing his eyes, Bikie breathed in the aroma of the whisky and smiled contentedly.

"I'm Isaac Leroy, but you can call me Isaac."

"I'm Bikie. Well, you know that already."

They drank to getting to know each other. Isaac told Bikie a bit about his bar and Bikie told Isaac about his, as well as about his Harley. He was very proud of his Harley and boasted about it as he gradually got more and more drunk. Over the third glass of whisky Bikie began a serious monologue.

"Dude, have you seen the latest Ducati? And the Honda? And the Harley? They're all almost identical now! Sure, they look real heavy, but they're all the same shit. The goddamn creeps are repressing our freedom of choice! Where is my choice? I want to make the fuckin' choice myself! I don't want to mount a Ducati by mistake when I'm wasted! And the music? All the lousy DJ's play the same thing! I could kill them all. How could they possibly fuck up their lives so badly?"

Bikie then spent about ten minutes cursing the Agency and its standardized technologies. What outraged him most of all was the almost complete loss of variety, even for the most primitive things, there was no choice at all.

"Those who have offloaded their OE have it even worse. God forbid I should ever turn into a Veggie," said Isaac.

"Well, even when they had their OE, Veggies were all stupid fucks," Bikie exclaimed.

"No, you're wrong there. My friend sold his creativity for love."

"That's like cutting your dick off for love 'cause it didn't get hard at the right time."

The joke didn't sit well with Isaac. He tried to explain to Bikie about Pascal, but Bikie interrupted and said that he didn't watch soap operas, read political newspapers, or listen to stories about stupid fucks.

"Listen to this then, will you! I almost became one of them, I just happened to be lucky, or unlucky, I don't know."

Isaac began to tell Bikie his story.

Bikie tried to listen carefully, but his head was gradually drooping and he was dozing off. When Isaac finished his story, Bikie raised his eyes, looked at him and said slowly.

"I propose a toast to... Elvis! For making an effort! To his resistance!"

Isaac was expecting a toast to Vicky's health, to his own story, to anything at all, but not to the crazy hobo.

Spotting Isaac's expression, Bikie cleared his throat and added:

"For rebellion and to Elvis! And we'll drink to you too now, boy."

"To Elvis," said Isaac, raising his glass.

"I vowed long ago to destroy this evil, and you appeared right in time. To have enough balls for fighting these days you have to be mad as a hatter or really, truly tough. As for me, I'm ready to fight and I will!"

And Bikie wacked the table so hard, his glass hopped up and broke.

COMUNA reacted fairly calmly to any protest demonstrations, which in time disappeared almost completely. Violations of the law were a matter for the police, and the Agency tried to keep out of such things and not participate in any open conflicts. People who had been cured of fatal illnesses came out voluntarily in support of COMUNA. They and their relatives were the Agency's most aggressive supporters, often showing up at meetings of protesters with poster saying: "You are advocating our death".

The relatively harmless attack carried out by Mr. Elvis-Henri was stridently branded an "act of terrorism" by the press, and was discussed for a whole week. The flames of interest were fanned by the site of the crime more than anything – calm, respectable and luxurious Monaco rarely came up in European crime reports.

When the Department of Orange Energy of the Paris police received the investigation report summary of the Monaco incident, no one took much interest in it. Only Commissioner Pellegrini, as the head of the department, was obliged to familiarize himself with the document. As he started leafing through the file, he saw that this was a standard case of an attack carried out by a solitary fanatic. Boring.

Pellegrini's father was from Naples; his mother was a Frenchwoman from Bordeaux. He was born and grew up in Paris, but he considered himself an Italian who had inherited the character traits of both nations. When necessary, his rapid, impulsive, Italian-style gestures coexisted quite comfortably with his subtle French tact.

Pellegrini's face seemed rough-hewn out of granite, with powerful cheekbones and a large forehead. Broad stripes of the bags under his small, brown eyes lent his face a masculine brutality and intense astuteness. Deep folds on his slightly sunken cheeks and around his mouth created the impression that his mind was constantly engaged in strenuous thought. He was tall and stately, and his bearing made it clear that he was a former military man. Pellegrini served in Africa for a long time before coming to work in the drug enforcement agency.

He worked very efficiently and could have become the department chief, but it didn't happen.

Despite everything, he did eventually rise to become the head of the new, prestigious Department of OE. Now everything was sure to change. Pellegrini thought he could really spread his wings and show everyone what he could do. How very wrong he was.

Six months after Pellegrini joined the Department, his friend Gautier uploaded his creativity out of patriotic considerations. He tried to persuade Pellegrini to go along with him and other officers, drawing wonderful mental pictures of how they would have a great life by the sea, somewhere in Bordeaux, while their creativity would continue working for the good of their homeland and the world. Pellegrini refused. He was finally getting up the career ladder, and in such a prospective department. His future looked very promising, and he wasn't willing to abandon his new position for rosy dreams of Bordeaux.

Initially, Pellegrini's work was interesting, with new technologies making catching criminals easy. But pretty soon the Agency grew so powerful that Pellegrini's job became pure routine. And not only his job, but all police work in general.

Pellegrini read the report of the attack without much interest, thinking that it would be good to feel the tenderness of the southern sun right now. He decided to take a trip to the scene of the "notorious terrorist attack" while the tracks were still fresh, while there was still something to delve into and someone to talk to. He phoned the Monaco branch of the Agency and asked them not to touch anything, explaining that he was on his way to conduct a supplementary investigation.

Isaac woke up close to midday. Despite his thirst and the hangover pounding at his temples like a sledgehammer, he got up quickly, because he was too hyped up to keep still. He downed two glasses of water and felt better. The adrenalin from yesterday's successful meeting flowed back into his bloodstream again, bringing with it pleasant excitement. Isaac prowled around the apartment like a lion in a cage, but couldn't make himself do any one thing.

Bikie didn't show up until one.

"What a dump," he grunted instead of saying hello.

"What?" asked Isaac, puzzled.

"I said, you live in a real dump," he paused for a moment and added: "Seriously, Isaac, it's like I just walked into my own place."

Isaac rewarded his irony with a wry grin.

They walked over to the computer, which was already switched on. Isaac opened the Agency's file and showed Bikie the database. Bikie whistled.

"Oh, wow! Databases are my soft spot, my true love," he said with a hint of smugness. " Literally. I see a database, get inside it, find the weak spot and crack it."

Bikie plumped down on the chair in front of the computer and ran rapidly through the list.

"Ah," he said disappointedly. "Nothing needs cracking here."

Isaac took the mouse from Bikie, moved it to find the cursor, and explained that the database was useful for finding accomplices. It was where he found Bikie and there were other people in it, who, Isaac believed, were of the same opinion than he and Bikie. Isaac explained about Wolanski and the other candidates. He felt too embarrassed to mention the girl, though.

Before Bikie even heard him out, he was hammering his fingers on the keyboard, digging through various social networks.

"Look at this dude Charles. A bit older than us, comes from a family with deep pockets. Moves in the highest circles, no problems with money. Yes, I remember, I remember," he said, once again interrupting Isaac, who was trying to say something. "You've already set your sights on this what's his name – Wolanski. But check it out – this guy's got a Harley. He's one of us, and there's an excuse for getting to know him."

"Just a rich showoff, I reckon," Isaac objected. "Bet you he only bought a Harley because he read somewhere how cool it is to have one."

"What are you saying, bro? Where do you think they write that it's cool to have a Harley? The Ducati Sport, now, that's never been like a Harley, and it shouldn't look like one, and that's why…."

"Okay, Bikie! But how are you planning to get close to someone from his circle? Are you going to say 'Hello, I'm a bartender with a Harley, what year's your bike? Do you have anything against COMUNA? Me too!'? I suggest that if it's a no go with Wolanski, only then do we contact this guy."

"Isaac, if you've already decided everything, then say so," Bikie snapped. "I figure, a normal guy will make normal conversation, with money or without. Although, I'm not sure what people consider normal these days, if ridding yourself of your soul has become the norm. Eh?

Especially if you don't happen to have any better way of doing as well as this guy with the Harley."

Bikie was so sure that Link's invention would ruin the world that it charged Isaac with confidence. Bikie regarded financial inequality and disparity of opportunities as the main reasons why it had become popular to be a donor. This way everyone got a chance, whether they were from Europe, Asia or Africa. The important thing was how well your head worked. Before *Collective Mind* came around, if you were unlucky enough to be born on some God-forsaken island in Asia-Pacific, all you could expect was the finger.

The first massive wave of creativity offloading came from countries with negligible opportunities to fight your way up without being connected to someone with power, to earn enough for your own house, or to get rich. A large flow of elderly but intelligent people followed from countries with a poorly developed social infrastructure: Latin America and Asia at the beginning.

In prosperous countries, the young followed the fashion of OE offloading. In Hong Kong, Greece, Italy and France, graduates who could not find a good job easily surrendered to *Collective Mind*. Yesterday's students quickly discovered how difficult it was to support themselves independently, let alone to earn enough for a decent house, start a family and live a stable life, no matter what high-level specialists they were. Most of the big-time positions were taken, and some had disappeared altogether thanks to the *Collective Mind*-generated technologies. Sure, you could scrape by on social support payments, but the money received for OE offered a real opportunity of never having to worry about anything again. That was why they studied, that's why they became educated, you could say. In America, masses of prisoners volunteered to sell their creativity. And it went on and on. After three years it was already impossible to single out specific groups. Everybody everywhere was offloading their OE.

COMUNA successfully campaigned for the abolition of capital punishment. Rather, an alternative was offered in the form of downloading of one's energy instead of electrocution or gassing. "Let every person serve the society" was the motto. It was a shame to waste the resource, if someone got executed his energy would be lost forever. COMUNA was keenly interested in increasing *Collective Mind's* capabilities, and didn't want a drop of Orange Energy to be wasted. It equipped prisons with download technology, and continuously increased the capacity of the network. Prisoners who offloaded their OE were offered significantly more comfortable conditions.

A popular Hollywood movie was made about a talented young 3D architect who, through a series of failures, takes the wrong path in life. His actions become more and more contemptible and mean. He loses his job. Hacking and drugs eventually lead him to a double manslaughter – the car he is driving while high on cocaine hurtles off the road and two passengers are killed. He sinks lower and lower and eventually becomes a killer. The hero becomes the antihero and the audience loses all sympathy for him.

But in the second half of the film, his profound repentance, and his study of the strong and weak sides of prison life lead him to voluntarily donate his creativity in order to improve the lives of prisoners. His OE rating was high and considered a valuable contribution to society.

No one knows what this man's real contribution to *Collective Mind* was. But the story looked really great on the screen, the movie won an Oscar, and the criminal was even pardoned, although he voluntarily remained in the prison boarding house since he didn't want to live anywhere else.

Hollywood is an ideal propaganda mechanism: it treats the public like a beautiful woman that wraps a man around her little finger, and gets everything she wants out of him by putting him through incredibly strong emotions. The audience cries and laughs, it lives other people's lives, and then it is ready to accept Hollywood's ideas and messages in real life.

Isaac and Bikie's home-region also had a chance to experience this miraculous quality of Hollywood. In 1956, the wedding of the famous American film star Grace Kelly and Prince of Monaco brought floods of tourists from all over the world to the Principality, instantly making it a beneficiary of the world's "Dream Factory".

Whether comedy or drama, corrupt cops or vigilantes, the mafia or patriotism: Hollywood has always steered people's hearts and minds any way it liked. And the movie "Energy of Prison" helped many skeptics change their opinion about COMUNA, increasing the flow of people wishing to upload their creativity.

Of course, there were exceptions. There were not very many donors among Russian Orthodox Christians and Israelis. Israel and Silicon Valley rapidly lost their positions on the high-tech market, surrendering leadership to COMUNA.

Any opposition of COMUNA was gradually disappearing. The opponents of offloading and pooling creativity did not have serious arguments to present to the public.

It took a long time for the Church to release an official statement on the matter. It remained neutral for quite a while, because it was difficult to go against the fact that the world was being purged of a great number of sins.

"You know what?" Bikie said eventually. "Why don't I phone this Charles anyway? The guy with the Harley. Maybe he'll be OK. We won't lose anything, and I promise to be very careful. And if it's a flop, we'll go to Wolanski."

For the sake of an amicable, collaborative relationship Isaac did not argue.

Bikie dialed the number and introduced himself. He said he was from a local club, and would like to meet Charles to talk about the rare Harley model that Charles owned and take a few photos for the club's site. Everything went smoothly and they agreed on seven o'clock that evening. Bikie made thorough preparations. He found a pair of old, tattered jeans, a black t-shirt with the sleeves crudely torn off and a biker jacket. He put on a bandana with a red Harley Davidson logo and a pair of Ray-Ban sunglasses. He looked really menacing and Isaac liked it. For this special occasion Bikie washed his bike, and even found a pretty good Leica camera somewhere.

"You know what I think? Why don't you skip the meeting and go straight to Hollywood? They'll put you in the movies without any auditions. Did you know that Harrison Ford worked as a carpenter up until he was spotted by George Lucas? When you end up meeting Lucas or Tarantino, at least text me to say that Bikie won't be back," joked Isaac, being quite impressed by his pal's appearance.

Bikie smiled his huge, broad smile and winked. He was happy with the way he looked, too. He had taken his time and great care in picking out his costume. He didn't get to go into town dolled up like this very often.

"Admit it, Bikie, you chose this candidate especially so you could have a costume party."

"Whatever! The time will come when I'll always be dressed like this. On a Harley, with a busty blonde behind my back. You'll see," replied the biker.

"Land this guy for us first. And then I promise you two busty blondes."

"Everything will be all right. Don't shit yourself!"

Hours later Bikie returned to the apartment quite despondent.

"First of all, that asshole was almost an hour late," he told Isaac disappointedly. "Then he spent a solid hour telling me how fucking cool he was. He didn't let me get a word in, peacocking his plumage like he was trying to impress some bimbo. I soon realized he was a trashy banker after all, because the speedometer on his super-rare Harley didn't even have a thousand kilometers on it. A beautiful thing but just gathering dust. Although better to gather dust than carry a dumb fuck like that.

"I tried about ten times to start a conversation about OE and *Collective Mind*, but the dick kept harping on about how bored he is and what he does to avoid getting rusty: Saint Barth, the Maldives, Bora-Bora, that sort of crap. He told me about all his chicks and how crazy they all are about him. Maybe there's some kind of error in your database? Or is all his creativity wasted on his stupid stories? I've never seen such a clown before."

"Don't let it bother you, Bikie, you looked like a million dollars, so he spread his plumage to impress you."

Bikie brightened up a bit.

"Seriously, Isaac, you're one of the few normal guys I've met just recently. Everyone else has gone cuckoo. Rushing about, no clue what they want in life. No goals, no ideals. Cardboard people. Let's drink some booze tonight, what do you say? Got any more whisky?"

"No whisky, but there's some awesome Seychelles rum."

"Never heard of that kind, but rum's even better."

"At this pace I will quickly become an alcoholic," sighed Isaac.

"In vino veritas, my friend. This is my way of protesting. I'd rather drink my creativity away than get downloaded. After I fought my drug-addiction, booze became my only ally and the way to forget that there was a day when I was supposed to be a great programmer. By the way, if you don't feel like drinking, that's fine, I'm not going to force you."

"Well, in that case I cannot but drink," Isaac, who decided to befriend Bikie, found it wise to keep him company.

"Tomorrow we'll get around to this Wolanski of yours," promised Bikie. "And I vow to take it completely seriously. We can't just go visiting anyone and letting them in on our plans. We can get into some real trouble this way. We don't need anyone else, but you and me. A bit of money won't hurt, but we'll somehow manage the rest..."

That night, drinking and reasoning, Isaac suddenly realized that it was not just the idea that was driving him, but anger and revenge for not being able to find his place in society. His failures, difficulties with Vicky, his poverty. Looking at the full-of-rage Bikie, he for a second saw himself and how he felt on the day of the attack. The failure with Charles has gotten his companion seriously wound up – Bikie was so full of hate towards *Collective Mind* that he even started to deny its undoubtful achievements. Isaac suddenly felt scared to have this weird outcast, whose aggression made Isaac actually defend the Agency, as his only ally. As he was getting drunk his thoughts started to scatter. Finally, having decided this all to be but a moment of weakness, he chased the unbidden doubts away.

"Our strong point is that they don't even suspect that we are fighting against them. We are a secret underground force! They aren't worried, thinking that everything has always been under control. Believe me, if this ever occurred to them, even a brief analysis of our search on the net would be enough to throw both of us in jail and force to offload our OE!" Bikie proclaimed.

Isaac didn't want to go back behind bars. The first time was more than enough, and as he remembered the tight handcuffs on his own hands, he came to the conclusion that, indeed, it was their luck that the enemy didn't know about their existence.

7

"Good morning, could I see Peter Wolanski, please?"

The young man who opened the gate looked at Isaac closely and enquired politely:

"Who's asking for him… and on what business?"

"My name is Isaac Leroy, and I'm here on a personal matter."

The young man looked Isaac up and down again, cast a glance at his scooter and opened the door wider.

"We-ell, all ri-ight," he said uncertainly, stretching out the words. "Come in," he added.

He moved aside to let Isaac through.

The house itself was not large, and set on a wide, flat plot of land – a rarity in the Cap d'Ail district. Six massive, dark-red columns, two of which ran down into a beautiful, sky-blue swimming pool. Windows down to the floor, lots of glass, lots of clear light and fresh air. The obligatory pampered palm trees on the grounds and lots of olive trees. A magnificent view of the sea. If someone lived in a villa like this, their life had come together very nicely. Through the glass walls Isaac saw a collection of modern art, both paintings and sculptures. He didn't know much about artwork, but even he recognized one of Andy Warhol's works.

"He's sitting pretty," thought Isaac. "It's a shame my parents weren't rich. But never mind, I'll make it anyway."

"Sit here," the young man told Isaac, pointing to a glass table surrounded by wicker furniture.

"Well, I'm listening. Tell me, what is this personal matter you have for me? I'm Peter Wolanski."

Of course, Isaac realized immediately that it was Peter himself who opened the gate. Although he hadn't found a photo on the Internet, the guy was the right age and spoke with an accent. From the dossier Isaac remembered that Peter had no brothers or sisters, and this guy had studied him too closely to be simply an acquaintance or friend of the villa's owner. Isaac was right to pin on his scientific society badge from school. Peter was clearly familiar with the badge and it had a favorable effect.

"So what exactly brings you to see me?" Wolanski asked.

"I just wanted to meet you and become acquainted. We went to the same university, although at different times. And we're members of the same scientific society. I'm an inventor."

"You are? And what have you invented? And what's the point of us becoming friends?"

"I've developed a couple of gadgets. Right now I'm planning to sell one of them."

"Not to me, I hope?" Wolanski enquired.

"Of course not," Isaac smiled. "Although you're capable of buying, I'm not here to sell you anything."

"Well, that's splendid," Peter added.

"The reason for my coming here, Peter...May I call you Peter?" Peter nodded.

"Is to invite you to join a recently formed, let's say... scientific society."

"A scientific society? Interesting especially in times like these. What society is that?"

"Obviously you're not a Happy," said Isaac, testing the waters. "They never show so much curiosity."

"Of course, I'm not a Happy. I don't have much faith in that piece of wishful thinking. And apart from that, it was a condition of my father's will that no one in the Wolanski family should become a donor. Not to mention that it's also the fundamental condition of my inheritance," Peter smiled ironically.

"I'm no fan of *Collective Mind* and the Agency either; although, my rating is 28015."

"How high?" Peter asked in amazement. In fact, Isaac's rating was more than twice as high, but he had named that number because it was Peter's level.

"Twenty-eight thousand and fifteen," Isaac rapped out, articulating each figure distinctly.

"Incredible... How did you find out my rating?"

"Ah, this guy's no fool," Isaac thought to himself. "No wonder he's a leader. You can't hold the smokescreen for long with someone like this. Better try speaking more openly, or else he will sense a lie, won't believe me and might even hand me over to the police."

"The information came my way," Isaac paused significantly, "from a very reliable source."

"What information? How?"

Isaac wondered whether to tell him or not. There was a pause.

"Okay, all right. You don't have to tell me. For now. Perhaps I don't want to know anything about it," Peter thought for a moment and added: "But since you're here on a personal matter, and this is the first time I've seen you, I don't promise to answer questions either."

Isaac was beginning to feel uneasy, his thoughts scattering.

"I read your student blog. I know you're not very fond of *Collective Mind*. And I'm planning to become a donor, so I decided to get some advice from people who are knowledgeable on the issue," Isaac lied.

"Rubbish! For that you can go on the Internet without ever leaving your home. Good bye," answered Peter.

"Wait! I invented this," said Isaac, changing the subject and putting the *V-Rain* on the table. "Turn on the lawn sprinkler and you'll see how it works."

"We'll get soaked."

"I don't think so," Isaac responded with a smile.

Peter took a remote control out of his pocket and turned on the sprinkler. Isaac pressed the "on" button, and not a single drop fell on them or the table between them.

"Some gadget! That's really cool!" Peter was impressed.

"With this size, the range is four meters. From four to five meters ten percent of the drops get through."

"Any restaurant would pay a heap of money for that gismo! It would let them keep the same number of tables out during a rainy day," exclaimed Peter.

Now it was Isaac's turn to sit there with his mouth ajar. Well done, Peter! Until this moment, it didn't even occur to Isaac that he could sell the device to restaurants.

"You're right. You and I have just demonstrated the possibility of collective intellect without offloading our energy," Isaac was impressed.

"Isaac, do you want to hear me say that I don't like the Agency? Well, I don't. What else?'

"No, Peter, I want to know just how much you dislike it."

"I dislike it very much. Why?"

"And I hate it fiercely. And that is the purpose of my visit."

"I don't feel fierce hatred, but I sense that this whole business will end badly."

"Perhaps very badly indeed. It's an epidemic. And epidemics have to be…"

"Halted?" asked Peter, again catching Isaac's thought in mid-phrase.

"Yes, and that's the goal of our scientific society. To find people who can do that."

Isaac liked Peter. What a pleasure it really was to talk to an intelligent individual. Memories of Pascal came flooding back.

"Don't be afraid. Tell me what's on your mind," Peter brought Isaac back to reality.

"You remind me of a friend of mine. He understood everything before I finished saying it too."

"Did he die?"

"To some extent. He's a brainless Veggie now."

"Well, it happens. What I dislike about this business is the general degeneration. And it's very strange that COMUNA doesn't publish statistics on the children born to Veggies. They publish all sorts of things, but they don't disclose that information. I rummaged on the Internet recently and discovered that Veggies' kids are all Veggies too. They're born without any Orange Energy. COMUNA is searching for the reason, for a cure. Now that it's surfaced, they don't try to conceal the fact any more. They say this is a new problem, but sooner or later they'll fix it."

"Yes, I read that too. Just how they intend to fix it isn't clear. An energy transplant? They have the technology but there's a lot they don't know about it. I don't think they'll be able to develop it further in the near future without Link." Deep in his thoughts, Isaac gazed into the sea, deep in his thoughts.

"They're hoping it's a developmental thing and the energy will come. And some children, just a few, are born with some creativity. After all, the oldest child born to two Happies is still only five. Anyway, have I answered your question? Drop this circus act and tell me what you came for, or is my answer already enough for you?"

"They really do not understand all about the system, because they haven't downloaded Professor Link's creativity. This is something I know for sure," Isaac added emphatically.

"You suppose so?"

"I know so."

"Wow! How could you know that?" Wolanski's tone told Isaac he can stop worrying about being kicked out of the house without finishing his story.

Isaac couldn't tell Peter about Link yet, or that he had seen the precise statistics on newborn Happies. Yes, some children did have creativity, that was true. But no one has performed a DNA analysis on those children. It wasn't certain that the mother and father were both Veggies. After all, there were enough cuckolds around, and maybe COMUNA implanted embryos from normal people into Veggie women, who could tell? The important thing was that the conversation with Peter Wolanski was encouraging and Isaac felt he could actually start getting to the point.

"Put it this way, now I'm prepared to ask... not just to ask my question, but to explain my idea."

Peter leaned forward, clearly eager to know.

"I want to find Professor Link. To know more about this technology. Then to demolish the system. Destroy it physically or ideologically. Or invent some kind of a virus. I want to stop COMUNA and the global idiocy."

"And how do you intend to do this? Is this a plan or just a naked idea?" Asked Peter.

"An idea Peter, as yet it's only an idea. I have no plan. But know that you have to fight fire with fire. I want to oppose collective intellect with collective intellect. But a living one. I'm putting together a team and looking for fellow thinkers to set the human race back on its previous path. That's my scientific society," finished Isaac.

"And you came to me with this?"

Peter was clearly astounded at the scale of the concept. He could see that Isaac was neither joking, nor insane. Which meant he was absolutely serious. Seeing Peter's response, Isaac regretted that the idea of the scientific society had occurred to him too late. If it had come sooner, perhaps he could have reached an agreement with Michelle Blanche and Abdul.

"You're crazy, because it's impossible. You're a genius, if you pull it off," Wolanski declared.

"Let's just say my rating is 57,555, and I'm by no means the biggest-brain box out there. There are much smarter people than me out there. Did you hear about the terrorist attack here in Monaco? I'm the fifth hostage that Elvis took, but they didn't write anything about me. The police took me for an accomplice at first, but when they figured out who I was, they let me go. The moment had passed, the journalists had lost interest, so I was left in the shadow. I learned something from that story, literally and metaphorically. First, I'll never set foot in that place again. Second, I decided to do everything I could to find Professor Link. And third, I ended up with the memory card of the branch's central computer, and there was some intriguing stuff on it. Your rating, for instance and not just yours, but hundreds of people's: brief CV's and all sorts of information that basically makes it possible to find others who think like me. The Agency is powerful, but don't forget that *Collective Mind* was invented by one man. Who, by the way, has not become a Veggie."

"Now I get it. I must say you intrigued me when you mentioned my rating. That really got me interested."

"And I've come to you for specific help."

"What kind?"

"I need money. I have no resources to implement my plan. I've left my job and the bank is about to foreclose on my apartment. From the list of people that came my way, you're not the only one with money, but you're one of those who have criticized the system openly. Some of the rich people have already moved somewhere else, some don't look trustworthy, some have already gone bust. Some are religious or too law-abiding. Basically, there aren't all that many options, but there are some. You and I are the same age, that's already a plus. Apart from the money, knowledge is important. You're a chemist and who knows, we might have to blow something up or dissolve something. I don't have a clue how the technology works. It's the closest kept secret in the world. But Link is the one who does know."

"Mmm, this is very sudden. And you only want money?" Peter's voice sounded a bit disappointed. "And has anybody else agreed to help you?"

"Yes, but we'd better just say that I'm alone."

"Well then, all right. That's even better," said Peter.

"And I'll give you back the money when I sell my invention."

Peter leaned back pensively in his chair.

"I'm no supporter of the system, but I've never thought seriously about destroying it. I have to think about it."

After that Isaac and Peter made some small talk about various other things. For the last fifteen minutes they simply drank coffee. Peter tried to be hospitable. Isaac was beginning to like the way his life had turned out more and more. Only a week ago he had to make do with the tipsy customers of the America, and his flights of fantasy were limited to how to find money for Vicky. But now he had an interesting, boorishly brutal partner in Bikie, and he found talking to Peter really exciting and, most importantly, he now had a big goal.

Both Isaac and Peter regarded this conversation as highly important. Each of them hedged his bets so that later, if anything happened, he could tell the police that the idea of *Collective Mind* destruction had only been mentioned as a light-hearted fantasy from the same category as "let's fly to the moon" or "let's move Mont Blanc". A trifling conversation, without the slightest intention of making it come true.

As the sun started to set, the two young men exchanged phone numbers and wished each other good luck. It was time for Isaac to go home.

As they parted, they agreed that in any case Peter would keep quiet about the visit. And if he decided to reject the offer, he would simply call and say he wasn't going to invest in Isaac's invention.

8

Peter called on the third day in the afternoon, and asked Isaac to come for dinner that evening. He said he had good news.

Even though the meeting with Peter left a good impression and the candidate inspired trust, Isaac was still a bit nervous. On the way there he kept glancing around anxiously. Bikie, who was entrusted with countering any negative consequences of the meeting, tried everything he could to calm Isaac down and cheer him up a bit.

Bikie approached the question of security very systematically and professionally. He tapped Peter's phone, hacked into his email account, and even undertook to watch the house in person. If Peter had contacted the police or lawyers, or if he had dialed a suspicious number, the two of them would know immediately.

Isaac assumed that Peter wasn't exactly part of the team yet, but he obviously wasn't refusing, either. So the news wasn't excellent, but it wasn't bad. Any help would be appreciated, and it could do no harm. Bikie, carefree as ever, suggested taking it easy and being cool.

Isaac and Bikie decided to go visit Peter together. Peter did not call a meeting in order to refuse to collaborate. Bikie remarked with a solemn face that Peter definitely hasn't called anyone at all. All he's done was call twice to order a pizza. And Peter didn't need to call anyone to make a decision. For that he had his own head on his shoulders, his own brains and his intact OE.

At seven in the evening they were at Wolanski's house. Peter again opened the gate himself, greeted Isaac and offered Bikie his hand.

"Peter."

"Bikie."

"Come in."

Large, comfortable sofas were laid out on the lawn, a barbecue grill was smoking, and several bottles of cold beer were glinting in the sun.

"I've arranged a little picnic. I invited you and one friend of mine," said Peter.

Isaac and Bikie exchanged glances of alarm.

"Don't worry, it's someone reliable."

"I hope you haven't told him too much?"

"No, I simply invited her to have dinner in a pleasant company."

Now it was clear that Bikie's surveillance failed and that he missed something. He had either tapped the wrong line, or did not have all of the numbers. Bikie was embarrassed at having screwed up, and kept glancing at Isaac with guilt. He clearly didn't expect that Peter could actually talk to anyone without him knowing, so his self-confidence quickly evaporated. It was obvious that Bikie has lost sight of something.

A car honked at the gates. Peter went to open and returned with a girl of about twenty years old.

"I'm Sandrine."

"Isaac."

"Bikie."

"Pleased to meet you," she said.

Isaac relaxed. He thought it funny to see Bikie looking like a spy caught red-handed.

"I'm not certain, but to judge from your name, you won't refuse this." Peter was holding a pack of dark Guinness.

"Thanks," Bikie mumbled.

"Help yourself. Sandrine is my very close friend, my girlfriend and, I hope, my fiancée."

Sandrine smiled and laid her head on Peter's shoulder.

"We're going away on a trip for a couple of months. First, to Stockholm, Copenhagen and the Baltic, possibly to St. Petersburg and Moscow, and then we'll decide where else. I haven't done any traveling for a long time, so I'll enjoy it a lot. They say summer in those parts is very pleasant and not as hot as here. I think I can get by without the sea for a while. I want to take a look at Germany, my grandfather's home country, as well as Poland. They say Polish girls are quite something."

The final remark earned him a light cuff to the back of the head from Sandrine.

"Anything's possible," he said with a smile, for which she pinched him too, quite painfully.

"Sandrine! Stop it!"

"What do you think is possible? I'll show you Polish girls!" Sandrine barked.

Bikie had already recovered from his error and was about to joke on the subject of Polish girls and Russian lovelies, but after glancing at Isaac, he decided not to.

Wolanski took his friends around the grounds and gave them a tour of the house.

"This is a safe place, but I'm going away for a long time and you never know if something might break down or someone might break in. In short, would you mind living here and taking care of the house while I'm away? I could even pay you for service," he added with a smile. "A little bit."

Well, how about that! The very idea that he could live in a swanky villa like this for a while took Isaac's breath away.

Bikie instantly forgot about the affront he had suffered and started gazing around intently.

"I'm sorry, but I have no secrets from Sandrine," Wolanski went on. "The two of us have decided to support you, but we won't get involved. In a few weeks I will acquire full control over my father's legacy. Right now, I live in a good house, I can afford to pay almost any expenses, but I don't have control over his fortune. I have free access to a large amount of money, which I can spend as I wish. So I don't want to put that at risk.

"And so, the house is at your disposal, I can even write you a check for a couple of thousand a month, you have Internet here, television, and a small chemistry lab in the basement, if you need it. As for financing and advice, sorry, but you have to handle that yourselves." Peter felt awkward for steering clear of the risks, and his voice had a guilty ring to it.

"You're here as security guards and sort of household help. I don't need to know what you are up to while I'm away. So let's agree that if I don't ask, you avoid discussing your business in my presence. I ask you not to involve any one else until you have at least a provisional plan. Naturally, I have cameras here, so if I see visitors, I'll ask you to move

71

out," Peter added. "And you must not use the main bedroom. Better not even go in there. And finally, good luck! And let's drink to that!"

For the rest of the evening the group ate meat, drank wine and beer, discussed music and never mentioned business again.

Isaac and Bikie were totally excited, and each of them chose a nice room on the guest floor. If you didn't count the small salary that Peter has set for them, he hasn't done anything to solve their cash problems. But on the other hand, no one knew if they would need more money, or if this would be enough. At least now they had food and a roof over their heads. And quite a nice roof it was!

Isaac and Bikie decided not to waste time, and move to Peter's place as soon as possible. Compared to Wolanski's villa, Isaac's old apartment looked like a dismal slum.

Isaac gathered up his things, looked around his old room, and thought that he would never come back here. He did not feel any regret.

"How weird," thought Isaac, "I have lived here for five years, but I don't have any particularly pleasant memories associated with this dump."

Isaac even tried not to bring girls back here, because he felt ashamed and thought it was better to go to their hotel.

"But even so I feel sad at the thought that I won't be back here any more. It's like I'm cutting off a big piece of my past, finally slicing off my youth and my student years."

Vicky wouldn't come back here again either.

Isaac walked into his sister's tiny little room. Her things had been tidied away a long time ago, as if she had known. Clothes folded away in boxes, a little bit of makeup, some books and textbooks, even an old doll. All he had to do was collect the bed linens.

"It might be useful. We'll stay at Wolanski's place for a while, but afterwards I'll have to rent something. Damn, I almost forgot about the kitchen and the bathroom. Glasses, plates, spoons, forks, knives... God, what a drag it is gathering it all up now and making sure nothing breaks."

Isaac lived an impoverished life, so he collected absolutely everything he could. He only left the furniture since it wouldn't have survived another move anyway, and Wolanski would have flipped at the sight of this old lumber.

Isaac hardly had any personal things at all: jeans and t-shirts, one suit from his graduation at the university, and his computer. Everything fit into two boxes. He also has a vintage poster of Einstein with his famous phrase: "Only those who attempt the absurd can achieve the impossible".

That aphorism was very appropriate considering the situation. Isaac took the poster down carefully, rolled it into a tube and took it with him. Bikie had a similar modest collection: apart from the fact that instead of a scooter, he had a genuine Harley, as well as a guitar.

"That Bikie guy is a true rock'n'roller," thought Isaac.

Wolanski met them at the gate. He had everything ready for dinner by the pool again: drinks and hors d'oeuvres. Sandrine was resting on a soft, white sun-lounger. She waved them hello and carried on relishing the beautiful sunset over the sea, while sipping on some kind of juice. Bikie and Isaac each took a beer.

"This is some life!" Bikie exclaimed, either making a toast or just thinking out loud.

They drained their bottles in one gulp, picked up their things and headed for the main entrance. Peter gestured them to stop and asked to go in through the side door.

"Guys, we agreed that you live in the guest section of the house, didn't we? No hard feelings?"

"Whatever you say, buddy, no problem," Bikie said amicably. "Don't think we'll have any use for your oval fireplace and swimming pool, anyway. We won't have time for long soulful evenings and swimming But the loungers… Can we invite girls?"

"Bikie!" Sandrine cried out, smiling. "No girls in this house! Guards don't invite girls to their work."

"I like you, guys. I really hope I haven't made a mistake by inviting you to take care of the house. You settle into your rooms and I'll wait for you here," said Wolanski.

The first thing Bikie did in his room was take his guitar out of its case and check that nothing had happened to it in transit. The guitar was fine.

"What is this?" Isaac asked.

"A relic."

"Meaning?"

"I bought it on the Internet. Keith Richards himself played it. He even signed it! I forked out a grand for it. It's a very rare item."

Isaac looked at the half-erased scribble.

"Are you sure this really is his autograph?"

"Positive, I saw a photo of him with this guitar."

"I see. Ever heard the word 'Photoshop'?"

"Screw you," Bikie growled.

"Just kidding. Surely it's original."

"Sure as death. They don't pull tricks like that in our crowd."

He then hit the strings so hard that the sound almost made Isaac jump.

Isaac went to his room, set his things by the bed, carefully hung up the Einstein poster and turned on his laptop.

"What's the Wi-Fi password?" He shouted out of the window.

"Alchemist28015," Peter answered.

"Your rating, right?" Isaac asked loudly.

"U-huh."

"Mine's bigger," Bikie put in.

"And mine's longer," retorted Peter.

"You boys are gross," Sandrine said and everyone laughed.

When Isaac and Bikie sat back down by the pool, the sun was already setting and the sky was scintillating with the most brilliant tones in the orange spectrum.

"Look, orange energy's draining away," the setting put Bikie in a poetical mood.

"Orange energy of the sky," Isaac commented pensively.

"The creativity of the sky, expiring at dusk, reborn the next day, with not a drop lost," Bikie commented rather neatly.

"Beautifully said! You're a genuine poet," said Sandrine. She and Peter were sitting beside the pool, with their arms around each other, also looking out to the sea.

"I write songs and play sometimes, but mostly rock'n'roll, not lyrical stuff. I even used to play in a rock band when I was in college."

"Peter, why don't you write me poems? Long ones," asked Sandrine.

Peter got up and pretended to be busy with filling everyone's glasses over by the table, ignoring her question.

"Friends, I declare the official ceremony to celebrate your moving in open!"

Peter knew how to create distance between himself and others when he wanted. He also knew how to shorten it quickly, which made you feel like a really old friend of his.

"Bikie, by the way, why are you Bikie?" Peter asked.

Bikie didn't like to answer the question about the origins of his nickname, because mostly it came from drunken customers at the bar. But he was still feeling pleased with Sandrine's compliment and decided to answer.

"The usual story, the name's been with me ever since school. I've liked bikes all my life. On my way home from school, I always looked at mopeds, motorcycles and choppers especially... I used to ask a lot of questions and even made friends with a few older biker dudes. I dreamt of getting my license as soon as possible and getting my own Harley. But let me tell you: there are different kinds of bikers. There are those who form gangs and deal drugs or guns. And then there are folks who are there for the love of motorcycles. I'm one of the latter. There used to be a whole group of us in school. The group no longer exists, though. One became a Veggie, one grew up and lost interest, one was killed in a crash. Well, as for my nickname, I got it when I was still a kid. My parents bought me a scooter, a red one, so I could easily be seen on the road. And I went straight into my dad's garage, where he kept his paint. That chrome stuff, you know. And black, too. I glued on a Harley emblem – I had a real one that someone gave me – and drove to show it to my friends. Didn't even wait for the paint to dry, got my trousers all soiled. Everyone said, that now I am true biker, only a little one. So they called me Bikie and it stuck. Bikie it was. Basically, I got to enjoy being Bikie and then, when I got to be this big, no one dared to give any other nickname to me, because people were afraid of me."

"When I was a little girl my mum used to call me Sasha," Sandrine said in her gentle voice. "Russian style. She got it from some Russian book. And I just couldn't understand, I kept asking: 'Mum what is this nickname of mine?'"

Everyone smiled except Isaac who looked morose.

"Isaac, what's up?" Wolanski asked.

"His sister, stepsister, has Russian roots," Bikie explained. "She's in the hospital now."

Sandrine put her hand on Isaac's shoulder.

"Don't be sad, Isaac. Everything will be all right. We have to give all these new inventions their due. Medicine has become excellent, a real breakthrough. I've never seen such equipment before. For instance, I recently had an x-ray or a scan – I don't remember exactly what it was called. I was roller-skating down a steep slope and fell, so I went to make sure that everything was all right. They put some kind of a special elastic suit on me, and a helmet. I stood in the middle of the doctors' office like an astronaut. And the doctor had a full 3D image of all my internal organs on his monitor. Yuck! And then he pressed a button – click! – and his screen showed my skeleton."

"My father was amazed that no one is afraid of dentists anymore," Peter added. "I told him: not only is no one afraid of them, no one ever goes back to them anymore. When they treat something or fix something, it's done once and for all. But that didn't stop dad from being opposed to *Collective Mind*. He lost a lot of money when it was invented, but he wasn't against it because of the money. He said we knew too little about all this OE stuff."

"Now they've completely beat AIDS," Sandrine went on. She obviously wanted to cheer up Isaac. "They can cure cancer, asthma and all forms of allergies. They can cure everything, Isaac!"

"Everything, but not quite," Bikie growled. "Some illnesses have been left out in the cold. Alzheimer's for instance – no one knew what caused the degenerative changes, and no one knows still. *Collective Mind* hasn't learned how to cure Parkinson's either. They can only cure the diseases on which scientists have already done lots of research. That hardware itself can do nothing! Just put together old crossword puzzles, maybe. Hell, why am I telling you, as if you didn't know all this?"

Strangely enough, it was Bikie who made Isaac feel better, not Sandrine or Peter. What Bikie said inspired Isaac, and he cheered up, recalling that his plan to find Professor Link had already started to become a reality. Everything was going really well. He had a team of, and maybe it was not very big – only him and Bikie – but Peter gave them a place to live and a bit of money. It was a good thing that Peter was on the sidelines since he turned out to be a great guy. It wasn't clear yet if they were going to do anything illegal. It might not work out at all, but so far it was working and Isaac was glad.

"And so tonight we relax, drink and socialize!" Isaac thought with a smile, reaching out for a bottle.

"Friends! Not another single sad thought today and not a single mention of COMUNA! You and Sandrine are used to this place, but I want to enjoy paradise," he cast a significant glance at Bikie and at his guitar. Bikie nodded eagerly.

"This time shall we set out to sea, or sail off on a drinking spree?" he sang, strumming the guitar, before reaching out for his bottle.

"Is that Byron?" Wolanski asked.

Isaac laughed so hard he almost choked.

Bikie gave Wolanski a severe look.

"That's not By-ron, it's By-kie. It's my song, you dorks."

"I wasn't joking, I actually like it."

"That's the most terrible compliment I've ever heard. Dorks like my music."

"I don't get you. I can't compliment you and I can't criticize you either."

"Why don't you just listen without any comments?"

"Okay, okay. Can I at least light up my cigarette lighter and stand beside you for a while, as if I were at a rock concert?"

Sandrine and Isaac laughed until tears came out of their eyes.

"You can lie down on the bottom of your pool with the lighter, if you'd like. The longer the better."

Bikie carried on strumming, sometimes the words were sad, sometimes really jaunty. There was a lot about women and drinking. Everybody enjoyed listening to him.

"She gobbled her food by the ton, and her figure was soon lost and gone. She crammed down that swill and GMO slop, in massive amounts, unable to stop," he sang.

For some reason the women in his songs were beautiful, but very fat, like a music version of Fernando Botero art.

"Her backside was just like a nut!" he continued, *"Tra-la-la. All big and rough to the touch, La-la-la. Her backside was just like a nut, Tra-la-la, that goes by the name avocado."*

Boom! A loud final chord.

The evening was so heartwarming that Isaac felt peaceful for the first time in a while. Great company of intelligent people and light-hearted mood. In a way, it was even better than hanging out with his university friends.

"Man does not live on Pascal alone," Isaac noted, recalling his evenings before his best friend became a Veggie. And he had never sat around with a guitar like this before.

Every cloud has a silver lining. If he hadn't had problems, he wouldn't have met Bikie or Peter, and he wouldn't be sitting here at this classy villa. He even saw the terrorist Elvis through a different prism now, and regretted that he hadn't talked to him while they were in jail together. Where was he now? Probably already in prison. But never mind, if Isaac pulled this off, they would let Elvis go too. He would definitely prefer to sit in prison for any number of years, but not volunteer for offloading.

The next day he went to see Vicky in the hospital. She was in relatively good shape. Her vitals were stable, and Isaac had two months to find the money for the surgery. Two months ought to be long enough for him. Fortunately he only had to pay for the surgery itself and for bringing the specialists from Germany. His sister's stay in the hospital was covered by insurance.

When he got back to the villa, Bikie met him with contrived cheerfulness.

"Well then, back already from your sweet little cutie?" Bikie really wanted to cheer his friend up, but it came out awkward.

"What are you talking about?" said Isaac, puzzled. "I've been with Vicky, my sister."

"Your stepsister. That's who I meant," Bikie chuckled. "Your little sister's high-class. I looked at your photos with her. A jaw-dropping figure and great smile. A real beauty! Got to get her cured quick. Why that acidic look, you guys have different parents, don't you?"

"We do," said Isaac slowly.

He felt a sudden, sharp sting. He wasn't offended by Bikie's offhand manner. He had simply never thought about his Vicky as a beautiful young woman.

"Vicky, a little cutie," he repeated to himself pensively. It was true. Neither hospital surroundings nor her wan complexion could spoil her looks. She looked so fragile under those hospital bed sheets and she was... beautiful.

9

In the morning, when Isaac and Bikie woke up, coffee was already waiting for them.

"The gentle cooing of this pimped-out coffee machine is akin to the noble sound of my Harley," declared Bikie, being in a poetic mood first thing in the morning. "I think I'll listen to it one more time. Isaac, make me another cup. Ah, I'll tell you what: genuine coffee is some mighty stuff! Not like that instant shit. You are one lucky guy, Isaac. Maybe there's some kind of lucky energy around you? Just think about it. You've got no money, but you will have soon. Your sister's sick, but only until you get your money, so it's a temporary problem. Your brains are in good shape. You went to upload your creativity, but Lady Luck saved you. You got a piece of computer motherboard and you didn't throw it out, you looked at it. Out of the candidates you found me and Wolanski. Hit the bull's eye again! I won't deny that I'm glad we ended up here, not after meeting that swanky jerk with the Harley."

"It's not entirely a fluke. I admit I was lucky with the uploading when Elvis showed up. But choosing you and Wolanski was shrewd calculation. A risk it was, certainly, but the analysis of the candidates was correct. Lady Luck likes hard workers; she doesn't do everything for you herself. And what's more, I had failures with a couple of other candidates."

"Dunno. I reckon you're lucky. And you've got good intuition. Sometimes I think about how many little details came together for me to be sitting here, right at this moment, and I realize that math doesn't explain it because it is unrepeatable from the standpoint of probability theory. I even ended up working in the bar because I love motorcycles. The owner of the bar is a biker too. If I were not a biker, I wouldn't have ended up in the bar, and you might have chosen someone else."

"You could say that about absolutely anyone, starting at least with the fact that every one of us is born from the victor in a race of spermatozoa. One out of tens of millions. It's like one person from all of France, one from Poland, five from America. So mathematics has nothing to do with it, its fate or something else. Maybe it is luck."

While they talked, they had no less than three cups of coffee each. Heady, exquisite aroma diffused through the air, and the delicious brew spread invigoratingly though Isaac's body, clearing his thoughts. Now it was time to sit down at the computer and do some work.

"Ok, Bikie. Any ideas on how to find Link?"

"Considering how much sugar you just had in your coffee, that's really a question for you. Sugar is the brain's main fuel. Your tank is more than full right now."

"About the ideas, I meant your professional skills, in the first place."

"Well, there are a few things we can do, and some we can't. As always, we have to try everything. You never know where you'll stumble across the right trail. Either he's a total hermit, which is quite likely for a scientist, or sooner or later he'll leave tracks. Provided he is alive and hasn't become a Happy."

"I still hope that he is present in the database not just by accident or mistake. He's definitely not a Happy, and clearly not officially listed as dead. Why keep data on the intellectual capabilities of a corpse?"

"Who knows? Many people searched for him. Although, we are special since we think outside the box. I start with most usual ways to search for someone."

Bikie considered himself a super-analyst and was sure he'd find Link if there was even the slightest chance. He downloaded all the information he could find, at the same time creating and running a file comparison program to eliminate identical content. In the end, he gathered a vast amount of relevant data.

He also compared articles that were almost identical, and copied any differences into his list of leads. In one place, he found the name of a hotel Link stayed in; in another, the make of car that he was driving there. Then he found out how Link was dressed. In all, he collected whatever could be found.

Leaving his partner to ruminate, Isaac went off to the next meeting about registering his anti-rain invention.

Isaac hated COMUNA more and more, and his desire to strike a blow at it was growing stronger. Five years ago, his invention would literally have been grabbed out of his hands, companies would have lined up for it. But now, he was going to meet the agent at the patents office, still not even knowing if this was the final meeting, or the first of yet another dozen bureaucratic discussions.

The bald, plumpish patent officer, who introduced himself as Serge Morell, was also an opponent of the Agency. He had his reasons. He used to be the boss of a large department, almost twenty people, a big wig, and a well-respected man. Now his department consisted of just him, and it was only still considered a department because no one wanted to waste any time and energy on renaming it a section. He loved inventors and creative personalities, but nowadays, they very rarely came his way. He felt awkward about Isaac's case and tried to excuse himself saying that he was overwhelmed with doing everything alone: register the applications, check them, and even record all the data.

He assured Isaac that the next meeting would be the last, everything was almost ready, and he hinted that he would be happy to leave his job and become Isaac's personal agent, marketing his inventions. Isaac promised to think about it. The agent added that his business card as a head of department still brought respect and simplified negotiations. And he knew everyone who would need to be approached and how to do it. After all, he had thirty years of experience.

The former Isaac, the one that was so unsure of himself, would have agreed immediately. The current Isaac felt like a different, hardened man, a man who wouldn't fling himself at the very first offer with open arms. So he only said he'd consider it.

When Isaac got back from the patents office, he glanced into Bikie's room. Seeing his friend, tired from the monotonous search, he decided to suggest an idea of his own.

"I can see you're tired. I'll take a fresh look at your provisional results, and tell you what I think and how we could approach the analysis. And you will tell me what's possible and what's not, and maybe add something else."

"Go ahead," said Bikie and turned back to the computer in his traditional style.

"We need to find things that could be important to Link: rare objects, or an old vintage motorbike, for instance."

Seeing that Bikie was really tired, Isaac wanted to cheer him up, and offered his suggestion with absolute seriousness. Bikie picked up on the gibe, turned his head and grinned.

"But seriously, though," Isaac went on. "Let's take a look at his credit card expenditures, his bank statements, habits and magazine subscriptions, and any other little details of his day-to-day life. What he loved and what he hated."

"The magazines could be a useful line, by the way. There are all sorts of things on the Internet, but everyone loves good old paper publications. That's easy," Bikie added. "And the same goes for phone numbers, his email account, favorite sites and digital subscriptions."

"If he's alive and well he might secretly be keeping in touch with a few friends, like Deputy Secretary-General Blake, for instance."

"I think I can find out Blake's mobile number, and if it's not a corporate UN phone, I'll crack all his calls. But if it is a UN phone, then it won't be easy, for sure. Probably even hopeless. Lots of companies' data protection programs are still not very good, but I can't say the same about the UN. Usually, it's the people themselves who are sloppy. They leave heaps of leads behind, without even suspecting it, either because they're negligent, or because they don't consider themselves important enough. There are still hordes of great hackers around, and get this – we programmers are actually amongst the lowest in percentage of OE donors," Bikie announced smugly.

"Yeah right, but lots of programmers are actually employed full-time by the Agency."

"If need be, a couple of my friends can crack any tough-nut system, and get the favorite porn movies off the computer of Secretary-General himself!"

"And then," Isaac continued his reasoning. "I think we should take a look at where Link went most often before he disappeared. I don't think he's in Africa or Antarctica. If you wanted to hide, you'd probably choose some place where you'd been before, the one you liked."

"That's easier. I can track travel, especially old travel dates. In those days, data protection programs were total shit, compared to today. Anyway, I don't think any travel company would pay millions on a super-program to protect data about its clients' destinations from a hundred years ago. I reckon I can easily get information from travels as far as ten years ago. I don't think Link had time to handle all the tedious ins and outs of traveling. More likely he used an assistant or a secretary."

"Then there are frequent flyer programs and maybe he used a car-rental company. I doubt they have mega-protection either."

"You can't be sure. But as far as I can tell, three assistants worked in Link's lab, two males and one female. He wasn't exactly the sociable type. There are only forty-two numbers that were called from the lab more than five times a year, and about another hundred from the phone of his assistant. And there are obvious front runners among them."

"Excellent, that'll be useful."

"Also," Bikie continued, "we have to find his old bank card and at least pick out the most popular transactions."

"Yes, we might see something unusual. Buying medication, for instance. And if it's rare, he probably still uses it."

"Get real. No more cancer, no more AIDS, remember? Or you think Link didn't get rid of some allergy he had?"

"Yeah, you're right, not much chance. But it really depends on when it happened. Everything wasn't invented, manufactured and distributed at once. But even so, please take a look. Meanwhile, I'll go down to the gym. Somehow, this place has given me the urge to work out. I used to think I wasn't the kind of a person suited for fitness, and now I just can't wait to pump some iron. It really clears out your head and calms the nerves. See how much stronger my arms are?" Isaac proudly displayed his slightly enlarged biceps to Bikie.

Bikie nodded without speaking. Wolanski's gym was certainly top-notch. It was put together by professionals, and was obviously very expensive. But Bikie didn't use it, he was as strong as an ox anyway.

The next meeting with agent Serge Morell at the patents office turned out not to be the last. There was some kind of a typo, and all the documents had to be signed all over again. The agent assured him that this was definitely the final stage, and next time, Isaac would receive a certificate for his patent. And so he did, two days later. Isaac couldn't believe his luck, it still wasn't money, of course, but he was in the last stretch. The agent congratulated Isaac on officially becoming an inventor, and solemnly presented him with the beautiful patent and a bundle of documents.

Smiling, Isaac gathered up the heap of papers. Just in case, the agent reminded Isaac about his offer to work with him, but Isaac didn't have time for that right now, he was too excited and delighted. He promised to think about it a bit later. Everything had ended well after all, and he set off back to the villa in a good mood. Bikie took one look at his glowing friend and asked:

"Well, how was the meeting with the im-patent agent?"

"Super! The invention's registered. Bingo! Look!" Isaac triumphantly raised the brand-new certificate with the big gold seal above his head.

"Well done! Cheers! Today we celebrate." Bikie gave his friend a tight hug.

"It's my treat!"

"From Wolanski's bar? Oh no! Today, we'll go to my McCarthy's. I'm on a long-term leave, but I still kinda work there. Itching to pour someone a beer and mix a drink. I haven't seen any chicks for ages, too. We live like monks! But I personally have never taken the vow. We're like a pair of doting parrots, we're perched in this gilded cage.

"Okay! Let's go into town!"

"You can be my customer, and I'll serve you! Live it up, it's your day!"

Early that evening they set out for the bar. Isaac put on his tattered jeans and a white shirt with skull cufflinks that he kept for special occasions.

"The skulls don't suit you, Isaac. I'll make you some cufflinks myself, real cool ones. Will be unique."

"Why, what's wrong with these?"

"Nothing's wrong with them, but nothing's right with them, either."

"The skull, by the way, is a talisman."

"I know. It's just that you somehow manage to look like a dumbass. But screw that, let's go!"

Bikie had washed and serviced his Harley for the occasion, and even wiped the dust off his biker's jacket.

"Just don't squeeze your tits against me too hard," he grinned, gesturing for Isaac to sit on the back.

"You have to offer a girl a drink first, before you can expect snuggling like that!" Isaac squeaked flirtatiously in reply.

With the old motor roaring powerfully, they hit the road and headed to the center of Monaco.

At McCarthy's Bar, Isaac felt jealous at first: it was his celebration, but everyone rushed to hug Bikie. They said hello to Isaac too, and Bikie introduced him to everyone. Then Bikie solemnly poured a mug of beer, switched off the music and made a ceremonial announcement.

"Today, we're celebrating the huge success of my friend Isaac, a great inventor who has conquered rain. He has registered his bizarre design with the patents office! Cheers!"

The entire bar roared thunderously: "Cheers!"

Hearing the sound of clinking glasses everywhere, Isaac felt a sudden rush of happiness. He's never been the center of so much attention, and absolutely everyone was shaking his hand and wishing him luck. These were sincere, genuine congratulations from people he didn't even know. Everyone smiled at him, and a pretty waitress even kissed him on the cheek. The bar was awash with festive cheer.

Bikie proclaimed that the next twenty mugs of beer were on the house, and people surged towards the bar. It wasn't so much that the guests were desperate for free beer, just that they all wanted to share Isaac's joy. Since they were caught up in his celebration, they wanted to be involved in it completely.

"*We are the champions...*" the speakers thundered.

"*Of the world*!" the entire bar sang, joining in.

"Hoo-ray!" Isaac raised the cry, and everyone supported him with a roar of approval. He was the happiest man in the world, a triumphant conqueror.

After drinking three mugs of beer in half an hour, Isaac felt the urge to go to the bathroom. At the table farthest away, right in the corner, hidden behind the columns, he spotted a solitary figure sitting in the semi-darkness, someone not participating in the general merriment. Drunk, either on happiness or beer, Isaac felt he had to dust off this melancholy customer's sadness, so he set off confidently towards the mysterious stranger. When he got closer, he saw that it was a girl.

"Dear God, it's Michelle Blanche!" Isaac thought in delighted surprise.

Michelle was sitting there, completely withdrawn and absorbed in her own thoughts. Standing in front of her was a half-empty cocktail glass.

"Michelle, is that you? What are you doing here?" Isaac asked.

"Ahh, hi, Isaac. It is Isaac, isn't it? I'm glad you're here. Do you think you could bring me some water, please?"

The realization that Michelle remembered his name sent a wave of warmth flooding through Isaac's body. He immediately forgave her spiteful look at their previous meeting. Looking slightly sad and relaxed, she seemed a hundred times more beautiful than before.

"Of course, just a moment, I'll be right back."

He realized the girl wasn't feeling well, and the drunken haze in his head dissipated instantly.

Isaac went in behind the bar, poured a glass of water, added ice and whispered to Bikie:

"Michelle Blanche is sitting in the corner. I went to her before I found Wolanski. I don't understand what she's doing here."

Bikie craned his neck to see who Isaac was talking about.

"I know her. That is, I've seen her here before. It's not the first time she's come. She doesn't come often, but she drops in. A strange girl, she's always by herself, never talks to anyone. Probably just taking a break from her jet-setter crowd. Maybe she's unhappy or maybe she's just pissed off at them all, and comes here to hide once in a while. Other people's thoughts are a maze, and women's thoughts are a maze to the power of three. At least to me."

"I see. She's so beautiful!"

"Her face is beautiful. But her figure... I don't like them that skinny."

Isaac brought Michelle water and she gulped down half the glass, then got up and asked him to show her to her car. Just when Isaac had started dreaming of getting to know her better, at last. He was terribly disappointed.

"Maybe you could stay for a while? Can I get you anything else?"

"No. It's time I went. I'm tired. Some other day."

Taking Michelle by the arm, Isaac carefully helped her towards the exit. People were still congratulating him, but Michelle didn't seem to notice that at all. That was a real bummer. He'd been enjoying a great triumph and she hadn't seen any of it. And now she was leaving! Isaac's mood was ruined.

Outside, Michelle didn't look tired. Her driver was waiting at the entrance, holding the door of her luxury car open for her.

"Thanks, Isaac, you're really sweet! I saw you were celebrating. Congratulations. Enjoy your evening." Michelle kissed Isaac on both cheeks, like a friend, said goodbye and drove away.

Isaac realized he was in love. Definitely in love with her. What a shame she had to leave. He could still feel the touch of her lips. He was totally shattered emotionally by how easily and casually Michelle had conquered him without even trying. Surely he wasn't her only fan. Most of the men in her entourage must have been in love with her. Isaac stood there in his loneliness for a while, he didn't want to draw a line under this unexpected encounter. Finally, he went back into the bar.

"Where did you go, Isaac? What's wrong with your face? What's got you so down?" Bikie asked.

"Just pour me a drink, will you? And not beer, make it a vodka. A double.

"Oh, your problem is clear enough," Bikie said with a jolly wink. "We've drunk to the patent, enough of that, now we're boozing to love."

Isaac didn't remember how much longer they spent in the bar and how they got back home. The next thing he felt was a fierce dryness in his throat and a splitting headache. He didn't feel like getting out of bed, but the intense pain in his head was so bad that he reluctantly got up and shambled into the kitchen to look for an aspirin.

10

After two weeks, Isaac and Bikie, having collected a ton of information and analyzed it forwards, backwards and sideways, were still stuck right where they started. They still have not come up with any theory concerning Link's whereabouts.

They discussed and argued, trying to persuade each other, but in fact, did not make any progress.

Isaac looked at the data they had and summed things up:

"So, our old boy didn't take many holidays and he loved islands. He was quite fond of Thailand, Corsica and Sardinia, and he had been to China. He visited the US, too, but mostly on business, for holidays he usually chose the Mediterranean islands. Sometimes he went just for a weekend, sometimes staying longer and, interestingly, often called a Dutch escort service before setting off. Well yes, sitting in the lab for hours on end does make it pretty hard to find a female companion. The rest is general information: date of birth, education – nothing that gives us any insight.

"Isaac, why are we trying to find him in the first place? Putting in so much effort? Maybe we ought to try studying the actual technology?"

"Intuition, Bikie. If we find him, maybe we'll find both our question and answer at the same time. In theory, the man who created *Collective Mind* can destroy it too. Many people who've tried to produce the technology have gotten nowhere, and we want to break it. What if we cause some disaster? It could be dangerous. Better let Link stop it when we find him."

"If he can, and if he wants to…"

"We'll make him. I'm sure he knows a couple of secrets how to persuade people to stop offloading."

"What if he's a big fan of his monster?"

"Stop cooking Link before catching him. We'll work it out. By the way, what about the woman he loves? If he's alive, she's probably somewhere close by. Analyze her data. Maybe it's not so secret, and anyway, women don't worry as much about security, or rather, they're not as careful as a paranoid scientist. If she's not from the science circle, she could easily have left tracks."

"Well that would be a good idea, except that I haven't really found any personal connections that Link had."

"And what about that escort service? Why don't you think he could have called and dated the same woman all the time?"

This secret side of Link's life could turn up some leads. Only they had to take into account that such a service probably didn't have a permanent website, or a permanent telephone number. But they didn't have anything else, and Bikie started on the analysis.

A few hours later Isaac looked in on his friend, and from Bikie's excited appearance, he realized they finally had some kind of lead.

"I think I know where our pal weaves his nest from time to time," Bikie was really excited, and Isaac saw that he was about to deliver some kind of an information bomb. "Every time after he called the agency from this number, there was another call, to a mobile or landline number. The mobile number's been out of use for a long time, unfortunately, but I wouldn't have spent much time on it anyway, because I came across something more interesting. The landline number is in Amsterdam, it's listed to an apartment at an address that came up once at the local immigration office. According to the report on this address, two girls lived there. A certain Yoshi Kato and a certain Hiro Okamoto. So, our man was not only fond of his laboratory flasks, he liked a touch of Japanese flavor."

"Right…"

"After that I came across Yoshi Kato several times."

"But Hiro not once, apparently," Isaac guessed with a smile.

"Bull's eye! Well done, kiddo, you catch on quick."

"And I'd even venture a guess that you've already gathered the info on Yoshi."

"Bull's eye again!"

"And you've found…"

"So far I've found shit," Bikie replied vulgarly. "Apart from the fact that she has a residence permit in England! But hang on, I haven't been digging for long."

"Well now, Amsterdam is not Tokyo, we can make an on-site inspection. Link had a cozy set-up, a one-hour flight and no prying eyes. I think I'll take a flight over there," Isaac summed up.

Thank God prostitution in Holland was legal, so they had a fair chance of finding the Japanese girl or her friend. Even though Bikie was working tirelessly and the search for information needed to be continued, it was impossible to stop him from taking a trip to Amsterdam.

"You know that we haven't got any money to spare, don't you? I'll manage on my own," Isaac assured him.

"I agree to a hotel with half of a star. I even agree to sleep with you in the same bed. I will not eat or drink, but I'm definitely going to Amsterdam, that's non-negotiable... Oh, and I'm taking back my vow not to drink."

Realizing that resistance was futile, Isaac called Peter and warned him they would be going to Amsterdam. Peter laughed and asked on what dates they would be away.

It is fifteen hundred kilometers from Monaco to Amsterdam. After a small argument with Bikie, who, having won himself a trip, promptly suggested going on his Harley, the alternative of going by plane was accepted. Because neither a car nor a motorcycle were convenient in Amsterdam.

Isaac bought the cheapest tickets and found a budget apartment with two beds using a popular app.

Bikie was so excited he wouldn't let Isaac sleep until three in the morning the night before their flight. Although they didn't really need to discuss their plan further, they talked it through briefly. They would contact the escort agency – there probably weren't many good ones, and they could not believe that Link had used a cheap one. They would try to find both the Japanese women there.

Assuming that Yoshi had disappeared together with Link, finding her would be no easier than finding the professor. But the other woman, Hiro Okamoto had no reason to hide. They would find her and see where the lead go from there. Bikie had easily figured out the old address of the two girls' apartment from the telephone number. The rest they would sort out on the spot.

Amsterdam. Dozens of canals divide the city up into a host of little islands, connected by hundreds of bridges of vastly different kinds. The main, and the most famous canal, is the Amstel. Amsterdam is also the city of tulips, but by no means their native land. The flower originally came from the mountains of Asia. The Greeks and the Persians loved them. And there was a "Tulip Era" in Turkey, too. It was from there that an Austrian ambassador brought back a few bulbs and presented them to a local professor of botany. They were then stolen and brought to Amsterdam. Isaac recalled the story of the famous tulip boom that followed these events. At that time you could get a good house for the price of a bulb of a beautiful tulip. Prices soared sky-high and everyone speculated in tulips, from bankers to ordinary housewives. Of course, in the end the bubble burst, dragging a whole bunch of people down to financial ruin. The boom of *Collective Mind's* popularity will probably fail similarly.

This was the world's freedom capital. Hordes of people once used to come here for a weekend to have a good time. There was everything here: the red-light district, loads of clubs and bars, and coffee shops. Nowadays, people still came here to smoke grass and have fun, although, vast crowds were a thing of the past. Isaac had been to Amsterdam three times but his most vivid memory was the King's Day at the end of April. The streets were transformed into torrents of orange – every single person was dressed in the national color to honor the festival. It seemed as if all of Holland had gathered in the streets of the capital. On the canals there were so many boats – large and small – and rafts, that you couldn't even see the water. And so many people crowded onto the boats, you couldn't tell where the pavement ended and the boats began. Everyone was singing, drinking and dancing. One of the best days in Isaac's past. He smiled at his pleasant memories as the plane made its approach for landing.

They decided to save on taxi and took an express train. Half an hour later they were standing in the central station. Bikie was amazed by the size of the bicycle park. There were thousands of bicycles, if not tens of thousands, in a three-story building. Bikes could be rented for peanuts, but the friends set off for the Old City on foot. Their apartment was conveniently located in the attic of an old house. There was no elevator, but that was no problem. Bustling and noisy Rembrandtplein was only a stone's throw away, and they could see the canal with a drawbridge that connected it to the Amstel.

"Isaac, let's have lunch first. The escort agency probably isn't open so early. I'm sure the girls are still asleep after their working day, or rather night."

"Okay, let's do lunch. That smell of pizza is making my stomach rumble. Do you mind a piece of Italy?"

"I'm all for it," Bikie answered, stroking his large belly.

Bikie prepared very thoroughly in an attempt to justify his presence in Amsterdam. He has studied the five most visited escort agency sites. Only two of them had Asian girls, and only one had Japanese girls. He also already knew the location of the apartment where the phone number found was registered.

"The phone number I dug up doesn't match any of the agencies. It's been changed since then but one of the sites said the agency has been in business for twenty-five years. I think that's the one we want."

Isaac's call was answered almost immediately by an extremely jolly voice.

"Decided to spend a pleasant evening?" A man's voice asked jauntily in English.

"Yes, thank you, but I have specific requests," said Isaac, feeling a bit awkward.

"Well, bear in mind that our prices are significantly higher than in the red-light district. And specific requests will cost even more."

"No, no, I don't mean that. I'm interested in oriental girls."

"Well that can easily be arranged."

"Not just any, but Japanese girls. That's essential for me."

"We don't have Japanese girls. Only Thai and Chinese, and a Filipino girl. There's a young Russian with slanting eyes, very beautiful."

"No, only Japanese girls. And, you know, a bit older. Over thirty, if possible."

"Listen, this isn't a supermarket, we don't have that kind of a selection. But you won't regret it if you choose a Chinese girl. We do have one a bit older, if you like. A very sexy and exotic woman."

"I want a Japanese woman," Isaac insisted.

"Are you a Japanophile or what? Or Japanese yourself?"

"No, I'm European. It's just that I was here a few years ago. And I was with this girl. I want to see her again."

"Sorry, lad, I've never had any Japanese girls here. If you want someone else, call us," the dial tone sounded in Isaac's ear.

"No luck," said Isaac, turning to Bikie. "I'll take a breather and call the other number."

"Hello," Isaac heard the same familiar voice say.

"Uhmm, this is me again…" Isaac didn't expect that different telephone numbers could belong to the same agency.

"You're a persistent lad. You must have had a really wild time back then," the agency manager laughed.

"But it says on your site that you have a Japanese girl."

"If you were drug-fuelled and I brought you a Chinese girl, you couldn't tell the difference. Anyway, I don't have any Japanese, and I never did. But I'll look for one. Do you remember the name of your Kamasutra? They often disappear, you know. I mean, they go away. Some guy like you falls in love, or gives her so much money, she doesn't need to work anymore. Sometimes they even get married."

"It's not a matter of Kamasutra. I don't remember her name exactly. Maybe Yoshi Kato, maybe Hiro Okamato or something like that."

"OK. If I find her, I'll call. What hotel are you in?"

"The Grand Hotel de l'Europe," Isaac lied. He didn't give the real address so the deal didn't go south. In this case, it was better to play a rich customer.

11

With nothing in particular to do, Bikie suggested they take a ride to the building where the girls have lived. They decided to take the bus, in case everything worked out with the escort agency. They didn't have much money to spare.

The girls' apartment was located in a pleasant looking district that was a bit outside the city center. Unfortunately, they couldn't find any cafes nearby that they could have used as an observation post. The building had no concierge, and the residents' names were scribbled next to the buttons of the intercom. There was no tab for Kato or Okamoto, but they found the name Akiyama.

"Look, Akiyama. Could that be our Japanese rose?"

"Let's check right now," said Bikie, pressing the call button.

There was no response for a long time, but eventually a soft, mewing voice answered. The friends didn't know what a Japanese accent sounded like, but the woman that answered definitely had some type of an accent.

"Can I speak to Yoshi Kato," Isaac asked diffidently.

"I'm sorry, there's no one here by that name," there was a brief pause and some bustling in the background. "Who's looking for her?"

Bikie jogged Isaac with his elbow. Isaac leaned towards him and Bikie whispered that if they didn't know Yoshi Kato, they wouldn't have asked who was looking for her.

"I'm an old student of Professor Link's. I'd like to talk to Yoshi. Are you her friend, Hiro Okamoto?"

There was a rustling sound and a different voice answered:

"Wait."

Bikie uttered a soundless "Yessss!" and slapped Isaac on the shoulder so hard that the latter winced in pain. When they were in the lobby, Isaac twirled his finger beside his head and told Bikie what he thought of him.

"Ouch! You're crazy? That hurts."

"Sorry," Bikie muttered guiltily. "I was so excited."

The girl – and it was Hiro indeed – proved to be very nice and hospitable. She didn't know to where Yoshi had suddenly disappeared. But she showed them her photo and said she suspected an elderly Englishman was involved. Thus, the most valuable thing the friends learned was what Link's girlfriend looked like. Hiro asked to let her know if they find her former roommate.

The men left feeling a bit disappointed. They didn't get any new information, apart from a confirmation of their guess that Yoshi was probably with Link. And it was pretty clear that the two were together, anyway. No leads yet again.

"Let's go have a beer at Smokey," Bikie suggested. "It's almost evening and I need to relax."

Isaac agreed. This was Amsterdam, after all. And Smokey was right on Rembrandtplein.

No sooner had the friends drank a mug each, than Isaac's phone rang. The number was not displayed, but he recognized the voice.

"I've found your Japanese girl, where shall I bring her?"

"Mmm, don't bring her to the hotel, we've rented an apartment."

"We?" the caller asked in surprise. "That'll cost extra."

"No, no, I'm the only client," Isaac clarified.

"Okey. I'll be there in forty minutes."

"Okey," Isaac replied uncertainly and hung up.

"What crazy shit is this?" Isaac asked, looking at Bikie.

"I don't know. Maybe Hiro was jerking us around."

"It didn't seem that way. But who can tell? Let's meet her anyway. It can't do any harm."

At the agreed time, a car drove up to the building. The manager introduced himself as Paul, gave the building a disgusted look and suggested they go upstairs. In the apartment, he looked around and sent a text message. Soon a woman of about forty came up.

"Here's your Yoshi," Paul said with a broad smile. "Give me the money."

"Do you know Hiro Okamoto?" Bikie asked the woman, smelling a rat.

She looked at Paul inquiringly and shook her head.

97

"It's not her," said Bikie, annoyed.

"How do you know if it's her or not? He's the one who fell for the Japanese girl," said Paul, pointing angrily at Isaac.

"But it really isn't her," said Isaac, trying to explain.

"I got you what you wanted, and she's got the right name! Isn't that right?" Paul was starting to get angry. "What's your name? Yoshi, right?" He asked, giving the woman a stern look.

This time she nodded.

"So let's have the money, guys, and she's yours. And no tricks. Don't even think of fucking us over unless you're looking for really big trouble."

Bikie jumped up off his chair with his fists clenched.

"Who's trying to scam here?"

"Look, lad," his opponent told him in an icy voice. "I'll leave calmly right now. And then I'll come back up and you'll leave here for the hospital."

Paul looked very confident and quite menacing – it obviously wasn't his first time doing this. Looking at Paul Isaac was beginning to get frightened by Bikie's quick temper.

"Wait. This is a misunderstanding. We wanted a different Yoshi. Let's settle this peacefully."

"Money on the table," Paul said quietly, calling a number on his cell phone. "We've got a problem here," he said to someone.

Bikie kept on crowding him.

"Don't give me this bullshit. I'll call the police and they'll stick you behind bars before you can even let out a peep. And then, they'll download you dry. No one is letting you rip off tourists. This town lives on them, and you'll get such a kick in the ass, you'll forget your name."

Isaac was already standing shoulder to shoulder with Bikie, feeling that a fight was inevitable.

Paul backpedaled from such confidence. He lowered his voice and started making excuses.

"I looked for the one you wanted. Hassled people and found you a Japanese girl. You guys are setting me up. I already owe the middleman."

"Do I kick you out, or will you leave by yourself?" Bikie asked, a genuine bar bouncer seething up inside him.

Completely deflated, Paul took the Japanese woman and cleared out.

They waited for another ten minutes, and it became clear that no one was coming back up.

"We need to get out of here," Isaac summed up.

"Agreed."

They quickly collected their things and went downstairs. Isaac's phone rang again and Wolanski's number was displayed.

"Hey, Peter! I'll call you back, we're a bit busy here."

"Surprise, Isaac! I'm here in Amsterdam, in the Sofitel Hotel. Shall we meet?"

"You know, Peter, your timing is just perfect. We've got nowhere to go," Isaac replied, turning in the direction of the famous hotel.

In Wolanski's room Isaac finally recovered his wits after the unpleasant incident. He told Paul about their search and the clash with Paul, making special mention of Bikie's heroism.

Wolanski listened avidly, once in a while throwing alarmed glances at the door.

"I swear I envy you, although you guys turned out to be real thugs! Your life is turning out to be really exciting and I couldn't resist flying up here. This is Amsterdam! And you, my friends, are here! How could I miss it? Especially since I was so close, in Copenhagen," Peter confessed in embarrassment. "Sorry I didn't warn you. I was afraid you would be against me coming," he added, speaking to Isaac.

"Against?" Isaac was amazed.

"Well yes, you're the boss, the ideologist, you decide what can be done and what can't," Wolanski explained.

Bikie nodded in agreement, reaching for the joint that Peter had rolled.

"I agree with Peter. I might have fired the shot, but you've got steel balls the size of melons. I am always prepared to knock the arrogance out of someone, but I couldn't have launched a global project like this, that's for sure."

"Who did you visit before me?" Wolanski asked.

"A lawyer. I sent some emails. Also a young athlete, Named Abdul. Bikie went to Charles. And Michelle Blanche, if you know who that is."

"I don't know Abdul, but I know Michelle."

"And Isaac wrecked himself on her, like she was an iceberg," Bikie explained in his usual style.

Wolanski laughed and Isaac blushed.

"To hell with wrecked ships and dashed hopes! We deserve a little party in Amsterdam. I don't fancy going out, but I wouldn't mind getting high," said Isaac, handing the others bottles of beer.

"Here's to Amsterdam!" Bikie clinked bottles with Wolanski and glanced suspiciously at the joint. "No tobacco in it, is there?"

"Of course not, pure grass."

Satisfied, Bikie leaned back in his armchair and let out a cloud of smoke.

"Peter, tell me," he added slowly, "Why did you decide to help us?"

"Honestly?"

"Well, of course, honestly. What do you have against the Agency?"

"Only if you promise not to laugh?" Peter felt a little embarrassed.

"2000 percent," promised Bikie.

"Same for me," added Isaac.

"Well," Peter hesitated a little. "I told Sandrine about Isaac's visit and his proposal. She hates the Agency, her parents are both Veggies. Before they offloaded their OE COMUNA ruined their company. So, I blurted out that I think I could help you, join the resistance. She looked at me with such admiration, I even somehow felt uneasy. She said she was very proud of me. So I just didn't have a choice. If I changed my mind, she'd think I was a coward. And she is just so stubborn, she could leave me immediately."

"In short, you just want to impress this chick?" asked Bikie suppressing a smile.

"Something like that. But now I regret nothing, honestly," Wolanski tried to justify himself.

Peter had such a guilty face that even stoned Isaac broke down with laughter, immediately infecting Peter and Bikie with it. The next morning Isaac woke up in the hotel, still in his clothes. Wolanski was sleeping nearby on the sofa, also fully dressed, and Bikie was snoring in the bedroom. Isaac splashed cold water on his face, ordered breakfast for three and woke up his friends. Then, he took a shower and felt better at once. There was still an hour left until they had to go to the airport.

They gave a warm hug to Wolanski one after another. Peter called and paid for a taxi.

"He's a good German guy," said Bikie, looking at the buildings flickering past the car window.

"I agree. And he has an excellent habit of showing up at the right time," Isaac added.

12

In the morning, Commissioner Pellegrini booked a ticket, put together his beach-going things and set off to the airport.

Four hours later he was in Monaco. He dropped off his luggage in a cozy hotel, and had a delicious lunch and a coffee at an Italian brasserie in the marina. He breathed in the delightfully salty sea air while walking to the local police department, where he was received very guardedly. The local officers were surprised at the attention from such a big wig, as himself.

"Those strange people, first they write a huge report, and then they're surprised that I've come," the commissioner thought in annoyance.

He inspected the scene of the attack thoroughly and took notes, which angered his local colleague even more.

"It's all in the report," one of the locals protested. The Monegasques didn't like it very much when the French interfered with their internal affairs.

"I understand," Pellegrini gave a dignified nod. "It's a good report. But it's always best to take another look. Who of the local officers dealt with the case?"

He was sent to Captain Robert, but the conversation did not produce anything new. The captain clearly had not found anything suspicious. The terrorist was a run-of-the-mill fanatic – you came across them, sometimes. He was probably crazy. He had spouted some total gibberish about "the heart of the devil" and smashed the computer at the Agency. Had he come across a cash register or a safe, he would have smashed that too. Robert gave out all the details, but didn't feel eager to deal with the uninvited guest.

"He's in a looney bin," the captain explained. "You can go there and check for yourself. A crackpot, if ever there was one. There are plenty like that. Some picket outside of buildings, some turn to frenzied prayer, but this one was violent. There's nothing more I can say. Here are all the witness statements as a bonus. Here's a pass for the looney bin, if you want. You can talk to this mental case Elvis as much as you like."

But Pellegrini wasn't able to talk to Henri Cavalier, AKA Elvis. The prisoner was silent as a fish. In the hospital, they said he was usually very talkative, and that he kept rambling on about the devil and his heart, saying it had to be destroyed. But he wasn't actually dangerous, at least not to people. He'd damaged some equipment, but that was about it. Other than that he was harmless.

The amiable nurse was really surprised that the patient refused to speak to his visitor and tried to help to get him to talk. But Elvis frowned, crossed his arms, turned his face away and said nothing. The girl told the commissioner that only an hour ago the man had been boasting that the heart of the devil would be destroyed, because he had managed to hand it on to someone he had enlightened.

"Elvis does have an attitude of a criminal, after all: say as little as possible at interrogations," the commissioner noted. There was no doubt about Elvis's insanity, and obviously nothing to do at the hospital, so, Pellegrini went back into the city. He strolled round the beautiful city, and admired various modern sculptures and vintage cars. Tired of walking, he dined in the famous Café de Paris, drank a glass of local rosé and went back to his hotel.

Pellegrini intended to fly back the next day, late in the evening, but from early morning to midday he had some time to lie out in the sun and take a swim. He had to make the most of his visit. The sea wasn't at its warmest, of course, but some people had already opened the season.

"And then," he thought. "Perhaps I should talk to some of the witnesses?" The commissioner quickly glanced over the records. "Yes, definitely! I'll have a word with them. I can go back to Paris any time, after all. I should take advantage of being at the Mediterranean."

All this time the strange phrase "heart of the devil" kept running round Pellegrini's head. His intuition, or perhaps experience, told him that there was something about these words, some hidden meaning. What if the madman talked about some object?

If the nurse reported what Elvis said correctly, someone else had this "heart of the devil", not Elvis. Was this the ravings of a lunatic, or an allegory that could be decoded to find his accomplices? But then, what accomplices could he have, except maybe another lunatic?

Accustomed to not discounting even the most absurd theories, Pellegrini went back to the COMUNA office to inquire about anything that went missing after the terrorist attack. He thought that Henri Cavalier had stolen something that he called "the heart of the devil". He was told that nothing had disappeared. The computer in the manager's office was only badly damaged. Pellegrini asked what was in the computer. Nothing special, just usual data, that was all. A pity. The "heart of the devil" turned out to be just a fantasy.

Boring. And boring was the modern criminal world, which consisted of nobody but dreamers, schizophrenics and freaks. There was nowhere to spread one's wings.

Time went by, but the promising "bombshell" dug up by Bikie still had not exploded. No clues and no interesting leads left by Link's Japanese girlfriend have been found. She was granted a resident permit and got a job in the same university where Link worked. All sorts of small stuff, but then, just like Link's, her trail disappeared. It looked like they were together, but their whereabouts remained unknown. Isaac tried feverishly to figure out a way to hook the big fish named Link and hoist him up out of the dark. What else should they look for?

Bikie was exhausted and frustrated, too. This made him start spending more of his time on things that had nothing to do with the project.

"Why don't we take a trip to England and visit the university at which he worked?" Bikie suggested out of the blue.

"To England?"

"Why not, we'll get on a train in Paris and scoot over for a day or two. Thanks to Wolanski we can afford to spend a little bit of money."

"Of course! An excellent idea! There's a chance we might find something new there!" Isaac exclaimed, obviously brightening up.

Bikie huddled over the computer and went to a website for railway tickets.

"Isaac, you don't mind if we go by train instead of flying, do you?"

"We can, but why?"

"I want to have a coffee in Paris. I haven't been there for a long time."

"Then Paris it is. Actually we could stay overnight."

They left on the earliest train, and slept peacefully for the five hours it took them to get to Paris. As Bikie had planned, they set off to drink coffee in Île de la Cité, at a brasserie not far from Notre Dame. They strolled round the center for a while and had lunch in Montmartre, but they simply couldn't relax. The hope that they would find a lead at the university urged them to go on in their search. They decided not to stay for the night, but went to the station, and exchanged their tickets for the next day for ones for the next train. In the last few years the length of the journey had shortened a bit, from two and a half hours to two.

"Not a lot, but in mathematical terms that's twenty per cent," Bikie calculated. He obviously wanted to talk, and there was almost an hour left to London.

"Isaac, what are you thinking about?" Bikie was ready to talk about anything at all to avoid traveling in silence.

"About how soon I can get the money for Vicky's surgery," Isaac replied. "I've almost sold the patent, but I think it'll be another month or two before everything is finalized. I should've asked Wolanski for the money. I would pay him back later out of my fee. What if something goes wrong with her? Something that can't be fixed?"

"Have you and your sister known each other a long time?"

"Yes, for ages. My mother got married for the second time when I was ten to a Russian immigrant. He brought his daughter Victoria with him. She's younger than me, but we became friends immediately. She's, you know... clever and cheerful, too. She was always kind and considerate."

"Yes, and beautiful as well," Bikie added. "With looks like that she'll be okay, she'll have a good life."

Isaac got that clammy feeling again, that anxious stinging sensation somewhere behind his lungs, like the first time when Bikie praised Vicky's looks. A beautiful girl, Isaac had known that before. He was happy for her, because she did not lack attention and had lots of admirers. The feeling Isaac had this time was completely new, and entirely inappropriate somehow. He tried to banish this anxiety and the thoughts that had begun distracting him more and more often. Before, he never thought about Vicky as a young woman. Meaning, a woman that could interest him as a man. Argh, dammit! That sounded disgusting! Even if she was his stepsister, she was still his sister. But controlling feelings was a hard task, and Isaac's thoughts kept turning back to Vicky more and more often.

He could not understand why he had not noticed it before. Vicky was nothing like any of the others Isaac had dated. She was a hundred times better! Because... because he loved her? That was not possible. It was the simple, logical conclusion, and he wanted to send it packing, and his feelings with it. But he just could not. Trying to think about it less only made it worse – the only thing he thought about was her.

Isaac looked too preoccupied, so Bikie decided to change the subject and distract Isaac by saying anything that came into his head. Seeing that Isaac wasn't responding, Bikie turned away to the window and started crooning another of his revolutionary songs.

... Steel rails like belts,
Constrain the world.
People are sleeping. All is quiet.
We rush to abyss, through the night.
There's nothing there to stop the flight.

We are inside the monstrous snake,
That has devoured the best of brains.
The two of us woke up in wrath
To wreak the choo-choo of its path.

So let the convoy miss a curve,
Cars break apart, disaster strike,
But wake and save all those who've there

Isaac's thoughts carried him further and further away. He recalled his chance encounter with Michelle, but then his imagination was gradually taken over by Vicky. This was a difficult dilemma, whereas he couldn't figure out even simple cases. But were there ever any simple solutions for someone in love? Everything immediately got tangled up and seemed totally overwhelming. Logic and desire contradicted each other and desire always won. If everything sorted itself out easily into neat pigeonholes in your head, then you were not really ensnared in passion. But if you were flung from joy to sorrow and back again, like a rollercoaster, and all your thoughts led back to the same person, then you are really in deep big-time.

Isaac believed there was no such thing as love at first sight. There was interest, which developed in different directions, depending on the two people involved. Especially, if a third butted in. A girl usually sensed any interest in her, and if there was even a drop of interest in response, she started turning the screw gently on her admirer. Not deliberately, but out of innate female flirtatiousness. So deftly and naturally, that it could make someone fall head over heels in love with her. She could make him furious or drive him insane. For no reason, other than to feel that she was in good shape and get a buzz of confidence in her own sexuality. Or maybe Isaac had made all this up and he was seeing hidden meanings in perfectly ordinary behavior?

One thing he did know for certain was that he did not understand anything about women. "Get lost!" could mean "go away" or "try a bit harder". If everyone left everyone the first time they were told to, the world would probably have become a drab place long ago. There would be no flamboyant couples like Elizabeth Taylor and Richard Burton. Mark Antony would never have conquered Cleopatra's heart. True love was only born by overcoming obstacles.

To win a popular girl, accustomed to all the very finest compliments and tired of constant attention, you had to fight really hard. You always had to fight for love. Everything was complicated.

But then, girls fall in love easily, too, and suffer over men that are definitely not worth it. Such was life.

"Bikie, listen," Isaac said, breaking the silence. "There's something I wanted to talk to you about, I've got this dilemma. I need an outsider's point of view. Only please, without your usual gibes."

"Talk," Bikie was all ears.

"From the age of ten I lived side by side with my stepfather's daughter. We basically thought of each other as brother and sister, and at the same time were good friends. But now I'm starting to realize that she's becoming more to me than a sister. What do you think about that?" Isaac paused, but then went on. "How does it look to you from the outside?"

"It looks okay to me..." not a single muscle twitched in Bikie's face. "I wouldn't bother about it. What could possibly be wrong? You're not related."

"We're not, but it's still not exactly the right situation for starting an affair."

"Isaac, you shouldn't get all hot and bothered over it. If you like her, I don't see any reason why you should not try and date her. Only I don't know how she'd feel about that."

"I don't know how she'd feel about it, either. I just want to get clear to myself, how weird I think it is."

"You know, Isaac, we have enough real obstacles in this life. There's no point in inventing more. If you love her, then love her. I've never really fallen in love in my life, so my relations with women aren't clouded by prejudices and fears. And believe me, lots of girls like guys who are direct and know what they want, without clouding the issue pointlessly. Although, of course, you have to be aware of the subtle line between directness and coarseness."

Isaac looked so gloomy that Bikie decided not to press him anymore and looked out of the window at the colorful patches on the fields. Those colors didn't arouse the slightest romantic impulse in him.

Great progress in agriculture was another achievement of *Collective Mind*'s work. "Energy of each person for the good of humankind," as COMUNA put it in its promotional material.

All the existing knowledge about agriculture, from the moment the primordial man first began working the land right up to the present time, had been systematized and integrated. A bundle of ideas from biological sciences, soil science, meteorology, astronomy, chemistry and God knows what else had been pooled together. And the result was that COMUNA could indicate precisely what to plant where, in order to produce the largest harvest of the most delicious fruit per acre of land. Even the demand and supply on the market was taken into account.

The technologies cost millions, and the first year saw a wave of protests from farmers, but then opposition subsided. The correct use of land produced such large harvests that, despite a general reduction in the price of agricultural products and the high cost of patents, farmers still made good profits.

Futuristic miracle-machines of gleaming metal worked in the fields. If something looks like it has arrived out of the future, it means the future is already here. The freakish combine harvesters with dozens of robotic arms droned as they collected and processed. Up on the hills, wind generators, with five propellers on each spun their curved blades silently. Hothouses with solar-battery roofs shimmered opaquely in bright light, like iridescent patches of petrol on water.

The contents of supermarket shelves changed instantly. From then on no one used GMO technologies. They'd been outdated by the arrival of new methods for growing organic produce.

Greatly improved in quality, fertilizers became more effective and were no longer harmful to people and animals.

In general, the environment had benefitted a lot. Chemical barriers and filters, waste disposal systems, technologies that reduced fuel consumption, high-power hydrogen and solar energy motors – these were all technologies that could not have been implemented without some powerful impulse. The world had definitely improved with the arrival of OE and taken an innovative leap forward.

Bikie was the one who hated the new order of things. This sweet, utopian world of smiling people had become too sterile to be regarded as real. It was more like a world of obedient, squeaky-clean robots. An advanced computer game.

Pleasant-looking, identical, nine-story buildings of a residential district flickered past the window. The little town looked lovely. It was a Happy Ghetto. Actually, these settlements were called Happy Cities, but Bikie's name for them was ghettoes.

At the Agency they hadn't immediately realized that by downloading energy from low-level individuals they would run into the problem of homeless Happies that no one would look after. Those, whose payment wasn't enough for a long, normal life in a boarding house or who lost the money they were given and proved incapable of adapting to the outside world. Nevertheless, the Agency didn't just cut these people adrift. A limit was quickly introduced, specifying a minimal level of creativity for offloading, and the donors were required to get insurance contracts for lifelong support, or at least have a guardian who had to obtain a license from the Agency. The homeless Happies were gathered together and housed in specially built residential districts. Of course, these weren't holiday resorts by any means, the apartments were small and simple, but even so they were quite adequate for the undemanding new residents. In any event, they didn't complain. Before moving to Peter's place, Bikie had lived in far more modest conditions, even if in Monaco. These little towns were built quickly, on inexpensive land, and dubbed Happy Cities. They had a pretty good infrastructure: sports grounds, parks and cinemas. There were even leisure and entertainment centers. The Agency chose jobs for the Happy residents, often building some factory nearby. The problem was solved and no more homeless Happies appeared.

The settlement and its residents were left behind. "The road to Hell is paved with good intentions," Bikie recalled.

"Listen, Isaac," said Bikie, surfacing from his reverie. "Do you think Link will agree to stop all this? If we destroy the system, we have to offer something to replace it. If you think about it seriously, for most people we're just ordinary terrorists, and death is too good for us. Wars and epidemics will start up again; lots of people will lose their chance in life. There'll be an economic collapse and chaos like the world has never seen before."

"Ah, but we won't destroy what has already been achieved. We'll just slow the world down a bit and reduce the speed of evolution. I'm not saying that *Collective Mind* is all harm and nothing else."

"There are so many benefits to it. I sometimes have doubts myself. Criticizing is one thing, destruction is a different matter altogether."

"The gap between COMUNA and the other corporations and governments is growing so fast, we'll have a dictatorship before you know what's hit you.

"That's just theory, but there's concrete, positive, practical achievement there outside the window. How many of these people will end up on the street? Die from overdosing on drugs? Wars and famine will start again. Sometimes I think we picked the goal out of anger for being losers," Bikie looked upset. "What if people finally created paradise on earth? They are stupid, they really are. But so what? As if in the nineteenth century everyone was smart. Veggies have no creativity, but they can feel joy – they watch movies, fuck, see no evil, obey the scripture. What if this is just the future that has come too fast? What is the future you want? What if *Collective Mind* saved us from a nuclear war, terrorist attacks that never happened, God knows what else? Lots of folks might not have been alive by now, but they are! Don't you tell me that it's better to be a dead smart guy than an alive Veggie. I don't mind the fuss, I'm following you, and I'm really interested in reaching the goal. But you, where the hell are you going? And why? Yes, there's theoretical danger in *Collective Mind*, indeed. But with this logic you can accuse the creators of the Internet, because terrorists use it to exchange information, or perverts to store child-porn. Or the creators of the cell-phone can be blamed that their gismo can be used to detonate bombs remotely. One can find potential threat in every goddamn invention! Actually speaking, this artificial intellect that Link invented is the safest possible. This machine doesn't work without people, doesn't make any decisions on its own."

"We'll find Link and then figure it out." Isaac was still absorbed in his own thoughts.

13

The train arrived at St. Pancras Station in London.

The friends got out of the train with its long, streamlined nose that reminded Isaac of his mother's flat iron, while Bikie thought it looked like a red-and-yellow Japanese dragon.

After they went up in the lift, they saw a huge bright dome of glass and iron, set on walls of red brick with archways and plastered columns. Beautiful and raw neo-Gothic architecture.

"Bikie, did you know that this place has the longest champagne bar in Europe?"

"I don't know what you're hinting at, girlfriend. Let's just have a coffee from the machine."

The machine poured them coffee in cups that had the number 2 printed on them. Soluble plastic. In two years there will be no trace left of those plastic cups. They each bought a sandwich from the next vending machine and sat down under a sculpture called "Meeting Point".

Passengers walking by seemed not to notice the tall sculpture of an embracing young couple, frozen in cast metal.

Not far away was another sculpture, a bit smaller: a respectable-looking man gazing up so intently at the dome that he had to hold on to his hat to stop it from falling off. It was Sir John Betjeman, a poet who adored railways and was feverishly active in the middle of the last century in the campaign against dismantling the platform of this station. He was a good example of a man who held on tight to the past. A good sign.

From the station they went to the university campus, which was a forty-minute drive from London. The university was now named after Jeremy Link.

The genial Hindu taxi driver asked if this was their first time in London.

"Yes, we've come to repair our karma," Bikie informed him.

The Indian gave a broad smile and said that one didn't repair karma, one restored it.

"My name's Rashid. Would you like me to explain what karma is and how it influences a person's life?"

Bikie nodded. Rather than travel in silence, he could listen to something interesting, and not just from anybody, but from a real Hindu.

Isaac didn't listen, he was again caught up in his thoughts about the ups and downs of love.

"Thanks Rashid, that was interesting." Unlike Isaac, Bikie had spent the entire journey discussing and arguing about his karma with the driver. "When we are ready to go back, I'll call you and you can pick us up. Did you get that, Isaac? If you spat in someone's face in a past life, you may get hit by your own spit in this one!"

"What?" Isaac had missed the conversation and didn't understand a thing.

"Look at you! What a blockhead with leaky karma you are! You've got two holes, in your left ear and your right one. It all flew in one and out the other. You missed everything!" Bikie explained disappointedly. "All that interesting stuff you were just told and you didn't pick up a thing."

"Sorry, I wasn't in the mood for listening. And I do know what karma is."

"In your case that's as much use as a straw hat against a meteor shower," Bikie replied acidly. "I'm not going to repeat it all. Listen to me next time, and I'll swap your karmic sombrero for a decent anti-grenade helmet!"

"It's a deal," Isaac said with a smile. "But can I have an anti-Bikie helmet?"

"There you go. You've just made another hole in it!" Bikie exclaimed indignantly. "What you've got isn't karma, it's a colander. And your head hasn't got cerebral convolutions in it, just spaghetti."

"I hope it's Italian, at least."

"Yeah, Italian, hard-shell noodle."

Isaac and Bikie walked up to the library building. They wanted to look inside – it had to be beautiful! It was centuries old and the collection of books had to be huge. All universities unofficially competed with each other to have the best library. Another depository of the ideas and thoughts of great people, only not computerized. If the Agency could have found a way to augment its capacity not by using people, but the books they had written, what immense power that would have been! The book-learning machine! Though there was nothing good about artificial intelligence either. All the films on that subject inevitably ended with a computer declaring war against mankind.

The university was beautiful and had a certain aroma of aristocratic dignity. Neatly trimmed lawns on all sides, with students leisurely lying around, discussing something or other, reading textbooks, or fiddling with their laptops. It was a scene from a fairytale. Of course, there were many attractive young women.

"I'd come here as a lecturer," said Bikie, impressed by two girls who had just walked by.

"And what would you teach? Rebellion and rock-n-roll?"

"Libertarianism and freethinking. Epicureanism, as well."

"This is a mixed university. You ought to go straight to a female-only school to do your lecturing. Although you're more interested in the practical classes aren't you?"

"Screw you. If you envy my high-flying imagination, just say so. You'll never reach such heights with that spaghetti of yours."

"Do I understand right that you won't take me as a lab assistant in your department?"

"In my department I conduct all the lab work myself," Bikie declared solemnly, lewdly adjusting his jeans. "But we'll find a sweet little fat girl for you."

Isaac's bad mood had evaporated. He absorbed the carefree student atmosphere floating in the air, and tried to listen in to portions of the students' conversations, recalling the time when he was in college.

The only thing making him worried was the task ahead – finding a lead to Professor Link.

"Look, Bikie, there's our target, the professor himself…"

"…with a bronze head! Enough with the jokes. We need a cover story. People could ask questions about who we are and why we're interested in the professor."

"That's not a problem, Bikie! The subject of Link's disappearance is still an event that intrigues people. We'll introduce ourselves as student journalists from the University of Monaco. No one will bother to check if our student journal 'The Principality and Science' actually exists," answered Isaac.

"OK, I was going to suggest something like that myself!" Bikie said with a nod, and then continued saying how envious he felt looking at the students in England. "Just look at that building, and how much land they have here, the lawns. Football pitches and handball courts – who are they training here, sportsmen or eggheads? And those golf courses we saw on the way here!"

"And those abandoned universities we saw on the way here," Isaac retorted.

"That's true," Bikie agreed. "Lots of students have given up studying. They went chasing after the money that COMA promised them, like sheep, which only proves yet again…"

"… that what we intend to do is right," said Isaac, completing the thought. "What did you mean saying COMA?"

"That's what one should call that darned COMUNA!"

Isaac and Bikie spent several hours searching for everything connected with Jeremy Link. They rummaged through the university publications and spoke with the professor's colleagues and former students, even with the cleaning lady of his study, which was now a museum. They also studied the publicly accessible archives, and asked everyone they came across about Link. There was zero new information. Everything they were told they already knew. Link had disappeared suddenly, without even completing the course he was teaching.

As they walked out of the building, a gallery of portraits of great scientists caught Isaac's attention. The great men looked down at him: Einstein, Leonardo, Galileo and right there among them was Professor Link. He had his head inclined to one side. His expression was sardonic, eyes narrowed. A true man of his time. Not a hint of glamour. Even on a portrait he'd been captured just as he was in real life.

"Bikie, there ought to be other photos of Link, right? Maybe we'll find a lead in them?" Isaac exclaimed in sudden insight.

They looked through what they had collected again, this time studying the images carefully. They asked students and professors about their photos. Some had photos of unofficial events, some boasted that they had "Link and me" selfies. People were glad to show the two journalists their photos with the great celebrity, and the pair tried to pick new details.

In his office in Paris, Pellegrini looked through the materials from the scene of the incident and the interviews with witnesses once again. In the report drawn up by the Agency's accounting department he saw that the computer had to be replaced and could not be repaired because some parts were missing. The computer had been written off as a loss as a result of the terrorist attack.

"A smashed monitor and keyboard with missing parts." Pellegrini was delighted: something had been lost after all! He could take another trip, an excellent pretext for a little more time by the sea at government's expense. But the most important thing was that new details had surfaced and he needed to know what parts of the computer had disappeared. This nagging little point had to be clarified, didn't it?

When Pellegrini showed up at the COMUNA office again, he was greeted with open arms like an old friend. When he asked bluntly which parts were missing from the damaged computer, no one knew the answer. The only person with that information was the system manager Simon Droit, and this was the third day that he hadn't been at work.

"The fact is he's going through cancer treatment," one of his female colleagues explained.

"Cancer?" Pellegrini was surprised. "And he's been away for three days? I happen to know that cancer is treated with a course of medication and no sick leave is required. One of my subordinates had the treatment last year."

"Yes, that's if you go to the doctor immediately, but Simon dragged things out too long, so now he had to take a sick leave. We told him to go to the doctor and get a prescription but he kept saying: 'I'm not going until I kill Trot'."

"Kill Trot?" Pellegrini repeated, alarmed. "I beg your pardon?"

"He was playing an online game World of the Worlds...or something like that, and he had this sworn enemy, Trot," Simon's female colleague informed the commissioner only too eagerly, and from all the details she knew Pellegrini realized that she had a crush on the person she was talking about. Or she happened to play this game too.

Eventually, they managed to get the administrator on the phone, and Pellegrini explained to him that he was investigating the terrorist attack and would like to know what part was missing from the smashed computer.

"The board was smashed and a large piece was missing. I could have just ordered a new monitor and a case but I had to replace the machine completely because of that piece," the system administrator replied blandly.

"So it was a board?"

"Yes, the base board. They used to call them motherboards. That was because the daughterboards were attached to it."

Pellegrini realized that now he would have to survive a flood of unnecessary information from a man who didn't have anyone to talk to about the things that interested him, so he preferred to say goodbye.

Pellegrini arrived back in Paris from Monaco, finally closed the case and prepared the materials to be sent to the archive. The last thing he needed now was for the trifling trips he had made to surface in an audit.

When the friends got back from London, they suddenly found themselves at a big party. True to his style, Wolanski arranged another surprise. Although he had not planned on returning home before he received his inheritance, he came back after all and organized his own birthday party. There were many people at the villa and the guests drank and made merry to good music. Isaac and Bikie were pleasantly surprised – Peter had turned out to be less cautious than they thought at first.

Their host greeted them like old friends. Isaac apologized because they didn't have a present, adding that they simply hadn't been expecting to see Peter here and they wouldn't like to cause him any trouble.

"No problem but I do have a present for you. You'll see it later," Peter said with a mysterious smile. "I thought about the security aspect and it's fine, I'm not taking any risks. Formally speaking, there's a month or a month and a half left until I get my inheritance, or a couple of weeks, if I'm lucky. I decided to celebrate my birthday, even though you are living here. To be honest, after Amsterdam, I miss our little group more and more. I didn't feel like celebrating without you, so I decided to come back, get a few friends together and have a party. Go change and join us."

The guys dumped their things, took a quick shower and joined the other guests, who gathered around the pool. A zany old DJ was playing music, which sounded different from the modern stuff. It was obviously the choice of a veteran of the underground, not some disc from COMUNA music label. It was like Isaac's good old student days, apart from the fact that the party was happening at a super-cool villa.

Isaac scanned the guests. An interesting crowd of those who were mostly from rich families. No Veggies around. People who had enough money for the good life were in no hurry to sell their creativity, although, many people who used to be rich had gone bust together with their companies when they couldn't compete with *Collective Mind*.

There were a lot of beautiful girls, all dressed very elegantly, not flashy. All were sleek, well-groomed, with lovely slim figures.

Maybe they weren't big fans of all the latest innovations, but they definitely used the new generation of creams and other personal care products.

Isaac sipped champagne out of a fancy glass, enjoying himself as he strolled among these representatives of high society. He met a well-known TV presenter, and a few girls who were famous models. Peter and Sandrine were sitting right there, surrounded by their friends. When

Peter spotted Isaac, he started making gestures that were hard to understand. Isaac eventually realized that Peter was pointing out someone sitting over to one side, behind the DJ's console. Isaac set off in the direction indicated, but he couldn't make out who was there through the flashing light that was pointed right at him. When he got closer, he realized what the "present" was that Peter set up for him. He had invited Michelle Blanche.

Isaac was totally delighted. If only there were more Peters in this life! He turned back towards the birthday boy's table and gave him a big thumbs-up sign! Peter smiled and replied with the same gesture.

Michelle was very beautiful with her hair gathered into a simple ponytail, just a little bit of makeup and a touch of lipstick on her plump lips. Small earrings, no watch or bracelets. The modest, short little black dress exposed her sharp little knees. Her outfit was completed by lacquered high-heeled sandals. Everything seemingly so restrained, but she looked stunning.

"Hi, Michelle! This semi-darkness adds some mystique to your beauty, mind if I join you?" Having drunk a glass of champagne after his journey, Isaac was in exactly the right condition – not yet drunk, but already feeling confident.

"Hi there! No, I don't. How are you getting on, Isaac?" Michelle moved from the center of the sofa to one side, so that Isaac could sit down.

"I'm good. Everything's going fine," Isaac said and kissed the girl on both cheeks. He pointed to Michelle's almost empty glass. "Maybe I could bring you another juice?"

"Yes please, only instead of juice, bring me a Bellini."

"How about I bring you a different cocktail? You'll like it. It's based on champagne too. I'm an ex-bartender after all, and there are cocktails that I invented myself."

"Alright, but only if it's not too strong."

"Well, they are just a little bit strong, but one or two won't cause any problems."

Isaac came back carrying two at once: one was of a bright golden color and the other had a bronze shimmer to it.

Michelle tried the golden one first.

"Whoa, that tastes good! What's in it? Wait, let me guess... Champagne, that's clear enough. Something orangey and maybe something with coffee?" she added, and then sniffed the second glass: "And this one smells of coconut."

"I won't tell you the ingredients, or you won't drink it! But you've guessed most of the smells," said Isaac, smiling. He was dying to boast about the recipe he had invented, but restrained himself. "I'll tell you, but first let's see if you can figure it out yourself."

"Well, the coconut flavor is clear enough. It's Malibu. I'll think a bit more about the rest. So you don't just invent cunning little devices, but cocktails as well?" Michelle asked with a disarming smile.

"How do you know that I'm an inventor?"

"Peter told me. He said he had a pair of interesting characters living at his place, talented inventors. He said one of them was an avid biker, and I'd seen the other one a couple of times. It was obviously you he meant."

Isaac flushed with embarrassment and pleasure. It was a good thing Peter hadn't introduced them as caretakers, who were keeping an eye on his house.

"Yes, I'm an inventor." That had a proud ring, and Isaac thrust out his chest. "And what do you do?"

"I wanted to be a designer. I was pretty good at it, and I developed a few fairly promising concepts. Unfortunately, it didn't grow into a business and remained more of a hobby."

"Why?"

"*Collective Mind.* They turn out excellent design concepts for quite low prices. It's hard to compete with them. It's possible, but the market has slumped badly. There's no financial motivation. It would be more accurate just to say I do creative work."

"That's not so very terrible for you; after all you're fairly..."

"Rich?"

"Well, yes. Well-off, you don't need money all that badly."

121

"Not strictly for financial reasons, no, but when your ideas die without ever being born, it's painful. I want to show what I can do. Show that I'm not just…"

"Devastatingly beautiful," Isaac put in.

"Thank you. To show that I'm not just another pretty face. Apart from a diploma in design I got top marks in many exact sciences."

"Oh! Heavy! I remember you have a high creativity quotient, but exact sciences – that's some cool stuff."

"But how do you know Peter? Quite an unusual person you are. Peter is no fool either, your friend is an inventor, and so are you. You came bouncing up to me that time with some kind of slogans. And now I learn that you have surrounded yourself with creative people. Have you got a special nose for them?"

"Something like that. People like that fascinate me."

Narrowing her lids, Michelle examined Isaac, finished her cocktail, put the glass down on the table and said in an affectedly stern voice:

"Now, tell me what you've drugged me with…some kind of love potion?"

"Almost. Unfortunately, it's just Brut champagne with Malibu and Cointreau in it."

"Delicious. Champagne and liqueurs. You villain! And what is it called?"

"Lucky Blonde."

"Ohhhh, is your girlfriend a blonde?"

"No, no," he protested. "I haven't got a girlfriend, it's just a name. I thought it sounded nice!" he said, deciding not to mention that he really had named the cocktail in honor of Anna, his undivided university love. Her name on Instagram was luckyblonde, so he chose it as the title of his creation.

"You're lying. Even in the dark I can see that you just lied. So you're a romantic too?" Isaac's cocktail tasted great, looked pretty and went straight to your head from the very first glass. Michelle was not an exception – she was joking and smiling, feeling the buzz.

"And the second one," said Isaac, primly deciding to change the subject, "is called 'Star Bridge'. It's champagne too, with Amaretto and Grand Marnier. Like a bridge to the stars. Those ones up there," he said pointing to the sky.

Michelle looked up too, at the pure black sky, spangled with bright stars.

It wasn't cold at all, but Isaac shivered, moved closer to Michelle and took hold of her hand. She didn't object, on the contrary, she put her head on his shoulder.

Everything was going so well, but then up walked Bikie and Peter, two romance-killers.

"Damn you to hell, Bikie, can't you guys see you've picked the wrong moment?" Isaac thought. But the moment had already been lost. Bikie had brought over four glasses of champagne.

"I want to propose a toast to Peter. He's a true character! Alive and natural, not some kind of a fake. You are young, and you're only just at the beginning of your road, so don't veer off it! Happy Birthday, as they say. Happy in the good sense of the word! Dammit, what a fine word they've ruined!" Bikie made a theatrical face and everyone laughed.

"To Peter!" Michelle joined in, getting to her feet.

"To Peter!" Bikie roared, after switching off the sound on the DJ's console.

"To Peter!" voices echoed on all sides, alternating with the clinking of glasses.

Sandrine came over and took the birthday boy away to dance. Bikie set off to get another glass and Isaac and Michelle were left alone again.

"Would you like me to show you my main invention?" Isaac suggested.

"Yes, please do."

Isaac went to his room and came back down with the *V-Rain*.

"A very stylish little tool. I tell you that as a professional designer." Her words were sweet music to Isaac's ears.

"The design's actually not the most important thing. Press this button here when it's raining, and not a drop will fall on you. It's as if you were under a dome."

"Oh, wow! Great! I've never seen anything like that before. That's a really useful item for someone in an evening dress with a fancy hairstyle," said Michelle, impressed. "I could use one of these."

"That's not all," said Isaac, glad that his invention had been appreciated, and moreover, by a girl he liked so much. "You can use it in all sorts of other places, as a personal umbrella or as a public one. You can keep the rain off restaurant terraces, or even have an exhibition of watercolor paintings out in the street. The patent has been registered."

"I see you really are an inventor. Peter wasn't exaggerating. Good for you! You are an interesting guy. Did you drop that glass at my feet deliberately that time?"

"No, by accident, sorry."

"I don't know. I'm not sure I can believe you. Every time I see you, you pull some really offbeat stunt."

"That's the effect you have on me. I get dizzy and glasses start falling."

Michelle put her arm on Isaac's shoulders. Isaac tried to kiss her but Michelle pulled away.

"I'm a strait laced girl. Let's move slower. You're too quick off the mark!" Michelle said, smiling.

Isaac couldn't tell if she was serious or not. He could see she thought he was cute and found him interesting. But he couldn't figure out if he should try to kiss her again or if it was better not to. Probably better not to, he could spoil everything. And today he could get to know her better. The party was in full swing, no one was getting ready to leave yet. These sober thoughts didn't linger in his head for long. A few minutes later he did kiss her after all, and this time she didn't pull back.

14

The next morning was a hot one, with the principality being scorched by the sunshine. At his old place, on a day like this, Isaac would literally have been gasping for breath. Usually, he preferred to go to the bar, where strong air conditioners buzzed quietly and it was relatively cool, earlier in the day. But that problem was behind him now. Wolanski's villa was a great place for days like this. Squeezed in between cliffs on both sides it was always slightly in the shade. On the other hand, there was always a breeze blowing from the sea, even on a completely windless day.

Electric cleaners hummed away steadily outside, tidying up after the party. Being in an excellent mood, Isaac and Bikie had sat themselves in the living room and were studying in more detail the photographs they had managed to get hold of at Link's university.

Isaac noticed that in some of the photos Link looked rather odd by modern standards. An American would have called his appearance "old-fashioned", and an Englishman would have called it "classic". In some of the photos Link was holding a cigar.

"Look, Bikie, at this photo here and this one too. Link smoked cigars. Smoking has already been conquered, right?"

"That's right, it has," replied Bikie. "I got cured myself. I never thought it would be so easy. I don't feel the slightest desire to smoke any more. In fact, it disgusts me. But there are some rich old farts that still suck on their cigars and pipes."

"And Link smoked! Maybe he still smokes. Link seems to be too stubborn to change his habits. That could be our lead. It is cretins like that, who think cigars aren't really all that harmful, who keep the remaining Cuban factories in business. Let's see what we can dig up on the subject."

Isaac remembered the world's exultation at the final victory over nicotine addiction. For three hundred years smoking had been a problem for ordinary people and a source of big money for the tobacco industry. The Agency didn't care about the influential tobacco lobby and released a drug that cured nicotine addiction, both physical and psychological, with just two pills. In a flawless marketing move, the Agency handed out the medication absolutely free, exchanging two tablets for a single cigarette of any brand. The tobacco conglomerates were crushed like pitiful worms; they went bankrupt in just a few weeks. The tablets flew off the shelves like hot cakes, people gathered in parks and burned their cigarettes together. There aren't very many ideas that can unite the entire world in a single impulse, but cigarettes were burned in parks from America to China.

The day they started handing out free pills was a global holiday, a celebration of independence. Independence from nicotine, which used to take a million human lives a year. People lost millions on their tobacco shares, some even committed suicide, but no one felt sorry for them. The hands of the tobacco company owners might not be bloodstained in the literal sense, but figuratively speaking, they were dripping with gore.

Anyone who still wanted to smoke could only find a tobacco shop in very biggest cities, or they ordered the old-fashioned poison on the Internet. Cigarettes already cost almost as much as cigars, their price rocketed as sales plummeted.

A month later the Agency spectacularly bolstered its influence by releasing a cheap remedy for cancer.

In those two months the popularity of donating creativity soared and more followed when *Collective Mind* struck a blow at drugs. This time, the Agency didn't forget its own interests – the drug-dealers and pushers were forced to "upload" as criminals.

Drug addiction had also been defeated. This applied to every kind of illegal drug apart from marijuana. The arguments about that were still going on, but the way things looked, it was going to be declared a drug, as well. The last bastions of legal marijuana, Amsterdam and Los Angeles were losing the battle.

So, smoking had been conquered. Only a few smokers were left, mostly rich people and members of the older generation. They were too old to listen to the warnings about how bad smoking was for you, and too arrogant to give up their beloved habit of puffing on a pipe or pulling at a cigar for any reason at all. For people like that, smoking a cigar was a matter of individual style, a hobby and a part of their life. There was a chance that the retrograde Link was the same. Everything seemed to suggest it. Like many geniuses, he was not very particular about his appearance, and grayish white traces of ash could be seen on his trousers and the sleeves of his jacket. Cigars could be seen in several of his photos. Although the tobacco industry was at its last gasp, it still existed because of people like Link.

Bikie came up with the idea of digging through the lists of clients on the servers of tobacco shops near the university. He asked Isaac not to bother him.

"I like to socialize and I get distracted when there's someone else with me," he explained. "So when I'm working, I'm a loner."

Isaac did not object since he needed to through the patent documents. The important thing now was not to sell too cheap. Wolanski's idea of using *V-Rain* on the open verandas of restaurants added a good two million to the price, if not more.

He went to visit Vicky in the hospital too. He wanted to see her all the time now. There was so much he wanted to say to her, but he couldn't. Neither could she hear. His beginning romance with Michelle didn't stop his feelings for Vicky.

Working on his new approach, Bikie collected the addresses of tobacco retailers in London. It turned out that there were a lot more of them in Link's time. First of all, he excluded the shops that were too far away, and then he picked out the ones that sold expensive cigars and were open twenty-four hours a day. He broke into their databases with no problem and focused on a tobacco shop that was located only a short distance from the university campus.

"We know when Link was in England. We know when he started giving his lectures or when he went away to conferences. I've highlighted the relevant dates. If he paid for cigars with his card, we'll see its number on those days," Bikie explained to Isaac.

Sales at the little cigar shop were pretty sparse, with not a single cigar being sold on some days.

"Good kids," Bikie growled. "Smoking is bad for you." There was a time when he was a heavy smoker himself and he had ignored all the warnings. It was hard to imagine how many cigarettes he would already have smoked sitting there like that and working on his puzzle. Now even during an intensive search he never even thought of smoking. Coffee was a different thing.

Bikie took a swig from his cup and looked at the results of analyzing payments by dates. Every time Link came back to England, a purchase for a substantial sum was made at the tobacco shop. Bikie compared the numbers of the cards used, hoping to see that it was the same customer every time. Then he could assume that it was the professor's card. But, alas, he saw that the cigars were purchased with at least two different cards. Did that mean that Link was the owner of at least one of them?

Bikie's analysis continued and he decided to break into the databases of local travel agencies. Even though the procedure didn't look too promising, he launched a card number comparison program, into which he entered the numbers that came up at the English tobacco shop. While the program was analyzing the data, Bikie decided to take clear his and see what his friend was up to.

Isaac had just come back from the gym and his hair was still wet after the shower. He was sitting on the sofa with the television on.

"I think you need to go down to the store and get a couple of new t-shirts for yourself. You've gotten pretty big since we've been living here. Good for you, of course, keep at it. But your old clothes are skintight on you now. They make you look like a dance teacher."

Isaac snickered and reached for the remote to turn up the sound. The jingle to introduce the news played and an affable presenter announced in a brisk voice:

"And now the latest science news! In Africa, new crops developed by COMUNA that are tolerant to heat and consume only small amounts of water are being planted. The food that is grown is already semi-dehydrated, and its volume expands several times over when liquid is added, making it extremely convenient for the region. The compressed harvest from one acre fits into a single small truck. It goes to the warehouse, from the warehouse to the shop and onto the shelf. The customer can easily carry the compact package home and then soak it in water."

"To deliver the amount of food that you get from one pack you would have had to hire a truck before!" An old shop owner announced briskly from the screen, leaning down to the journalist's microphone.

Then the news switched to the latest news in medicine. In a discussion about a large number of conveniences and innovations available to the disabled, the developers presented a new generation of artificial limbs, which were practically indistinguishable from real ones.

At the end of the bulletin they showed a brief glimpse of a demonstration against downloading OE in Delhi. The protesters carried placards saying: "Veggies have dimwit children".

"Not all of the children are born as Happies, which shows that the situation can be corrected. In any event, *Collective Mind* is certain to solve this problem, as it has previously solved other problems of mankind," the presenter summed up.

Isaac knew that the Agency was tracking the problem; he had seen the table of Veggie children's creativity levels. But it wasn't true simply to say that their level was low, because most of the children were born without any creativity at all, and it would be a good idea to have paternity tests for the ones who did have some. So COMUNA lied. Isaac was furious, but there was nothing he could do.

After the advertisements came the sports news. In sports, Happies performed no worse than ordinary people. Physical ability was still the determining factor here. Veggies simply kept themselves in good shape under the guidance of a trainer, and basically accomplished with ease any task they were instructed to do.

Suddenly Mick Jagger's voice started singing in the room where Bikie's computer was at work: "I can't get no satisfaction!"

"What the hell's that?" Isaac started in surprise.

"The program is signaling that it's found a match!" Bikie said with a sly wink.

The friends dashed to see what had been discovered. It turned out that the numbers of both cards used to buy cigars were found in the payment database of one travel agency. They had been used several hours apart to pay for two different ticketsone-way to Sardinia. The charge to both cards was exactly the same. But the most exciting thing was the date of the payments. It coincided with the period of Link's disappearance, the very same day when he didn't show up to his lecture.

"Both cards again?" Bikie exclaimed, as if he was talking to the monitor. "Why two cards?"

"Have you forgotten?" Isaac asked, turning his blazing eyes towards his friend, who was so proud of his discovery but at the same time had failed to see the obvious. "Link had Yoshi with him. I'm sure she bought him cigars occasionally. And they flew to Sardinia together. I'm sure they paid at different times to keep the conspiracy a secret."

"It sounds convincing! It *is* convincing, dammit! But was Sardinia their final destination?"

"Let's take a look at the tobacco situation on the island, shall we Bikie?"

"Already looking."

Until quite recently there had been two cigar shops left on the island, both quite excessive for a dying economic sector. One shop had already been closed, but the other was still operational. Bikie opened the databases of both and rummaged around in the accounts section to see if the two familiar cards showed up there. Alas, the numbers weren't in the databases.

"But look here!" Bikie exclaimed. "Literally two days after Link's disappearance a really big purchase was made in one of the shops. It looks very much as if someone stocked up well in advance before going into hiding. As a former smoker, I can tell you Isaac, that when your nerves are stretched you smoke a lot more."

"Obviously, Link couldn't use the old cards for purchases. He must have had new ones ready in different names."

"If we assume that Link hunkered down on Sardinia and he has a new card, he must have used it a few times."

"Bikie, this is a lead, this is our chance to find him. Check the purchases for the last seven years on the card that came up, and check that the card used for that large purchase hadn't shown up in the shop before then and I'll go and pack. If I'm right, we'll go to Sardinia, keep the tobacco shop under observation and lure Link out into the open."

While Isaac was packing, Bikie shared the news with him: no one had used that card before the date in question to buy anything at the tobacco shop, or anywhere else on the island. But after that date, the number showed up again later at that shop and in several supermarkets. Deliveries had been ordered on it too, but Bikie did not manage to discover the delivery address.

"Delivery companies have been flourishing, they have the money for good data protection," said Bikie, making an excuse.

At last they had a theory about where Link was that was based on more than mere hope. It was much better than the straws they had been clutching at before. With their computers and their own two heads, they could set up a brainstorming session even in New Zealand, if necessary, and Sardinia was relatively close. Not Asia or North Africa, luckily. The only thing keeping Isaac here was Vicky. His heart ached at the thought of having to part with her again and this time he did not know for how long.

With their plan set, Isaac and Bikie felt better. The nervousness that had dominated them for the last couple of weeks subsided. A concrete decision clears things up, switching one's thoughts over to the new challenge. Neither of them wanted to admit that the logic for the journey was rather flimsy, that Link could have moved on from Sardinia, so without talking about it they supported and encouraged each other.

That evening Isaac had yet another good sign. He got a short but very encouraging text message from Michelle Blanche, asking him how he was doing. He decided that today luck was definitely on his side. Forgetting about Vicky, he immediately remembered the unbelievable evening that he had spent at Wolanski's place with Michelle, chatting and discussing things like old friends and even kissing. That was the first time she had shown any real liking for him.

Isaac answered that he was doing great, and even plucked up the courage to say he would be glad to see her again. The sooner the better, because he was going away and didn't know for how long. As he waited for Michelle's reply the minutes stretched out into hours, and when she finally replied: "Yes, I've freed up my evening, so we can meet!" – Isaac was engulfed by euphoria.

Everything was coming together incredibly well. At last, they had a serious lead and his nascent relationship with Michelle was getting on track. It felt really good to fall in love, and have the memories of their first real evening together.

On days like this he thought there were quite a lot of good things in his life. As he packed his suitcase, he remembered how he used to go camping with his family. They drove there, and those trips were always real adventures! His mother and stepfather took turns to drive, while Vicky and he gazed out of the windows, spellbound.

Remembering Vicky again, Isaac realized with some confusion that his feelings for her were similar to what he felt for Michelle.

"There'll be time to figure things out," he decided.

Now that they calmed down a bit, the two friends started thinking about what they needed for the journey and how they were going to get there. Isaac had a clear opinion about that, but knew Bikie would not agree. His friend dreamed of going on his motorbike, and Isaac spent a long time choosing his words before bringing up the subject. As if he was thinking out loud, he said they would need some old and inconspicuous to survey the shop. It would be better to drive to Sardinia in the van, as well, because they couldn't do much talking on a motorbike. They could take everything necessary and have a roof over their head. And if everything went well, they wouldn't be coming back alone. In the end Bikie realized, that Isaac had already made the decision. The only obstacle was that they only had his bike, so the question was where to get a van.

"Look, Bikie, what if we try borrowing some kind of a van from someone in your crowd? Or maybe swap something for it, something that your friends value?"

"Isaac, you don't want us to go on my Harley, and you're dropping hints, wondering where we could get a van, aren't you? And since there's nowhere we can get a van for free, you are driving at that I have to sell or exchange my Harley, right? Now tell me....are you totally nuts?"

Isaac nodded guiltily, as if to say, thank you, Bikie, for sparing me the need to suggest it.

There was a brief pause and then an argument followed. Bikie protested heatedly, screaming that his Harley was his life, his brother, his love and destiny. The type of thing you don't sell or exchange, either temporarily or permanently.

"I'll never, ever lend out my friends, my women or my motorbike!"

In reality, Bikie was arguing with himself, since he was the one who had voiced the idea of swapping the Harley. Bikie was a pretty sound analyst, and he realized that he was stuck between a rock and a hard place. His logic was backing his own wishes into a corner.

"Now listen, Isaac. You talk about imagination and creativity. Everyone who isn't a Veggie wants to express himself, not everyone tries, but they all want to. Musicians express themselves through music, scientists through science and I express myself through my motorbike!" Bikie went hyper. "It's more than just a piece of machinery. It's my alter ego! I can't sell it or swap it. It is me! I wouldn't sell me! We bikers aren't like that.

"There was this guy in the bar who had a sports bike and he was summoned to court for speeding. He managed to convince the judge that at a speed of two hundred and seventy kilometers an hour it's impossible to read the speed-limit sign. The judge, who used to be a biker himself once, awarded him the minimum fine and just gave him an official warning instead of confiscating his bike. That's the way we do things.

"My Harley is my membership in a big family, my attachment to people who aspire to freedom and don't rely on rules and authority for this freaking system that we fight against... It's my comrade-in-arms. Do I have to lose my comrade for the sake of the struggle? What would you choose, Isaac? We're not them, we've got hearts!"

Bikie talked on and on, discouraging himself more and more and cursing the situation. He turned sullen and angry, realizing that he had no way out.

"All right Isaac, let this freaking system choke on my Harley. It's decided, I'm selling it. It won't be a sacrifice, it will be an iron bone stuck in their throat. Only I can't do it myself. I'll send you to a friend of mine, he's been asking about my bike for a long time. He's bound to buy it. Better let him have it than some other creep, even if I'll have to give him a discount. At least he's a straight up guy. My brother will be in reliable hands."

Isaac nodded without speaking. He knew firsthand what it was like to sell a part of oneself.

15

The next day Isaac called the prospective buyer for the bike and they agreed to meet in the evening. In the meantime he set his eye on a roomy American-made van. It was a hell of a machine, working on the archaic fuel combustion principle, guzzling gas like a crazed horse. The benefit was that there were only two windows in the front, so they could carry whatever they liked in the back and no one would see it from the outside.

Before setting out to close the deal, he dropped in to see Peter and outlined the situation.

Wolanski was upset for Bikie, he couldn't buy the bike, it would have been a violation of his father's will, and they couldn't put off the journey until he received his money.

"There's an operational Volkswagen in the garage. If you guys can find a way to destroy it – burn it or smash it up – I could receive the insurance reimbursement and buy the van to replace it. But that's a couple of weeks' hassle, or maybe ten days, and extra risk for you. You decide," Peter suggested.

"I feel sorry for Bikie. As soon as I get my first *V-Rain* payment I'll buy him a new Harley."

"Don't be in a hurry to sell the rights to your invention, Isaac, I'll soon have money and the situation will change. You're no longer a crazy stranger to me, so let's see, maybe we can agree on a partnership. I had time to think a bit about your invention and take a closer look at you. I am ready to do business with you. As for Bikie's Harley, let's do this...you agree with the buyer that you have the right to buy it back within two or three months, to be on the safe side, with a mark-up of twenty or thirty per cent. Bluff and say you won't sell otherwise. I think he'll agree."

"All right, I'll try it. Thanks, Peter! Bikie will be crazed with joy. He's desperately miserable right now and gloomy as night."

When Bikie heard about Peter's idea and his willingness to buy back the motorbike he turned extremely happy. He went back to his room and asked Wolanski to come over. Bikie didn't know how to express thanks, but it was a very long conversation, and Isaac could only guess what he said. When he came back to the living room, Bikie was very serious and declared that Peter was like a brother to him now!

With that burden off their shoulders, things started to move fast. Bikie changed his mind and went with Isaac to close the deal. At first the buyer was upset, but he agreed to the buy-back condition and promised to be very careful with the bike.

The van they bought turned out to be pretty good. Bikie bought a fuel combustion enhancer at a wrecking yard and attached it to the engine. With such a gizmo, gas was heated by oxygen and entered the engine at an increased pressure, which cut the fuel consumption by a third. An essential, albeit short-term gain: this way the engine wore out sooner, and rubber gaskets and spark plugs needed to be replaced earlier.

Isaac was responsible for their everyday needs on the journey, so with the rest of the money from the Harley he bought a couple of sleeping bags, some blankets, a little stove and other things that might come in handy. They were intending to work, cook and sleep in the van. Since they had no idea how long the trip would last, thorough preparation was essential.

The two friends packed their things in silence. Bikie was still sulking about losing his Harley, even if temporarily, so he didn't talk much. They just exchanged occasional remarks about important things, keeping quiet about everything else.

Bikie was worried that his Harley would end up in an accident or break down. He imagined someone blithely racing it too fast with the engine roaring, so every now and then he started grumbling like an old man suffering from gout, venting his emotions on his friend.

"Don't forget to take your ski boots, Isaac!"

"Don't forget your pink bathrobe, Isaac!"

"Will you survive a week without your favorite porn sites, Isaac?"

Isaac tried to ignore the gibes and focus on essential things. He realized that for Bikie traveling to Sardinia in a van then on a ferry was a blow. Especially without any prospect of being on his bike for a long time. It was like a senior VP of Boeing flying on business in an Airbus.

"Isaac, take the umbrellas," Bikie gibed yet again.

It seemed he just couldn't calm down. Finally, he said he was going to write a song about a proud Kenyan marathon runner serving in a foreign army in big, clumsy boots.

"That's it, Bikie. Stop it right now. I tell you what, you love everything American, don't you? So look, we are traveling in a classic American van, we are going to live in it, and I agree to listen to nothing but rock'n'roll the whole way. How about that?"

"Okay, fine! It's a different matter all together with those terms," said Bikie, suddenly breaking into a smile. "You surrendered easily after holding out for no more than an hour!"

They hooted with laughter and never mentioned the subject of vans, motorbikes or marathon runners in boots and swim fins again. Bikie packed a full box of rock'n'roll discs, enough to last them for a year on the road. There was no point in objecting, the old van didn't have any slots for modern phones or memory cards, and there was no time to look for an adapter.

The friends were fully ready that evening. They downloaded maps and made some notes on them, set out their route and went to celebrate a job well done at McCarthy's. Michelle was surprised that Isaac had chosen an unromantic bar for their next date and invited his friends on it, but agreed to come anyway.

Bikie persuaded Wolanski to come along. Michelle arrived a lot later than the others, putting Isaac through some serious turmoil. When she finally showed up she looked absolutely stunning with her hair done in a ponytail emphasizing her long neck, not wearing much makeup again. Her look was completed with a stylish biker jacket of soft leather. Isaac clutched at his heart melodramatically, but Bikie immediately outdid him by putting his hands over his fly and starting to slip slowly under the table, groaning and gasping. Wolanski spluttered with laughter. Michelle gave him a scornful look, folded her hand into a pistol, set it against Peter's head and said "Boom!" Theatrically blowing away the smoke of the shot from the barrel, she glanced smugly at the scene and asked:

"I'm not sure, should I stay here?"

They all instantly came to life and started to convince her that she should.

"I'm mortally wounded, but I'm still alive," Peter exclaimed solemnly.

"And no one has ever died from an orgasm!" Bikie added.

Bewildered by this torrent of compliments for Michelle, Isaac couldn't think of anything to say. He kissed Michelle on both cheeks and moved her chair closer to him.

"I'll sit beside you, I hope you don't mind?" Michelle indicated to Peter.

"Sandrine would mind, only she's not here," Bikie responded merrily.

"Why not beside me?" Isaac asked.

"Because you're punished!"

"For what, Michelle?"

"You invited me out... to a bar! You could have chosen a restaurant, a café, a park, anywhere at all. Who asks a girl on a date to a bar with a bunch of guys?"

"Um, well," Isaac found nothing to say.

"Please forgive him, Michelle," said Bikie, intervening for his friend. "I agree that he is a moron, an idiot, a blockhead and a fool. He's gotten his chance by mistake. But then that's why he's unique! If you are cold to him, I won't be able to bear his sour face tomorrow. It takes almost twenty-four hours to get to Sardinia. And what's more, today he saved my iron buddy's life, so now I'm simply obliged to come to his rescue."

Isaac was not even slightly amused by all these jokes, he felt despondent and miserable at his blunder. He had imagined Michelle as his girl and then bungled their first date so badly. In the hustle and bustle of packing he hadn't even thought that it was a real date.

"Okay. Quits! Let's say we're even for the way you helped me that time in the bar."

Michelle moved over to Isaac, who, delighted at his redemption, tried to put his arm round her waist.

"Oh-oh-oh! Don't get too excited!" said Michelle, gently removing his arm. "Quits doesn't mean you're completely forgiven."

"Oh come one, Michelle. You're a real piece of work!" Bikie exclaimed. Turning to Isaac, he added. "I don't envy you, old buddy. But I envy you just as well."

"OK, a bar it is! I'll have a Mojito," Michelle kissed Isaac on the cheek and said affectionately: "Bring me that, please. And you Bikie, tell me about that iron buddy who was saved and why you are going to Sardinia."

"Long Island for me, Mister Leroy," Bikie added solemnly, getting into a role of a social advocate.

"And me," Peter put in.

The longer they sat talking, the less Michelle was mad at Isaac. Eventually he managed to put his arm around her waist and bring her closer to him. She didn't resist. Isaac felt he was drowning in his love for her. As soon as his panic was gone and the adrenalin from the fright left his blood, the alcohol took effect and Isaac suddenly got very drunk. As a matter of fact, they all, except Michelle, got totally zonked on the deceptively sweet, but very strong Long Islands, flinging out toasts about individual freedom and fine creative gals like Michelle Blanche.

Wolanski shelled out three grand in cash for the journey. Bikie promised to take him on as the frame drummer in his Banksy-Band – the rock group he was going to set up after the job was done. It was named in honor of the great English graffiti artist who "bombed" the streets of cities all around the world with his witty and acutely political paintings, and had never been caught.

"And if you refuse to be my frame drummer, you yourself will be drummed. If you don't play rock I will clean your clock!" He added laconically, tripping over his tongue.

They talked a bit more about Banksy, his sense of humor and how distinctive his works were, about the way he managed to remain incognito, the cunning way he inserted his graffiti into the environment and how municipal boards, signs and peeling walls turned into pop masterpieces once one of his drawings appeared on them. The police had never once caught him at work, and they wondered why. Was it because he thought out thoroughly how to avoid getting caught, or was it plain, dumb luck?

"Anything worth doing is worth doing right," Bikie quoted. "Hunter S. Thompson said that. You know what about? If not, I'll tell you. You are not bikers, after all. In the 1960's that guy, Hunter Thompson, did something fucking awesome. Back then he had an old Jaguar, no bikes, and he had absolutely zilch connection with bikers. But he found them, I mean us, interesting. Normal folks have always associated us with freedom, rebellion and real adrenalin.

"Those were the days of bike-clubs. One ferocious name competed with the next: 'Gipsy Jokers', 'Grim Reapers', 'Galloping Geese', 'Pissed-Off Bastards', and so on. Brutal, leather clad dudes with tattoos all over them. They swilled beer and roared along highways but one group among them really stood out – Hell's Angels. They drove the law-abiding society crazy with terror. There were rumors that they smear their bike suits with shit to make leather stiffer and that they would rape all the women they came across. The newspapers constantly wrote rumors about them. Well, you know how low-grade journalists can both terrorize and confuse. The girls all squealed and waited for the Angels to drive round and start raping them.

"So Thompson wondered what this national bogeyman was really like. He had a friend, a former Angel, some kind of a news reporter, a colleague basically. And through him Thompson got access to the bikers' get-togethers. It was useless to tell the Angels 'Hello there, I'm a journalist, I want to write about you'. But Thompson was no goodie-goodie, he was a man who broke the rules. He got an advance from a publisher for a book, bought a bike and spent a year riding with the Angels, recording the way they lived. He stuck with the pack, cruising round the cities, tearing along the highways, interacting like crazy, smoking pot, lying on lawns, listening to cops ranting about his rights and ending up in the slammer. He was beaten up with the bikers and he buried their gang bosses with them. In short, he plunged headfirst into the subject matter. And when he resurfaced, he published his book and it became a sensation. He didn't just say how much beer a biker drank a day, he dug deep and came up with the causes of the confrontation between bikers and the American society – he figured it was all to do with the post-war period.

"By the way, those damned Angels totally flipped out from all that fuss. They started reading the news about themselves over their morning beer, and they learned how to extort money for interviews, photos or videos. So when they found out about the book, they demanded a share of the author's fee and beat the shit out of Thompson, but that was nothing new to him. It wasn't the first or the last scandal in his life. Scandal drives the media. That was the way he lived," concluded Bikie what wouldn't be his last story that evening. "A new term was even coined in his honor – 'gonzo journalism' – he was a real heavy guy. A legend."

"He also wrote the book Fear and Loathing in Las Vegas, I've read it," Michelle added with a smile. "You're not the only one here who knows Hunter Thompson."

"If you get bored with that blockhead Isaac, I'm always at your disposal," Bikie added respectfully, after a brief pause. "You're a totally fucking cool chick!"

"You could have left out the swearing, but coming from you, Bikie, it doesn't sound crude," Michelle laughed, winking at him flirtatiously.

"You can't have her!" said Isaac, coming awake and drawing Michelle closer against him.

A ray of light, feebly shining through the peep in the curtains, woke Isaac up. The night was just about to surrender. The clock showed five in the morning. He looked around – he was in a beautiful, nicely furnished bedroom.

By his side, on the large soft bed, Michelle was sleeping. Isaac gently drew her close against him. She sighed but didn't wake up. Her warmth, her scent, she was so sexy! Isaac didn't remember how they ended up in one bed, but now it didn't matter.

As if accidentally, he moved, sliding his hand along her body – she was wearing some sort of a long thin T-shirt, tiny silky shorts and nothing more. Carefully, trying not to wake her up, Isaac began to kiss her neck, shoulders, her stomach, squeezing her closer against him, at the same time taking her clothes off. He caressed and kissed her more and more persistently, barely able to control himself.

Not opening her eyes, Michelle smiled, hugged Isaac, letting him cover the two of them with the blanket and take off the rest of her clothes.

For the first time in many years Isaac was making love with somebody he really wanted. Spilling all the accumulated passion, he again and again kissed and caressed Michelle, then without hesitation, climbing under her blanket. Sleepy Michelle obediently allowed him to do what he wanted, smiled without opening her eyes, reciprocating. The night was endless and there was no time to sleep.

16

After the best night of his life Isaac arrived to Wolanski's villa only at noon. He woke up Bikie and Peter, and made them a big cup of coffee for each, followed by a large serving of fried eggs.

Having woken up at night at Michelle's place, Isaac didn't sleep close his eyes again. With last night's liquor wearing off, his headache was getting worse. He felt like lying down but it was time to set out for Italy.

Peter suggested putting off their departure for a day. Isaac did not oppose, of course. In the morning, Michelle had sent him a text message with no words, but three kisses and a little heart. He wanted to see her again. Just the two of them, without his friends. The memories of the previous night were warm and inspiring. But iron-willed Bikie showed no sign at all that he'd been boozing heavily yesterday and insisted on going. He said they should not allow themselves to relax, that he was fine and ready to take the wheel. It wasn't his first binge, wouldn't be his last. Isaac really wanted to stay, but he had no arguments to object to Bikie, especially since he knew that Michelle was the only reason he didn't want to go. He made a feeble attempt to argue, explaining what he had with Michelle definitely was a relationship, passion and, probably, love.

"All the more reason for us to go! Michelle won't run away from you. As an expert on women's hearts, I can tell you Michelle is spoiled with men's attention, so she'll find an original little character like you especially interesting. You caught her eye the way you are, stay that way. The ones who jump through hoops for her probably don't catch her."

"But all the same…"

"But all the same, we're going," Bikie interrupted. "Trust me, you can't think straight about her in any case. Get in the van and let's go!"

They set out five minutes later. Isaac only remembered about Vicky as they were driving past the hospital. He felt ashamed for forgetting to visit her and for letting Michelle drive her completely out of his mind. The second reason bothered him less. Maybe Michelle really could help him forget his sudden crush on Vicky?

It was sunny and hot already. Bikie was driving and Isaac asked him not to turn on the music, as he wanted to try and doze off. Even in silence, it was impossible to fall asleep on the winding streets of Monaco. Eventually the van climbed to the very top, where the local road merged into the highway. Bikie was feeling great, and Isaac, having taken a pill for his headache, cheered up, as well.

There was no point in driving in silence any longer, and it was strange not to talk at the outset of a new journey with the road stretching out ahead. Both friends were filled with contradictory emotions from the anticipation of adventure and a good hunt to a vague, indefinite fear of failure.

Ventimiglia was the first Italian town on their route. Like all the less prosperous inhabitants of the border regions of France, Isaac often visited its large local market. The low, modern buildings of the resort town were modestly mute about the ancient Roman consuls and emperors who used to frequent the area. The local Roman amphitheater, of which only ruins remained, once had been a place where humble slaves amused the rich.

Things were shaping up much the same way now, Isaac thought. Now the Veggies were the slaves, only by virtue of their intellectual abilities, not their physical ones. Their OE had been sold to those who had plenty of money and didn't need to donate their creativity. Isaac knew from history that the Roman Empire didn't fall in a single day. First it split into two parts – Western and Eastern. The Eastern part, which was also called Byzantium, was destined to flourish. Maybe that was because they stopped regarding slaves as things and started seeing them as people? Isaac was still absorbed in his Ancient-Roman thoughts, pondering the idea of liberating the world from modern-day slavery, as they approached San Remo.

"Have you ever been to San Remo?" Bikie asked.

"Strangely enough, I haven't. But I've heard it's not as good as our resorts."

"No resorts are as good as ours, but that's no excuse for not going."

"Then I'll go see it one day."

"I've been here, on my bike."

"And where else have you been?" Isaac asked.

"Not many places by car. But on my bike I've been as far as Venice and Geneva, and Paris, naturally. The farthest points I went were Amsterdam and Copenhagen. In Copenhagen I lived for a whole week at the famous Freetown Christiania. And in Amsterdam I had such a wild spree in a coffee shop, I was afraid to go near my bike the day after. My head was spinning. And you probably know yourself – it's the kind of city where you're always looking for a reason to stay an extra day."

"True. After our last trip, we definitely have to go back there. We could go on your Harley, like you wanted and take a look at the windmills and tulips and all the other stuff."

"I've never seen any old windmills, only the modern wind turbines. There are loads of them everywhere now, not just in Holland."

In confirmation of these words a row of immensely high wind turbines appeared on their left, smoothly taking in the air. Isaac counted eight of them, brand new ones, with multiple propellers. Fifty meters tall, if not more. Once they all used to be white or grey, but these were painted all different colors. A pink one with black blades looked the zaniest. Where the row of turbines ended, an elevated road began with a tunnel following it. There was a gas station where the tunnel ended, and Bikie reduced speed, getting into the right lane.

"I need an Italian cappuccino," he explained. "And bathroom."

The friends ordered a delicious doppio cappuccino, and sat down on plastic chairs under a sunshade outside. It was amazing, you only had to cross the Italian border and cappuccino, even at a filling station, was totally different. Either the Italian milk tasted better, or the water was purer, but the brew was divinely delicious.

"Italian cappuccino and a panini – not just a snack, it's a party!" said Isaac, smiling with pleasure.

"I don't like paninis," replied Bikie. "I'm more a pizza man. I once read that Italians prefer Margarita to any other kind because it's impossible to spoil."

Before that I used to take 'four cheeses', or seafood. I liked it with salami too, and never took a simple Margarita. What for, when there are such delicious kinds with all sorts of toppings and fancy doodads? But after I read that article, I ordered a Margarita. And I didn't regret it. It really was delicious, and the cheapest too! Since then I only eat Margarita; although, I used to laugh at people who took it, I thought they were stupid."

After they had their snack and cleared the table, Bikie and Isaac moved on. Anyone driving along this autostrada for the first time must surely think it the most beautiful freeway in the world. On the right side the sea and endless little Italian towns; on the left, luscious mountains buried in greenery.

Isaac was feeling much better. Every kilometer the van dived into a new tunnel and shot back out into the sun again. A dark stretch and a bright stretch. After the party at Wolanski's he had begun a bright stretch, and he wanted it to be a long one.

"Driving into a tunnel is like dying, and the heavenly light at the end is like being reborn into a new life," he said pensively.

Isaac believed in God, but not in a specific God He regarded himself as agnostic and didn't believe in Christ, Allah or Buddha, but he served the commandments: thou shalt not kill, thou shalt not steal, and thou shalt not commit evil. He liked the idea of karma, too – it was like a shield over one's head. Good deeds strengthened it, which is why villains' karma is rotten and leaks. Too bad, though, this leakage was not immediate. Sometimes, it took years for the shield to begin to leak.

It was probably karma that had rescued him when he went to download his OE. It had saved him, or the angels had, the words made no difference. He would have become a Veggie a long time ago, if not for Elvis's fortunate appearance. And then there would never have been Michelle, or Bikie, or Peter, or the long-awaited patent in his life. He felt the urge to share these thoughts with Bikie.

"You know, I've thought about God many times. My parents were killed, Vicky is sick. But they were very good people, and there was nothing to punish them for. I can't say I feel glad about ordeals like that. I'm grateful for what he's given me, but he's taken away plenty of things too."

"It depends what God means to you," Bikie responded.

"As a scientific mind, I think of God not just from the viewpoint of faith, but through the prism of science. For me, God first and foremost is justice and conscience. The ultimate justice based on the actions of each man. And from the standpoint of science, God is infinity."

"I don't get it. What's infinity got to do with it?"

"Well look, what's more potent and universal – infinity of space or time?"

"Can you really compare them?"

"Yes. As being impossible for our awareness to grasp, you can. Both of them are inconceivable to man, and above all, they're infinite. No matter how far you go, no matter how long you live, there's always something beyond, something still to come.

So it turns out that time and infinite space are almost identical. Is there anything bigger than infinity? Longer than time? No. You can say the same thing about God. What could be bigger and mightier than God? Nothing. So God is both infinity and time. Those are his different manifestations. You can't say that there are lots of gods in infinity.

"And it turns out that God didn't create time and space, but he gave them to us to exist in. They are a part of himself that he has shared with us."

"So God is time?"

"Yes, and he is space too. When I was a kid I went to a planetarium for the first time, and saw an incredible show, a 3D film on the dome of the building about Earth, the solar system, outer space, the galaxy, and the Universe. There was loads of interesting stuff in it. And in the end, they showed an ordinary man on the screen. The camera started pulling back and the man became a spot compared with a skyscraper, the skyscraper turned into a spot compared to a city, the city - compared to the planet, the planet to the sun.

"Soon even the sun seemed like a microscopic speck compared to other stars, and in turn they were transformed into dots compared to other big stars we know today. And so on to infinity. Our galaxy is a mere speck compared to the Universe. There could be hosts of universes. Because, if it is not so, then what comes after our Universe if you fly an infinite distance away from it? There'll be other universes and something much bigger. Possibly. The Universe is a little piece of one of the atoms that make up the wing of some fantastic insect, sitting on some fantastic flower. And the flower grows…"

"In your imagination," Bikie joked.

"Let me finish. At the end the film, the screen shrank to a tiny dot and disappeared. They turned the lights on and I was dumbfounded, I didn't think anything could astound me any more at that moment. My stepfather added something else, 'Isaac,' he said, 'I can see you've realized how small we are, that there's something much bigger! But that's not all, you can go in the opposite direction, too, with things getting smaller. We're huge compared with some things, as huge as the Universe is compared to us. Just imagine, we consist of molecules, and they consist of atoms, but if we had an immense, mega-powerful magnifying glass, we could enlarge an atom and see what it's made out of – a host of complicated pieces, each consisting of particles that are made up of a huge number of universes, which consist of hosts of galaxies, stars and planets, inhabited by someone or something. And so on to infinity'."

"Yeah, infinity's mighty stuff," Bikie declared. He had listened to the theory of God with genuine interest. "You know, Isaac, they should put you on a stake! I'd even lend them my Zippo lighter to light you up." Just a second ago Bikie was serious too, but now he started hooting with laughter in his usual manner.

"A gaping black hole has just appeared in your karma, and the remains of your clueless brain have started evaporating out through it, Bikie," said Isaac.

"No problem, it was you who just said that my brain is infinite. And even after it has evaporated almost to a frazzle there'll still be something left. A handful of thoughts, my last three hundred Spartan soldier thoughts, will kick ass of your legion of Persian fantasies."

"That's right! A battle of minds. Only, to be more accurate, your last three hundred thoughts will all be about chicks. So your regiment is Spartan women, not Spartan warriors."

"Please stop fucking with my brain!"

They roared with laughter and cracked jokes, teasing each other, although, the conversation had supposedly started with a serious subject. God probably invented humor and jovial people especially so that we wouldn't go insane trying to understand what comes after the Universe or die of boredom.

"Isaac, tell me how does your idea of God and infinity fit together with karma?"

"I don't know, I haven't thought about it."

"Well, I'll tell you. Karma is your identification number, your coordinates in infinity, God can see you, after all, in the context of infinity, and you're totally insubstantial. You're a tiny piece of space, empty space."

Isaac couldn't tell if Bikie was serious. It could easily be a joke.

After two hours of traveling the van eventually reached Genoa.

"The great Genoese were born in this very city," thought Isaac, remembering Christopher Columbus. "The man whose curiosity and love of adventure, combined with impudence, gave the world the discovery of America and brought gold flooding into the treasury of the Spanish crown, causing the deaths of thousands of Indians."

At first, what they saw looked like a fairly run-of-the-mill port and an industrial city but when they reached the historical center everything changed and the city became magnificent. Leaving the van in a car park, the two friends set off to Ferrari Square to have a cup of coffee and a light snack. There was plenty worth looking at here.

"Isaac, the spirit of pioneering endeavors dwells in this city," said Bikie, obviously thinking about the same thing.

"Our goal is different. To find another pioneer. To sniff out his tobacco smell."

This was the first and last large city on their route. The friends were in an excellent mood, the jokes were as feeble-minded as in the morning, and the sun was scorching, forcing them to squint or shut their eyes. Isaac and Bikie were on a high. As for the goal of the journey, it could wait, they thought. After all, they were not in the army, they did not have a precise schedule to go by, and were not expected to be stern and serious, not having the right to down a couple of beers along the way. So they did. The mug of beer invigorated their philosophical mood.

"Bikie, we have a chance of becoming prophets or terrorists. The world has become cleaner and less aggressive. There are no wars, less crime, a whole heap of achievements. Even the fact that Veggies' children are stupid doesn't mean that it cannot be fixed. We now see the world striving towards an ideal utopia. Should we fight that? We're certain to be regarded as villains. The funniest thing is that a couple of months ago I would have tried to stop a pair of schizos like you and I."

Bikie was already getting used to his friend's fits of self-doubt. Unlike Isaac, he had no second thoughts.

"The world won't lose the technologies it has already gained from OE and there's nothing else good left to look forward to. And don't quail, before we hack in, we'll weigh everything one more time. Our goal is to find the professor but we don't know yet whether we'll convince him to help us. Now, why don't you just take a look at those lovelies?"

At that, Bikie strolled rakishly toward two female tourists and introduced himself.

The girls turned out to be Swedish from Stockholm, Stephanie and Carla. They had arrived in the morning on a cruise liner that was leaving for Rome tomorrow. In three days of sailing they had become thoroughly bored and were glad to keep Bikie's and Isaac's company. They had a great time as Bikie spun tales about the dangerous journey through Africa that the guys had ahead of them, all the way down to Johannesburg, and invited them to look over the van, in which he and Isaac were going to live, sleep and cook as they cut across the dark continent, all the time bewailing the fact that they'd probably miss European women terribly on the journey.

It wasn't clear if Stephanie and Carla believed in the African trek, but they went to look at the van. Isaac preferred to leave the van and the free-and-easy socializing entirely to Bikie, despite the beer he had drunk and the obvious interest he felt from Stephanie. Michelle Blanche was firmly stuck in his head… and Vicky too. He definitely wasn't interested in other girls. Isaac tried to drive away his lustful thoughts of Vicky by recalling memories from their childhood, telling himself that they were friends and virtual brother and sister.

"No, a confession of that sort will definitely shock her," he thought. And the last thing he wanted to do was to unsettle Vicky and drive her away from him. He had to admit that even when he started thinking about her, when thoughts of love came up, he caught himself switching back to Michelle. That was probably for the best.

Isaac went for a stroll through the Old Port of Genoa. In the meantime, Bikie, without batting an eye, raked both girlfriends up in his arms, promising to tell them about the dangerous hippopotami, as well as the cannibalistic customs of some tribes. He began by saying that a male lion usually had several females at once and they made love up to seventeen times a day. The last thing that Isaac heard as he clambered out of the van was the beginning of a story about how girls in Africa often didn't wear any blouses, preferring the natural look.

"The vanquisher of Africa" didn't bother to call or text Isaac when the girls left, he fell asleep right there in the middle of the van on top of a crumpled sleeping bag. That was how the furious Isaac found Bikie, after freezing outside until four in the morning. He was forced to go back to the van, even though his friend hadn't answered any of his calls or texts.

The next morning they boarded a ferry to Sardinia.

"Just look at that view! I wonder how Monet or Picasso would have painted it."

"He'd have painted it wonderfully. He'd have painted you yesterday pretty well too. With your pants down in a van littered with all sorts of garbage and beer bottles."

"No one drove you away yesterday. You went yourself. You have no damn reason to be angry. Why don't you just look how beautiful this is?"

"I think I'll postpone the nature for a while and get a couple of hours' sleep."

But Isaac couldn't go to sleep – the van was stinking of the fumes of alcohol consumed by Bikie the night before – so in the end he had to join Bikie on the deck.

"Nature is an infinity of masterpieces, and any work of art attempts to create the composition, colors and depth that are equal to nature," Bikie said with a wink, emphasizing the word "infinity".

"I wonder," Isaac ignored his words, "how much creativity Picasso had? Must have been a lot."

"It would be funny to find out that he was average, while the people who promoted him had a level that was much higher. Now that would be a hoot."

"Remember the artist who became famous after he became a Veggie? After he offloaded, it turned out that he had a really high level of OE, he was one of the highest rated donors. The journalists blew up the story, and people started admiring his paintings. He was immediately declared one of the greatest geniuses of modern times."

"It has always been that way – people often start idolizing a genius only after he dies in misery. Not just painters. It happened with Mozart, who died in total destitute. And since he was writing his Requiem when he became fatally ill, a popular rumor spread that he was writing it for himself. Public relations, although it wasn't called PR in those days. If people weren't so fond of spoofs, who knows, maybe all his brilliant compositions would have sunk into oblivion."

"Wouldn't it be great to find out Mozart's rating?"

"Forget about the dead. We've got to worry about the living."

The fairy danced slightly on the waves of an oncoming ship and Isaac felt sick at once.

When they reached Sardinia, Isaac and Bikie went straight to Porto Cervo. The cigar shop was located somewhere in its vicinity. Their stomachs were rumbling and they decided to eat something before putting their plan into action.

They took a table at the veranda of a little restaurant that caught their eye and started discussing, once again, what the connection between Professor Link and his assistant might be.

The sickly aroma of gossip hung in the air, but the two friends felt that they were obliged to understand the role of the Japanese woman, not out of curiosity, but for the good of the cause, and so they could not avoid the subject.

Everything suggested that the professor was bound to her by more than just sex. She bought his cigars for him, so she could not be just a plain call girl. A lover, friend, assistant? What was she to the professor?

Isaac suddenly stared, wide-eyed, and his lips stretched out into a broad smile.

"I think that's her," he said, jabbing his finger towards a woman walking nearby. She looked Filipino or Malaysian.

"Oh, sure, the first Asian woman we see will turn out to be the very one we're looking for! Of course, you're a fluky bastard Isaac, but not that fluky."

"What does flukiness have to do with it? It's just analysis and precise calculation. With your rating you can't possibly understand me," Isaac snapped.

"Right, right, definitely. If you multiply the length of the equator by the number of Japanese and divide it by the number of Chinese, take away the square root of ginseng, then you're bound to get thirteen. If you get bullshit, it means your calculations were fuckin' bullshit too."

"Hey, cut the swearing!"

"I'm not swearing even though your calculations make me feel like it."

"No Bikie, swearing is really the lowest of the low."

"Stop bitching, you're just jealous of me."

"Why, I wonder, would I be jealous of you?"

"You're jealous of my light-blond locks."

"What blond locks, you've got dark hair."

"The light-blond locks those pretty little Swedish girls left on my sleeping bag!"

"No, Bikie, I rather feel bad for you, my dear friend!! What sort of pain in the neck do you have to be to make girls' hair fall out?"

"They tore it out in the heat of the moment! But don't be upset, I promised to be your mentor in handling women. I think that after a couple of years' of intensive training, I'll let you move on to practicing and we'll begin with tender kisses."

"You can kiss my ass...tenderly. Why don't you record your advice on how you trimmed the Swedish girls' hair so sweetly. If it works so well, I'll just hold the recorder up to my face and use it to shave with."

After they stuffed their stomachs, they walked round the sunny little streets of the town, feeling very happy.

The superb resort town really lifted their spirits. Every step brought into view hosts of bars, little restaurants, cafes and other pleasant establishments.

Bikie stuck a bandana on his head, slipped on a pair of sunglasses and put on long black shorts. Isaac dressed even more lightly: his entire outfit consisted of a t-shirt, flip-flops and shorts. There was no shower in the van, but they could walk to the beach and take a dip.

17

Having returned to the van, Isaac and Bikie started the engine and drove to the cigar shop. It turned out to be in the outskirts of the town, although previously, it was located on an upmarket shopping street. There was an upside to the location – unlike in the center, there were convenient observation sites where the friends could easily park and begin their surveillance.. The shop window displayed hookahs, wine bottles and all sorts of bits and pieces including a cigar box and a humidor.

Driven by the thrill of the chase, Isaac suggested going in, but Bikie objected.

"How could you be so careless? We obviously don't fit the part of rich smokers or their couriers."

"Cool it! Half the store window is filled with cheap garbage. It's a long time since they sold anything but cigars. Come on."

Getting into the shop turned out to be impossible. A note stuck to inside of the glass said that the shop would open in half an hour. How long ago it had been put up was not clear, and the disappointed friends went back to the van. It was stuffy inside so Bikie parked the van under some trees to keep cool.

Bikie took out his laptop and fiddled with it, trying to find a Wi-Fi connection. Isaac watched the entrance, waiting for the owner or a shop assistant to show up. Long after the lunch siesta crowds flooded the street, there was not a soul around, just the baking sunlight and hot asphalt frazzling the air. Bikie started the engine to feel at least a small blast of coolness from the air conditioning. The two friends didn't feel like talking. You might have thought they have been overcome by holiday-resort lethargy, but they were really trying to focus. It felt like at any moment Link would come to the shop and everything would work out just fine.

Eventually, an elderly Italian man came up to the store, opened the door and took the note off the glass. Five minutes later the friends were already inside. They saw that it was just an ordinary little shop, nothing remarkable. Bikie asked about an Internet connection, and a secondhand mini-router was unearthed from among the masses of odd objects on the shelves. While the shop assistant checked to see that it was still working, Isaac pointed out to Bikie a large humidor with a glass door, with neat rows of cigars inside, in boxes and loose. Bikie smiled contentedly. The cigars were found, all right – the only thing left was to wait for the buyer.

After they spent several hours in the van and not a single customer entered the shop their excitement evaporated. They noticed a policeman coming in their direction. He walked up to the van, peered inside vigilantly, knocked on the window on the driver's side, and when Bikie opened it, asked an unambiguous question:

"What are you doing here, boys?"

"We're tourists," Bikie replied brightly, keeping his grip on the laptop. "First day on the island. We still haven't figured out where to stay, so we're sitting here arguing and looking at hotels nearby."

"Move on, guys, will you," said the policeman, in a genial mood. "We've had a complaint from the old woman in the house opposite. She says some strange characters got out of a van and then mysteriously went back, and now they're sitting there with the engine running, stinking up the air, and are obviously plotting something. I understand everything, but she's an old lady, why upset her?"

"OK, chief," Bikie responded. "Already gone."

The policeman walked away. They drove the van farther down the road, and Isaac nodded in the direction of the shop. The owner locked the door and was twirling the handle of the shutters, covering the display window. The guys could leave without any qualms of conscience: the first day of surveillance was officially over.

They stopped a kilometer from the shop, at an empty lot where the van was concealed from the road by bushes. Bikie came up with an idea – let technology do the surveillance. In a blink of an eye he had linked a web camera from his arsenal to the laptop and fine-tuned the image.

It was almost dark when the friends got out of the van to stretch their legs, grab a bite and install the web camera opposite the cigar shop.

When they reached the site, Isaac noticed an old woman on a chair in front of one of the houses. She was either dozing or enjoying the long-awaited coolness of the evening with her eyes blissfully closed. Bikie caught Isaac's glance and nodded. They would have to wait. There was a little grocery shop on the ground floor just behind the woman.

"Clear enough, life teaches proprietors to be vigilant," Bikie explained to Isaac. "Or maybe she's just feeling bored."

They took up a position on a municipal bench, pretending to be tourists resting after a hike, and ate the pizza they got on the way. The old lady couldn't see them, but if they turned around and craned their necks, they could see her.

It took quite some time before the woman finally got to her feet, yawned, grabbed her chair and retreated into the house.

"I'll take the chair inside, so the damn thieves won't steal it," said Bikie, imitating an old woman's voice so convincingly that Isaac could barely hold from laughing.

Mindful of their earlier mistake, the friends took their time. They waited until the light came on upstairs, which meant the old woman was in her bedroom, and went out again, indicating that she had gone to bed. Only then did Isaac and Bikie get up and stroll gently in the direction of the cigar shop.

Pretending to take an intense interest in a blossoming bougainvillea, Bikie quickly fixed the camera on the fence, hardly even slowing his stride. To look even more natural, he theatrically sniffed in the air from one of the lush purple flowers, breathed out noisily and walked on, whistling. Isaac teased his friend, saying that today Bikie had indeed revealed his acting talent.

The entire next day they observed the shop remotely. There was only one customer in the morning, an elderly gentleman with a cane and another three in the early evening.

"Now that's what I call a rush of customers!" Isaac quipped acidly. "Bikie, maybe we need to think of something else?"

"I already have," Bikie replied. "I've written a little program that responds to changes in the video image. It will be activated every time someone goes into the shop. Something like a remote motion-detecting sensor. Then at least we won't have to spend the whole day staring into the monitor. When someone goes in, the computer will chirp. And tomorrow we'll visit the shop again and I'll put another web camera inside. We'll be able to see who's buying what."

The third week of surveillance was coming to an end, and the friends were gradually giving in to despair. The program that observed movement at the shop was working excellently and had no glitches, but in all this time cigars had only been bought on eight occasions. The demand for smoking material really was drastically subsiding. They took turns keeping watch, making periodical visits to the marina.

They even wanted to talk to a salesman from the cigar shop to ask about the buyers, or with that watchful old lady, but they were afraid to scare off the Professor. You never know if the seller knows Link, and could warn him. So much wasted effort wasn't worth the risk. This shop was their only lead, to risk it was impossible, so they decided to be patient and wait.

Sometimes customers came in and bought cigars.

Isaac followed the first customer, who turned out to be a steward from the luxury yacht Carbonica. This was obviously not the right lead. Isaac had decided that they would follow all the customers who bought cigars. The next box was bought by some local individual with a beautiful villa in the town's center. On three occasions cigars were delivered to different yachts, and once to a hotel.

Once, Bikie had to drive off in a hurry and follow a young guy on a scooter to the nearby town of La Maddalena, while Isaac kept watch from the bench with his laptop. And on one occasion they had to drive all the way to Cagliari, which was three hundred kilometers one way.

It took them almost seven hours to come back. The damn van guzzled so much gas that they had to fill the tank and then hurtle furiously down the road to catch up with the buyer. They did, but it was a dud of a lead, yet again.

On three occasions the owner of the cigar shop delivered cigars himself, every time to different yachts.

Isaac saw the humidor at the shop so often that he started dreaming about it. And Bikie knew the exact number of cigars in it, so he could easily tell how many one or another customer had bought.

Meanwhile the money Wolanski gave them was running out. The island of Sardinia proved to be far from cheap. Eventually they decided to sell the van, since living in it had become unbearable – it was very hot and constantly burning gas by using the air conditioner was getting too expensive. They made a serious loss on the sale of the van, but didn't really have any options. They moved into a budget hotel three hundred meters from the cigar shop and rented a cheap scooter for operational movements around the island.

Their frustration and despair would have taken the best of them long ago, but after living in the van, the cheap little hotel they moved into seemed almost like heaven. The relaxing atmosphere of the cozy Italian island also helped keep their dark thoughts at bay. The evening walks they took immediately after the cigar shop closed was better than any therapy. Every morning and every evening Isaac jogged five kilometers to the sports ground where he worked out for an hour. A little longer and he would have to buy new clothes again.

Their days were exhausting, but their evenings, after the shop had closed, brought great relief. In the evenings they could walk to the marina or take a swim, and that inspired them with hope for the next day. The backdrop of luxury yachts and laid-back people had a calming effect on them. Now and again Bikie picked up another female tourist, while Isaac and Michelle exchanged phone calls and messages more and more often. He lied to her, saying that Bikie and he were already in Palermo, fearing that Michelle might decide to come to Sardinia. She probably had many friends here. He really did not want her to know that Bikie and he were living in a two-star motel with a communal shower and a kitchen in the corridor. After Wolanski's villa, his room seemed like the ultimate slum.

After all, the womanizer Bikie had been right. After Isaac's promising start with Michelle, the involuntary separation only enflamed their mutual feelings. This was especially true with Michelle, who was accustomed to men dropping at her feet. The mysterious Isaac had gone zooming off on his own business for nearly a month, which made him all the more interesting in her eyes. And the sort of business he had was a mystery too, but he obviously didn't look like a criminal or a scam artist. No matter how hard she tried to find out where he was and what he was doing, she got nowhere. She got nothing but excuses and evasive explanations from Isaac.

Isaac was not happy to be stuck on the damned island either. From what the doctors said, Vicky was improving, but there was still no question of recovery without surgical intervention. He wanted to see Michelle really badly, but then he would have had to tell her everything and he couldn't. It would be bad for the cause, and there was no point in opening the girl up to unnecessary risk.

Every time Isaac phoned Vicky's he had to explain that he was her brother, a fact which gradually returned him to feeling that role for real. He decided that his temporary lust for her was a result of stress and purely brotherly concern. Apart from everything else, meeting and falling for Michelle could not have come at a better time.

There was still one detail that was bothering Commissioner Pellegrini, so he decided to call the Monaco branch of COMUNA to find out of what the board that had disappeared consisted. The system administrator, now fit and well, told him that the most valuable part lost was the memory card, something that really ought to have been backed up constantly, but the instructions were not to do that, in order to protect the classified data from being copied.

Pellegrini frowned with the man's ability to bore one to death with his work talk, thanked him for assisting the police and hung up without waiting for more explanations. He hated people who talked too much and off the point. In fact, he was afraid of them. That was just about all that he feared in life.

As an experienced army officer, he had been through a lot and had a reduced sense of fear. The commissioner had also conducted hostage negotiations at least three times, all of which were successful. Even though the last time the success was relative – he had to shoot the captor in front of a teenager. The predator had let his guard down after Pellegrini promised to meet his conditions, and the commissioner shot him in the head. It was perfectly legal since the criminal was using the kid as a human shield and threatening to kill him.

There was also a similar incident, when a deranged drug addict was so desperate for a fix that he demanded his wife sell their only daughter, yelling that she was no good for anything anyway. He was so badly disturbed that he couldn't even explain to whom he thought the girl should be sold. He just yelled with foam on his lips, holding a knife to the girl's throat.

A neighbor saw the quarrel from the window opposite and called the police. The situation was critical – the junkie's hands were trembling, leaving scratches at the child's throat. He could blow his top any moment.

The commissioner decided to act without waiting for the backup team. He assessed the situation and suggested to the junkie to take painkillers while waiting for heroin to be brought.

Holding out his open left hand with the pills, the commissioner coaxed the perpetrator to make a couple of steps towards him, so he can see what he was holding. Seizing the moment when the junkie loosened his grip to transfer the little girl to his other arm, and the knife lowered some distance away from the child's throat, Pellegrini flung up his right hand and put a bullet straight into the man's heart.

In two swift bounds he reached the man before he fell down and grabbed hold of the little girl. The knife and the body fell almost simultaneously. The knife sprang back off the wooden floor with the blade pointing upwards and at that instant the body fell onto it. It was a ghoulish sight. The little girl didn't even scream, she was completely stunned with fear. The commissioner liked and, at the same time, disliked to recall this story.

Later he visited the girl, made sure that she received free psychological care and even gave a part of his bonus to the mother, so that she could at least buy something for herself. Their home resembled a garbage dump: everything that could be sold or exchanged for drugs was gone and they used all sorts of trash as household items. The atrocious father brought home from the dumps everything that could have any value. There were even two old cassette players there, which he obviously couldn't get rid of.

Two years later, when the little girl turned seven, she started calling the commissioner daddy, and he called her his goddaughter.

The most repulsive memory was the way the dropped knife ripped open the man's stomach, with guts spilling and feces flowing out on the floor. Sometimes, when he stayed on late at work and there was nothing around to eat, the commissioner summoned up this picture from his memory to suppress his hunger.

Right now it was time to end the work-day, but Pellegrini kept on sitting there, going through his notes again while suppressing his hunger. The notepad fell out of his hands and opened on the page with the names of the attack witnesses. One of them was a dark horse, who had been overlooked somehow. Not even Captain Robert had said much, just that he was an ordinary young guy and the captain had checked him out and let him go. Pellegrini arranged another working trip to Monaco in order to meet him.

However, the search for Isaac Leroy was worthless. Laughing at the fact that the local police took a victim for an accomplice, Pellegrini obtained a copy of the interrogation report and went over it. There also was a registered report from someone named Bongardt, a lawyer, and Leroy's explanatory note to that report. Captain Robert thought that Isaac had post-traumatic stress syndrome, which is why the incident with Bongardt occurred. Pellegrini agreed. As a real professional, he very soon dug up a whole heap of information about Isaac, though the guy himself was nowhere to be found. Through phone records, the commissioner learned that Leroy's phone was used in roaming in Sardinia.

"So, you are in Italy. All right," mumbled Pellegrini to himself.

The fourth week was coming to an end without any developments. After supper they felt sleepy, so decided to go back to the hotel. Every day they put off this moment for as long as possible, because even the bench on the street was more comfortable than their room.

"Oh, it's time to get up," Bikie moaned. "Get up or get it up? My smartphone always used to confuse the two meanings, automatically switching to 'get it up'. The software developers were obviously men with a lewd sense of humor."

As always, Bikie had the urge to talk about women.

"It would be good to get it up and in right now. The last one I had was really wild. Well, you don't remember, of course... but anyway, she doesn't count. As for an all-nighter, there were just the two Swedish girls, and a really long time ago a girl from the beach who was really drunk and took a mighty effort to entice me."

Bikie told the story with all the details, but Isaac wasn't listening. Now it seemed to him that all their conclusions were far-fetched, that Link wasn't there. They were running out of money and their future seemed very obscure.

Another two days passed in surveillance of the cigar shop, and their hopes for success dissipated. They started looking for an alternative lead, and reviewed the reports about Link over and over again but no new findings or ideas came up. A couple of times they took off on the scooter following buyers who left the shop. It was all pointless. The first time, the cigars were delivered to a yacht again; the second time, to a villa drowning in greenery, where a respectable looking little old man met the courier at the gates and immediately lit up a one of the cigars from his purchase. It was the same house in La Margarita that Bikie had already been to. This time they even saw the smoker, and it was not Link.

The fifth week of surveillance was just beginning. The laptop chirped – a fresh delivery of merchandise was brought in. Almost immediately, the computer signaled again. Isaac looked at the screen. He saw the door of the little shop closing behind an elegant woman in a light dress.

"Bikie! A girl, a girl has gone into the shop! She looks Oriental and quite young, as far as I can tell. She hasn't been there before. You can't see her now, but the salesman is rummaging in the humidor!"

They ran out of their hotel, hopped on the scooter, started the engine and stood by waiting. Within a minute, the girl came out and walked towards her car, holding a large package. The friends managed to get a good look at her as she got into the driver's seat. It was Yoshi! Her car set off without much hurry. Bikie and Isaac followed.

18

Pellegrini found out that Isaac's apartment had been repossessed by the bank for bad debts, and that it was unclear where he was residing since. Questioning the neighbors didn't turn up anything. Isaac hadn't been on friendly terms with any of them.

Isaac's sister was in a coma. Pellegrini visited the hospital and asked the personnel to call him immediately if Monsieur Leroy shows up.

The commissioner had a pleasant, warm feeling in his chest — as always when he was not idling but focused on a case. Events and facts looked strange: Isaac moved out and lives nowhere, came to the Agency, but didn't offload his OE. All other donors injured in the attack went through the procedure afterwards, and this guy never returned. Though his need for money didn't disappear. Maybe his sister is just a cover? On top of that, he was held in the same cell as Henri Cavalier, who suspiciously refused to communicate. And there was the strange report written by the lawyer. Also, judging by the roaming charges from his phone, Isaac visited Amsterdam, and London, and not just in anywhere in London, but the university in which professor Link worked before disappearing.

Pellegrini was pacing around his hotel room like a tiger in a cage. He had a long-forgotten, but familiar feeling that he will soon find and reveal the offender. He couldn't believe that it was all a coincidence and thought Isaac's behavior to be very fishy.. "Suspected to have taken part in the attack," the Commissioner made a mark opposite to Isaac's name in his notepad. After writing that, the commissioner decided to speak with the physician of Isaac's sister. He thought that maybe this conversation could shine more light on the situation.

"Let's go through it again." Bikie was a bit nervous.

"Again, we're reporters from a student journal and we've come to interview Professor Link." Isaac wasn't nervous, on the contrary, he had calmed down a little. "That cover story works just fine."

They were standing near the gates of a high wall around a mansion where Yoshi had dropped out of sight the day before. In the last few days they had thought of many different options. The absence of an intercom seemed strange. They could not see any security cameras either. Bikie wanted to launch a small drone, but Isaac was afraid its noise would alarm their target. Additionaly, they did not have the money for such an expensive machine.

They thought that a request of an interview would astonish anybody who opens the gate and throw them off guard.

If the staff in the villa didn't know for whom they were really working, then they must know him by a different name. They would probably repeat the name "Link" and tell the guys they had the wrong address, but if the person who opened the gate knew, he would be startled, thus giving himself away. He would ask who had come and say they were mistaken, or something of the kind only after a pause. Since there were no cameras, someone had to open the gate in person and a person's face could say a lot.

In any case they would ask to pass on a note that said the following:

"Dear Professor Link,

We kindly request you to grant us an interview. You need have no concern that your whereabouts are known to anyone but us. We are neither enemies nor friends of yours, but we need your help. We ask you to meet us as a token of goodwill. If you turn us down, it will be pointless for us to keep your location secret.

Yours sincerely, Isaac and Bikie.

"PS. Please call the following number. We are staying in a hotel not far from you."

In the case that whoever opened the gate refused to take the note, Isaac and Bikie planned to leave. They also planned that in case of an initial failure, half an hour later a pizza deliveryman would drive up to the house and hand over the note together with the bill, while Isaac and Bikie remained at a safe distance.

Bikie thought they had to give Link three hours to consider, assuming that he wasn't likely to contact the police, and if he had any backup, it could only come from the Agency. But that was unlikely. In any case, it would take at least three to four hours for Link to get any type of help to come up to the villa.

The friends shelled out for a second hotel room that was located on the ground floor and had an exit that led into the garden. The hotel was by no means a cheap one, had air conditioning and a mini-bar, which, of course, were totally useless for the operation. But there was one big advantage – the hotel was located by a market, and several tourist cafes and souvenir shops. A very busy spot. Bikie bought more video cameras and a local mobile phone - a prepaid one for visitors, that didn't require registering.

They set up their laptop and a web camera in the room. The broadcast signal went directly through the Internet, and it was impossible to determine quickly who was watching it and from where. The telephone number in the note was cunningly redirected, and the phone itself was linked to the computer.

Bikie had done something to ensure the anonymity of their location: after a minute of the ringing tone, a program cut in that sent the call through the web. But the phone carried on ringing, and you could still answer it, or you could answer via the Internet.

"In short, it's not possible to tell exactly where we are," said Bikie, explaining his scheme.

He hung a mirror over the door so they could see the window. He blocked off the keyhole on the inside with three layers of tape and covered the crack under the door with a rug, on which he placed a night table. It was impossible to get into the room without being noticed.

Very soon Isaac and Bikie were standing in front of the fancy hammered gate of Link's supposed villa, which was when they saw the first camera. It wasn't located on the wall, but hidden inside the garden. This explained why they hadn't noticed it yesterday – they never came that close to the villa then. Isaac hesitated for a moment and rang the bell.

"Good afternoon, who are you looking for?" A voice that obviously belonged to an older woman, answered in Italian a minute later.

There's no denying it, you live and learn. Sometimes you lose sight of elementary, but important, details. The friends were so carried away with designing a plan of retreat, preventing a professional from finding them, that they had overlooked a simple contingency that no one would open the gate at all. The call button was on the door, but the intercom was hidden on the other side of it.

Bikie shrugged in confusion. Isaac feverishly tried to think of something.

The pause started dragging out and the voice asked again, this time in broken English:

"Pardon me, who are you looking for?"

"We, we… is this house number five?" asked Isaac, playing for time.

"Yes it is. Are you looking for someone? Who are you?"

"Could you please ask the owner to come to the intercom?"

"Who? The owner? What for, on what business? Stop playing games, young people, or I'll call the police."

"We have a personal letter for him."

"There's a letterbox on the left. Drop it in there."

"It's a confidential letter, we'd like to be sure it won't get lost."

The only reply they heard was the entry phone being switched off.

They stood there for a while, bewildered, not knowing what to do, whether leave the letter, ring again, or just go.

Finally Isaac pressed the call button once more.

"Now what?" The voice was by no means as cordial as the first time.

"Signora, I've dropped the letter in the box as you requested. It is a letter from the owner's home country, we have travelled thousands of kilometers to deliver it. It's very urgent and important. Please be sure to pass on greetings from Elvis."

"Very well."

The line went dead again.

"What has Elvis got to do with this?" Bikie asked.

"Nothing at all. This is just to make them curious. To make them read the note sooner."

Once they were sure the envelope had been collected from the box, the guys dashed to a café they had chosen earlier to watch the web camera.

19

The next three hours seemed like three days. No call came. No one came to their hotel. No one drove out of the professor's villa. Nothing.

"What if he's not home?"

"Sleeping?"

"Or they didn't give him the letter?"

Many questions, but no answers. Both friends were nervous.

"All right, let's think. If it's not Link, then whoever it is would clearly have called the police by now. The letter can be interpreted in various ways. It could even be perceived as a threat."

"That means Link either hasn't read it yet, or he doesn't know how to react."

"Or maybe they took us for pranksters?"

"Take a look at us, we're obviously not street riffraff. We're too old to be monkeying around."

"Let's see again: if it's not Link, anyone who got the note would call either the police or us. Or they would get one of the staff to call, just to be on the safe side."

"True."

"Then if there's no call, it is Link after all."

"I hope so. Yes, it's definitely Link! We saw Yoshi."

"And how long can we wait for him to react?"

"Let's wait until morning. We were there around lunchtime, so it's possible that he got all the morning papers and the next time he picks up the mail, including our letter, won't be until tomorrow morning."

"What if he doesn't read his mail at all, just emails?"

"We said quite clearly that the letter was for the villa's owner."

"All right, we'll wait until morning, but what do we do then if he doesn't call?"

"Look, I don't have a clue!" Isaac was starting to get annoyed.

"Whatever you say," Bikie shrugged.

Suddenly the phone rang and the ring made Isaac and Bikie almost jump out of their skin. Isaac waited a few seconds to pull himself together and answered the call.

"Hello?"

"Good evening. I've been handed a very strange letter from you and, to be honest, I don't understand a thing." The voice had a slight nasal twang, as if the nose was squeezed shut by something.

"A-ah, yes, I sent you a letter."

"Perhaps you'll explain what it means?"

"It means that we want to meet you."

"Me? What for? I think it must be some kind of mistake."

"No, Mr. Link, it isn't a mistake." Isaac was confident again. "We put in a lot of work to find you, and we did. There's no point in playing games with us. You're dealing with a couple of pretty smart guys here. Believe me, it would be best for us to meet and discuss everything. I recognized your voice, I've listened to your lecture on YouTube, so there's no doubt. Either you meet with us or I post my conclusions about your whereabouts on social media. It's your choice. I'm sorry if it turns out that I'm wrong. The police will come and you can try to prove that you're not Professor Link, after all."

"According to my calculations, you should have done that a couple of hours ago. But you haven't," answered Link.

"But..."

"Of course, if the meeting really is so important to you, I don't think you're ready to flush the results of your work down the pan because of an hour or two's delay."

"True, but it doesn't mean I'm not prepared to flush them down the pan at all. I quite definitely am. If the result is negative, it can be discarded."

"All right," said the voice, losing its nasal twang. "Let's not waste time on words. What do you want?"

"I told you, I want to meet."

'I'm afraid that's not possible."

"Why not, I wonder?"

"You're probably in Sardinia now?"

"And aren't you?"

"Not any longer. I'm in Capri. Or maybe in Corsica."

"Won't you get tired of running? We found you once, so we can find you again. But the next time we do, we won't keep your location a secret. How did you sneak out of the villa, by the way?"

"Now that, young man, is none of your business. So let's manage this by phone somehow. By the way, it's your fault I had to leave Sardinia."

"Professor, the questions I want to discuss are not for the telephone."

"You mean you want to discuss something illegal with me?"

"That depends how you look at it. I'd prefer to say we are fighting an epidemic."

"You've probably got the wrong man. I'm not a specialist in that area."

"Well, I think there is one epidemic where it's impossible to find another specialist of your level."

"Ah, I think I'm beginning to understand what you're driving at, young man."

"Professor, think about it. There are plenty of clues to your presence left at the villa. Fingerprints, hair and all sorts of things. You're a very public individual. How far away can you go? To Japan?"

"That's enough," said the professor. "We can meet. My driver will pick you up at the hotel tomorrow morning and bring you to me."

"Straight to Capri?"

"Straight to me."

Isaac didn't feel much satisfaction after the conversation was over. Finding Link should have been a cause for celebration, but the talk did not go well.

Bikie nervously ran through every idea that might enter the professor's head.

"What if he decides to get rid of us? Poison us? Or hand us over to the police?"

He hastily wrote a computer program that would send a pile of information to all his friends if a cancelation password was not entered at a specific time. He thought that would keep Link under control.

In the morning, Isaac went to a pharmacy and purchased an absorbent digestive gel used in cases of food poisoning. He ate half a tube of the Jell-O-like goo himself and made Bikie eat the other half.

"It ought to neutralize a dose of poison or a sleeping draught," he explained. "I'm more concerned about sedatives."

Bikie laughed and said that in any case he wouldn't accept any tea or coffee from the professor's hands and Isaac shouldn't either. In addition, after inspecting the contents of his bag, he took a knife out of it and stuck it behind his belt. Being armed, he felt a lot calmer.

"He won't try to kill us. What's the point? He realizes we can put out information about him. He doesn't know how many of us there are. I didn't need to swallow that gel of yours. If we found him, it means we're not idiots, so we would take precautions. And you pressed him hard on the phone. I liked that."

"You know, to be quite honest, I really feel like having a drink."

"With that gel in your stomach?"

"Yeah, that's a bummer. Seems like we do things right, but something always gets overlooked."

"Don't worry about it. The important thing is that we found him."

Isaac nodded and began writing a text-message for Michelle. Sensing danger ahead, he wanted to write to someone really close to him.

Morning was almost over – the clock showed past eleven – and Link's driver still hasn't showed up. The friends decided to go to the lobby and have a cup of coffee – they needed to kill time somehow.

20

The car arrived at the hotel at midday. It was an ordinary taxi. The driver spoke neither English nor French. He said they were going to Porto Cervo, smiled at all their questions and answered in Italian. Italian is very similar to French, so Isaac and Bikie were able to understand that he had been called in a usual way, asked to pick up two men at the hotel and take them to the seaport. Mostly mega-yachts moored at Porto Cervo, the driver explained. But in every luxury port, one could always find ordinary fishing boats and smaller yachts too.

Isaac and Bikie were met by a gloomy-looking man who introduced himself as the professor's assistant. His dour look sat strangely with the jolly red color of his beard and a gleaming bald patch. His sudden appearance confused the friends even more: how would Link deal with them? What should they expect?

Meanwhile, the assistant handed each of them a package containing shorts, t-shirts, and flip-flops. There were also two baseball caps with the inscription "Sardinia".

The man also gave them a key to a locker located at a nearby beach, where the friends could change and leave their things. Once changed, they looked quite funny in their new outfits. In fact, the clothes fit Bikie, but hung baggily on Isaac. Bikie tried to conceal the knife in his shorts, but couldn't, so he left it in the locker.

Redbeard waited for them to get changed and led them along the berths. Isaac examined with curiosity the little boats and the large yachts and ships standing a bit further off shore. They came to a rather large sixty-foot sailing yacht, old but well-kept. The sail was furled, the engine running.

"Board the yacht, please," Redbeard said.

They walked across a springy ladder to where an Italian captain was waiting for them. As soon as they were all on board, he cast off the mooring rope and the yacht set out to sea.

There was a slight swell and Isaac started feeling sick. The captain noticed and handed him a pill.

"For seasickness," he explained.

Isaac thanked him, pretended that he was feeling much worse, leaned over the side and flung the pill away.

"Boss, I could do with a pill too," said Bikie. He took it and tucked the pill in his pocket inconspicuously.

"What for?" Isaac asked him quietly.

"Maybe we can check to see if it's a poison," Bikie whispered with his lips barely moving. "Maybe even test it on our professor. Or on Redbeard there."

Bikie was upset at being left without his knife, and he felt calmer knowing that at least he had a pill of "poison".

The yacht kept sailing away from the shore. The friends sat at the bow and gazed at the sea's blue, rippling waters. This was not the direction to Capri. Perhaps the professor was coming to meet them on another yacht?

Suddenly a sharp voice behind them said:

"Well then, congratulations! You managed to do what no one else could. You found me."

Isaac swung around. A short man of about sixty was emerging from a small cabin that Isaac had thought was empty. He straightened up to his full height and the guys immediately recognized the cunning glint in his narrowed eyes that they've seen in photos so much.

His had thick, combed head of hair with receding temples that glinted in the sun, dividing the upper part of his head in two, which gave him a somewhat diabolical look. Fine lines radiated around his eyes, making his expression cunning and good-natured by turns, and several deep lines on his forehead testified to exceptional intellectual capacity. He was attractive and scary at the same time, which was exactly what Isaac had imagined the professor to be.

Isaac eventually replied to the professor in the same tone:

"I think we really wanted to."

"I can see you did. Well done, well done."

"And I see you weren't really in Capri?"

"Of course, I wasn't. I never left the villa. You're still young, you have a lot of weapons in your arsenal: passion and unflinching determination. But in mine, I have experience and bluff."

"That all comes with time, but we have youth in our arsenal."

"Now you're offending me, that's in poor taste."

"I'm sorry, it just slipped out. I don't like to back down."

"That's a good quality, but have you ever heard of aikido? Why go head on, if sometimes it's better to make use of your opponent's energy... Would you like some wine? Local, homemade."

"Professor, why did you choose such a strange place for our meeting? Why a yacht? Do you think you're safer here?" Isaac parried.

"No, not because of that. I have nothing to be afraid of, and my experience tells me that wasting nerve cells on stress causes far more harm than the actual danger that so often fails to materialize. I enjoy fishing. Sitting there, catching fish, thinking."

"I booked this yacht last week. And I decided not to cancel it, I thought we could talk perfectly well out here."

"And what if we'd been seasick?"

"There are pills for that," the professor said with a smile, holding out his hand, into which the captain placed exactly the same kind of a pill he had given to Isaac and Bikie earlier. The professor closed his eyes and tossed the pill into his mouth.

Isaac and Bikie exchanged glances and the professor continued.

"And then, even if you were seasick, we wouldn't be far from shore and could get to the marina in five minutes. We could easily continue our conversation in the evening, eating what we catch today for supper."

"Great! You live the good life alright!" said Isaac, beginning to feel less tense. He finally realized that he had achieved an incredible goal. He has found the man he had been searching for so methodically for so long. Found him alive and well. Out of all the people who had searched for the professor, only he and Bikie found him!

"The grass is always greener... That rule always applies without exception. This life has its cons too. I do not go to big cities, and I miss their bustle and energy. I miss my students. They are very intelligent and great listeners. I'm actually glad to see you. I'm sick of hiding. I pass the time splendidly, but it flows along too smoothly.

"And so, young people, I shall listen with pleasure to what you have to say to me," the professor summed up. "And then you'll tell me how you found me and why," he added, puffing on a cigar.

"The little magic key is right there in your mouth," Isaac thought, then he spoke out loud:

"We need your help."

"You wrote that already and I understand everything the first time around. I don't like it when someone tries to explain something to me five times, as if I were some slow-witted schoolboy."

"All right, I'll try not to repeat myself. Professor, what you have created is both wonderful and appalling. But in the future, the appalling side could become a whole lot worse. You have created an epidemic, a ticking time bomb. The technology you have created will get humankind to complete totalitarianism in no more than a couple of decades. We want to stop that."

"Appalling and wonderful. Interesting words," said the professor, smiling wistfully. It was a long time since he had been involved in a serious debate.

"And you will help us do it. Help us stop your own creation," Isaac continued. "Whether you want to or not. And even if you didn't give a damn about your own life, we can always find a weak spot, something that is really important to you. Today, only two of us are here, but we have allies. If necessary, they'll find you again. So it's not just a matter of us. By eliminating us or handing us over to the authorities, you'll only gain a little time."

"There's no need to threaten me, Isaac. I don't intend to do you any harm, God forbid. I created the technology for honorable purposes and it has brought no less benefit to humankind than electricity or penicillin."

"But it will inevitably lead to catastrophe."

"An interesting theory...continue. You're intelligent young guys. I could have done more with students like that. And you actually bluff quite well. Concerning the 'allies'," the professor smiled good-naturedly, "you're a bit short of practice. Tonight I will give you a book on poker, written by a friend of mine. It was published in a small edition and is very popular with the pros. It's not as boring as textbooks on the theory of lying, is much more popular, and better describes the gestures people make when they lie or tell the truth."

"That's in theory, professor, but you are going to run up against the reality. Then we'll see how true your conclusions are."

"Shush, calm down please. Our conversation has gotten off on the wrong foot. So far there are no reasons for an argument. I can see that you're rather high-minded individuals, and so am I. Let's relax and start over again. How about some rum and coke?" Link poured a dark, foaming liquid into a glass and added rum from a dark, heavy, thick-walled bottle.

"Professor, I'm not really in the mood for drinking cocktails," said Isaac, pushing aside the glass held out by Link.

Link apparently guessed they were worried about poison and took a relaxed swallow from the glass he had just offered to Isaac.

"For starters, I've realized that you're Isaac, right? You work out a lot, I see?"

Isaac nodded. The worldly professor was trying to lull their suspicions with his apparent kindheartedness, slipping compliments into the conversation.

"And, judging from the hardline tattoos and the stubble, you are Bikie?"

Even in beach clothes, it was obvious who was Bikie and who Isaac.

"And I, as you know, am Professor Jeremy Link. But please, young people, just call me Link. Using the first name is a little too hobnob for me, and Mr. Link is way too official. So, simply Link."

"All right, Link. So now what do you have to say? Seven years is a long time, you're a clever man, and you watch TV and read the news. What's your opinion?"

"You want to destroy the system for gathering Orange Energy – you do understand that we're talking precisely about the system? It's impossible to destroy an operating system if it's installed on too many computers. Either physically or with some cunning virus. It's a program. It is sold in thousands of shops. And Orange Energy is a program too, a technology. I'd even call it a form of knowledge. Knowledge is impossible to destroy if it has spread around the world. It's like trying to convince people all over again that the sun is nailed to the sky."

"If you want to destroy it, you have to make everyone stop using it. Make it unpopular. That is possible. I'm sure that you, being the most respected man in the world and a celebrated inventor, will be paid attention to." Suddenly, Isaac realized why he actually had been looking for the professor so persistently. The man was the top authority, the one to make people follow him. "But to find the weakest point, the key con, we have to understand how the technology works, and you are the one who can help us. You can present this final "key con" as a fact, and do so clearly. Can you tell us if, hypothetically, you will be able to help us?"

"And this is why you searched for me…"

"Yes. We decided to find you in order to understand the system. As Gogol says in Taras Bulba: 'I gave you life, and I will kill you'. We want to know everything you know about the technology. Its strong and weak aspects, the principles it works on, basically everything. The plan is to destroy it, to switch it off. We'll figure out how as we go along. The world hasn't been destroyed yet. Even if you refuse to destroy it yourself, you'll give a chance to the opposition, meaning to us. And we, by the way, may be right in our conclusions."

"The world cannot be destroyed. Sooner or later a tyrant dies. If a new tyrant takes his place, he will die some time too. Sooner or later there is a revolution. Even if the world goes completely to the dogs, humankind will survive in some places, invent everything all over again, and a new surge of evolution will begin. We don't know what heights were scaled by the inhabitants of Atlantis, if they existed. But the fact remains that mankind survived and was resurrected, and invented everything all over again. We fly into space, we talk to people living on other continents by ways of miniature wireless devices. We've surpassed Atlantis, that's for sure.

"In the same way, the hypothetical crisis that I've created will pass sooner or later. Even a nuclear war, capable of reducing cities and civilizations to dust, sooner or later will be forgotten. Life will start over again and completely restore itself. Where will the new cradle of civilization be? Maybe somewhere on the outskirts of New Zealand, maybe in Africa, or on Mauritius," said Link thoughtfully.

"That's empty rhetoric, Professor. We're talking about here and now, not ten thousand years in the future. We want to win today, not through the whim of time's endless flow. Our task is to halt evolution in the wrong direction. My sister is sick today!" Isaac started shouting.

"What's wrong with her?" the professor sounded considerate.

"Something your *Collective Mind* couldn't deal with or didn't want to. Neither it nor the Agency are interested. She's nothing for them, a blob! But she's a person! And she doesn't have anybody but me!"

"I'm sorry to hear that."

"That's what brought me to the Agency. It was a miracle that I remained myself. Now I have a first-hand experience of your super-computer. I want to know if it is possible to bring it all back? Return to people their creative energy? All those who came to the downloading office along with me are normal people, deprived of their choice in life. By you!"

Professor grew pensive. He closed his eyes and it looked like he was weighing hundreds of pros and cons. His face was tense.

"I've had enough time to assess the consequences of my invention. I disagree with your conclusions, although there is a grain of sense in them. In fact, it is hard not to agree with some of them. If everything were in my hands right now, I would use the technology differently. I agree that there are no guarantees. No matter how a system is constructed, sooner or later a villainous scoundrel will control it. This is quite possible. So what then?

"Every system is run by people. People get old and die, and new people take their place, it's an endless process. And in infinite time, the probability of any event occurring is a hundred per cent. Sooner or later. If God exists, then probably he alone never changes and can offer guarantees, because he is eternal."

"I agree about eternity. I think so too. But God helps those who help themselves."

"Scientists are often faced with a choice: to give a technology to people or to destroy what they have created. Everything has an upside and a downside. Electricity is a good thing, but lots of people have been killed by it. Not to mention nuclear power. There are nuclear power stations and there are nuclear bombs. You can say the same about radio and antibiotics, GMO and many other things. "

"We are in the present. Seven years have gone by. And everything is still in your hands. And ours. You can correct or adjust the world that has been steered off course by your invention. We believe that it's time to stop. You got the world addicted to this morphine, which is now causing harm after being helpful for a while."

"You can't stop scientific progress! Might as well try to hold water in your palms! Don't be so primitive, for God's sake!" Professor was clearly about to blow.

It looked like the professor wanted to add something else in favor of his argument, but, having studied Isaac and Bikie closer, he changed his mind. His face was stiff with disapproval but then a little smile touched his lips and he continued with a soft voice, a bit sadly but amicably.

"Yes, everything that has happened is a catastrophe for me as the inventor. I created a universally accessible drug that is instantly addictive. The technology itself is unique and mega-useful, only there aren't any instructions and my idea is not used as I wished."

"Professor, I understand that you're disappointed, I understand about electricity, and about the drug, I just don't understand how determined you are to put right the mess you have caused," Bikie interrupted

"I didn't cause it, young man, I invented a technology. God creates and humankind causes certain events. We always get what we deserve." Professor's voice instantly changed from soft and feeble to icy cold, he looked at Bikie with ill-concealed contempt.

"Professor, let me repeat more courteously, as you requested. Sorry, Bikie got really tired looking for you and took things a little bit too far. Are you willing to try, let's put it this way... to reboot the program? To correct its malfunctions, especially since the program has already done a lot of good, and all the achievements will be retained?"

The professor sighed and started pondering, shifting between happiness and sadness. In the end, he glanced at his watch and replied:

"I have devoted the last five years of my life to this and I'm willing to devote all the time I have left. Of course, it's annoying for me to hear about the negative aspects of my invention from a pair of young pups, no matter how intelligent they are, but I'm a scientist and I studied the consequences intensely myself a long time ago. And I'm prepared to try to correct them."

The professor was writhing out uneasily. There was clearly a struggle going on inside him. Agreeing to help Isaac and Bikie, he would cross out all his achievements, acknowledging their extreme danger.

Hearing that the professor was willing to help took a huge weight, a massive burden, off Isaac's mind. The immense rock that had been hanging over his head crumbled to dust. He struggled to contain the emotions welling up inside him. Until today he had been obsessed with the idea, and now he saw hope ahead. He was successful in generating an opposition. Not a radical opposition of fanatics, but a powerful, conceptual opposition by intellectuals. Even "intelligent pups" sounded flattering when it came from the lips of a genius. He felt terribly sorry for the professor, understanding him very well as an inventor. He was aware that at that moment Link was renouncing the apple of his eye.

Isaac suddenly felt ferociously tired. It seemed that he couldn't lift his arms or legs. As if the burden has been lifted, and his body demanded rest, a well merited time not to be disturbed for a while. Now that the constant influx of has stopped, he felt exhausted.

Link's spirit was as hard as granite. Having taken hold of himself and processed the new information, he quite soon gathered his wits and continued the conversation with Bikie, who had apologized. Isaac could no longer be a part of the conversation, but Bikie and Link continued arguing and agreeing about things. Several times the professor commended on his opponent's intelligence. Isaac saw Bikie take out his mobile phone and press something on it. He was sending the text message to cancel the publication of information about Link on the Internet.

As for Isaac, he simply looked at the glitter of the waves, incapable of either listening or thinking. At that moment, he was not even thinking of Vicky or Michelle. There was only peace, peace and the splashing of the clear blue water.

He could not see land or the yachts beyond the horizon. Only occasional silhouettes of fishing boats, and a distant expanse of light-blue. The tabula rasa of the sea, he thought. Genoa was somewhere over there, not far away.

"I will definitely reach my shore, I'll reach it and discover my own America, completely new and not fucked-up, and I'm going to build a new life there," Isaac decided firmly.

His mobile phone rang. The number did not display, but Isaac answered it reluctantly. Something might be wrong with Vicky.

"Good afternoon, my name is Pellegrini, I'm a Commissioner of police and the head of Orange Energy Department. I need to talk to you about the incident that happened in Monaco."

"I think I already told everything," began Isaac, but the Commissioner interrupted him sharply.

"I inform you that you must appear for interrogation at your local police station."

"I'm not there," said Isaac. "I'm in Spain... at a friend's place," he lied.

"When are you coming back?"

"I don't know yet."

"Young man!" Pressed forward aggressive Pellegrini. "If you do not come voluntarily, I will declare you wanted, and I promise you will be delivered to me nicely cuffed in small iron bracelets. I do not advise you to argue with me!"

"I... I'll be back to Monaco in a week, and I will go to the police station," promised Isaac.

"Okay. I'll wait." The Commissioner disconnected. He was pleased with himself. He heard fear in Isaac's voice and did not doubt that he will break him instantly.

Isaac's comfort and fatigue vanished as if by magic. Who was this damn Pellegrini and what did he want? It was more than two months since the attack at the Monaco branch of the Agency. Why in the world can't they all just relax at Cote D'Azur?

Although did he really need to worry about it when professor Link himself promised to work it all out and put an end to OE offloading? He had Michelle and Bikie, and soon, when he got the patent money, he would be able to pay for the surgery and dear little Vicky will be fine.

Isaac shivered – what if Link lied and will disappear again? Isaac couldn't relax just yet. He needed to make sure everything was done right.

Link looked quite relaxed, talking to Bikie, who, in his turn, seemed rather nervous, asking his questions in a cocky manner, as if trying to offend the professor. Link didn't seem offended at all. He spoke calmly, using facts where needed to support his claim. He was behaving in a very friendly manner, clearly happy to welcome his guests. He also was quite lavish with praise, comparing Isaac and Bikie with his students and lab-assistants. When he found out that the friends were staying in a cheap motel, he invited them to move to his villa.

After returning to the marina in the evening, the professor's assistant took them to fetch their things. While packing, Bikie looked sullen, as if he wasn't happy to have found Link. Isaac asked his friend what happened and if he was ok, but Bikie just grumbled that he was fine.

The professor served them an amazing dinner made from the fish they had caught during the day. It was delicious, especially after their usual daily pizza, of which they were so tired by now. After eating all he could, Isaac went to sleep in a cool air-conditioned room the professor had offered him, and immediately passed out on a very nice and soft bed.

21

Hardly had the morning smile faded from the commissioner's face when his mobile rang. The number was that of Monaco. "Must be from the hospital," Pellegrini thought and answered.

"Commissioner Pellegrini? Good afternoon! We didn't have the chance to speak a few days ago, sorry about that. This is the attending doctor of Victoria Frank, you asked me to get in touch with you."

"Yes, thank you for calling back. The thing is that her brother, Isaac Leroy, is our suspect," Pellegrini had already made his decision.

There was a lot of background noise from all the machinery at the hospital, which is probably why the doctor didn't hear Pellegrini's last words.

"Yes, Isaac... why, her only relative, I know him well. A kind-hearted man. Selfless. He sold everything he had to pay for the treatment of his sister. I really empathize with him in this difficult situation. He has signed a contract for the operation and left us a check. The money he was supposed to get from offloading his OE was to pay for the surgery. But this terrible terrorist attack! He didn't get the money it time and now his sister is in a coma. He's got another couple of months, though, because of that. He said he has found the means to pay for the surgery, so I hope they will both be fine!"

"How did he find it? Where?" Pellegrini stiffened.

"It seems that he sold his invention. Said, the money will be there soon."

"Are you sure? For how long has his sister been treated?"

"Nearly a year. Her health went down a lot right around the time of the attack. What are you implying?"

"Nothing. Thank you. I'll call you back."

The commissioner could not breathe. It was true that he wanted to sell his creativity to get money for his sister. Isaac is not a felon, but a decent human being. Pellegrini was terribly embarrassed that he so easily judged a good man. The commissioner opened his cabinet, poured himself some whiskey and quickly drank it. He had never made such mistakes. The damned Agency had led him, an experienced police officer, to make such a horrible mistake! He created a criminal and offended a good man.

Calling back with apologies wasn't in the commissioner's manner. His job didn't really suggest things like that.

Something was dragging Isaac down from behind. He tried to turn and failed thus waking up. With surprise, he found himself sitting on a chair, with his hands bound behind his back. Next to him he saw Bikie, also tied to a chair.

"Bikie, wake up!" Isaac screamed, realizing that they are in serious trouble.

"What? Where are we? Isaac, is that you?" Waking up slowly, Bikie couldn't think clearly yet.

"We are restrained! Professor! That jerk!" Isaac tried to free his arms, cut couldn't.

"Damn it!" Echoed Bikie.

The red-bearded assistant emerged from behind their backs silently and left the room. Isaac tried to understand where they were. Apparently on the same Villa, only now they were in the basement. The walls were dimly lit, along them were various boxes, some wine racks, and a large cigar humidor. There were no windows and Isaac smelled mold.

The Professor entered the room and turned on the light.

"Good morning, boys! I trust you slept well?" He asked as if nothing had happened.

"What is this, Professor?" Bikie asked angrily.

"Nothing. A small precautions. I can't tell you anything right now. We need to wait and see," replied Link.

Redbeard brought in some equipment with sensors on it, which he connected to them right away.

"What are you going to do with us?" Isaac cursed himself for his gullibility. "What is this?"

"We'll have a chat. This is a polygraph. More precisely, a lie detector of my own invention."

"And what are we going to have to tell you?"

"Everything. Everything that I decide to ask you."

"And if not?"

"Then I will connect another equipment to you. I have been doing neural research for many years. An electrical impulse here and there. At a small level. And then I'll let you go."

"Just let us go like that?"

"Of course! You can do with a small artificial amnesia. Unfortunately, it doesn't work in chronological order. Memory loss will be random, and until I see that you have really forgotten who I am and that you've been here, I will have to proceed."

"So, we can forget not only you but something else too?"

"Unfortunately, yes. I'm really sorry. I didn't invite you here. You came at your own risk."

Isaac was terrified. The professor discourteously placed the creativity meter on his temple, gave a hum of approval and then measured Bikie's creativity, as well. Isaac didn't doubt that the crazy scientist could do as he said. He could erase their memory! Childhood, youth, parents, Michelle, even Vicky! God, Isaac could forget that Vicky needs an urgent surgery!

"You are such an asshole, Professor," muttered Bikie. "We come to you with good intentions at heart and you do this!"

"That's what we are about to do – check that heart of yours," replied Link. "Isaac, you can start your story. How did you find me and why. Everything. Everything in detail. It's in your best interest."

Isaac started his story from the time of the attack. He concealed neither how they found Yoshi, nor their trip to England nor their hacking of the cigar shop database. Wanting to protect Peter, he explained that Wolanski did not know where they are exactly and that he doesn't know they found the professor. Michelle wasn't aware of their business at all. After the story, Isaac answered some additional questions. He didn't know how to work around the polygraph, so he couldn't lie to the machine, but he had no bad intentions on his mind, so it was all right.

"I think you have something to add," said the professor looking at Bikie.

Bikie moved uneasily and replied firmly:

"No!"

"It's a simple choice – you either answer my questions or stay silent. If you are silent or lie, I erase the memory of you both."

"No," repeated Bikie. "There's nothing that I have to add."

"Think," professor sighed. "It's not just about you. This is also about Isaac, about his sister. Or are you satisfied with the role of Pascal-2? This time, it's in your hands, not his."

Isaac did not understand what was happening, but judging by Bikie's grim face, his friend was stubbornly silent about something.

"Isaac's motivation is clear to me. But yours... How far were you going to go?"

"I was going to kill you," suddenly calmly replied Bikie.

Isaac caught the professor's expressive look: "You see, Isaac, what's your buddy like. I bet you didn't even suspect it." And that was the truth!

There was a pause.

"Bikie, are you serious? You lied to me all this time? But why?!" Isaac felt betrayed.

"Because of his father," calmly replied Link instead of Bikie.

"Yes. I was going to kill you. My dad was addicted to heroin. And he was downloaded. Not cured, but downloaded. Then he died and I vowed to take down whoever is responsible," Bikie's voice was hoarse.

"But it's now in the past. And I won't kill you, as much as I would love to do that. You are the key to ensuring that this all stops."

"Why do you blame me?"

"Whom should I blame? *Collective Mind* is your brainchild."

"Come on, Bikie! Let's say that everyone who lost someone from electrocution will blame, I don't know, Volt, for example. Or we'll blame Columbus for tobacco. I discovered orange energy and learned to use it. I have saved millions of lives!"

"Don't compare yourself to Volt. You won't find more that one percent of families in the world who haven't lost someone they love because of you."

"That's a fact," thought Isaac. There were Pascal, himself, Sandrine, as it turned out, and also Bikie, who lost his father. Isaac wasn't happy to realize that Bikie isn't quite the straightforward man that he thought. Bikie was a secretive, insincere man who used Isaac for his own motifs.

As if reading his thought, Bikie gave a guilty look to Isaac.

"Forgive me. You never asked me why I hate them so much. You were too focused on your own problems. And I don't really like to talk about my drug-addict father. That's why I drank. Because there was nothing I could do. It was my only secret from you. I swear! I hope, no, I'm confident that this will not end our friendship. I wouldn't anything even now, if only my life was at stake. But it's not, it's yours and your sisters," said he.

Isaac was upset, but he immediately nodded in approval, allowing Bikie to understand that he doesn't hate him. Perhaps this is a real friendship. One doesn't have to turn the other inside out, getting into the innermost corners of the soul to be considered a close and trusted friend. Isaac also felt guilty that he didn't know and wasn't particularly interested in what motivated Bikie.

Bikie continued sitting there with his head down. Judging by the fact that the professor did not ask any more questions, everything was clear. Bikie's original purpose was to kill Link. However, the fact that he changed his mind was also true.

"Link why did you disappear?" Isaac asked, trying to be casual. "Is your secret location important enough to kill us? My sister is being killed now, you know that."

"It's all very simple. I ran away because I was frightened. Secret Service agents came to see me and 'have a talk.' The government wanted to learn everything about the technology and then make decisions on whether they wanted to make information public. I was forced to quickly set up the conference and present the technology, handing it over to Blake at the UN. Immediately after that I got a call asking me not to leave the country. But I was all prepared. When I realized that the government would stop at nothing to get hold of the technology, even if it was an exact copy that they can replicate, I panicked and ran.

"Think about it yourself. How much time would pass before they downloaded my own OE? I possess knowledge that is deemed top secret. Or somebody would order a commercial built of *Collective Mind*. A private one, so to speak. Then people would start kidnapping and downloading scientists all around the world. This would create a creativity race.

"I was far too tempting a morsel for everyone, from the military and the big corporations to ordinary terrorists. But if I were to vanish, there would be only one computer in the hands of people who had spent their lives at least trying, if not always successfully, to maintain peace on earth.

"I thought about it a lot and realized it was an absolute certainty that someone would get the idea of downloading me. It was only a matter of time until they arrived at that brilliant idea.

"But had they laid their hands on my ideas, I'm afraid there would have been a few surprises in store for them." With a restrained smile, the professor raised his index finger and narrowed his eyes. "If energy can be pumped out, then a way can be found to…"

"Pump it back in," Isaac murmured.

"So again, it was just a matter of time until, sooner or later, someone unearthed this idea of mine. And that was something I definitely couldn't tolerate. But now we have everything developing according to a fairly positive scenario. The technology belongs to the UN, where there are decent people in charge. Things could have gone differently. If not for my reputation, I wouldn't have been able to get to the Secretary General so quickly.

"Thank God, my old friend understood me and the implications of my invention instantly." Sweat beaded down the professor's brow. "I was lucky. The last thing I wanted was to become a man who had invented a super-powerful weapon," he added confidently. "If the military had gotten their hands on the technology first, then… I'm afraid the word "democracy" would only exist in textbooks, although, not for too long."

There was a minute of silence as each of them imagined a future with the military in control.

"But couldn't you have thought about that beforehand?" Bikie pulled himself together.

"I did. I was funded by the university. My laboratory assistants wrote reports on our work and expenditures. Someone obviously overdid it, and the authorities took an interest in my invention. I only had a week to organize the conference and my escape before the Secret Service paid me another visit. Everything started slipping out of my control. But all's well that ends well. It probably never even occurred to them that a highly respected fifty-five-year-old scientist can just go on the run."

The professor moved away to light up a cigar.

"You know, Isaac, when the professor starts talking, I listen to him and realize that compared to him you're a dumbo," Bikie said very seriously and immediately got a friendly punch from Isaac.

"Friends," the professor intervened, coming back with the cigar in his hand, "you shouldn't overestimate an old blockhead like me. In fact, everyone warned me that the technology was extremely dangerous, and that it could be dangerous for me. But who were they to tell to me what I should do? It's interesting that you found me. Anyway, I'm glad my refuge was cracked by truly intelligent individuals.

"My refuge!" The professor continued. "How sick I am of this settled life in this lousy dump, pardon the expression, the cloying syrup of identical days. There was a time when a journalist came to see me every month to publish an interview about my invention. Frequent scientific conferences and debates. I used to feel the way explorers and pioneers felt, the way the greatest minds of humanity felt at the summit of their achievements. The world seemed to revolve around me! Everyone on the planet seemed to be concentrated on me."

The professor's eyes were glowing demonically. He felt great pleasure remembering it all.

"Professor, that's exactly the way things were," Isaac remarked. "And I'd say they still are. A great deal depends on you in the life of mankind."

Still smiling, the professor frowned.

"It's boring," he said, continuing his skeptical complaint. "I'm so bored to live this way. All my memories, pangs of conscience, fears – they don't count. That's all trivial compared to the boredom. It's all trivial compared to the peak I've reached."

"Who said you've reached your peak, Link?" Bikie asked, trying to make the question sound as intriguing as possible. "You have taught the world how to download OE, but you haven't taught it how to give it back to people. But you said yourself that it is possible! Now that would be the highest peak, Professor, returning creativity to those who have lost it. Is it feasible?"

"Theoretically," said the professor, brightening up. "I've had enough time to think and I can picture how to do it. Only, as you know, theory is theory, but implementation requires experiments and trials. We need a real Veggie. Practical tests, you know…"

"Professor!" Isaac had a glimmer of hope. "We have to make it a reality! And I even have a candidate for the experiment. I have… I had a friend, Pascal, I told you before, he offloaded and became a Veggie. You could use him for your experiments. If you return his creativity, we can all be sure the theory works. We have a great base in Monaco! There's enough room for everyone. We can conduct any experiments there. And Pascal lives very close."

Link was obviously very interested in this proposal and went straight to the specifics: when and where did Pascal offload his OE? What was his rating? What kind of life does he lead now?

Isaac replied briskly. For a while he forgot about danger, the uncertainty and the possibility of failure. It all paled beside the idea of pulling his friend out of his vegetable condition, bringing the first Veggie back to creative stage!

By the end of the evening their plan of action took shape. It was simple and precise. Give Pascal back his creativity and thereby justify their struggle against the system.

Link felt similar elation. He felt that a great experiment was on its way, that a new frontier would be conquered. He got so excited that Isaac's last doubts evaporated. He knew that the professor was not going to disappear because he needed them just as much as they needed him. A scientist's fascination with his work is as addictive as a drug and Isaac knew that Link was not going to miss his chance.

Part 2. Creator vs. Creation

Prologue

Being interrogated is frustrating, even scary. If you are simply being questioned, you are a witness. If you are being interrogated, then someone has decided that you are a criminal. And if you have no alibi to convince the police that their hypothesis is wrong, things become difficult. After all, they, by default, believe that you're lying.

Everything is complicated if you're not guilty of your charges but are still afraid, because you've committed some other crime. Not the one the police think, but another one. It's kind of like trying to convince the authorities that you didn't kill someone, because you were busy robbing a store.

Isaac didn't kill anyone in the attack that interested the commissioner, but he came into possession of something that incriminated him, nevertheless, and needed to hide that. He had to think carefully about his answers and find the right words. He needed only to answer the questions that were asked of him, and try not to provide any other information.

Commissioner Pellegrini took notice of everything. He caught small, forced pauses, excessive nervousness, suspicious facial expressions, thus understanding that something was wrong. He was becoming more and more convinced of his version – this guy was somehow involved. And confidence gave him extra strength. The offender's motive was clear, as he urgently needed the money for his sister's operation. The fact that the direct connection had not been yet found, only added excitement. There was no connection just because the picture was not complete. It only takes to restore the picture correctly and then the commissioner can prove to himself that he hasn't lost his bite.

On the other hand, Isaac had to convince the commissioner of his innocence so that he could get back to his business as soon as possible. Any extra attention from the police was completely unnecessary. It was unfortunate that even though the attack took place two months ago, the interrogation was happening only now. A week ago, he would have confidently replied to any questions, with nothing to hide. He didn't do anything illegal.

Last week everything changed when Isaac found Professor Link in Sardinia after a long and fruitless search. Now their plans, to put it mildly, didn't fit in any social norms.

1

"Isaac, what's the value of your creativity?" Bikie was obviously bored spending another day visiting Professor Link.

"Almost twenty million. Why?" He reluctantly looked up from reading a message from Michelle.

"Big bucks. It's a shame that there is no more slavery and you're not my slave. I would sell you creativity," dreamily added his best friend. "I'd buy a new Harley and go around the world with some chick. Would lie with her on the beach, drink beer, listen to rock."

"Well, thank you! You make that sound terribly sincere!"

"That's the truth. Don't like lying over little things."

"So now I am a "little thing"?"

"That *is* the truth. Don't like lying over little things," Bikie repeated.

"You yourself have to be sold. For meat. You do not have to be cooked, as you are already marinated with beer. The famous Bokassa would definitely admire your greasy body parts," shouted Isaac.

"I'm not fat, but big. But why are you so angry?" Bikie was confused. "And beer, by the way, it's an inspiration. Inspiration that comes in a liquid form. You, as always, do not understand. You always..."

Bikie didn't have the time to continue messing with Isaac, because they were called to dinner.

After the friends went through the professor's complex tests their relationship with Link improved dramatically. Isaac knew that Link, after hiding for so long, won't too excited to hold his experiments to miss out on the opportunity. It seemed the professor was nervous that Isaac and Bikie would suddenly change their minds and leave, depriving him of the opportunity to test his ideas. So he introduced the new tradition of eating breakfast and dinner together, trying to establish an utmost trust, conversing about the pros and cons of his invention.

The guys spent more than a month in Sardinia searching for the professor, and both of them wanted to go back to Monaco. Bikie toiled from idleness, and Isaac had an unresolved problem with his sister back at home. The two to three months that he was given before the money needed to be paid for her surgery were evaporating, leaving him less and less time. And there was still no money.

Such long a separation and secrecy began to spoil their relationship with Michelle, as well. Isaac was forced to lie to her constantly, and she felt that he was concealing something from her. In addition, Michelle planned to go to Miami for a month, and Isaac needed to be back before she left at any cost. She made the first move, inviting him along, and he had to refuse without providing an explanation. Michelle, was very offended and wasn't responding to his calls or text messages second day in a row. Isaac was nervous and felt down.

"I have a big day today!" Unlike his guests, Link was energetic. "I am happy to celebrate it with you!"

"What is it?" Asked Isaac.

"It's been exactly eight years since I created my *Collective Mind*!" Happily declared Link.

"Is it a holiday? It seems to me we are going to fight it, not support it," said Bikie, not appreciating the occasion.

"In any case, this day should be noted. It is not necessary to look at *Collective Mind* from a one-sided perspective. To many he gave life. We must be objective in our conclusions. We are scientists, and not some biomass," softly replied the professor.

"Your invention breeds biomass everyday." Bikie just couldn't let go of it.

"Why is everybody so sad? We will return creativity to the first donor and decide what to do next. By the way, a few days, and I will have finished my calculations." The professor sipped expensive cognac, holding in his free hand his traditional cigar.

"Just wait and we'll conduct this unique experiment! First of its kind!"

"I want to go tomorrow," firmly said Isaac. "We have spent far too much time here. And you can finish your calculations and join us later."

"As you wish. Bikie, what do you say? Will you stay or go?" The professor turned to Isaac's friend.

"I love freedom of choice, risk and a variety of options, which the world is promptly losing. I like to make mistakes, to gain experience. The Agency's world is a beautiful long-legged rubber girl that cannot be impregnated, and from which you can't pick up an infection. Boring as hell."

"Bikie, please don't be such a downer, everything has already been discussed," said the professor, sick of hearing about the disadvantages of his brainchild. "And you are still talking about the same thing! You should go with Isaac."

"Both of you are willing to partake in the experiment regardless of the consequences!" Bikie was annoyed. "By the way, Isaac, do you even remember that our future lab rat is your best friend? Aren't you scared that such an experiment can melt his brain and he can die?!"

"I am. But, there is no choice. I'm not doing this for the sake of lying on some beach with a girl and drinking a beer," said Isaac, recalling a recent joke.

He wasn't happy that the only Happy, on whom they could run their dangerous experiments, was Pascal. He was the donor, who became the necessary connection point between Link and the friends.

"That's right Isaac," the professor was happy. "You are reasoning like a scientist! No real scientist can be stopped! In science, there are no friends, only discoveries. I'm ready to try to return creativity to Pascal. To download his orange energy back and see what happens. I have been theoretically ready for a long time, but there wasn't the right occasion until you came along. And the chances of success are very high. I need a little more time to finish and then I will be ready to visit you in Monaco. We can figure everything else out as we go. How does that sound?"

"Alright," said Bikie, this time without sarcasm. "I'm always up for turning a Happy back to a normal dude!"

Isaac wasn't pleased with Link's compliment. He did not wish to become a person for whom science is more important than friendship, especially when there was risk to human life. He nodded, deciding that there would be more time to deal with such risks before the actual experiment begins.

2

Link suggested that Isaac and Bikie take his van so they can bring along his things and a small laboratory. When they thanked him for the car, he remarked, with his typical directness, that it remained to be seen who was doing whom a favor. He could not bear traveling in that old banger, he said. In addition, the van was the best, if not the only place, where they could carry out the experiment on Pascal. So the little wagon would have to be driven back anyway, but Link was quite content it wasn't him who'd need to worry about this.

Although the professor was not supposed to set out until a week after Isaac and Bikie, and the experiment could not begin without him, the friends wanted their time on the road fly by as fast as possible. Even though they were not late for the ferry, Bikie drove at top speed. Their impatience had them all tensed up, and each was absorbed in his own thoughts.

Isaac thought about Vicky and Michelle. For the first one, he had to get money, whereas the second one required ... the right words. Michelle didn't answer her phone, apparently offended by Isaac's rejection of her offer to go together to Miami. Stepping over her pride, she called him to go together, and he... he should better tell her, she'll understand. But for that, he must first at least get a hold of her.

Returning to their temporary home, he should let the owner know about the imminent arrival of Link. Isaac decided to consult with Bikie. He believed that saying something was not necessary, recalling Peter's request not to get him involved. And so the less he knows the better.

"Moreover, if Peter says no, then there's nothing we can do," concluded his partner.

Isaac felt better from this logical answer. He smiled and slapped Bikie on the shoulder.

"Thanks for being you, my friend!"

Bikie looked at Isaac as if he were crazy, rolled his eyes and growled:

"Put the sun visor down. You are having a heat stroke."

"You fool, Bikie, I'm just happy and delighted with life."

"For now, be delighted at being dealt a good hand at the beginning of the game. You still have to make the right moves."

"No, Bikie, I wasn't dealt it, I pulled it out of the deck myself. Card by card. So sorry, but it's not a matter of luck, just the right approach. A rational approach and precise calculation and reliable partners, of course. I was just thinking that everything could have turned out differently. How many coincidences had to come together for us to be driving along like this from Link's own villa! Just think about it! It's unimaginable." Isaac continued, counting on his fingers, "I went to COMUNA on a particular day, and only because Vicky needed surgery, and what's more, her illness is extremely rare. Secondly, that was the very day when Elvis went there to carry out his terrorist act. Thirdly, for no particular reason, I got up and they thought I was an accomplice. Additionally, out of the entire heap of rubbish Elvis picked out the memory unit and decided to give it to me. Then, I found the database there…"

"Twenty-fifthly, twenty-sixthly, and twenty-seventhly, blah-blah-blah. You can say that about anything in life. Absolutely anything, starting from conception. Everyone knows there are millions of sperm, and only one will reach the egg. Although, in your case it obviously wasn't the very best of the bunch that made it there."

"Apart from the fact that the first card I pulled out of the deck was a low one with tattoos on it, I can't imagine what you're criticizing me for."

"You're the low card. I'm the ace of spades!"

"Yeah, an ace of shovels, that's right. A sequence of events like that does not happen every day."

"It does. Every life is a correlation of unique, unrepeatable events and coincidences. The domino principle, only in a hundred dimensions and all directions. It's chaos. And the dominoes come rushing at you from all sides, knocking each other over and creating new chains of events. It's a funnel stuffed full of moving dominoes, and that chaos is called daily life."

"Sometimes you're an incredible drag. Let's just stop to fill the tank, then go to the café and get something decent to eat so we don't have to run to the buffet on the ferry."

"My God! The youth saw the light and started talking sense! Hallelujah! A miracle! And the blind shall see, and the poor in wit shall wise up a bit."

"And Bikie's sexual maturity shall come to pass."

"I'll show you maturity! You need to take lessons from me, young man!"

"Oh yes, professor ace, big-fat-face, quickly, do tell me, how you get within a mile of a girl with a beer belly like that?"

Bikie swung the wheel abruptly and turned into a gas station at a high speed. Isaac banged his head against the van door.

"Shit, you moron!"

Bikie cracked with laughter. Rubbing his bruised head, Isaac summed up:

"It's true, apart from the external similarities, rockers and Neanderthals have identical behavior patterns."

"Clear out and get me a double espresso, swiftly. I'll fill the van in the meantime."

Isaac bought croissants, a couple of chocolate bars and tuna sandwiches. Despite the filling breakfast they had at Link's place, he was still hungry. He filled two plastic bags with all sorts of food, and gazed around for something interesting. The tank was not yet filled, so he decided to take a look at the magazine stand. As usual, nothing interesting there, the magazines were all like clones from an incubator.

He paid, climbed into the driver's seat, and the van drove into the port to board the ferry. Now back to Genoa, continue along the highway into France, and then his own dear Monte Carlo. Ah, Monaco, Monaco, will you be the cradle of the new world?

"Well, bro," said Bikie, biting into a sandwich. "From the look of things, you're home already. What are you thinking about?"

"That's obvious. Our plan. We have to give Pascal his OE back. Then he'll be the way he was before and so will our friendship."

"Friendship, friendship," Bikie mocked. "The one thing I couldn't understand was why we didn't go to him for money, instead of Peter."

"Go to Pascal for money?" Isaac asked, frowning. "Believe me, I tried several times. He always refused and the last time I hated him for it. I wanted to smash the nose of this asshole of a Happy when I went to borrow money for Vicky's surgery. He promised he would if his administrator told him to. However, she explained that the contract with COMUNA has a clause that specifically prohibits lending or giving away money that belongs to a Veggie.

"The Agency's got a really smart set-up. It has its own bank, and it has probably been the most powerful bank in the world for a long time. All the large fees paid out to the Veggies just lie there unused. The Veggies sign a contract, and afterwards, with rare exceptions, they don't spend much. Pascal said that if it wasn't allowed, there was nothing he could do. I tried to explain to him that the administrator wasn't allowed to do it, but he was. I even said I'd pay it back with interest. And this asshole asked: 'Why would I want interest?'

"It's like they've erased his conscience. And you wouldn't believe it, but he can laugh at the jokes in a TV show and watch a movie. He is a great soccer player. Only he doesn't have jokes of his own any more, just enough brains to go ask his nanny, as I call her, to do anything he cannot handle himself.

"It's ludicrous, but he has some really good gear at home, all these latest computers and gadgets. And it all gets replaced regularly. He stipulated in the contact that it would all be the very latest technology. Before he offloaded, he said his girl Eva deserved the very best, and he was going to do everything to make sure she and he had that. Only Eva took off, and the gear is still there. He doesn't even turn it on now. And he doesn't have the wits to stop them from delivering new stuff.

"He watches TV all the time, plays sports in the evening, when his nanny tells him to. He is a vegetarian now. That's in the contract too. He has everything he needs and he is happy with everything. A kind of happy bus-driver. Riding along the same route all day, being happy as a clown with life.

"At first I tried so many times to shake him out of it. Looked through our school photo-albums with him, remembered adventures we had together. He remembers everything. 'Those were great times,' he says. 'I've changed now,' he says, 'and I like different things.'

"I hate the stinking *Collective Mind*. And I started hating Pascal too. We were like brothers, and Vicky was like a sister to both of us. I trusted him like I trust myself. And his indifference now is like a knife in my heart."

"So you've succeeded in making me waste several minutes of my life on listening about this worthless idiot," Bikie responded, but the sympathy in his voice was clear.

"Losing creativity made him like that, and when the professor pumps his OE back, who knows what will happen?"

"That professor has some brain," said Bikie, changing the subject. "He really radiates charisma. A real predator! He seems like an ordinary middle aged guy who's getting on a bit, with this strange expression on his face. Drinks his coffee, puffs on his cigar. But when you think of that juggernaut he blitzed us all with, it's terrifying!"

Isaac understood what he meant. It always feels a bit strange when someone you have only known by reputation actually talks to you, accepts you as being no fool, someone worth talking to, even working with. Especially such a behemoth of science! Associating with someone like that sets you on the next step in your life. You are not the old you any longer. You are a new and updated version, you have a different level.

It's especially flattering if that person is a genius who has made his mark in the history of mankind. The name Jeremy Link was inscribed in the annals of the age to which he belonged. The generations to come would undoubtedly venerate his greatness, study his life in school, and name streets, buildings and stars after him. He was a living legend who had put the world on its head. Isaac's head started to spin at the thought of Link becoming a member of his team. Just imagine!

Finally, they got to the border between France and Italy. Monaco was just twenty kilometers away. After passing the border, Isaac remembered his promise to call the police upon his arrival.

"Hey, Bikie, I didn't want to mention it in front of Link, and then it slipped my mind. I got a call from the police about that old incident. Some commissioner Pellegrini, who emphatically requested me to contact him when I get home."

"You were right not to tell Link. The old fogey would have shit himself. What was it they wanted?"

"I don't know, nothing special. Just, call us when you get here."

"Well, that doesn't mean a thing. Why would they scare you ahead of time? What have they got on you?"

Isaac told Bikie about the events of that day, recalling all the details he could. The only thing that could interest the police was the fact that when he was at the police station, the terrorist gave him a computer board. Nobody but him and the terrorist behind bars could know about this.

"So no one knows that you got that piece of the motherboard?"

"Nope. That crazy Elvis-guy isn't likely to have told anyone. Again, in their eyes he's just an ordinary madman."

"OK, I'll think about it. So far I don't see any problems, to be honest. I was surprised how easy it was to copy the lists onto the computer. Usually information like that is kept on the server or on a cloud. The guy in the office who copied it onto his computer is a common idiot. He either won't remember what was there, or just to be on the safe side, he won't admit he kept the lists on his own machine instead of on a protected server. I found all sorts of other trash on that card, terabytes of files and folders. The absolute mess some folks have on their computers is worse than the history of the Middle Ages."

His friend's reasoning reassured Isaac. Nothing terrible could happen.

Isaac asked Bikie to drop him off near the hospital – he wanted to immediately visit Vicky, to make sure her condition did not change and she was still stable. He felt relieved to find out that she didn't get worse while he was gone. He still had a month to find the money.

Previously he spent all his time thinking about her surgery and the money he didn't have. Now his head was more occupied with Link and Michelle. It came to his mind that it was cowardice on his part to be glad that everything was still the same, that Vicky had not gotten worse.

He sat down by her bed, the sensor measuring her pulse rate chirped quietly. The transparent mask over her mouth and nose made it hard for Isaac to imagine that she was simply asleep. Isaac realized how badly he missed her. He took Vicky's hand and started talking to her quietly. Isaac told her everything as if she could listen to him. Apart from one single thing – that he'd had a hallucination, a moment when he thought of Vicky as not his sister, but as a coveted girlfriend. That absurd delusion was completely gone by now, thanks to Michelle. He told his little sister about his new relationship too.

As he finished talking, Isaac felt relieved. He kissed his sister and went to Michelle's house. She still hasn't answered his calls or text messages and he new that he was two days late to still have an opportunity to join her in Miami. But he has decided to tell her everything, being sure that she would understand..

Concierge recognized him, and although he wasn't allowed to do that, he said that Madame Blanche left a few days ago with two large suitcases.

What happens with a heart in love when receiving dismissal is impossible to describe. In Isaac's enamored soul there was a mixture of love, despair, remorse, and resentment. It was so unfair! She didn't even want to hear him out, and he could explain everything! The bright side of the deal – the fact that Link was found – turned out to be the dark side, as well – Michelle has left Isaac.

In such a state, he still had to make the one phone call to Commissioner Pellegrini. He felt no fear, he didn't care.

The commissioner, who was going to finally return to Paris, was surprised to see Isaac Leroy's number popping up on his phone. He has already closed this promising case that turned out to be a dud. He remembered how he scared the young man for no reason and felt embarrassed. So he decided to answer the call.

"Hello. Are you already back in Monaco?" He was trying to sound friendly to mitigate the guilt.

"Hello. Yes, I'm back," Isaac's voice sounded depressed.

"Did something happen?" asked Pellegrini.

"No. Got seasick on the ferry from Sardinia. The sea was stormy. Then the road again. Just tired. I can come visit you now."

"Sardinia?!" the Commissioner felt struck. Memory didn't fail him, he quickly looked at his notes and saw that Isaac, in a telephone conversation, said that he was in Spain.

"I'll expect you tomorrow at eleven. Don't be late," Pellegrini chose the place of meeting, and again being upset with the conflict in his schedule, cancelled his flight to Paris.

Then Pellegrini called Grace Kelly Hospital. He had learned that Monsieur Leroy had come to visit his sister. In the most polite tone that he could muster, Pellegrini asked them to always call him in the future when Isaac shows up and also, if he does not come alone, to take a note of the names of the people with him.

In the evening, Isaac and Bikie discussed the summons to the police, but came to the conclusion that if Isaac insisted that he hadn't been given anything – and no one could prove he had – there wasn't any particular problem. He could go with a lawyer, but that would raise the police's suspicions that something shady was going on. They decided that Isaac would go alone, but just to be on the safe side Bikie promised to clean up the computers and erase all traces of the lists including the results of their search and other indirect evidence.

Such interest in Isaac had to be put out before it took hold. The last thing they needed was for the police to decide to visit Isaac at home, with Link just about to arrive.

3

The commissioner asked various questions, all of which were seemingly innocent. Isaac had the answers to most of them prepared.

"Have you remembered anything after the terrorist attack that you didn't mention before?"

"No, nothing."

"Have you suffered any post-traumatic syndrome?"

"No, I'm fine, thanks."

"Any nightmares?"

"No, they don't bother me."

"Where are you staying now?"

"At Peter Wolanski's villa."

"Just taking it easy at Wolanski's place?"

"Working."

"What do you do?"

"Security, we keep an eye on the house, the pool, the lawn."

"Who with?"

"Bikie, just a friend. We work together."

"Have you known him for long?"

"No, we met on the job."

"How did you find the job with Wolanski?"

"From an ad."

"Who do you spend time with?"

"No one in particular."

"Where did you go to?"

"To Spain, to Ibiza. To see a friend."

"What's the friend's name?"

"Alfredo."

"Does he have a surname?"

"Yes, of course. Martinez."

"It must be a nice place."

"For a break, not for working. Of course it's nice."

"Did you talk to Elvis?" suddenly said the commissioner, changing his tone abruptly.

"Who is Elvis? That schizo?'

"Yes. The terrorist. You were in the same cell for several hours. Did you talk on that day?"

"My head was killing me. Your idiots – sorry for that – clouted me so hard I got a concussion."

"You mean to tell me you didn't say anything at all to each other?"

"He muttered something, the screwy freak, but I didn't listen to him. I just wanted him to shut up."

"Did he give you anything at all?"

"No, he didn't."

"Maybe he did and you don't remember?"

"How could I not remember? I came home afterwards. They gave me back my things. If he'd given me anything while I was out of it, I would have found it afterwards for sure."

"You, I heard, found the money for your sister's surgery?"

"I hope. My employer Peter Wolanski is a rich heir. One of his bankers promised to consider a loan application for my invention. It is a portable device against rain. Something like electro-umbrella."

"I don't have any more questions. On behalf of the police, I apologize for the incident once again. I hope you're well already and your sister recovers. Here's my card and if you remember anything, call me."

Isaac left the police station in an excellent mood, thinking the devil wasn't as dark as he was perceived. He went into a café two blocks away, where Bikie was waiting, briefly told him everything, and handed over Pellegrini's card. Bikie decided to look up just who this commissioner was.

Isaac said goodbye until the evening and set out for a stroll. He called Michelle's number but she didn't reply.

Pellegrini successfully lulled Isaac, he didn't want to frighten him prematurely. First, he wanted to follow him, to understand who were Bikie and Peter Wolanski. The animal must be observed to find out where he goes, what he does, where he feeds. And the commissioner needed to see if his future victim was alone or if there was an entire team involved.

That same evening he was convinced that the suspect lives in the place he says he lives. There also lived Bikie, known as Laurent-Marie Afr. None of them appeared on any crime reports. Bikie's father was repeatedly arrested and, in the end, got imprisoned and forced to get downloaded. His potential role was not clear. According to tax records, Isaac and Bikie were hired by owner Peter Wolanski on the same day. Nothing suspicious at a first glance. But to jump to conclusions fast is also not wise, so he wanted to watch them closely to see what will happen next. Let them, as they think, off the hook. The commissioner decided to return to Paris and tap Isaac's and Bikie's phones, as well as the lines at the villa for two weeks. You never know what turns up.

4

Isaac prepared the room he was staying in for Professor Link and his assistant. He cleaned and made sure they had everything they needed ready for them. He himself moved in with Bikie.

"I don't understand why you haven't put their beds together," said Bikie, glancing into the room Isaac was getting ready for Link.

"Why don't you shut up, stop making vulgar little jokes and help…"

The professor happily observed the territory, walked straight across the lawn and disappeared through the glass doors of the main entrance.

He settled into Wolanski's master bedroom and sent his assistant to the guest room. Isaac tried to protest, saying that Peter, the owner of the house, had asked them not to occupy his room, but the professor ignored these comments.

"Just say you're upset because the idea didn't occur to you first. When Peter comes, I'll settle everything with him if necessary," said Link.

"Professor, it's an intrusion into his personal space!"

"Isaac, I'm an old man, I cannot sleep in a room with a bad view. I would be tossing and turning all night long, thinking about how I could have settled in more comfortably. It is bad for my nervous system. Why don't you just find me a set of fresh towels?"

"We are pretending to be servants of some sort to the authorities. Taking the master bedroom will blow our cover."

"Well, so keep playing servants. I'd rather play the master. You have to have someone to serve, after all, don't you?" the professor chuckled.

It was pointless to argue. Like all geniuses, the professor was slightly off his rocker. Isaac would have to clear everything up with Peter later. Hopefully, he would not descend on them out of the blue in his typical manner. In any case, it was good that Isaac hadn't told Peter about the professor moving in with them.

For Isaac, security was the top priority, but the professor easily ignored things as long as they didn't bother him personally. He made quick decisions and generally did not change his mind. But then, his fast judgments have not let him down so far, so Isaac told himself he would let the professor do what he wanted.

"Sorry, Peter, every contract comes with an overhead," he thought.

That evening they had supper by the pool and talked. Link, having finally escaped from the bounds of Sardinia, was on a high, enjoying the new place, and even reciting poetry.

Bikie, picking up on the professor's inspiration, hummed and whistled another of his rock composition about women.

"I've never seen you in my nightmares,
So could not make you out that day.
Your fat paw pinned me down real hard
So I could never get away.

You captured me by hitting hard
Just like a boot, between the eyes,
But I shall make it to my Harley
And open up the throttle wide…"

"How's your sister?" the professor asked Isaac.

"It's not exactly clear. She seems stable, but I'm worried, of course."

"And what does the doctor say?"

"He says there's a cyst in her head. I am having a meeting about a potential loan tomorrow."

Bikie, an expert in changing grim subjects, immediately intervened.

"Link, please explain on an advanced level what this process for pumping back creativity is."

"All right. Do you know the principle behind collecting orange energy? The basis of the technology is a special kind of magnet. A human being also generates a magnetic field, which retains OE, to prevent it from dissipating away.

Within the computer, there is a supping magnet, whose field is much more powerful than that of a human. Essentially, the following effect occurs: imagine two magnets, one much stronger than the other, the more powerful magnet attracts all the iron filings on the table or, in our case, energy. If you turn it off, the filings will instantly stick back to the other magnet. In our case, it will return to the human energy field.

The trick is that the big magnet is universal, attracting all energy while the human magnet is specific, so the energy will revert to the source from which it had been taken."

"Heavy! Brilliant!" Bikie summed up.

"What's brilliant?"

"Not the system for collecting the energy. The presentation is brilliant, the apotheosis of metaphor!"

"Then I'll continue with my thought." The professor wasn't flattered at all by Bikie's clumsy compliment; in fact, he seemed rather annoyed at having been interrupted. "A human being is a rather weak, feeble magnet. If we want to return your friend's creativity, then we need to reduce to a minimum the distance between him and his orange energy and amplify his field or switch off the main magnet. Or best of all, do both. But don't you young people worry about that, I think this can all be done. In your situation, I'd be concerned about something quite different."

"What?"

"What's the name of your Veggie friend….Pascal? Have you already thought of how to persuade him to cooperate with our plan? Persuade him, deliver him here, and attach the equipment, and, of course, we would need to take him to Paris, as close as possible to the Paris OE storage server. We don't need to go inside, but we will have to get very close. Let's suppose I can put together an amplifier for his field, I still won't be able to switch off the magnet in COMUNA's branch."

"Persuade Pascal? I don't know, Professor," Isaac said uncertainly. "I'll try it when the time comes."

"Well, do try," Link smiled. "There are no other options."

The next morning Isaac went to the bank, which serviced Wolanski. Peter assured him that with his recommendation there was nothing to worry about and the loan will definitely be given.

In high spirits Isaac left their home way ahead of time. He could not wait to resolve the issue that was so pressing in his mind for so long. He happily walked down to the center of the city and entered the bank's air-conditioned office.

He had to wait for a long time, almost an hour, before a clerk finally appeared. It was fat man in a sharp suit who looked very worried. He briefly apologized to Isaac, explaining that all employees were summoned to an unscheduled meeting, and announced that the bank was sold to a new owner today. Operations with existing clients' accounts were carried out in the usual mode, but any loan transaction were suspended.

"I'm sorry, I don't understand what that means?" the anxiety of the banker infected Isaac.

"Unfortunately, the bank suspended all lending operations."

"You deny me the loan? You promised Peter Wolanski! He's your biggest client!" Isaac became desperate. "He won't just let it go!"

"I'm sorry. It's very tough on me, as well. Now I can be let go. But I have a wife and son!" The fat man trembled.

"Yes, my sister is dying! What don't you understand?" Isaac switched to shouting.

"I want to talk to your supervisor!"

"He is no longer empowered to make such decisions. The new owner will send his team, which will determine the bank's further strategy."

"Well, at least let me speak with them! I will let them know!"

"They are not here yet. No one is here yet. We're just a branch. At first, the changes will be applied to the central office and its top management, and then they will start restructuring everything else. They will let go many employees, their priority is automation. They say the programs created by COMUNA can significantly reduce costs."

"What programs, I'm sorry?"

213

"COMUNA. The Agency is the new owner of our bank. They bought us."

Isaac sat down.

"It just can't be! Damn bastards! They are to blame!"

In Isaac's heart there was nothing but hatred. He wanted to strangle the fat man. The man was not guilty, but rage blinded Isaac. He slammed his fist on the table and rushed out into the street. He had to calm down and think of something. In desperation, he called Michelle, leaving her a message that he urgently needed to talk to her. For the sake of his sister, he was ready to beg money even from the girl that just left him.

The professor easily felt at home in the villa, working on his device, often leaving his room only in the evening.

Isaac agreed to another meeting with his patent clerk, Serge Morel.

"I see you went on a vacation? Looking good, so refreshed! Did you go to the beach?" The patents manager was trying to be as endearing to Isaac as he could.

"No, Serge, I went to the south of Italy, there's more sun there than shade. Let's get down to business if you don't mind," Isaac replied.

"Yes, yes, of course," Morel agreed fussily. "The essence of my proposal is this: it's always hard to sell your own product, work, or invention. It is your personal creation, so you may feel embarrassed to praise it or even exaggerate slightly. But a good agent is always worth his commission because he squeezes better terms out of the buyer. I was going to suggest ten percent. If that's too much, I could actually accept seven."

"And you have experience with successful deals?" It was the first time Isaac had ever conducted a business negotiation of this kind, and in the role of the hirer too.

"I haven't worked as an agent before," Serge replied. "But I have imagined myself in that role many times. I'm sure I can do it quite well. You can trust me, that is important too. We've known each other for a long time, and while you look for another candidate and come to grips with all the procedures, you'll lose a lot of time."

"And how soon, do you think, until we receive the first payment?"

"In less than a year!" Serge replied triumphantly. "I'll try my very hardest to get it done in seven or eight months."

"A year? Seven or eight months?" Isaac exclaimed, dumbfounded. He was expecting the money to start coming in much sooner.

"Within seven months for sure!" said the agent, frightened by the reaction.

"I agree to sell the invention very cheap. Really cheap. Not at half price, ten times cheaper." Isaac himself was surprised at how calmly he announced the new proposal. "But the money is needed in three weeks, no later."

"I'm afraid that's impossible. Even if we get in touch with potential buyers, the tests will take at least a couple of months. You only have one sample. There are a few technologies here, the magnetic field generator and amplifier..."

"Pascal helped me with the amplifier," thought Isaac. "He may need to patent it too."

"Such a low price can scare a potential buyer," continued Serge. "They might decide to double-check if it's some kind of a trick."

Isaac suddenly felt unwell. His head was spinning and the earth started shifting under his feet. He felt as if he were about to pass out. He planned to pay for Vicky's surgery with this money and he was not expecting it to take so long to get it. It was impossible to imagine that he would be denied the loan. Thus, selling his invention was the last option.

"Are you ok? Have a drink of water. It's so hot in here!" The agent ran to bring a glass of water.

"Yes, I'm fine," Isaac's voice suddenly went hoarse. "Is there any way to get the money sooner? I need it in two or three weeks, a month at most."

"Believe me, seven months is already quite fast. To meet that deadline, I'd be working round the clock."

"I have a month at the most," said Isaac, thinking out loud now. "I accept," he added hastily. "Where do I sign so we can start immediately?"

Serge was absolutely delighted and he shook Isaac's flabby hand for a long time, trying to add something, but Isaac was in no mood to listen.

It soon turned out that Isaac didn't even have a month. He got a call from the hospital and the doctor wanted to discuss things with him in person. The bad news kept coming. Vicky had developed complications. Despite the medications she was given, her body started adapting to the prolonged coma, and these changes threatened to affect vital organs and could afflict irreversible damage. The surgery had to be performed within the next few days.

Isaac was desperate. No sooner had his life come together that it started falling apart again. The doctor said he had a week at the most and hinted that Vicky had a rather high OE level. Isaac didn't want to hear anything about that and interrupted the doctor in mid-sentence.

But where could he get the money like that on such short notice?

First of all, Isaac phoned Wolanski, just in case he could help. Peter listened attentively, just mumbling something in response. He was very sorry, but everything he could put together from all available sources would barely cover half of what was needed. He would have been glad to pay it all but most of his money was still beyond his reach.

Isaac called the hospital and offered to pay half. They refused, they wanted the whole amount.

Isaac feverishly ran through all possible options. He had absolutely nothing to sell and Bikie didn't have any money either. Was he really too late now, had everything been in vain? Going back to get downloaded sounded totally crazy. In theory, Link or Michelle could have that kind of money. But Michelle didn't call back, it seems she removed Isaac from her life. He left her a note with the concierge, describing the problem with his sister. If Michelle gets it, it might help.

Isaac dashed back home and knocked on the professor's door. Link was there, as always, working on his device.

"May I come in?"

"Yes, just a moment and I'll open up. Wait downstairs for a couple of minutes and I'll join you straight away."

The professor soon appeared in the sitting room.

"What happened, Isaac? You look terrible. Pale as a ghost."

"It's Vicky. She needs the surgery urgently. I have a week at the most, and only half the money."

"And how much more do you need?"

Isaac told him, and the professor whistled.

"I'm afraid I don't have that kind of money. I'm only a fugitive scientist who didn't get a cent for his most important invention."

"Tell me, what do you still need to finish assembling the input device?" A desperate idea was taking shape in Isaac's head.

"Actually, it's ready. The problem is that there is no one to test it upon."

"What if I get Pascal to you quickly and we can perform the experiment on him? Do you think you are ready for that?"

"Yes, I'm ready to try. In theory, everything ought to work."

"Good. Then you'll have Pascal. I guarantee it."

The idea of performing the experiment on his former friend scared Isaac. He didn't want to do it, hoping that some other option would turn up by chance. But it had not and now there was no choice. The other option was selling his own orange energy.

As Isaac set off to Roquebrun, he was raking his brain over what could persuade Pascal to take on this dangerous adventure. Of course, it was pointless to lay all the cards on the table, but Isaac did not want to lure him in by deception either. He chose a middle course.

Before he entered Pascal's luxurious house, Isaac switched on the web camera that Bikie attached to his sleeve. He said hello to Pascal and immediately blurted out:

"How are you doing? Still sitting here, turning musty? Look, I'm going to Paris, so I decided to ask you to come along. Would you like to go to Paris, bro? Just imagine, the evening, the Eiffel Tower glimmering with sparks of electricity, you and I sitting in a street bar with a beer. Like in the good old…"

"Hi, Isaac. Thanks for the invitation, but no, I don't want to go," said his old friend, greeting him with a smile. "Come in!"

"Aw, come on, I can see you want to!" Isaac thought maybe he ought to pressure Pascal a bit. He might succumb to persistence. He had never tried any psychological tricks before.

"You can see I want to? Nah, thanks, I don't. Not really interested," Pascal said melancholically.

"I tell you for sure, you are interested. When was the last time you got out of this place?"

"Ages ago, but why get out? It's great here anyway," Pascal replied with a polite smile.

"No, wait! Travelling is so much fun! Just imagine this: Paris, strolling along, pretty college-girls sitting on lawns with heaps of books. And food! Isn't food delicious there? Remember that nice little restaurant we found once and it turned out to be simply great?"

"I remember. But no thanks, don't hassle me." Another smile. "Would you like something?"

"Yes, I would, actually. I would like to know is there anything at all that interests you now." Isaac was trying hard not to get wound up, but he was already starting to feel angry.

"I am interested in everything. There's the TV, there's food, there're sports. I can play football. Fresh air. I don't understand why I should go anywhere."

"But it's Paris, Pascal!"

"Well, so what? There's Moscow, too, London, New York. What next, should I travel to all the cities in the world? What for?"

"Pascal, this is a specific trip to Paris! And you should be interested if you're interested in everything, as you say. Let's go, I guarantee you won't regret it."

The word "interested" was starting to make Isaac feel sick.

"That's right, I am interested in everything."

"Then let's just go," said Isaac, delighted that he had manipulated his friend's opinion so easily.

"No."

"But why not?"

"I don't want to, and that's it," Pascal replied. "I have to call my administrator."

"No, no, no …" Isaac protested, but Pascal was already dialing the number.

After talking to his "nanny", Pascal looked at Isaac with the smile still on his face, blinked several times, either in apology or in attempt to force out a speck that had got into his eye, and said:

"I won't go. My administrator says that the sanatoriums in Paris are worse than in Nice. Want a coffee? The broadcast of the Brazil-England game is just about to begin. Do you want to stay and watch?"

"Total déjà vu!" thought Isaac, remembering the time Pascal refused to lend him money and sent him to the administrator, and she sent him back to Pascal.

Isaac made a final attempt, realizing that it bordered on insanity.

"Pascal, would you like to stop being a Happy and become normal again?"

"Would I like to? I don't know. I guess not. Definitely not. I'm happy. Everything is just fine. I like my life very much, without that eternal search for money and the tiny, cheap apartment. I don't see any point in changing everything back."

Isaac was exhausted, he gulped down the coffee Pascal brought him and grimaced. Lousy garbage. Decaf.

"Have you regular coffee, with caffeine?"

"Caffeine's bad for you, Isaac. Everyone's known that for ages."

"Living's bad for you in general. You keep getting older."

"Follow a healthy lifestyle and you'll live a long time."

"You say that as if you're reciting propaganda."

"But it's obvious, Isaac, look after your health. Why drink and eat what's bad for you and expose yourself to unnecessary risks? Live right and you'll live to be a hundred."

Isaac said goodbye and left. He promised to call in again after a couple of days. Pascal smiled and said he was always glad to see his old friend.

"Isaac, brother," Bikie said after he heard the story of the failure with Pascal, "as for me, I don't see any problem here. Of course, you can study textbooks on psychology, the latest articles on behavioral stereotypes of Veggies and search through all sorts of bullshit. But I'd prescribe our patient with my perfectly ordinary left hook. A minute of guaranteed blank brain, no broken bones, and a slight headache."

"I'm not sure, Bikie…"

"As a matter of fact, our professor is preparing a little something that is far more terrifying than my fist. He and his assistant are putting together an amplifier that will draw OE towards your astute friend. That's the dangerous crap here. If they fry your Pascal's remaining brains, now that would be a problem."

Of course, Isaac was worried about Pascal. However, this concern was mitigated by the professor's unshakable authority, his own strong desire to save his sister and get his friend back, and the realization that there was simply no other way. He wanted to talk about the risks with Link, but the professor announced that he wasn't feeling well and asked not to be disturbed.

All said and done, Pascal was the only chance of getting the money for Vicky, after all.

5

It was early evening and Isaac and Bikie drove the professor's van in the direction of Pascal's house. All bases were covered and the friends were definitely counting on success. They didn't ask themselves what would happen if the operation went sour.

It was good they had Link. He immediately said that whatever happened, his house in Sardinia was at their disposal. Could they hold out there for long? Link had for seven years.

Isaac was very focused and Bikie was as carefree as ever. The conversation was circling around risks they were taking and their possible consequences. Bikie told Isaac about Gregory Roberts, who escaped from an Australian prison and lived in India for ten years. Roberts managed to hide from Interpol for all that time, until he finally got caught in Europe. He had a Harley too. After he got caught and imprisoned, he wrote his autobiography entitled Shantaram, which became an international bestseller, and he turned into a living legend.

"Haven't you read Shantaram?"

"No, I've never even heard of that book."

"You're just an oaf who understands nothing about life. If you haven't read it, you live blindfolded. You don't know how to spend your life."

"I'll read it. I hope I won't read it in the same place where he wrote it."

"Don't shit yourself, Isaac. If anything, we'll slip off to Link's place and sort things out there. This is what brains and unexpended creativity are for."

"What about Pascal?"

"What about him? He's already a Veggie, just might become a little bit more stupid. He won't even notice."

The prospect of Pascal losing his mind really frightened Isaac. Uneasily, he had to admit that ending up in prison frightened him even more, though.

"By the way, Isaac, I don't know what the law says about what we're doing, it probably doesn't specifically mention artificially induced insanity. They'll probably just download us. But I'm sure that everything will go fine."

"I wish I had your confidence."

"We'll live long, long lives as normal people, on the run, we'll buy Harleys and we'll rob banks."

"Don't talk garbage. It isn't funny."

"Just please relax. Everything will work out fine. Don't get scared, we're almost there."

The plan was simple: the journey to Paris would take ten hours there and ten hours back. Isaac would drive as far as Lyon while Bikie slept, then they would swap. When they got there, they would tie Pascal to the seat, put the helmet on him and hook him up to the professor's equipment. Then they would wake him so that his magnetic field would be at its maximum strength. They would pump creativity in quickly and give Pascal another injection to make him sleep for a couple of hours. Bikie would then drive them back. Isaac had to be beside Pascal at the moment when he finally woke up, just in case. They had a first aid kit ready in the van, and a defibrillator, in case Pascal's heart stopped. No one knew how the body would react to OE being pumped back in, so they'd decided to take everything they might need in case of an emergency.

The van drove up to the house and Isaac got out. He decided to go in alone in order not to rouse any suspicion, and not drag everyone into jail with him, if things went wrong.

In one hand he had a syringe with a strong sedative. The dose was calculated for eight hours – the time it could take them to get to Paris if they drove fast and didn't stop. In his pocket, he had a note for the administrator, which he had written in Pascal's name: "I'll be back late. I'm going to play soccer and watch a movie". Isaac pushed the front door gently. It wasn't locked and opened almost soundlessly.

Walking through quietly into the sitting room, he saw Pascal, who was sitting on the sofa, watching TV. The program was about the successful testing of the new generation of hydrogen-powered engines. Pascal was watching with interest.

Creeping up from behind, Isaac grabbed Pascal's head, swung his arm and sank the syringe into his friend's neck.

After the injection, Pascal broke free, turned around and stared at Isaac. He even had time to smile, not realizing what had happened, but he immediately grimaced in pain and grabbed hold of his neck. The next moment his face relaxed, his eyes closed and his body went limp. A few seconds later he was soundly asleep.

Isaac whistled to Bikie and they carried Pascal to the van. They sped off to the spot where Link and Redbeard were waiting. The professor leapt into the passenger seat beside Isaac and the assistant got into the back beside Pascal, who was sleeping sweetly.

"How did it go?" Link asked.

"Smoothly," Isaac replied. "Let's go." The van set off.

Link's eyes were glittering insanely in anticipation of the experiment that he had dreamed of for so long. That kind of insanity probably comes over all scientists when they are on the threshold of important discoveries.

They drove fast but without exceeding the speed limit. Bikie wasn't able to get to sleep – the van swayed on the infinite road turns. Pascal's sleeping body swung about in the back, so Redbeard had to hold him with both arms.

"Isaac, you actually aren't such a soft touch as you seem," said Bikie, looking at unconscious Pascal. "Good thing I'm not your old friend."

"I thought you were for it?"

"I still am. Your obsessive persistence and your toughness on the verge of cruelty both scare and fascinate me. When it is needed, you are like that. Well, I guess all leaders are."

Isaac didn't like those words at all. It was easy just to speculate when someone else was there to make tough decisions.

"Everything is fine, Isaac, bro. Cheer up! I would do the same. It's just that you have more balls. And this is a compliment indeed, don't you think so?"

Isaac actually was feeling quite uneasy. He didn't show it, but the doubts were there. He didn't know if it was the right thing to risk Pascal like this, or destroy everything that's been created so far. He didn't have a clue what people wanted: be free but live in poverty, or be blissful and rich? Yet, to show lack of confidence was risked ruining the team that was motivated to stay together by a single clear goal.

Then Isaac sank back into thoughts about Pascal and what he wanted from him. On the one hand, it was clear that he wanted to see his old friend, whom he loved. On the other, to tell him about everything, about his resentment. Of course, Pascal had been locked in a brain jail. But Vicky! How could he be so unconcerned about her life?

Another question was what he would be like after all this. What if he didn't give a damn about their idea? Or he might say: "What have you done, you fools? I was so happy! What have you dragged me into without even asking?"

And what if he died as a result of the experiment? Or became a total idiot, not even a Happy? Isaac tried to drive these thoughts away. God was on their side, as they say. There was no reason things should go wrong.

Somehow he did not believe that Pascal would tell them to go to hell. He offloaded his creativity for the sake of his girlfriend and now he lost her. Surely that was a reason to hate the Agency.

Isaac had started to hate Pascal, and maybe Pascal had already changed a long time ago. What made Isaac think his friend would be the same great guy as before? What would he say when he discovered that they had risked his life for the sake of an idea? The video that Isaac shot in the times when he was a Veggie should help.

The doubts and questions tormented Isaac so badly that he was even afraid to share them with Bikie. He would only twist everything again.

"Bikie, have you ever had any real friends?" Isaac asked, coming at things indirectly.

"I had one. Even two."

"And where are they now?"

"One went to California. His parents moved there. We were teenagers back then. We stayed friends until twenty-one. We used to race our mopeds like crazy."

"And the other one?"

"The other one turned out to be a scumbag."

"How come?"

"I thought he was my friend. But apparently he was not. David Suleiman. I trusted him, and he used my trust to rob me. Turned out to be a bastard. When I was restoring my Harley, he offered to buy some spare parts for me. Said it was interesting to see how to make a super-stylish bike out of an old frame and a heap of metal. And then I found out he had been ripping me off big-time on the parts. Bastard. Some friend. Like they say, with friends like that, who needs enemies? I would have smashed his head in, but he didn't cross my path for a long time, and I cooled off. Screw him, I reckon it's bad for your karma to touch filthy scum."

"I see. I've only had Pascal. And to be honest, it's really bothering me right now. We're putting his life on the line. It's not a friendly thing to do."

Isaac started telling Bikie again about their friendship, how they had fun and fought shoulder to shoulder. He got so carried away that Bikie started getting angry.

"How come you guys didn't get married, if you loved each other so much?"

"Drop it, Bikie," said Isaac, catching the note of jealousy. "He was a great guy and you would have liked him."

"I doubt it, you make him sound so perfect, and it's sickening."

"Not perfect, just my best friend. He was," Isaac added, after a moment's thought. "Until he became a Veggie."

"I don't give a shit. Right now we need him for business."

"Bikie, I'll tell you honestly, I don't know what he'll be like after being a Veggie. He might even go running to the police. He's so straight and proper now. We can't imagine what changes have taken place in his brain these last few years."

"Then I'll definitely smash his head in."

Isaac stopped talking and didn't bring the subject up again because Bikie was too crabby. But the thoughts about Pascal didn't go away.

Bikie was clearly also musing on the possible consequences, but neither he nor Isaac wanted to discuss them.

He couldn't afford to show his uncertainty though, this way he would risk destroying the team, which was supported by only one thing: their distinct goal.

The highway to Marseille ran along the shoreline, then it turned uphill in the direction of Lyon. The sunset was bright orange again, like on the first day at Wolanski's villa. Isaac saw this as a hopeful sign. It looked like orange energy spilled out across the entire vault of the sky! Beautiful! But the conspirators couldn't really afford to admire the sunset. Driving past Avignon, Isaac couldn't help recalling the words of a simple prayer, and he whispered them soundlessly, barely moving his lips. The papal residence was located here once.

They drove in silence, and Isaac fell asleep. A few miles later Bikie shook him and asked to switch. Isaac got behind the wheel after drinking some coffee from a thermos.

"Isaac, you couldn't," said Bikie.

"Couldn't what?"

"Couldn't go and offload your creativity for the sake of Vicky. Then it would have all fallen apart. You're now more valuable than thousands of Pascals, because it is not in this one man, but in all the mankind. I understand that this is a difficult choice, but it is the only true one."

"I know," quietly replied Isaac.

The moral issue of Pascal stayed in his head, tormenting him and paining his conscience. He could go back to the Agency and offload his own creativity without risking his friend's life. But that would be the end of the resistance. It was important to hear this not just from his own internal voice, but also somebody else, and Isaac felt much better after Bikie's words. Now he will prove his usefulness to society.

"What kind of world do you want to live in?"

"You keep going on about the world. Take it easy, don't make your life too difficult. Why don't you think about chicks instead? Or about how to sell your invention for more dough? If you have money for drinking and eating, you can live in a world of dreams if you like, or in

Hollywood, or set up Hollywood at your villa, like Wolanski. You and I don't have any money, we have different concerns, but we can live in a world full of struggle and adventures. For a good job, for a girl, for our own thoughts and ideas. Or you can become an ordinary nine-to-five guy, living on a schedule like a robot. But then what's the point?"

"What are you talking about?"

"Richard Bach has this book called Running from Safety. At fifty-nine, Bach mystically meets his nine-year-old version and spends time with him. The boy questions him very strictly about the life he's lived: What he has achieved, has he stayed true to his principles, has he realized any of his wishes, and, most importantly, which of their dreams he has achieved. The grown-up Bach can't really answer, he just makes excuses.

"Almost in everything he got caught up in work and the problems of the day-to-day life. He didn't achieve much of what he wanted as a child, he forgot all his childhood dreams. He tries to prove something to the little kid who is he. He gives him advice, explains something. But he can't overcome the starry-eyed boy's disappointment, and the boy rejects this version of himself in the future.

"Gradually they start patching things up and then, looking back over the years, the man points out his own mistakes and gives the boy tips.

"The main conclusion of the book is that one should not live a sated, contented life in a straight line, but take initiative. Life is not a preset route like a railway. Life is a movie and living it like a humble extra is the most boring thing that can possibly happen to you. Run from a full belly, tranquility and safety. By the way, that is what our Prince Albert is like: he's been to the North Pole, competed in the Paris-Dakar rally, even taken part in the Olympics five times."

"Why are you telling me all this?"

"So you'd realize that by taking a risk with Pascal, you're doing him a favor. He's playing an extra's part with no highs or lows. If you offered him a chance to switch from being a desk drone to being the lead character in a wild financial venture, what do you think he'd say? You'll be betraying him the same way he did you, if you don't hoist him out of his state, or, at least, try. What sort of friend are you if you won't lend him a hand?"

Isaac said nothing for a long time, then he pulled over onto the shoulder and gave Bikie a hug.

"You're a real friend, Bikie."

"More slobbering. I already know I'm a real friend," Bikie remarked, but without a drop of his trademark acidity.

The sun quickly disappeared and evening set in. On the whole, the journey was going well, and there were no incidents. Soon Lyon came into sight and they had a bite at a gas station in town.

Bikie replaced Isaac at the wheel. Exhausted by the monotonous journey, Isaac fell asleep. They only woke him up after they passed the sixty-kilometers mark to Paris. It was almost four in the morning. In two hours it would start to get light.

After some more hot coffee from a thermos Isaac moved into the front beside Bikie. In the windshield they could see a searchlight running along the horizon, shining upwards and to one side from somewhere far away. They still had quite a ways to go before Paris, but the Eiffel Tower was already announcing its presence.

"A ray of light, cutting through the darkness – yet another optimistic omen," Isaac noted to himself.

The Eiffel Tower was built for the 100th anniversary of the 1789 French Revolution. Even back in school, Isaac had liked that date, because it was easy to remember: seven, eight, nine, a sequence. In honor of the anniversary of the American Revolution, France gave the USA another towering monument: the Statue of Liberty. Gustave Eiffel was involved in creating that, too.

"Revolutions, revolutions... And what date is it today? Is it easy to remember?" Isaac thought and laughed. "What if the school kids of the future would have to learn it by heart, too?"

As a matter of fact, when the Eiffel Tower was built, many people objected and attacked the project. Three hundred famous individuals, including Guy de Maupassant and Alexandre Dumas, demanded the removal of the structure, calling it an ugly iron monster. Fortunately, no one listened to them and thank was good. How could you possibly imagine Paris now without its most important symbol?

"People, even the clever and talented ones, can make mistakes and take the wrong attitude towards innovations," Isaac pondered. "We will give Pascal his creativity back and find out if we are right or not in just a few hours, I hope."

Half an hour later, Bikie turned towards Versailles, close to where Europe's main *Collective Mind* server was located. The little LED display on Link's device started blinking, indicating that there was a major energy source nearby. Link put the helmet on Pascal and his assistant switched on the download system.

"No connection yet. We need to drive closer," Redbeard said. "We need to drive north."

The location of the reservoir was no secret, there were even signs on the road. For safety reasons, they wanted to try downloading Pascal's energy from as far away as possible to minimize the chance of being noticed.

The steady connection couldn't be obtained just that easily, and eventually, the van drove up quite close to the server building. It was guarded, but not like a military site, thank God. Only the fence around the facility was kept under surveillance. They drove around until they found a spot with a more stable connection, got off the road into a car park, and switched off the engine. Bikie and Isaac moved to the back of the van with everyone else. Pascal was sleeping peacefully. Link finally adjusted the receiver on his helmet and they heard a long squeak.

"It's time! We have a steady signal," Link declared, picking up a voice-recorder. "OE download test number one. Subject Pascal Dean, twenty-eight years of age. Physical condition normal, no apparent medical problems. Distance from the reservoir approximately four hundred meters. Visible interference hazards: a concrete wall and metal fence. Internal obstructions unknown. The output of connected battery – two kilowatts. Check the straps," Link added. "One minute remaining. Hold him, just in case."

Pascal lay there, strapped to the seat. He was firmly tied, but crude force might still be required to deal with… no one knew what. Redbeard directed the radar towards the storage server, increasing the signal power again.

"Thirty seconds! Ten... Five... Go!"

"OE download initiated," Redbeard announced, keeping his eyes fixed on the helmet indicator.

Isaac and Bikie held Pascal's arms and legs. The helmet started buzzing. Pascal shuddered but didn't wake up.

"Download interrupted. We've lost the signal. The signal's back." Link exchanged curt phrases with Redbeard.

"Test number two. Increasing power output to four kilowatts." Link made a second attempt, recording everything on his voice-recorder.

The second attempt was unsuccessful too.

"Test three. Maximum battery power at six kilowatts." Link turned the switch again.

Pascal jerked abruptly, the suddenness of it frightened the friends and they pressed him down harder against the seat. Pascal tried to shout something and groaned harshly. But this attempt failed.

Redbeard took a t-shirt out from somewhere, folded it silently into a gag and stuffed it in Pascal's mouth. Frightened, Pascal writhed about in the seat like a snake. He couldn't see anyone or understand what was happening to him because the helmet covered his eyes.

"Link, let me give him an injection to make him sleep!" Isaac shouted.

"No, don't! We're not getting anywhere as it is. When he's asleep, there's less chance, his brain became active just now and his magnetic field strengthened. So we'll have to wake him up."

"Is it working?"

"No. The power's too low. Bikie, quick, remove the backup car battery and bring it over. Isaac, climb up on the roof and install the radar higher than the fence, point it at the biggest window in the building. Quick, before your friend goes totally gaga!"

Two minutes later they were all back together.

"We might not get a second chance. Let me fill you in on the situation. Last time we almost succeeded in returning his OE, now I'm going to double the power. That's slightly more than the calculated safe level. I don't know for certain what will happen to his brain afterwards. He could even die. So if anyone is against it, speak up now. I think it is worth a try."

"Go for it!" said Bikie, large drops of sweat streaming down his face. "Let's take a chance!"

"Sorry...!" Isaac groaned and pressed Pascal down harder against the seat.

"Twelve kilowatts. Go!"

Isaac slapped Pascal on the cheeks and he woke up, trying to escape. Everyone expected crackling and sparks, heat discharge, groans and convulsions, but it was all quiet. No sound followed as orange energy finally smoothly went into Pascal. As everything was done, or, at least, it seemed so, Pascal immediately fell unconscious again.

Redbeard dashed to put back the car battery. Isaac carefully removed the helmet from Pascal and Bikie stuck some ammonia under their subject's nose. Pascal opened his eyes and looked at the people staring at him, his gaze gradually focusing.

"Pascal, how are you?" asked Isaac, trying to give him a drink of water.

"Isaac, is that you?"

"Yes, yes, it's me. How are you?"

"My head hurts... and I feel dizzy. My whole body's tingling and I can't move."

"I'm sorry, Pascal, you're tied down."

"What for? What's happening to me? Where are we anyway? My head's itching! On the inside. As if insects have gotten into it."

His mouth was dry and his tongue wouldn't obey him.

"What rubbish," Pascal thought, "your head can't itch on the inside."

Focusing his attention on the other people leaning down over him, Pascal made out an elderly man with a beard whom he had never met before. But the face seemed vaguely familiar. And a peculiar face it was! Its expression kept changing all the time, from attentive and tense to bursting with delight. The man lit up a cigar, glancing at Pascal with an impish smile.

"Seems like it worked then?" another stranger enquired. "Did you get that quip about insects?"

Pascal turned his gaze to this man, a young, unshaven lout covered in tattoos. Although his head was still spinning, Pascal realized that, other than Isaac, these were people he didn't know.

Intent eyes studied Pascal's pupils, the elderly man's fingers tapped at his cheeks and then took his pulse. Pascal felt these touches and they left behind a trail of pinpoint prickling.

"Pinpoint prickling. What a strange term, what could it mean," Pascal said to himself.

"He seems to have come round," the unshaven guy said.

Pascal heard that absolutely distinctly. His head felt as if it was filling up. If it was a kettle, then this would probably be the sensation of water coming under pressure from the tap, roaring down, seething and glittering, gradually filling the empty space.

"Tell me, Pascal, can you picture a pink sunset on a sandy beach?" Isaac asked.

"What a strange question," Pascal thought.

"Come on, Pascal, try and concentrate. Can you?" Isaac insisted.

Pascal nodded. The three men in the truck broke into jubilant exclamations, hugging and congratulating each other.

"What are you gaping at? Congratulations, you are not a dumbo any longer!" The lout rubbed his hands together, took his gloves off and slapped Pascal on the shoulder.

"You can get up gently. I'll untie you now," the elderly man said with a broad smile.

"What's happening to me and where am I?" Pascal's own voice mumbled feebly.

"Your old friend will tell you all about that. He's bursting with impatience already. There, look for yourself," said the lout, gesturing indefinitely to one side.

Pascal tried to turn in the direction indicated, but he felt a prick and sank back into sleep.

"Let him sleep for a while. His brain is overstressed. He needs a rest now. Bikie, help me untie him. If we get stopped, God forbid, we'll have a hard time explaining why we have someone tied up to the seat in the van."

"OK, one moment," said Bikie, deftly unfastening the straps.

"I'll sit with him for a while, and you drive," said Isaac, moving his friend's head to a more comfortable position. "How long will he be sleeping?"

"About three or four hours," Link replied. "Half the way there. Then you'll have time to fill him in on what's happening."

It was preferable to get back before the administrator became seriously concerned. The risk wasn't very great, but the less time she searched for Pascal, the better. It would be good if she didn't call the police. Pascal's mobile phone was here, charged. If she called, Pascal would say he was all right.

After a sleepless night and the nervous strain, the monotonous journey exhausted Isaac and he fell asleep. He was woken by someone tugging on his sleeve. It was Pascal.

"Isaac, where are we?" he asked.

"Are you awake? Well, thank God. In principle, you ought to be as quick-witted as you were before. You just need to wake up a bit, have a coffee. Right now you feel like you've woken from a deep sleep, plus you're reacclimatizing."

"Who are these people?"

"This is Bikie. And there's Professor Link himself," Isaac said with a smile. "We've brought you back from being a Happy."

"From where?"

"Have you forgotten? You became a Happy. Now you're normal again," said Isaac, glowing. "My God, Pascal, I can't believe it's you again."

"Isaac, I don't remember how I got here. Where are we going, and just what has happened?"

"It's hard to explain. What's the last thing you remember?"

"I remember going to the Agency. And where's Eva? Why isn't she here?"

Isaac went silent, bewildered. Those questions sounded a bit strange, especially the one about Eva.

"Pascal, do you remember your awesome house?"

"What house? You mean the apartment?"

"Hang on a moment, I'll explain everything."

This was troubling. Could it be from the sleep? Or the download operation? Isaac shook Link awake and shared his ideas with him. Link frowned and sat down beside Pascal.

"Pascal, I'm Professor Link. Yes, yes, that professor. You were a Happy. Yesterday evening we transferred your OE back into you. Do you remember what year it is, or the date?"

"Of course, I do." Pascal confidently named the date when he parted from his creativity. "I offloaded my creativity yesterday. You don't forget that kind of thing."

"Hmm, I see. You have amnesia, Pascal... Isaac, stay with him, I want to check a few things."

Isaac didn't know what to say or how to behave with someone who had lost his memory. Maybe if Pascal wasn't a Happy any longer, and could think clearly, it was best to tell him exactly how things were? He would have to learn the truth anyway.

"Pascal, it's two years since that happened."

"Two years since what happened?"

"Since the day you went to the Agency."

"What? Are you making fun of me?"

"Hang on, let me tell you everything in the right order. I've got a bottle of old whisky ready. Will you have some?" Isaac pulled the bottle out from under the seat.

Pascal nodded.

"If you are up for a drink, you're definitely not a Veggie anymore. It looks like we're in for a very long conversation," Isaac said with a sad smile.

The conversation ahead would prove a lot more difficult than expected. Two years of amnesia is no joke. Isaac had to try to jolt Pascal into remembering something. And it was really important to figure out the reason for his loss of memory.

Link sat down beside them. He was holding a downloading helmet, which as they now knew, could also be used for re-inputting OE. A few new little wires had appeared on it.

"Pascal, I need to take a tomographic image of your brain. To see if there's any damage, tumors or any other anomalies. We have to find out the reason for your amnesia."

The professor put the helmet on Pascal's head and attached various sensors to it.

"Try to move as little as possible. That way the image will be sharper."

Link ran various tests, took notes and compared diagrams. While the professor turned his back Bikie, distrustful, seized the moment, took the creativity meter from the shelf and pressed it against Pascal's temple. The ex-Happy's creativity level was high again. Half an hour later the professor had finished and disconnected all the wires.

"There's good news, very good news and bad news. Which shall I begin with?"

"The bad news," said Pascal, alarmed.

"I don't think we can call your loss of memory amnesia. You won't recall anything, because… because you don't have any memories of the last two years. The good news is that your brain couldn't be in a better shape. It's absolutely fine. We didn't damage it during the input process. The right hemisphere, left hemisphere, and cerebellum – they're all perfect. And the very good news is that your level of creativity has not changed, you got back everything that you had before."

"What's the conclusion?"

"There are several. As far as you're concerned, you're absolutely healthy. The input process works magnificently. But you don't have any memories from your period as a Happy, as if you'd been in a deep sleep. You could say – and I congratulate you – that you have emerged from a long-term coma. Since the brain is fine, I'm sure the loss of memory is a consequence of being a Veggie." The professor started pondering. "I'll have to make sense of that myself."

"But what about the two years?"

"Forget them for now. But then, you don't remember them anyway. It's strange, of course. You should just live and enjoy life and be thankful we've pulled you out," said the professor, glancing at Isaac in concern.

"Be thankful to you? You're the one who invented all this! It's all because of you."

"Pascal, please, calm down. The professor's a member of our team. That's why he's here. And our common objective is to put things right," said Isaac, also trying to assimilate what had happened to Pascal.

"But I lost two years!"

"Some people have lost seven. And they will lose even more if we don't intervene. We're acting illegally. No one forced you to offload in the first place. And you were paid a whole heap of money. What's important now is that you are well. Consider that you've been reborn. Or survived a global catastrophe."

"Have some whisky, you'll feel better," said Bikie, handing Pascal a plastic cup.

"Thanks." Pascal sipped the whisky and winced, the taste was so unfamiliar now. But the atmosphere warmed up a bit.

Isaac really wanted to discuss their discovery with the professor and Bikie. But he talked to Pascal all the way back, telling him what had happened during his effective absence. About how the world had changed even more, how it was still averaging down and getting more boring. Pascal listened in silence. The longer Isaac spoke, the gloomier Pascal became, as he realized how much time had really flown by.

"I'm sorry, but you've missed a lot. Everything's averaging down, total globalization is continuing. The main obstacle – the language barrier – has almost been erased. There's a modern electronic interpreter far classier than the ones that used to exist. You stick a wireless earpiece in your ear, and away you go. No problems. Go to Japan if you like. Go to Peru.

"There are plenty of different pros, but various cons have come up too. Happies' children are born without any OE, for example. The most terrible thing is that the Agency doesn't have any opposition. There are individual dissidents, but until yesterday evening, no one had any proof of the negatives."

Isaac told Pascal about how he had gone to download his own OE, but, in the end, had not done it. How he got to know Bikie and how they had found Link. Pascal listened attentively. He didn't remember anything and he was horrified. Two years cancelled out of his life. Isaac told Pascal how he behaved when he was a Veggie. Calm, polite, always smiling and not interested in anything. He showed Pascal the video taken with the web camera.

"And where's Eva?" Pascal asked warily. He had obviously wanted to ask that for a long time, but couldn't bring himself to.

"I'm sorry, Pascal. But Eva left you ages ago."

"Left me? What does that mean? But when? You mean, she... dumped me?"

"No, she just left. I'm sorry." Isaac was still apologizing as if he were to blame for something. "You haven't been together for a long time."

"What about me? Did I try to do anything? Stop her?"

"No. Nothing bothered you. Absolutely nothing! My Vicky needed a surgery and I was flat broke. You told me to take a walk."

"Vicky needed a surgery? What's wrong with her?" Pascal asked in alarm.

"Yes, Pascal, she did. And she still needs it badly now. It was because of her I went to the Agency to offload. But before that I came to you, a millionaire, and you gave me nothing. Your contract said you weren't supposed to, you see."

Isaac finally poured out everything to Pascal. Everything that had seethed up inside. He ran through all his unsuccessful attempts to persuade Pascal. He told his dumbstruck friend about his resentment, all the sore points, and he had accumulated a lot of emotions.

"Isaac," said Pascal, rubbing his neck: the mark from the sedative injection was no longer visible, but it still hurt a bit, "please forgive me and thank you, my friend, for saving me. Give me the number of your account at the hospital and I'll pay off everything today. I'll have a lot of other things to make right, too. I'm sorry I keep asking, but where is Eva now?"

"She's still living in Monaco. Only she doesn't mingle and party anymore. She got herself a job."

That day at lunch the administrator did call the Agency after all. She saw the note from her ward and decided to seek advice. The elderly woman realized immediately that Pascal hadn't spent the night at home: the bed was still made up from the previous day, the TV remote control was in the wrong place, and the same food as yesterday was still in the fridge. He definitely hadn't gone to bed and he hadn't eaten breakfast…the first time in two years. Her other wards had never disappeared like this, and they always laid out all their things neatly in the right places.

She didn't go to the police since Pascal hadn't disappeared after all – he had answered her call. He said he was OK and would be back soon.

After spending half a day with the team at Wolanski's place, at almost five in the evening, staggering slightly, Pascal went home. To a home that he didn't recognize. Half of the bottle of whisky he had drunk with Isaac was sloshing about in his stomach, and raging fury with the Agency had matured in his head. For the lost years, for the loss of Eva, for being awoken purely by chance. He transferred the money to the hospital account as the first step in correcting the mistakes he had made. It was the very least he could do for the time being. Link had carried out another dozen measurements and tests and was finally convinced that he was right: Pascal was healthy, and the amnesia was the result of being a Happy.

Approaching the villa, he saw through the window the anxious administrator in the sitting room. He didn't remember her, but he recognized her from Isaac's description: constantly red face, plumpish, with grey hair in a bun. Pascal opened the door and walked in, glanced around his home, looked at his computer, which had obviously not been touched for a long time, and at his "nanny", who wanted to ask him something, and walked into the bedroom without saying a word.

The administrator, astounded by the smell of alcohol, called the Agency and told them everything was alright, the Happy had come home.

6

That evening, at the villa, Isaac's team triumphantly celebrated their great victory. Initially, he wanted to invite Peter, but then changed his mind. First, he had to discuss everything with the professor and Bikie.

After downloading Pascal's creativity, the professor changed a lot. He joked, inspired by the successful experiment. He happily agreed to move on, namely to hack one of the *Collective Mind*'s servers and return orange energy to thousands of Happies. The Professor wasn't trying to defend the benefits of his invention anymore, agreeing that the loss of memory is a good enough reason to turn it all around.

But at Pascal's villa, Pascal was alone with his second bottle of whisky. He could have joined Isaac later, when it got dark and the administrator has left, but he wasn't in the mood. He was drinking alone and did not want anyone anywhere near him. Apart from the girl who had left him a long ago.

It was already some time since he realized that he was not dreaming and that Eva, his beloved Eva, for whose sake he had offloaded his creativity, was not with him for two whole years. It would be wrong to say that he did not remember his Veggie period very well. Rather, that period didn't seem to have taken place at all. His memory stopped dead at the moment when he offloaded his OE.

When he woke up he was the same as "yesterday", a twenty-something-year-old guy, head-over-heels in love with his girl. "Yesterday" she hugged him and kissed him, they made love, he cracked jokes and she laughed vibrantly in response. It was impossible to grasp that she had left and was living with someone else, eating breakfast with someone else, having supper with someone else, sleeping with someone else, making love to someone else. The pain was appalling. Pascal flung his unfinished glass at the mirror above the fireplace. A spray of glass and liquid flew across the sitting room and the mirror tilted over and cracked right across, with a gaping hole at its center, as if from a gunshot.

Monstrous cubic pictures goggled down at him from the unfamiliar walls of his luxurious home. A few old photos on a chest of drawers, only one photo of Eva. Before, in his little old apartment, there had been many of them.

Pascal picked up the photo. Eva was so dear to him, so precious, so unbearably beautiful. That smile of hers… Pascal poured himself another glass.

Isaac told him she has been seeing a doctor for a year already and has moved in with him. That gave Pascal a strange feeling. Betrayal? Almost. Something like betrayal, probably. His rational mind understood that a lot of time had gone by, that it was really all in the distant past. But for him it was all as if she had dumped him just yesterday. Yes, dumped him! That was the way it was for him. Yesterday he had hugged Eva, said goodbye cheerfully and promised to get rich before the evening came. He wanted to surprise her.

That bastard of a doctor! The Count of Monte Cristo and his Mercedes surfaced from the depths of Pascal's memory. His Eva did not wait for him either. The feeling of pain consuming Pascal was amplified sequentially by love, hate and a whole slew of other emotions. He compared himself to an abandoned cripple, a missing person, a shipwreck survivor cast away on an uninhabited island, whose love had left him for someone else. His heart refused to accept that he had been a living vegetable with no chance of experiencing emotions and mutual affection.

How long had she waited for him, how long had she been with that doctor? Why? Where did they meet? These pointless and agonizing questions were literally eating Pascal. The bottle was empty. His body, not used to alcohol, struggled to get through it. Pascal suddenly felt sick and went dashing to find the toilet.

After taking a shower, Pascal went back to the sitting room. He felt dizzy and he did not want to drink any more. He would not be able to get a drink down. There was a foul, bitter taste in his mouth. And in his soul.

For a while Pascal pondered over whether he would get her back, even though she was with someone else. In his despair, he decided that he wanted and was able to forget. But the alcohol had embittered him. No, she used to be his woman, only his. Now he couldn't say that anymore, remembering that lousy, rotten doctor all the time. His mind conjured up pictures of her in passionate embraces. Her and that creep of a doctor. No, he could never come to terms with that, he could not live with it, he was too self-respecting. If he has lost her, then let it be.

An egoistic inner voice whined despairingly: you're a smart, attractive young guy, you have money now and you will forget and find yourself another one, lots of others. The voice of reason argued: forgive her, she is not to blame! It is all your fault! His feelings muddled reason: he wanted only her, he wanted to turn time back and delete this period from his life. A kaleidoscope of love, hate, grief and alcohol…

Pascal fell asleep in an armchair in the sitting room. He had a dream that had no torments or love in it. But it was still some kind of a nightmare. He dreamed of airplanes, crashes and wrecks, a conflagration. All in color, and all so lifelike. His brain could not blank out the anguish, but it had blocked out the original cause, in an effort to protect his nervous system the best it could.

Isaac came to wake Pascal at half past seven in the morning, half an hour before the arrival of the administrator. He had to help his friend to convincingly imitate a Veggie. They have not yet decided what to do next, so for the time being it was best to keep everything secret. The door was not locked, so Isaac walked in and saw the terrible mess in the room.

"Pascal, what have you done? Get up, your nanny will be here soon! Where do you keep the vacuum cleaner? God, you reek of stale whisky, like an alcoholic. You'll give yourself away and all the rest of us too. Veggies don't drink!"

Pascal jumped up and looked around. A completely unfamiliar pad. He remembered absolutely nothing about living here for more than two years. All this electronic gear everywhere. He didn't have any clue where the vacuum cleaner was, or even the mop.

Ten minutes later the mop had been found, the broken glass removed and the bottles thrown into a garbage can in the street. Isaac poured half a liter of strong coffee into Pascal and forced him to eat two cheese sandwiches to make the smell of alcohol disappear.

The administrator was five minutes late. Walking into the sitting room, she stared in surprise at Isaac, then turned her eyes toward the broken mirror and Pascal's slightly puffy face.

"Hello! I broke that, I'm sorry," Isaac said confidently. "How are you doing?"

"Hello, Isaac. I'm doing fine. But what are you doing here so early?" The administrator's voice was thick with suspicion.

"Pardon me, but I came to see Pascal, not you," Isaac snapped back. "We're going out for a stroll. Will be back this evening. Or tomorrow morning."

The administrator glanced at Pascal in surprise, but he nodded in confirmation.

"Let's go, Pascal. You wanted to visit Vicky, right?"

And before the administrator could ask another question, they left.

Commissioner Pellegrini read the report on the call that Pascal Din's administrator made to the Agency, reporting his overnight disappearance. Strange that she haven't called the police. Pellegrini already knew that Pascal reappeared.

"This is becoming very interesting," he thought. "He didn't spend the night at home, and that smell of liquor. Veggies don't drink. This needs to be figured out. I'll have to talk with this Pascal and the administrator, too. And with that liar Isaac, of course. These events could all be connected."

The commissioner rummaged through the police reports that came in the last few days, and everything seemed normal. A couple of broken windows and a stolen scooter. He checked COMUNA's records just in case. All quiet there, too. There'd been a minor computer glitch at the Paris storage server, probably an electrical surge, nothing of interest. He only had to wait for the report from Isaac's and Bikie's mobile providers, to check where they've been and whom they've seen.

The leather couch, on which Pascal was sitting all alone, seemed to sway from side to side. He poured himself another whisky. The upholstery stuck annoyingly to his arms, legs and back. His entire body, outside and inside, was turning flabby and unresponsive, but not his brain that carried on erupting, neuron by neuron. Alcohol is a conductive medium and its thoughts are the electric current. Even if you get as drunk as a skunk it won't help you, as your brain still keeps working.

Pascal felt as if he had offended Eva so he gave in and called her. He was not able to control his contempt and fury and tried not to give himself away, but he slipped into barbed, acrid sarcasm and tossed from one extreme to another. In the end they quarreled. He could tell Eva was relieved to end the conversation. They agreed to keep in touch. Eva said they'd better not see each other just yet, Pascal's absurd grievances were too fresh and there were too many emotions. She did not feel guilty at all and was not prepared to listen to any reproaches, which she did not think she deserved. At the end of the conversation Pascal had almost said what his aggrieved ego wanted, that he was not a Veggie any longer but he had checked himself with a struggle and limited himself to simply saying:

"OK, see you, talk to you soon!" Eva had wished him all the best and hung up.

The phone fell out of his hands, clattering loudly on the tiled floor.

"Hey you, lush, who did you just call?" Pascal heard Bikie's menacing voice ask.

"No one."

Bikie picked up the dropped phone and looked up the last number dialed.

"Fu-uck it, are you totally mad? You idiot! We're risking everything here for your sake! Want to go back to being a Veggie?"

"You risked my life, too," Pascal protested weakly, already quite tipsy.

"We have to keep an eye on this jerk! Isaac!" Bikie was in a violent fury.

He dashed to fetch Isaac, who was tidying up his room in preparation for his sister's imminent arrival. Isaac rushed back to his infuriated friend, tried to calm him down, said he would sort everything out and sat down beside Pascal.

"Old buddy, hold out for just a little while. Soon you'll be able to drink as much as you want whenever you want. You'll get to see Eva whenever you want…but not right now. We've got a lot to do, and you can help. I'll make a quick trip to the hospital to see Vicky, have a word with the doctor, then come back and I promise you we'll get drunk. Today. Just the two of us, like in the old times."

With a sigh, Isaac dialed Michelle. Silence. Even the messages were not delivered... He called the concierge of her building and got an answer – Mademoiselle Blanche has not returned. Bikie, seeing that Isaac is too sad, dug up her e-mail address. Isaac did not dare to write everything that happened in an e-mail. He only apologized, made excuses and said that she will understand everything and forgive him when she returns and he has an opportunity to tell her what has happened.

Isaac realized long ago that he completely messed everything up, but didn't want to admit it, didn't want to give up, did not want to return to the gloomy solitude in which he lived the last years. Michelle was so cool, how did he manage to lose her? Was he just a hookup for her? Even in Sardinia they were constantly calling each other. She sent a ton of messages to him and he to her.

This put him in a very bad mood. Even the fact that they had finally paid for Vicky's surgery couldn't make him feel any better. In the end, he and Pascal started getting drunk together at lunch by the pool. Just the two of them, drinking sincerely. Bottoms up! And both out of love. Even Bikie stopped being angry, seeing how pitiful they both were.

"The thing is, Pascal, all this whisky, vodka and rum doesn't help. On the contrary. At first, you drink and you feel better, but then the heartache only gets worse, so deep that you think all the problems you had before were bullshit. Nothing runs as deep as heartache. Feelings are infinite and nothing compares with heartache except more heartache.

You think you still have everything ahead of you and life goes on. Your reason suggests all sorts of solutions but everything collapses again. Heartache is a mudslide that smothers your heart and your soul.

"This mudslide sweeps away the flowers of love. But they grow back again, even on rocks, even in the desert, even in a nuclear dump! The flowers of love are the most resilient ones in the world. They grow out of your heart, out of nowhere, they build beautiful castles in the air, and your reason immediately moves in there. You live within an illusion and hope moves in there, too."

"Right, hope never dies. It's immortal!"

"That's right! Faith and love can die, but not hope. It survives again and again and resurrects love."

"I don't have hope any more. Only despair. I lost everything. I lost Eva. I did it myself!"

"But you can get her back. Or, at least, try."

"I don't want to. It's disgusting. She betrayed me, so she's a bitch."

"No, she didn't. It wasn't her who forced you to offload, was it? You went on your own. What do you blame her for? You've seen the video of yourself. Can anyone live with that?"

"Looking for support from you is like treating a wound with brine. It only gets worse. Her hope died kind of quickly. She abandoned me."

"You're just selfish. A great, narcissistic egotist, who won't admit his own mistakes."

"Ah, to hell with her! And you can fuck off, too!"

"Pascal, it is quite possible that she still loves you. Why else would she talk to you on the phone for so long when you're drunk? I'd be only too happy to get Michelle back, only I don't believe it would work. I've screwed things up so hopelessly. And she's so... totally unbelievable! I just got lucky, didn't I? Like, once in a blue moon. But I blew it all."

"I'm sorry, that was because of me. I blew everything, too. But I'm not going to admit it!"

They clinked glasses again and drank. A pause ensued, then Bikie arrived with more beer.

"I wonder, does it even matter to them that we are suffering like this, Bikie? Or don't they give a shit?"

"No clue. What I'm sure about is that chicks don't like crybabies. Watching the way you two have been whining is disgusting."

"Michelle told me to go to hell. Haven't heard from her in the last three weeks. Not a word! Not even 'get lost'. She just disappeared from my life like she'd never been there in the first place."

"Don't fret, Isaac, it'll be fine. Just don't bother her too much, don't annoy her and don't send her too many messages. She clearly likes you, that's obvious."

"Oh, well done, you've set everything out neatly on the shelves. Like in a supermarket."

"Have you told her even once that you love her?"

"No."

"Well, you're a fool. Though it seems to me she took a liking to you precisely because you are such a fool, an unusual cretin. Spaced out."

Bikie was strumming the strings of his guitar, Pascal was falling asleep, and Isaac tried to write a message on his phone.

"Michelle, I miss you so badly.
Forgive me for being such a fool.
Being with you was the happiest time of my life.
I'm terribly afraid that I have lost you,
That I'll never be able to hug and cuddle you.
I love you, I love you, I love you.
You are a miracle that happened in my life.
I will always love you.
I want to take care of you,
My hopes and thoughts of you are my life.
Let's see each other again, darling, please give me a chance.
I need you very, very much."

Isaac read the message through obtusely several times, and then deleted it without sending.

"Morning. I'm desperate for water. Lousy sunlight blinding my eyes. Why aren't the damn curtains closed? The phone is ringing, but it is easier to put up with it than get up. It's ringing again! What could somebody want so early in the morning? I don't want to get up at all. I have to try to get some more sleep." Isaac turned his face to the wall and fell asleep again.

At the other end of the line was Commissioner Pellegrini, displeased. He decided to summon Isaac for another interview and wanted to make sure that he was not going for another journey to his pseudo-Spain.

"Never mind, I'll call later," the commissioner thought as he got ready to leave for the airport. He planned a three-day trip to Monaco; besides Isaac, he had to talk to Pascal, Pascal's administrator and the staff at the hospital. He knew that the operation for Isaac's sister had been paid for out of Pascal's account. Formally, there was nothing wrong with it, but too many strange coincidences came together around this Leroy-guy, who, according to the report from the mobile company, went to Pascal's every one of these days.

Formally still a Happy, Pascal was a very rich young man. He had his creativity back and the money was still there. The disappearance of his orange energy from the server must have gone unnoticed. Even though the amount retrieved was substantial, dozens of other people uploaded their OE on the same day, so the overall level of energy in *Collective Mind* shouldn't have fallen. It would take them a week to figure out the exact details of creativity transactions on a given day.

People love statistics, and the data on the aggregated creativity of the planet was reported every Monday in the weekly magazine "Science and People". No one on the team really knew how this system of statistics worked, but it was clear that even if someone noticed a deviation, they would not immediately realize where the leakage had taken place, or whose brains the energy was from or – most importantly – how this OE had leaked out.

In any case, the law had no provisions for the theft of OE, and it was not possible to compel Pascal to download his creativity again. At least, it was impossible to do it quickly. The legislation included quite a lot of ideas that came from OE donors, and among them presumption of innocence prevailed.

Even if the police or COMUNA officials came after him, Pascal could play the fool pretty adequately. Bikie had him watch dozens of videos of Happies and socialize with his neighbors at the settlement. He learned their habits pretty well so it would not seem too difficult to imitate them. But Pascal's imagination worked excellently by now, and he thought of dozens of ways how he could be outed by a serious investigator.

What if they made him check his OE level again?

He had both – his brains back and the money, although, now it was no longer his money, but an operating fund, the team's fund, which was just sitting in his account. He had offered that himself. But it was not so easy to spend it: if a Happy came in to buy a transistor and not a teapot, the salesman's jaw would drop.

The professor has firmly concluded that Pascal did not have amnesia, but the absence of memory, which resulted from downloading his OE back. They all agreed to get together that evening and decide what to do next.

The next day the preparations for Vicky's surgery began. Isaac arrived at the hospital, accompanied by Pascal and Bikie. The girl at the reception smiled at them, asked the names of the patient, the relative and the other guests and entered them all in the visitor's book. She was clearly nervous, but Isaac took no notice. His mind was focused on other things.

He was delighted that at last his sister had a chance to get well. And not just a chance, but a very high probability of returning to a normal life. Of course, he was nervous and agitated, as anyone would be

249

in his place. Besides, he still felt embarrassed that while she was in a coma, he had almost fallen in love with her. He still wanted to say the same words to her as he did then: that he loved her very much.

They went towards the lift and did not see the receptionist dial the commissioner's number.

Vicky's room was on the third floor. The blinds were up, and through the windows one could see a magnificent view of the sea and the city. It was probably the only hospital in the world with such an insanely beautiful view.

Vicky was lying under a sheet, with various tubes and drips attached to her body. Her chest moved calmly and evenly as she breathed, with the sheet rising up and down just a tiny bit. Even with those closed eyes and pale skin she looked tremendously attractive. Someone in the future would be very lucky to meet her.

His thoughts were interrupted by the doctor, who came to explain Vicky's surgery and recovery plan.

There were still several days before the operation. A brain surgeon would specifically come from the US to perform it. At this moment, they were introducing markers through the IV to color the tumor so that it could be better seen on the monitors. The actual surgery would take no more than three or four hours, then the patient would gradually be brought out of her comatose state followed by another week of rehabilitation. Her muscles had atrophied, so massage, physiotherapy and injection of stimulants would be needed to restore body-tone. The recovery process used to take at least a month, but now it was quicker, thanks to COMUNA. Then they would allow Isaac to take Vicky home and continue with the physical therapy there.

"And when will I be able to talk to her?"

"In about ten days. Might be a bit sooner or a bit later. We should not hurry with bringing her out of the coma. But don't worry, you will have plenty of time to talk," the doctor reassured Isaac.

After lunch, the group split up and Pascal went back to his villa. He needed to review the significant events of the past two days, get a clear idea of what was kept where in his house, check the state of his finances, and practice Veggie behavior just in case. His body, accustomed to daily workouts, was literally itching to get on an exercise machine.

Bikie went back to join Link at Wolanski's villa and Isaac bought a bouquet of flowers to sent to Michelle's home.

Pellegrini sat at the table and looked through his notes, Pascal Din goes along with the others to visit Isaac's sister in the hospital. That was not typical for a Happy. Well, theoretically possible, just a bit strange. The money Isaac suddenly got to pay for his sister's medical expenses was Pascal's money. That was even stranger. Then the administrator had reported an alcoholic episode. Again, more than unusual for a Veggie. Looks like they got him drunk to get the money. Maybe it was not alcohol, but some new chemistry, that suppresses your will? They live with Bikie at Wolanski the Chemist's villa...

Theft from Happies was a new crime for the new age and, strangely, in seven years there were no cases of this sort. Perhaps there have been, but they have not been reported or solved.

Pellegrini felt prickles of excitement inside, like in the old times. He was looking forward to cracking Isaac and creating a precedent of catching someone who dared to take advantage of a trusting soul, to take candy from a baby, so to say. He must look into everything to see if there had been any similar cases before.

It took Pellegrini twenty-four hours to comb through the archives in search of reports that somewhere, at some time, a Happy had voluntarily transferred money to a third party, but he did not find any. Donors had always faithfully kept their money in the bank, hardly spending any of it. Pascal Din appeared to be the only exception. This just looks so much worse for you, Isaac.

When the commissioner checked the whereabouts of Isaac's mobile phone on the night when Pascal went on a bender, he did not find anything. The phone was switched off. But Pascal's mobile showed up nine times in the region of Lyon. In Lyon? What was he doing there and how did he get there? It was time to clarify all this. Everything suggested that they had got the poor Happy drunk and forced him to pay for the operation of Isaac's sister.

7

Michelle still was not answering Isaac's calls and text messages. He left the flowers with the concierge and asked him to pass on a little note:

"How can one speak of love
in words both clear and simple?
Must ample words be borrowed from above?
In the surrounding world I'm seeking an example,
To tell you all. But how, I do not know, my love.

Much easier by far than framing your description
Is finding words to tell about the skies and sea,
So I will take your hand and share my silent vision
I will be numb and let my kisses speak for me.

Please forgive me."

After a futile attempt to get the concierge talking about mademoiselle Blanche, Isaac was going to return to the villa. The elderly man asked not to pester him with questions that he cannot answer, as he can be fired for giving such answers.

"Young man," the wrinkles on the face of the gray-haired concierge were speaking more of his kindness than of rigor. Taking pity on Isaac, he carefully looked around and added quietly, "I will give the flowers today."

It was at least something. So Michelle is back and he has a chance to find her.

As always, Bikie was growling over a computer. Pascal couldn't stay at his home, so he came too. All they had to do was to call the professor.

"What are you looking for?" Isaac enquired listlessly.

"Nothing much, various garbage. Reading about a new motorbike that just came out. Real high-class. What's wrong with you?"

"Nothing much. It's because of Michelle. She is back, but, she doesn't respond.... Right, let's talk about something else. Where's Link?"

"Hey, professor! The pea-brain is here, and Isaac is back! We are waiting for you!" Bikie shouted loudly.

"Dear Students! I was looking into how one can plug into the COMUNA computers. There are two pieces of good news, and one of bad news," Link said pensively. "I've figured out how to get close to the servers. We need to discuss this."

"What's the puzzle?" Bikie barked cheerfully.

"The good news is that COMUNA has four servers, containing identical copies... The first is located in New York, the second in Moscow, the third in Hong Kong and the last one, the European server, is where we were, near Paris. I myself once sent Blake my ideas on the location of the servers, when I handed over the technology. We don't know where precisely the central computer and the equipment room are located in the buildings.. But never mind, we'll figure that out. The best news is that I have studied the amplifier that Pascal created for Isaac's anti-rain device. It is small, but very powerful! In theory it is suitable for my hacking-in device. Pascal and I can dig a bit deeper, adapt it a bit and combine the devices together to get a really powerful hacker and transmitter. If everything goes well, all the Happies within several kilometers will get their OE back."

"That's awesome!" Isaac and Bikie exclaimed in a single voice. They were inspired by this news, Pascal was smiling too.

Pleased, the professor puffed out a cloud of cigar smoke. This was a familiar, but forgotten situation for him from his past, when his student expressed enthusiasm. Sometimes he called his new friends students.

Link smoked a lot, sometimes not taking the cigar out of his mouth for days on end. The house already stank pretty badly. The cigar ash left marks on the floor, the sofas and even the computer keyboard.

"What's the bad news, professor?"

"The fact that three of the four servers are unsuitable for our purposes, even theoretically. Of course, we could just try our luck Russian style, without being sure of anything, but a bunch of Frenchmen in a Moscow institution might look suspicious. Hong Kong is heavily guarded too and the staff there is all Chinese, no Europeans. So Russia and Asia are out. I've been in the Paris building from where we retrieved Pascal's creativity, only once, before they installed the server. I'm sure we could take it over, but there's no point. The facility is surrounded by forests and fields. The signal won't reach the city, even with Pascal's amplifier. There will be no one within reach to return the energy to, so we either have to gather a crowd of Veggies around the Paris storage server, which isn't practical, or go to New York."

"So what's the bad news?"

"That I won't be able to go through US passport control unnoticed. And it is risky for Pascal to go without a cover story, as well."

"Then let's split up. Pascal and you deal with the amplifier, and Isaac and I will explore the New York facility. And we'll think about the border. How's that?" Bikie suggested.

The professor nodded, agreeing.

"Hang on," objected Isaac. "I want to tell you about my plan too. My suggestion is to go to the police."

Bikie and Link gaped at Isaac in amazement.

"We don't really need any plan," Isaac went on. "We'll tell the police everything. I thought about it and realized that we haven't done anything wrong. On the contrary, everything was right. Let's stop taking risks and carrying this burden. Of course, we won't tell them all of the details. There's no need to say where your house is, Link, so don't worry about that. We can say that Pascal joined the experiment voluntarily, no one coerced him. He will confirm that. Wolanski's role doesn't have to be explained. So we worked for him, who cares about that?"

"Isaac, I don't trust them," Link said calmly. "We'll present our proof, but even with my reputation on our side, there is a risk that the situation won't develop the way you think it would."

"And what if some villain has already hijacked the Agency? But no one knows or realizes that?" Bikie said in support of the professor.

His rebellious spirit hadn't disappeared, after all. "Our plan is safer. That way we don't risk running up against malevolence inside COMUNA or the police."

"The Agency could react in a hostile way," the professor agreed. They could start lying and say that our OE upload did not take place, that we simply erased Pascal's memory and that the energy was returned to him in some other way and incorrectly. Even sue us for theft."

"But not the police, why would they want to do that? And the police still have enough power to stop anyone at all, whether it's terrorists or the Agency."

Pascal supported Isaac, affirming that, in his opinion, his testimony and Link's conclusions would be enough. Professor Link himself! The creator of the invention, whose opinion should be regarded as the most authoritative in the field! And if several more people were brought back from being Happies that would definitely be enough for the police to prohibit any further offloading.

Bikie retorted with a macabre observation that Pascal would be turned into a "lab rat".

To enhance the effect, he sang in a morbid voice:
"Happy, happy end,
All the Happies will have their Happy ending!"

Thus, opinions were divided, so Isaac had to make the final decision and accept the responsibility. He thought things through again, weighing up the pros and cons deciding that informing the Agency was definitely not a good idea. He recalled that even though children born to Veggies had zero creativity, the Agency hasn't stopped, but buried the problem under a mountain of endless tests and analyses.

And now they might not stop, but launch an endless search for errors in Link's method of back transfer of OE. Yet if that was true for the Agency, it was not for the police and, thank God, so far the authority rested with the police. On the other hand, there was some logic in what Bikie and Link were saying. The professor declared that he had not agreed to anything like that, that his freedom and even his life would be in danger, and if Isaac went to the police, he would leave immediately.

Without the professor, their case would collapse, and keeping him here by force wouldn't be a smart thing to do.

Big money was at stake, the contributions of COMUNA were too innumerable, and the Agency's influence too immense. Of course, the truth was on their side, but it had to be taken across. Skillful counter-propaganda could easily distort all the facts.

And really, no one knows how the world actually works. Which people would turn out to be good, and which bad? Who could be trusted and who couldn't?

Of course, Isaac was tempted to go to the police and tell everything. It would all be over, he could calmly take care of Vicky, and find Michelle. If they didn't say anything now, thousands more people would offload and turn into living corpses.

Intellectually Isaac had already accepted his friends' reasons, but he wanted so badly to shrug this problem off his shoulders. The police were closing in on him, and if he told them everything, he would be a hero instead of a suspect!

"We take the professor's plan." Isaac's voice was decisive again. "And we'll get this done as quickly as possible."

"Hoo-ray!" Bikie exclaimed and the professor sighed in relief.

Isaac and Bikie didn't waste any time and immediately started analyzing the information on the American facility. And there was a lot to go through. The COMUNA branch was in a building beside Central Park that used to be the Guggenheim Museum.

"I have an idea…" Bikie began, but stopped short.

"Then tell me," Isaac urged. "You know, popcorn's for chewing on, ideas are for telling."

"The Americans are smart chaps. They make money on everything! They could have put the storage server in the UN headquarters, but no, they put it in a public place and now make money on guided tours as well. And that gives us a definite chance. A lot of people work in the building and some are stationed there permanently, some visit from overseas. They don't all have access to the underground central storage server, but I think there must be a few dozen: the director and his deputies, lab assistants, security men, technicians, cleaners, etc.,

etc. If you think about it, the list could be even longer. And what's more, I think the security is not serious. More to deal with fanatics and vandals, so most of the activities take place at the entrances to the building."

"Yes, look. The Agency branch used to be located at the intersection of First Avenue and 42nd Street, and they only moved to the former museum last year. And there haven't been any serious attacks on the Agency for at least four years."

"Here are some photos," said Bikie, leaning back in his chair, pleased with himself. "I got them all on social media. In some, you have a great view of the central hall, the cloakroom and the restrooms. The security at the door is serious, of course, but there's basically isn't anyone in the hall."

Bikie was incredibly good at his job. In fifteen minutes he dug up all the statistics for attempted attacks on the storage servers. Official data wasn't too comprehensive, but he found a mass of information in the press and social media. In the past, the servers had been attacked regularly, and often by extremely well-prepared groups. But that was before. Now it was loners like Elvis, who were easily neutralized by standard security measures. The "Monaco terrorist attack" had been the most notorious case that year.

"First let's look at those people who might need money. There must be a lot of cleaning ladies for a building like that," Pascal suggested.

"You're wrong there," Bikie replied. "While you were a vegetable marrow, cleaning ladies were replaced by automatic robots. A cleaning lady is probably someone who controls the automated vacuum cleaners."

Pascal could see that Bikie disliked him, even though they were on the same team. Pascal hadn't actually done anything bad to him. Well, he phoned Eva once when he was drunk, but that was understandable, he'd lost two years of his life and the girl he loved. Isaac mostly ignored Bikie's attacks. He knew that calling someone a vegetable, a pumpkin with brains or a sardine out of the tin was part of Bikie's style, especially if that someone had once offloaded his OE.

"Come to think of it, Pascal's idea is pretty good. Pascal, you're rising to the occasion, as always."

"More ideas than seeds in a watermelon," Bikie droned.

"Bikie, why don't you just dig up the names?" said Isaac. "I think the chances of finding ourselves one ally, or at least a gullible blockhead, out of thirty or forty people are close to a hundred per cent."

"One blockhead is already an ally of ours; we can put a whole team together!" Bikie chortled.

"Pascal, please take no notice of him," Isaac forced out through his laugher. "Bikie got a tattoo on his head, the ink percolated into his brain and darkened his sense of humor."

"The important thing here is to do the search for the blockhead right," Bikie persisted. "We should listen to Pascal's advice and do the opposite."

"Bikie, before I was a professor, I was a lab assistant, and I earned the money for my experiments at poker. Leave this to me, I won't get it wrong," boasted Link, who had just walked up.

"Professor, I'm checking the stakes, show me your bluff," Pascal joked.

Everyone laughed at last and the tension hovering in the air between Pascal and Bikie evaporated. Whether Bikie liked Pascal or not, he was a high-class technician and recognized Pascal as a talented inventor. He appreciated that the amplifier created by Isaac's old friend was now the key element of the operation. He was impressed by the way that Pascal and Link discussed reconfiguring the device to enable OE transfer over long distances. So, now it turned out that the rebirth of the biker movement and the reanimation of the good old, uniquely designed Harley-Davidson were in Pascal's hands. And nothing infuriated Bikie more than picturing the shops of the future, where they sold almost identical, averaged-out Ducatis and Harleys. Bikie envisaged the difference in the future as existing only in the emblems, and for some reason the Ducati's was white and the Harley's was red. Or maybe these companies wouldn't exist anymore and there'll be just one, combined. "Collective Bike". Damn! Things were already heading that way.

"Actually, it would be cool to break into the New York branch," Bike declared pensively. "America is the motherland of rock'n'roll. Jerry Lee Lewis, Chuck Berry, Buddy Holly! I'd like to take a look at this country. But what I love most about America is Elvis, Harleys and the know-how for making money!"

"We'll do it," said Isaac, slapping his friend on the shoulder. "You can be sure of that. It is the only option. Dig up as much useful information as you can. I think you can even find a plan of the building. After all, it used to be a museum."

Isaac's mobile phone started chirping. A text had arrived.

"Yes! From Michelle!" Isaac exclaimed delightedly and read the text avidly. It was very brief and rather strange.

"The Monte Carlo Bay Hotel in 30 minutes. Dress code –white. If you're one second late, I'm leaving."

"Who's got white trousers," Isaac shouted. He had a white shirt, but no white trousers.

"Are you joking?" Bikie chuckled.

"I do," Pascal responded. "I found some pretty good outfits at my place."

"Pascal, please, let's run!"

"Where to?"

"To your place, of course! For the trousers!" Isaac commanded. "Sorry guys, but our conversation has to wait a while! See you this evening!"

8

Twenty-eight minutes after Michelle texted, Isaac screeched to a halt at the hotel. He was wearing a white shirt, white slacks, with the bottoms rolled up slightly, and light-colored shoes. Pascal's pants were a little too long and baggy for him, so they slipped down slightly, but with the belt tightened up they were basically okay. The shoes fit him perfectly. The ex-Veggie's wardrobe held about a dozen pairs of different-colored pants and half a dozen pairs of shoes.

He did not see Michelle by the hotel. And she has not shown up two, five, and even ten minutes later. Isaac was getting nervous. He texted her: "Hi! I'm here" – but got no answer. He reread her message again and again. Everything was right. It was from Michelle. The Monte Carlo Bay – there it was. There couldn't be any mistake. "Maybe her text got delayed," Isaac thought anxiously. "Maybe it wasn't even from today? Maybe it's just a nasty trick?" Theories flashed through his love-struck mind with ferocious speed. Some of them frightened him, others gave him hope.

After twenty minutes Michelle finally emerged from the hotel. She was dressed all in white too: a short, semi-transparent frock, white Roman sandals with straps that wound round her legs from the ankles almost up to her knees and two large pearl earrings. Everyone turned to look at her, both men and women.

Stopping two steps short of Isaac, she spoke to the parking attendant: "Park his scooter please. And I need my car." Then she turned to Isaac. "Well done. You can do it when you want to. I saw that you arrived in time. I was finishing my coffee in the lobby."

Isaac turned a bit sulky, imagining her examining him indolently through the dark glass of the lobby in his nervous, emotional state, twisting his head in all directions. To anyone watching, he looked rather funny and stupid. But he did not reply or show his hurt feelings. He waited to see what was coming next.

"Don't be offended. You were so amusing and terribly charming." Michelle cast an eye over his outfit. "I see you didn't have time to buy flowers? Or you think the ones you left with the concierge will be just enough?"

Isaac could not help blushing. He should have guessed! What a fool! He could not really have done it in time, but she had a point. He blundered again, dammit! Even one simple rose would have been enough.

The parking attendant brought up a silvery Jaguar Silverstone. The classy old-time convertible was in perfect condition. Retro cars like that are quite usual in Monaco, although in other places you hardly ever come across them.

"Will you drive?"

"Yes, of course," Isaac answered warily – that car was worth a fortune. "But where are we going?"

"To Saint Tropez."

Isaac got in the driver's seat without asking any more questions. Not about where exactly they were going, or what kind of white party this was, or when they were supposed to come back. The important thing was that Michelle had forgiven him, or at least given him a chance to put things right. What was really important was that she was finally with him, and he would figure out the rest later, somehow.

They arrived at Club 55 in San Tropez. It was a fancy party, with people in white dancing, drinking cocktails and champagne, running to the sea now and again to take a dip. A great DJ fired out hit after hit.

Isaac took Michelle out to stroll along the beach in the dark. The long, sandy arc ran off into the night, seeming as if it would never end. Along the shoreline, little white craft and beautiful motorboats bobbed about on the water, and a bit further, luxurious yachts were riding at anchor. Among them Isaac recognized the black and white beauty "Michelle" that belonged to his girlfriend. In hopes she was still his girlfriend.

The owner of this opulent floating home had thawed out and wasn't angry any more. Over the course of the two-hour drive to San Tropez her coldness has diminished. She radiated affection and warmth, although she was trying not to show it. When she thanked Isaac for his beautiful poem, he decided to tell her everything. From beginning to end. Starting with how he almost became a Happy, and ending with stealing back Pascal's creativity.

Michelle listened attentively, not believing her ears, occasionally asking a clarifying question. As he spoke, Isaac sensed how he was gradually transforming in her eyes from an ordinary guy into a serious, ambitious man who was risking his freedom for an important cause. She was very intelligent and Isaac enjoyed the conversation. By telling her everything he shrugged a mountainous load off his shoulders: now that nothing was being held back any longer, he was not afraid of losing his girlfriend because of yet another unplanned emergency.

"You know, Isaac, you're turning out to be a really cool guy," Michelle's admiration was genuine. "Somehow I never expected this kind of thing could really happen. That anyone was capable of something like this."

"Oh come on," he replied, embarrassed. "This is a team project. Everyone supports each other."

"Yeah, I can imagine. And what are you going to do next?"

"At first we wanted to tell the police everything, but we decided not to risk it and to hack into one of the servers. So next up is America, New York. It's not practical to get to the servers in the other branches. How and when we are going to do it isn't clear yet. There's no hurry, the most important thing is to prepare properly. Now that we have Pascal's money, everything has become much simpler. And then Pascal waking up, his reaction… now I feel sure I'm doing the right thing. While we were rushing to fetch the white pants, we almost crashed at a turn and you know what? He shouted 'oops, fuck!', and then he smiled. I mean, really smiled."

"Why didn't you tell me all this earlier?"

"I really wanted to, honestly. You can't even imagine how much. But it was too dangerous. And above all, it would have been stupid. I would have felt worried about you. If anything happened, you'd be an accomplice and could have gone down with the rest of us."

"I'm going to New York, too!"

"No, that's out of the question. We don't know how all this will end. We're men and we can stand up for ourselves. Everyone joined in voluntarily and knows what he has gotten himself into. The very thought of you ending up in a cell gives me cold shivers. So you better not come."

"I can stay in a separate place from you. You have no right to say I can't."

"Let's not talk about that right now. We are alone together, strolling along the beach at night. I don't want to talk about this anymore. I've missed you so much!" Isaac turned towards Michelle, took hold of both her hands and added: "I love you."

The girl looked at him, thinking about something else. Isaac suddenly saw that she was crying.

"Michelle, Michelle, what's wrong with you? What happened?"

"You have no idea what it is! You order yourself not to respond to calls or texts, and within five minutes, break your own promise. It's humiliating when you constantly look at the phone to check if there is a text from you but there is nothing! And in despair again and again you check the phone. And there is nothing! To wait for the time when you are back. To live through these days is suffocating. You just don't breathe, as you understand, that there is no air, your chest feels like it was strapped with a belt. And you just feel so unhappy."

Michelle wept, and Isaac was lost, not knowing what to do.

"And you lie to me time and again, I can feel it, but just can't help myself, because I need you. Can you imagine what it's like? Be ready for any humiliation, just to be there for you. And I'm not just some girl, I'm strong, and you took over me and crushed me. It seems to me that even if I found out that you were not alone, even then I didn't have the strength to throw you out of my head. This is real torture, and the tormentor is the one you need most! Maybe for you, the time flies, but for me, every minute felt like an hour. The hour of torment, without hope! Every thought, every minute, whatever it is, ends with you.

"I was in a terrible state, I drank sedatives, and went to Miami to a clinic. And you, even knowing that I'm leaving for a long time, just did nothing! You're so callous, thinking only about yourself, you felt nothing! You're awfully cruel, what did I do to deserve this torture?"

Michelle finally burst out crying.

Isaac had no idea that someone could love him so much. He hugged her and held her very close, petted her. She kept crying, and he couldn't calm her down. He kissed her hands, eyes, quivering lips, cheeks, forehead, he hugged and caressed her.

"I am sorry, sorry, sorry," he said, kissing her lips, feeling an incredibly strong surge of tenderness.

Michelle did not respond to his kisses. Isaac felt pain, but it seemed like nothing to him compared to what his girl has experienced. All of that was his own fault.

"I love you, my dear, I promise I will never cause you so much pain. I will tell you things. Just don't leave me. I love you very much. Forgive me, please."

"Take me home, please."

"Please don't leave me," taking her hands in his, Isaac got on his knees.

Michelle, swaying slightly, looked at him. In her tearful swollen eyes was fatigue. And love. Her hysteria passed, she tried to pull herself together.

"Stand up, Isaac. It is not necessary to me. Just remember that I am the person for whom you are like air. I don't want to be dying like that anymore."

"Never! I swear to you! Never!"

Michelle leaned on Isaac's arm, and for a long time they wandered along the beach. Isaac was happy. Happier than when he found the professor or when they downloaded Pascal's OE back. Even the moment when he paid for Vicky's surgery couldn't compare to this. It was a different happiness, not a sense of relief or victory, but something bigger and stronger.

Michelle wound her arms round his neck and kissed him. That night they did not go back to Monaco – they were picked up by a boat and taken to Michelle's yacht. Isaac did not have time to take a good look at the gorgeous yacht or the huge bedroom. Drowned in Michelle's tender embraces, he did not even feel the slight rolling of the waves.

This night was very different from the first one that was filled with passion. This night was filled with tenderness.

9

"Where's Isaac?" Pascal asked uneasily the next day, when he arrived at the villa earlier than usual.

"He texted to say he'll be back after lunch. He spent the night in Saint Tropez."

"Doing what? I've got some urgent news."

"If it's urgent, out with it. What's happened?"

Pascal told the others he had been summoned to the police station where he was questioned for a long time. What interested them most was why he had given money for Vicky's surgery. They also inquired where he was on the night when they downloaded his OE. Whether he drank alcohol or had something else. Pascal had played a Veggie the best he could, answering briefly in monosyllables. The video that had been made of him when he was still a Veggie was really helpful. He didn't really know how plausible this show was, though. The commissioner was very considerate and had not pressed him at all.

"Oh, yeah," Bikie chuckled. "He's a real tender-heart for sure. But he keeps digging and just won't give up."

"Digging?" Link was surprised. "You mean this is not the first time?"

"No. Isaac's been to see him once. But everything went OK. We thought there wouldn't be any more questions."

"That's not good. Bikie, call Isaac and find out exactly when he is coming."

Two hours later Isaac hurtled into the sitting room. Michelle followed him in, gazing around curiously. She said hello and sat down quietly in the corner.

Bikie gave Isaac an inquisitive look.

"She is in the loop," said Isaac, answering the silent question. "What has happened?"

"I was questioned," Pascal answered. "Commissioner Pellegrini called me in. He suspects you of forcing me to pay for Vicky."

"What about you not being a Happy?"

"I don't think he realized that. Or if he did, he didn't show it."

"What exactly was he asking?"

"Many things. Like where I was that night, what I was doing between Lyon and Paris, why I smelled of alcohol, why I gave the money for the operation. I said I didn't remember that night. I thought maybe I'd been riding in a car. About the alcohol, I said I didn't drink and I don't drink at all. About Vicky, I said you'd been trying to persuade me for a long time and I agreed."

"I see. And how did he find out that you were between Lyon and Paris?"

"I don't know."

"Dammit," Bikie grunted.

"Maybe he figured it out from my mobile. You switched it on at about nine, when we were expecting a call from my administrator."

"We left our own phones at home, but we didn't think about Pascal's. What a fuck up!"

"Okay, we'll wriggle out of it somehow. What else did he ask?" Foreseeing another encounter with the commissioner, Isaac wanted to know all the details.

"Nothing else. I asked him if I was entitled to a lawyer under my contract. The commissioner gaped at me, of course. He was really surprised. He said there was no need for a lawyer. After all, I was the potential victim. At the end of conversation he gave me his card and wrote down his personal mobile number. Asked to call him after every time I see you. That's it, now I remember! He asked me about the hospital and with whom we went there. I said it was a friend of yours, but I didn't remember his name."

"Shit, looks like the hospital's snitching on us! Bastards!" Bikie was not that worried about having been spotted, rather just mad.

Before Isaac had time to digest the information, his phone rang. It was Pellegrini, asking him to come to the station.

"Stay cool," Bikie reassured him. "We'll think everything through right now."

At about five o'clock Isaac walked into the station harboring a couple of moves up his sleeve. Pellegrini was waiting; he greeted Isaac and started talking about Pascal right away.

"So Pascal is completely OK, isn't he? You haven't noticed any changes recently?"

"No, nothing particular. What do you mean?" Isaac knew that he had to ask questions too. That way he might also fish something out of the commissioner.

"Why did he suddenly go and pay for your sister?"

Isaac was not taken unaware.

"I was trying to persuade him for quite a long time. Talked to him about a hundred times, and finally succeeded."

"What persistence!"

"She's my sister! I was ready to upload my creativity for her sake!"

"Yes, yes. I remember. Very laudable. But even so, how did you manage it?"

"Manage what?"

"Well, to persuade Pascal. You didn't threaten him by any chance?"

"My God! Of course not!"

"That's strange. Going to upload your OE is fine, but threatening a rich friend for a relatively small sum of money was not? Have you been drinking with him?"

"What are you getting at? I didn't threaten anyone! Or get them drunk."

"All right. But even so, sould you possibly remember the last words you spoke to him before he agreed?"

"I don't remember. I implored him. I recalled lots of things we did together in our lives. Vows we made. And it seems to me, Commissioner, that the questions you're asking are too personal for a witness interview! Maybe I went down on my knees! Do you need to know that too? I can refuse to answer, after all. You know that I'm no idiot, far from it, and I might not have been at an interrogation before, but I've seen movies and I more or less know my rights!"

Isaac got carried away in earnest and was about to start shouting.

"Calm down, Isaac. I'm doing my job. I'm not accusing you of anything," the commissioner said very gently. "But that's for the time being! And if I don't understand something, I'll keep asking as long as I like," he added, suddenly raising his voice.

Pellegrini literally hovered over Isaac, who was not really expecting this abrupt aggressiveness after the soft beginning. Movies are one thing, real life is another. This was the first time Isaac had been in a situation like this.

He shrank away from the commissioner.

"I'd like to hire a lawyer. After all, I have that right."

"You'll hire one when I want you to. Or will you get the money from Pascal again?"

"Where I get my money is my business."

Isaac tried to behave confidently, but he did not really know how to behave: whether to answer politely or aggressively, or not answer at all. He thought in any case it was best not to get the commissioner angry.

"Isaac, we're not enemies," the commissioner continued gently. "You raised your voice at me. I know how to speak loudly too, as you can see. Let's just get on with it calmly and peacefully. Everything's all right, you haven't broken the law, have you?"

"I haven't." Isaac was clearly glad of this change of course. He was afraid of being too impolite and getting himself charged with something like insulting an officer in the course of performing his duty, or something of that sort.

"If you haven't, then good for you! But what Pascal did is very unusual. Not really a Happy style."

"All people are different. And anyway, I got the documents for the patent on my invention. And I guaranteed that I would pay back everything down to the last cent sometime very soon."

"Of course people are different. If Pascal gave you the money, I am only for it. Why should I be against people doing good deeds? You've got a great sister, a fine girl. She will recover, you'll see!" Pellegrini gave Isaac a friendly slap on the shoulder. "Don't worry. She'll recover."

Isaac relaxed a little. If warm words about anyone could win his sympathy, then that person was Vicky.

270

"Have you ever thought of joining the police?"

Isaac was completely confused by Pellegrini's questions.

"I never thought seriously about it. But I like stories about good cops," Isaac added, just to be on the safe side.

Pellegrini grinned.

"Just another couple of minutes, Isaac, and then you go home, OK? As for me, I'm already getting hungry. Feel like going to a little Italian restaurant."

Isaac was really glad that the interrogation was finally about to come to an end. He realized he also was ravenous and exhausted, so he shifted closer to the desk.

"Two minutes, I'll finish filling out the papers and you can go."

"Thank you."

Commissioner Pellegrini wrote quickly and Isaac waited. The commissioner finished, loudly slammed down on the desk, which apparently signified the end, looked at Isaac and suddenly painfully squeezed his shoulder asked in a casual voice.

"Tell me, where did you put the board from the computer?"

Isaac had probably slipped up somewhere. He guessed immediately that the commissioner had spoken to Elvis. Had Elvis given Isaac away or not? Apparently he had, since Pellegrini asked Isaac the question. And the cunning commissioner had slipped it in so underhandedly, when Isaac was already thinking about where to go for supper. He wasn't ready for this sudden U-turn.

"Surprised? I know everything, Isaac. I'm only interested in certain details. It was interesting to watch you lie to me."

The commissioner raised his voice, speaking with regret and disillusionment at the same time.

"A lot of things depend on me. But your lying made me upset. I could help, if you had done something stupid by mistake. But that's not the case here. You clearly acted consciously and deliberately."

Isaac felt like he was drifting. Thank God, he couldn't say anything, his thoughts were in a hopeless tangle. There was only fright.

"Sign," said Pellegrini, handing him the sheet of paper.

"What is this? I didn't do anything with any board. I don't understand what you are talking about."

"You understand perfectly well. Sign it. It is an undertaking not to leave the area. Or I'll keep you here as a potential fugitive from justice."

"What would I run from and where?"

"From having lied to me."

"I haven't lied to you."

"Of course not. Clearly you spent three weeks in Ibiza, as you testified the last time, while your mobile phone roamed about Italy and even took a holiday on Sardinia."

"What do you mean, Sardinia?" Isaac asked, unable to stop himself, although he knew it was best for him not to say anything.

"It's called mobile roaming, Isaac. Haven't you ever heard of that old invention? Where you phoned from, where you phoned to. Where you were. You lied, Isaac, and that's included in the report. So read it and sign it. We'll continue this conversation on Monday. And don't even think of shooting off anywhere. I'll find you quickly anyway and you'll get an extra five for attempting to flee. Your gain is plain – the money for your sister. But what you did with the board and why you went to Sardinia still remains to be figured out. Perhaps you were Elvis's accomplice after all, and Captain Robert just didn't notice? Haven't you been to Lyon with Pascal? Where were you that night? Or you have a witness, that being Bikie?"

The commissioner was clearly pleased with himself. In reality, he couldn't have kept Isaac at the station - that required a warrant, and getting that on Friday evening was no easy matter. It could wait until Monday. Where would Isaac run? His sister was here and he didn't really have any money. And if he did run, then that would be even more interesting. No, Pellegrini himself couldn't be bothered to request a warrant from the prosecutor. Oh, that South of France! It would soften anyone into utter laxity. And then again, it is all guesswork as yet, unfortunately. Or rather, he was quite certain, but did not have enough evidence for an arrest. There was a victim, all right, but he was a stupid Veggie, and working with him was really a drag! But never mind. Now that it was clear that something fishy was going on, the questions of the victim and the charge will fall in place eventually.

Isaac read the report of the interview. He broke out in a cold sweat at the part where he talked about Ibiza, and the commissioner made a handwritten addition that this was a lie. There were no other notes. And even though his thoughts were confused, and it was hard to read, and his head was splitting, Isaac tried to remember as much about his answers as he could. It was strange, by the way that the commissioner had singled out the section with the lie in it. Isaac felt a brief flash of hope that it was just another police trick to exert psychological pressure on him.

At last everything came to an end and they let Isaac go. He walked home as if he were drunk. Bikie caught up with him about ten minutes after he left the station.

"Well then? How did it go? Why so long?"

"Not so great."

Isaac stopped and leaned against his friend. He was emotionally drained and was already eating himself away for being caught out like that. In retrospect, he realized that even if Elvis had given him away, his own word carried exactly the same weight as Elvis's. He should have refused to admit anything and stuck to his guns. And the commissioner has also given himself away when he suggested that they were accomplices. Most likely it was a trick, and Elvis hadn't told Pellegrini about the board. Or maybe the old commissioner, insidious as he was, had managed to trick him too? Damn, he'd thought he was well prepared. The team had worked through heaps of questions about Pascal's behavior. But Pellegrini hadn't even asked about that.

"Come on, tell me. I'm a total nervous wreck. Even the guys have already called twice."

In reply Isaac handed Bikie a copy of his undertaking not to leave the area. Bikie whistled.

"All right, just pull yourself together. Here, have a drink," said Bikie, holding out a flask of rum.

The rum scalded Isaac's throat, going down into him with an agreeable sensation, and he instantly felt drunk.

"We forgot about the roaming. From Sardinia."

"I get it. What else?"

"He knows I ended up with the memory card. He called me out when I was getting ready to leave. I didn't admit it, but he is certain. He definitely knows, but I can't say from where. Maybe Elvis gave me away, maybe there were cameras at the police station. I don't know, but he knows for certain that I have it. I think. Also, he knows about you, the fact that we are working together."

"What else?"

"He was surprised about Pascal and Vicky, but I was prepared, and I think I answered that perfectly."

"Is there more?"

"I think that's all."

"Try to remember, Isaac!"

"That's definitely all. I read the report of the interview before I signed it, fifteen minutes ago."

"OK. Never mind. Let's go home quickly. We'll think of something."

The commissioner, who had trailed Isaac from the police station all the way to where he met Bikie, thought to himself delightedly:

"And here's another character, an accomplice. It's Bikie himself. So they're working together. Well-well. He matches the description from the hospital. He was there with Pascal and Isaac." Taking out his mobile phone, he entered a note: "Who is Bikie?"

After that, pleased with the interesting case and successful interrogation, he went to a restaurant and ordered a scallop carpaccio with truffle oil and his favorite lasagna.

The scallops were magnificent, but he had to wait a little while for the lasagna – the Pulcinella restaurant was crowded. Pellegrini's hunger reached its highest point, and when they eventually brought the steaming plate, the commissioner attacked it with great appetite, washing the food down with a light Provençal rosé. He was savoring his meal and the successful ending to the day when his phone rang. The screen informed him it was Pascal Din.

Pellegrini chuckled contentedly and answered the call:

"Pellegrini speaking."

"Commissioner, please, they're threatening me!" he heard Pascal's frightened voice.

"Who? Why? Who is threatening you?" the commissioner's smirk evaporated.

"It's Isaac. He called me. He is very strange! He's gone crazy. Very aggressive! I think he's drunk. I want to call the police!"

"Calm down! Everything will be fine! Hang on a moment. Can you lock all the doors?"

"Yes, of course I can. I already have."

"Don't call the police - you'll frighten him off. I'll be there in ten minutes. And don't open the door for him no matter what! What's your address again? "

Pellegrini darted across to the waiter, taking out his police badge on the way.

"You got a car? Or a scooter or motorbike? It's urgent!"

"Yes, yes. A car. It's out there in the car park, the company car."

"The keys, right now! I'm from the police! I'll bring it back later."

The waiter ran to get the keys and a minute later the commissioner was hurtling in the direction of Pascal's home.

A dumbfounded patron watched the car go with his mouth hanging open. He had never seen anything like that in respectable Monaco.

Pellegrini pushed the car at top speed. He stopped one block from Pascal's house and ran, keeping as close to the wall as possible. He was barely visible in the evening light. He glanced at his watch – eleven minutes had gone by. Everything was quiet at Pascal's house. Aha, so he had gotten here ahead of Isaac! He knocked on the door quietly, dialing Pascal's number at the same time.

"Pascal, it's me. Everything's fine, open up. But quietly."

"Just a second."

First of all the commissioner glanced quickly around the room.

"Turn off the light, so he won't spot me from the outside."

Pascal meekly turned the light off.

"Phew," said the commissioner, catching his breath. "Bring me a glass of water, please."

Pascal went to the kitchen for the water. The commissioner watched him go, feeling annoyed.

"Oh, these Happies. I dashed here, but he's moving like a tortoise. In no hurry to get anywhere." Pascal came back, carrying a glass in trembling hands.

"Don't worry, I'm here now," the commissioner reassured him, and downed the water. "Did he call again?"

"No, he didn't call. But he said he was coming. You got here very quickly. Thank you, commissioner."

The commissioner's legs and arms suddenly felt heavy. His eyelids were closing – he was falling asleep.

"Why, you bastard," was the last thing he had time to think before he blacked out.

10

Pellegrini woke up with his head throbbing violently. He tried to get up, but couldn't – his hands and feet were bound tightly to a chair.

"You've come around, dear Commissioner," he heard a polite voice say.

Pellegrini peered at the speaker. A late-middle-aged man holding a cigar... And then a jolt of recognition seared Pellegrini like an electric shock: sitting there in front of him was the famous Professor Link in person! The one who had disappeared without a trace!

The professor continued calmly:

"At last you and I can talk in a calm setting, since, you know, you're always in pursuit. On your side, Commissioner, you have all the technology and thousands of brains, including the best in police. On our side we have only four creative, high IQs and a longing for a free life. Almost even odds, right?" The professor winked slyly. "But we have won. How are you feeling?"

"Does that matter?" the commissioner asked venomously.

"Of course. We're human beings, and exceedingly humane ones. Which cannot be said of machines. Computing machines."

"In that case, I wouldn't mind a glass of water."

"Sparkling or still? Local or Italian?"

"Without any poison!"

"What poison? It was a standard sedative. The latest generation. Your head will stop hurting in a couple of minutes. So would you like French or Italian water?" asked Link again with a smile.

An Italian being the head of the French Police Department. Apparently, the professor knew about Pellegrini's career setbacks due to his Italian name. But how did he, the commissioner wondered. It was Pellegrini's secret grudge, one he had always kept to himself and never shared with anyone. And from out of this grudge grew a great and powerful resentment of all nationalist blockheads. With his professional attention to detail, Pellegrini realized that, for some reason, this was no secret to the professor.

"When did you go digging into my head?"

277

The commissioner forgot the condition he was in for a moment and almost barked at the professor in his stock interrogation voice. He had been an interrogator many times, but this was his first time in the position of a detainee. Well, or a prisoner, which wasn't all that different. Checking himself, the commissioner relaxed his shoulders slightly and glanced imperturbably round the room. Isaac, Pascal and Bikie were here. So they were all in it together. Pascal wasn't a victim at all!

"Bring me a double espresso with brown sugar and a croissant," Pellegrini said in the most brazen and provocative voice he could manage.

"Isaac, bring the commissioner some water and a cup of coffee. With a straw," Link added and turned back to Pellegrini. "I haven't been digging into your head. That would contradict our basic principle. At this stage we are opposed to the use of other people's thoughts or collective thoughts. It is simply that, as often happens after the sleeping drug that Pascal slipped in your water, you were slightly delirious and you let slip one of your closest secrets.

"In this case you spoke abusively for a long time, expressing your grievances by using the words 'Frenchmen', 'Italy' and 'surname'. As your opponent, I have studied you quite closely, and it wasn't hard to guess what you meant."

"That's contemptible!" said Pellegrini, turning scarlet.

"You've got nothing to worry about – it is of no interest to me, and I didn't eavesdrop on you deliberately. I simply came in to check on your condition. In a moment you'll have your coffee."

The captive's face muscles relaxed slightly, forehead lines smoothed out. The professor saw that the commissioner was starting to calm down.

"Will you give me the croissant through a straw too?" Pellegrini drawled caustically. "Is there anyone here to chew it for me, apart from rats?"

"There now, see how useful it is to have imagination," Link commented in the soothing voice of a pediatrician. "You can even compare people you don't like with rats. Soon you'll be able to eat whatever you want – that's if you want to, of course. Very soon. So you'll have to wait a little bit for the croissant, especially since it's evening now, and croissants are only served at breakfast here."

The skilled policeman in Pellegrini suddenly had a bad feeling. Link was standing there in front of him, alive and kicking. Pascal and Isaac weren't hiding the fact that they were working together: this all meant trouble.

"Dead men don't eat whatever they want," the commissioner summed up.

"Dead men? Oh, come now, Commissioner! We're scientists, not murderers! We're not going to kill you."

"Oh, sure. Then why have you suddenly decided to reveal all your secrets? To make my job easier?"

"Firstly, we don't intend to reveal all our secrets to you. And secondly, by morning you will be entirely harmless to us."

"A good rat catcher is always dangerous to rats," the commissioner hissed through his teeth.

"Isaac, is the helmet ready?" Link asked, then turned to the commissioner and continued collectedly. "We tried to decide what to do with you for a long time, and then we had an idea, which, as you'll appreciate, is rather brilliant in its own way."

Pellegrini was really annoyed by the professor's smile, but he didn't show it, not blinking an eye.

"We are humane individuals. Of course, we can't let you go, but we won't keep you prisoner. We'll hold a 'Link court' over you, they used to 'lynch' people, now we'll 'link' you…" the professor smiled at his own joke. "And you'll go back to your job."

Despite the commissioner's most intense efforts, an expression of surprise appeared on his face. Isaac put the helmet on Pellegrini's head and explained.

"Now your experience and creativity will serve the world together with many talented minds, but separate from you, unfortunately, or more precisely, from your brain. You're a great supporter and even defender of the program, now you'll have a chance to be involved in it for a while."

"You won't dare," the commissioner said in a dry, tense voice.

"Why not? Believe me, it will all be done fair and square. We'll measure your creativity level and calculate its price. See, I have just prepared it." The professor showed the creativity meter to his prisoner and continued. "You'll sign a standard contract with your instructions and wishes. And Pascal will transfer the standard fee to you. You'll find him very interesting to talk to, by the way. He was a Happy too, not so very long ago."

"What do you mean, '*was*'?"

"He *was*, but he isn't any longer. Now he's a normal person again," Isaac said, smiling.

"But how? That's impossible."

"Impossible for some, entirely realistic for others."

"You won't dare," hissed the commissioner again, turning pale.

A large piece of the jigsaw suddenly fit into place in his mind. If not for his hundred-per-cent certainty that Happies didn't come back, of course he would have realized that Pascal was too strange. It was obvious that his behavior was different. Right through the interview with Pascal, the commissioner had been haunted by a strange feeling that he was normal. But who could ever have thought it? The commissioner had clung so tightly to the idea of extortion that he had totally neglected this suspicious point.

"Why not, commissioner? Surely it is only humane to bring you closer, so to speak, to your ideals?" said Isaac, calmly continuing to attach wires to the helmet, but Pellegrini was already thinking of something else and didn't try to argue.

"Hey! Commissioner!" Pascal called, rousing Pellegrini from his stupor. "I have something to tell you. I'll reassure you. I was a Veggie and I looked happy. You will too. I spent over two years as a boiled vegetable, it was like a dreamless sleep, you know? I don't remember anything about those years, anything at all! Being a Happy is like being in a coma. You won't feel a thing and you won't understand a thing. And where there is no understanding, there is no fear. You'll become a blissful fool who won't be bothered by any discrepancies in the behavior of that liar Isaac, or that strange Pascal. That's what it will be like. Now isn't that wonderful?"

The commissioner followed Pascal's words with a struggle. He was barely in a fit state to listen. For probably the first time in his life, he was genuinely frightened. He realized they wouldn't let him go.

Initially, when he understood that these people were not planning a murder he somewhat relaxed, but what he heard after that made him change his mind. They won't let him go, it was clear, because otherwise, they wouldn't have told him the whole truth. And was it the whole truth?

"Hey, Pellegrini, wake up! There is one piece of really good news," said Isaac, trying to bring the commissioner to his senses. "Our ultimate goal is to return orange energy to all the Happies, so think of this as a kind of sabbatical – six months to a year, I hope no longer than that. Fill out the contract, please. Write the instructions, and I promise to deliver them to your relatives. They'll take you to California, or Hawaii, or Florida, or Goa. Nothing personal, this is a battle of ideas."

A foggy swamp, a thunderstorm. That was how Pellegrini could have described his train of thought. Flashes of light and total confusion, a kaleidoscope of pictures flashing through his mind: his sister Janette, his god-daughter, the Eiffel Tower seen through the window, salmon fettuccini, his office in the Department, and a Happy settlement. Himself together with his colleague Gautier who had sold his creativity long ago.

"I'd rather shoot myself. I'm an officer and I have the right to choose."

His mouth seemed to pronounce the words on its own, as if it was his sub consciousness speaking.

"An interesting shift in your life philosophy," said Isaac, surprised. "Only half an hour ago you were prepared to tear us to pieces for the sake of your ideals, and you've renounced them so easily."

Pellegrini's mouth went dry, he had to respond to that.

"My ideal had always been a world in which there is no crime or violence. I'm not renouncing that world. And I'm not the only one in this room who has shifted his philosophy of life! I think this is your invention, Professor Link?" Pellegrini glowered at the professor. "Why have you suddenly changed your mind and organized an entire underground movement as well?"

"Unfortunately, Commissioner, I created an awful problem. It has given the world many things that are beautiful. The planet has taken a miraculous booster pill, you could say. Became healthier, stronger. But I'm afraid the remedy has side effects that I now have to put right."

"What are these side effects, if you will pardon my curiosity?"

"Pascal has told you everything already," the professor replied sadly. "The condition of being a Happy is not a real life. It's a new form of coma. People die, not physically but emotionally, so to speak. The brain doesn't work any longer. They have no memories, as it turns out. We've given Pascal his orange energy back, as you see. But what we've really done is brought him back from the afterworld. Believe me, it wasn't easy for me to admit that."

"Maybe you did something wrong when you returned his energy and accidentally erased his memory?"

"Now that is why we didn't go to the police," Isaac answered for the professor. "Someone would say we returned the energy incorrectly, someone else would suggest we were conducting additional research. Do you think it would be easy for the Agency to renounce power like that? Can you recall any similar instances from history? And what if they declare us insane and stick us in a madhouse? The fact that all children of Veggies have a zero level of creativity doesn't seem to have stopped OE downloading."

"But not all the children are born Veggies!"

"It's ironic you call them Veggies just like we do, and not Happies. Have you done any DNA paternity tests on them? Why have you decided that both parents were definitely donors?"

"Well, that's really getting ridiculous, Leroy," Pellegrini tried to protest.

"No sir, I'd call it 'assessing the risks soberly'," Isaac replied firmly. "If we give another thousand Veggies their creativity back, it will be an indisputable fact. Not an isolated case that they could interpret any way they like. Think about it. Without the Professor, the back transfer will be declared unscientific, because it wasn't carried out in

282

proper laboratory conditions, for instance. And if we present the Professor to them, we know where they'll put him away the next day. And who'll actually do it? The terrorists or the security services? And they could even cast doubt on Link's statement. How can you prove that uploading OE back was carried out correctly? They could dispute the fact that Pascal was ever a real Veggie. Maybe he's a con artist who got hold of some money and then coolly pretended to be a Veggie? If our plan fails, of course we'll tell all of this to the police. And to the journalists as well."

"Well, yes…" Pellegrini couldn't help but agree with Isaac's reasoning. Going to the police didn't guarantee anything. Except that to start with, they would all be placed under arrest. After all, a theft had been committed, even if it was an unusual one.

"Listen, Isaac, I have a god-daughter, I have a sister. I have to think about them, take care of them."

"No problem. Think. If everything goes smoothly, you won't be a Veggie for all that long."

"And if it doesn't?"

"Commissioner," Isaac said with a smile, "it seems to me that you are starting to root for us to succeed!"

Pellegrini caught himself thinking that that was exactly right. He was worried they wouldn't succeed, and he would remain a Happy forever, and this thought was unbearable.

"Just imagine, practically all the donors had relatives, people near and dear to them, friends. Had. Because someone who becomes a Veggie is an emotional corpse," put in Pascal, who didn't want anyone to become a Happy, not even his enemy the commissioner. "The most terrible thing is that someone who has turned into a Veggie is no longer himself. And you must admit, Pellegrini, that the only thing a person has is himself.

"Ultimately, every person is an immense world or, to put it less grandly, every person is a radar station. He radiates waves around himself – these are his actions, ideas, interactions with other people. And from the way these waves come back to him, from the feedback, a person evaluates the way he lives. So there are billions of radar stations on earth, each one radiating and evaluating. Each one living by making sense of the signals that it receives. Each one of a billion separately, and all doing it together. Thinking about it can drive you crazy. A Veggie is a radar station that can't send out radar beams. I wonder, is it possible to imagine a crueler act of violence than taking away a person's own self? Turning him into a walking device for processing food?"

Pellegrini listened attentively to Pascal, trying to imagine his own future condition. He had come to terms with the idea that he was inevitably going to become a Happy, although still dreaded it.

"I decided to upload for the sake of the woman I loved," Pascal continued. His hands were trembling. "But she left me in less than three months. And I didn't even try to stop her. I couldn't care less! I really, really care now, but that ship has sailed! She's been with someone else for ages! You can't imagine what it's like to fall asleep in the arms of the woman you love, then wake up in the morning and realize that she's already been with someone else for a year!"

Pellegrini lowered his head. He wouldn't have wished on his worst enemy the fear he was feeling now. How he hoped that everything would work out for this damned Isaac!

Bikie saw that the commissioner was trying to keep it together, but turning over inside. So he decided to intensify the effect and thus, picked up a pile of clean sheets of paper off the table and held them out to Pellegrini.

"You can write a letter to the top management of the Agency. You're important for them, you work in the main department that collaborates with them directly. Write and tell them they've made a mistake and they have to put it right. And write to the Minister of the Interior too. It might help us if the operation fails."

"We'll leave you for a short while," Link concluded, taking the helmet off the commissioner's head. "I'm sure you need some time on your own."

They all went out, leaving Pellegrini alone with his thoughts. It turned out that there had been a girl in the room as well, and she went out last. All this time she had been sitting somewhere behind the commissioner. He didn't see her face, but one glance was enough to take note of the long, black hair and the mind-blowing figure.

The first thing he did when he was left alone was try to free himself. That didn't get him anywhere. Only his right arm from the shoulder down was free, so that he could pick up a pen and start filling in the documents lying there.

The entire team gathered by the pool, as far as possible from the house, so that Pellegrini wouldn't overhear them accidentally.

"Looks like he's ours," the professor declared with a pensive smile.

"I hope so," Isaac agreed.

"Professor, you really are a genius!" Bikie exclaimed excitedly. "What a fabulous plan! I swear, being on the same team with you is not only an honor, but the most fascinating event in my life. And Isaac, you're some kind of megastar actor! Really convincing! I believed it all! It was a pleasure just listening to you."

"Thank you, my friend," said Pascal, hugging Isaac. "You're like a brother to me. A genuine one! By taking those risks, you effectively saved my life. I've been reborn!" And he added with a smile: "So now you're like a father to me. A godfather! Very scary!"

Instead of praise, Michelle rewarded Isaac for his acting with a long kiss.

"Bikie, Isaac, guys, working with you is a pleasure too," the professor said with a smile. "My best students ever! The most important thing in any partnership is the buzz you get from succeeding together. You have someone to think things over with and have a drink to celebrate."

11

The professor's plan, which they have now carried out, was as simple as all ideas of a genius: after listening to Isaac when he got back from Pellegrini, he immediately supplied Pascal with a little packet of sleeping powder and sent him home. Pascal had to call the commissioner and tell him about the threat in a frightened voice. Naturally, the overconfident Pellegrini, like some super-hero, would prefer to arrest Isaac in person, without assistance from anyone else, and he would immediately go dashing to Pascal's home. In order not to frighten Isaac off, he would probably dump his car a couple of kilometers away and run for a short distance. Which meant that he would be thirsty. Even if he wasn't thirsty straight away, Pascal would offer him water or coffee. That was the first part of the plan, and it went like clockwork.

The commissioner fell into the trap just as Link had predicted. While he was sleeping, they brought him to Wolanski's villa, where they had emptied one room of everything that might give Pellegrini a hint of where he was. They curtained off the window. After that, they had to get him to believe that they were planning to download his creativity. They had a downloading helmet, but they had nowhere to download anything to. According to the plan, they had to win him over to their side. A man with a police badge, and one who held such an influential position, could really help them a lot. Whether they had managed it or not should become clear in the next couple of hours.

"What do we do next?" asked Pascal. "What's going to convince you he's ours?"

"We gave him a contract and paper to write letters. When he crumples them all up and tosses them away it would mean he realized that it's pointless writing to the top. That would be the right moment to sow the seed of hope!"

Half an hour later, Michelle walked into the room where Pellegrini was sitting. He had crumpled sheets of paper lay around him.

"Commissioner, do you need any help?"

Michelle could barely hold her smile. She obviously played with dolls as a child, but a human puppet was so much fun!

"No, thank you," Pellegrini replied sadly. "I've already finished half of it."

"Would you like me to sit with you, so you won't be so lonely?"

"Yes, please. Do sit for a while, of course."

"My name is Michelle. Michelle Blanche."

"And I'm Luca. The fact that you tell me your full name only confirms that I'll be downloaded."

"Don't you worry. They're already flying to America next week. I'm sure they'll pull it off. They're so clever."

"Yes, I'd like to believe that. Although right now that probably sounds strange, coming from me."

"It's not strange at all. I understand everything. Now you know what it means to be a Happy, I understand your attitude towards downloading. You'll most likely agree that it's strange. More recently, we were so glad to see *Collective Mind* at work. At first, I was also shocked and couldn't believe it."

"Listen, Michelle. I wouldn't want to tell them..." Pellegrini paused. "The Professor and Isaac, that is... but they need to go sooner."

"What do you mean? What for?"

"I wrote a request to the prosecutor for Isaac not to be allowed to leave the country. It will be processed on Monday, and he won't be able to fly anywhere. And bearing in mind that I've disappeared, I think he'll be arrested. They need to fly sooner."

"Whoa! What a good thing you told us! I'll warn them immediately. You don't mind?"

"No, I don't. Tell them," said Pellegrini. Although his whole being cringed, he did not have a feeling that he became a traitor.

Michelle walked out to tell everyone the important news. Bikie immediately started checking the options for a flight to America that weekend.

"But what about me? Have you thought of anything?" Link asked.

"Not so far, Professor, sorry. But there's still time," Isaac replied.

"What's the problem with the Professor?" Michelle asked.

"He's wanted. We don't know how to fool the US border patrol. Three months ago they installed new devices that identify everyone by their DNA. We don't know how to get round that. Link will be spotted immediately."

"That's strange," Michelle replied. "I recently was in America, and my DNA wasn't checked at all."

"Which airport was it?" Isaac asked.

"I flew Nice to Miami. I was modeling for a lingerie photo-shoot, I think," caustically added Michelle, in response to Isaac's smile.

"What kind of flight's that, I've never heard of a direct flight from Nice to Miami?"

"It's not a commercial flight, it was a private jet."

"Hell and damnation!" exclaimed Bikie, exchanging glances with Isaac.

"Could you tell us about that in more detail, please?" Isaac said.

"Sure," Michelle readily agreed, with a pleasant feeling that she was fitting into the team. "Well, I'm not a poor girl," she said with a slight sense of guilt. "Sometimes I travel on private jets. There's a separate terminal in Nice where they fly from. They can take you anywhere at all. I landed in Miami, at the main international terminal. But I didn't cross the border where the passengers of commercial flights do – there is a separate terminal for that. Without crowds or lines. They have nice VIP rooms there. You give them your passport and a few minutes later they bring it back, already stamped by the customs and the border patrol. Before you exit, of course, they check you against the photo in the passport, but they don't take your DNA."

"Enough said," Isaac commented, giving Michelle a peck on the cheek. "Professor, it looks like the problem can be solved. I think that so far, the new system is only located in the major terminals, and they haven't gotten around to the private flights yet. Now, where do you get these private jets?"

"There are lots of different brokerage companies. And by the way, since they fly all around the world, they're not limited by time zones. They work right around the clock. You could call right this minute."

"It can't be true," Bikie exclaimed in delight. "I'm going to fly to America on a private jet!"

288

"Michelle, honey, you're just a marvel! Could you give me the phone number of one of these brokers? Now, since that commissioner's opened up to you so much, you'd better go back to him, will you?"

Michelle went back to their prisoner. He hadn't made much progress with filling out his application.

"Thanks for the warning, the problem has been solved. They'll fly out tomorrow or on Sunday."

"And Link?"

"Link too. It's a pity you're on the other side, Commissioner. But don't worry. We'll manage."

"It's hard not to worry. Isaac will be a wanted man starting Monday in any case. They'll soon figure out where he flew. I'll be missed after a couple of days. It won't be easy for him to avoid being noticed in New York. He's taking a great risk. If I had a chance to cancel my request, it would simplify everything," said the commissioner, testing the water.

"And is that possible?"

"It is until Monday."

"But to do that we'll have to let you go?" asked Michelle with a smirk.

"Yes. Can I trust you, mademoiselle Blanche?"

"That depends on what you have in mind, Commissioner."

"You're Isaac's girlfriend, right? Or Bikie's? Maybe you could have a word with them?"

"Be more specific, Commissioner. I'm not a stupid girl."

"I'd like to come to an agreement with them. I've done some thinking in here, weighed everything up. I'm willing to cooperate, to help," he added humbly.

"To help us?" Michelle asked, trying to show genuine amazement.

"Yes, you. If the Professor isn't lying, if he has returned Pascal's energy correctly, then I understand his desire to stop everything. And I understand that going to the police is too risky. I'm not trying to trick you. If there was a lie detector here, you could easily make sure of that. I'm being sincere. I always quickly figure out the new circumstances,

I'm a policeman – skilled and experienced. Could you act as intermediary in negotiations about this?"

"You know, I believe you. Realizing what is really going on, any decent person would join our side. But why would you need an intermediary? Just talk to them directly! Just don't lie. We studied your profile: Isaac knows that you were awarded as a skillful negotiator. Speak for yourself."

"You think so?"

"I'm certain of it."

Michelle returned to the pool and told the friends about Pellegrini's offer. Bikie suggested they use the lie detector, but they didn't have it with them in Monaco. The professor could assemble another one, but then he'd have to take apart the hacking device and it takes too much time.

Five minutes later everyone gathered once again in the room where the bound commissioner was sitting.

"Isaac, Professor, I want to help you. But for me to do that you have to let me go."

"Why would you help us, Pellegrini?" Bikie asked. "Are we supposed to trust you immediately and let you go? What if you are lying?"

"It doesn't look like he's lying," Link added. "I can tell from his gestures and expressions."

"I'm definitely not lying," Pellegrini replied. "If I were lying, why would I have warned you that you are wanted?"

"In order not to become a Happy forever."

"Of course, I don't want to be a Happy, especially after what you've told me. But there are other reasons. If I don't recall my request, you'll have almost no chance in America."

"But if we let you go, then you're not risking anything."

"You can let me go after you've flown out and landed. You will be on the wanted list if I've lied to you, but if I have not, you have a chance. You don't lose anything."

"You've seen all the others. They're taking risks."

"I give you my word as an officer. Who was the first person you gave back his OE, Isaac? Your friend Pascal. I have many old colleagues among the Happies now. Do you think I don't give a damn for them? I joined the police to fight crime. I worked at the DEA for a long time and have never sworn an oath of loyalty to the Agency, I did swear it to the people, to my friends and to myself."

"You sound convincing. But I've learned from personal experience that you know how to say what's needed to convince a person or put him at ease."

"Yes, Isaac, I'm a professional. That's true. And believe me, I'm willing to do more. Not just cancel the request, but also help you carry out your plan."

"Commissioner, think about how to reduce our risks. You know the weak spots of the police best."

"Very well. I'll think about it. But you think about it too."

"Agreed. I'd like to trust you. But it's not easy; after all, I am putting my friends at risk."

They all went out to the pool to consult, leaving the commissioner with Michelle. They really wanted to believe him. And after all, it wasn't clear what to do with him if they didn't. They couldn't kill him, could they? And they had nowhere to download him to. If they left him tied up here, of course, he would be missed and sooner or later he would be found. His notes probably included the facts about where Isaac worked, he had asked that at the first interview. And who would stay behind to feed the commissioner and give him water?

What they needed badly was some proof that the commissioner was ready to switch over to their side.

"The Commissioner and I have an idea!" said Michelle, coming back to the pool.

"Both of you? Are you already in a league together?" Isaac laughed.

"No. But I trust him and I'm concerned about you."

"And I'm concerned about you, hon. I shouldn't have dragged you into this."

"Don't worry about me. I've got good lawyers, and I haven't done anything wrong. I didn't kidnap the Commissioner, I didn't participate in anything. Yes, I was there. But whoever said I agreed with what you were doing? My lawyer will definitely get me off. What could I do about what's going on? I'm just a frail, beautiful girl." Michelle wound her arms around Isaac's neck again and kissed him.

"OK, let's go and listen to this idea of yours."

"My laptop is in my hotel room," Pellegrini began. "It is locked but I will give you the password. But you'll have to bring in here anyway. The key to my room is in my back pants pocket. The Marriott Hotel, Room 414."

Isaac nodded to Bikie, who reached into the commissioner's back pocket and pulled out a plastic key card.

"Please bring the laptop, Bikie."

"OK, boss," said Bikie, saluting Isaac playfully.

"Then what, Commissioner?"

"Next comes the second level of protection – my iris. We'll scan it in with the web camera to gain entry into the database. Then the third level – my fingerprint. That has to be scanned in too. Then we'll enter the 24-digit password for the database, and you'll gain access to it. That's the highest level of security! It's only accessible to some department heads, as well as the Minister of Defense and his deputies, and the Minister of the Interior. Only files with individual access are have higher level of security If anyone finds out that I gave away the codes, I'm done for. I will be an encyclopedic example of treason that will get into all textbooks on criminology. I will go under trial and suffer terrible shame. There can be no reason that would justify me revealing this information. With my password, you can even look up undercover agents. You'll be able to cancel the request about Isaac and alter all the interview reports. I'll show you how."

"Do we still have undercover agents?" asked Isaac.

"We do. And the remnants of the mafia still exist. In Japan, I recall, OE downloading is prohibited. Tattoos are prohibited there as well," said the commissioner looking at the blue skull tattooed on Bikie's shoulder. "After that, consider me your hostage until the end of my life. If anyone ever finds out that I gave you the passwords, I am history. They would have shot me for that before. But even now it's a sure court-martial. And the sentence for treason will be downloading."

"Very convincing. Just one question. How can we check that the 24-digit isn't a false one, one that is used as an alarm signal?"

"There's no way you can check. But then, you can do all of this when you are already in America. And if you fly out tomorrow, we will have enough time."

Despite Bikie's protests, he did not get a chance to fly in a private jet. They decided that it would be too risky for everyone to travel together, so Isaac and Bikie would take a commercial flight two hours after the private jet carrying Link and Pascal leaves.

Still the commercial flight to New York's John F. Kennedy airport would arrive earlier than the private jet. Isaac and Bikie had only a brief connection in Paris, whereas Link and Pascal were going the long way via Miami. Not to mention that the most time gained would come from Isaac and Bikie taking the brand-new supersonic Concorde-100 between Paris and New York, an upgraded version of the famous old Concorde that was in service in the late 20th century. Thanks to *Collective Mind*, the shortcomings of the previous version have been eliminated, and three hour long transatlantic flights again became a reality.

Michelle had to stay in Monaco. Someone had to make sure that Pellegrini would indeed cancel the request. She promised not to fly to America, but Isaac didn't believe her. He suspected that she wouldn't keep her word. He was worried about it, of course, but on the other hand, he felt glad.

"We'll be in the US – the homeland of Harley – tonight!" Bikie exclaimed, interrupting Isaac's train of thought. "I've waited so long for this!"

"Me too," Isaac said with a smile. "We're almost there."

Pellegrini had offered to follow them to America, which was a major breakthrough. He would help avoid suspicion in the US. They had very little information about the New York storage facility and a lot of things would have to be assessed on the spot. Pellegrini promised to arrange an official visit for himself to the New York branch of the Agency within a couple of days, and that would give him an opportunity to examine the building from the inside.

"Well done Link," Isaac thought. "What a brain!"

Isaac himself had been going through agony, trying to think of how to break away from the policeman's pursuit, but the professor succeeded in turning him into a teammate.

"The former enemy is now an enlightened ally," Link announced triumphantly as he shook Pellegrini's free hand in farewell. "And 'former' is the important word here. The fact that the Commissioner has come over to our side is a message to the world. We are on the right track, my friends. If the system is overthrown, no one will ever want to download OE again. Veggies look happy and satisfied, they are often rich, and so people got confused. But it's a deception, isn't it, Pascal? You are also a vivid example testifying that the system must be destroyed."

12

On the Paris-New York flight they managed to get a couple of hours of sleep in comfort. Pascal was generous enough to buy business-class tickets for his rescuers. They didn't run into any turbulence and were able to get some rest and put their thoughts in order. Before they found themselves working together, each of them was used to being a loner in his own way, Isaac thought. During the three months together they had too much of each other and some tension was creeping in, despite their high spirits. Bikie was absorbed in his own thoughts too. Each of them felt like resting alone.

Isaac was pretty exhausted by Vicky's illness and the search for Link; the dangerous operation to return Pascal's creativity felt like the final straw for him. But then it continued: the police interviews, the undertaking not to leave the area, the need to make quick pivotal decisions. Even the relationship with Michelle didn't make it easier: positive emotions are still a stress on the nervous system. Three months of regular exercise had shaped him up; he looked trim and fit, but had fatigue bags under his eyes.

Isaac has assembled the team, they all saw him as a leader and that was far from being simple. They were all temperamental, self-assured and egocentric. He thought it was hard to carry this weight, when each of them had his or her own opinion and sometimes didn't actually regard Isaac as the boss. They were all equal: Bikie totally independent, Link a genius, unaccepting of any authority.. Pascal had come from the past, when they were friends and on equal footing. He was not disposed to appreciate the subtleties of a command hierarchy; he was too often immersed in grief over loosing Eva "just yesterday". And now he was the source of the team's funding, which put him in a privileged position too.

In addition to urgently saving the world, Isaac was looking forward to going to America to zone out and unwind a bit. Vicky's surgery has now been paid for, so why should he be in a hurry?

In the meantime, Link and Pascal have also done their part of the work – they combined the hacking device with the amplifier, so OE could be now returned to all Happies within the radius of thirty to forty kilometers. In densely populated New York, that ought to be enough for thousands of people to get their former creativity back. And that would be enough to spark off a massive wave of protests.

Focusing on his own condition, Isaac was surprised that he had absolutely no fear of failure, probably because he was so tired.

"Don't relax, just a bit longer now," he told himself in an effort to liven his spirits up. "Get a grip on yourself, pay attention and be cautious! The last thing you want is to wind up in jail right at the finish." Of course, America was not China, where even relatively minor crimes were punishable by compulsory downloading, but they were not particularly fond of terrorists here either.

The John F. Kennedy Airport looked different from the airports he'd seen in Europe. A bit on the dirty side, without superfluous luxury, but very functional. It had impressive dimensions; before reaching passport control, he and Bikie walked at least a kilometer. The flow of passengers was immense, with flights coming in from every corner of the world. They could see crowds of Asians, Europeans and Latin Americans. Judging from the tags on the hand luggage, there were arrivals from Tunisia and Kenya. Everyone was eager to come to America. And a whole heap of automated systems was used in the airport to process these crowds rapidly.

The corridors were full of cameras, detectors and scanners with red crosses measuring passengers' temperature for signs of infection and viruses. The scanners often blinked green. A monitor responded to Bikie with a yellow signal. Paramedics immediately approached him and asked to walk through a glass door into a parallel corridor.

"Why?" Isaac protested. "What's happening?"

"Everything's all right, sir. The sensor indicated that your friend has a high temperature. We have to carry out an additional minor check," a paramedic replied politely.

"Can I go with him?"

"No, sorry, you'll meet up again later at the meeting point after you go through customs. He'll be just fine, I assure you."

"Everything's OK, Isaac, I really am feeling a bit funny," Bikie muttered morosely. I'll call you when I'm out." And the paramedics led him away.

Isaac started walking faster. He wanted to get out of this airport with all its bells and whistles as soon as possible. After a hundred meters, the corridor widened out and everybody walked, one at a time, into the gateway for hand luggage check. There were several dozen gates.

"Exactly like a highway toll terminal in France," thought Isaac. Hanging on the walls were numerous posters warning of things that couldn't be brought into the USA.

Isaac joined one of the lines that had about ten people ahead of him. While he waited he could watch the way the gateway worked. The booth was made completely of glass or some transparent plastic. A newly arrived passenger went in at one side, the door closed and some kind of scanner swiveled around him. If everything was fine, the door on the other side opened and the person could walk on. Occasionally, a light on the booth started blinking, and police officers walked up from the other side. In the next channel a passenger was found to have food products that were illegal to import. They confiscated them and led the poor wretch away to file a report.

The next passenger also turned out to be an offender – the gateway sounded a piercing and revolting alarm. Half a dozen police officers rushed to him from the exit side. Another two elbowed their way through the crowd from Isaac's side.

The young guy in the gate started thrashing about and cursing hysterically, trying to break out. He pounded on the glass with his fists and kicked it, but it didn't even shake.

The policeman standing beside Isaac giggled fiendishly. He and his partner were talking quietly and Isaac tried to listen in, but he couldn't make anything out properly, except for the word "cocaine". The policemen were absolutely calm, and it was soon clear why. Gas was fed into the gateway through an opening from above. The criminal jerked a couple of times and rapidly went limp. The gas was immediately pumped out, the door was opened and the body was carried off along that parallel corridor. The policemen went back to their places. The entire operation took no more than five minutes, and happened right before the eyes of the astounded public.

"Mmm, yes," thought Isaac, "rapid, effective and very instructive."

Having successfully passed through the gate, Isaac joined the line for passport control. After that, all he had to do was collect his luggage, which he brought along more in order to avoid looking suspicious by traveling light, than for any real need. Standing there on his own, Isaac felt nervous about Bikie. Sunday became six hours longer. In theory Isaac could not be put on the wanted list until Monday. Pascal and Link texted him that they had successfully crossed the border in the VIP hall for private flights in Miami and were waiting for a flight to New York. Everything was just as Michelle said it would be.

At last it was his turn.

"What is the purpose of your visit to the United States?" the border patrol officer asked.

"I want to see New York – the museums, Central Park, Broadway, everything. Tourism, basically," Isaac replied politely.

The officer twirled Isaac's passport in his hands and read the form that Isaac had filled out. He was in no hurry.

"What a job! This could drive a person crazy!" Isaac thought. "The speed you work at makes no difference to your chances of getting the job done quicker and going home earlier. Flights are coming in every minute, and people just keep on arriving. Just sit here as if you are chained to your seat until the shift is over. And it doesn't matter how many passports you've looked through. A thousand or ten thousand. At least in the bar I used to get tips…"

"Place your palm on the scanner…"

Isaac patiently set his palm on the transparent little window that glowed blue. It felt as if someone gave his palm a gentle pinch. The officer looked at his monitor, then at Isaac's face and stamped his passport with a loud thud.

Bikie was all right. They took a couple of tests and gave him an injection that rapidly relieved all the symptoms. He was waiting for Isaac at the entrance and already had his suitcase.

"Wow! You were even faster than me! I was worried about you."

"Yeah, they did everything pretty fast. I'm actually glad they hooked me out and cured me so quickly."

"So it's Hail America, then?"

"Precisely! The future cradle of liberty!"

The U.S. held first place among countries for the number of orange energy downloads. And what's interesting, the average level of creativity was higher there than in other countries. The answer to the question of why the Americans were leading in the amount of creativity per person was fairly obvious.

Ever since WWI the U.S. has imported "brains". They were the receiving end of the so called "brain-drain" of other countries. Many people came here during WWII, as well, and many more afterwards. America created good conditions for qualified specialists, so talented scientists from many countries yearned to come here. They knew there were laboratories, grants, abundant opportunities and decent money waiting for them here. The perspective of fulfillment and advancement prompted people to make the move. The more lenient tax regime was also a powerful stimulus for European entrepreneurs, while the strong legal framework protecting private property attracted businessmen from Latin America, Africa and Asia.

Today, the Agency had the lead in most places, but not so long ago everything was simple: if you're a talented programmer, then welcome to Silicon Valley! An artist? Go to Miami or New York! A hot-shot actor? Try your luck in Hollywood's most prestigious studios, making the best money you could make anywhere.

The U.S. posed a choice of two options before a gifted individual. Option one: stay in your own country and vegetate in half-empty laboratories, struggling to find financing, sometimes living in poverty and maybe even dying in some military conflict. Option two: immigrate to America and take advantage of many opportunities available, feel that you are needed and become a U.S. citizen.

No doubt this was a cunning policy. The best minds produced the best technologies. The best technologies produced the best economy. The American dollar, backed by these minds and technologies, is the symbol of stability and the universal reserve currency.

Like a cheapskate who ends up paying twice, the generous America often earned a double profit by eagerly exporting arms and offering refuge to the finest minds of countries at war. Of course, wars were not permitted in or around the U.S. itself.

Until the invention of *Collective Mind*, the whole world knew that if you did not know where to find the latest cutting-edge developments in one field or another, you should look in the States. Now the brains that had flowed into America were benefitting the country's image. The Agency was growing more and more powerful elsewhere, but its influence wasn't really yet felt in the States.

"I think I'm going to love this country," Bikie declared when they walked out of the airport. "I'll just get a breath of the air of freedom and rock'n'roll, and fall in love immediately."

Bikie theatrically filled his lungs and held his breath.

"Take care not to burst with delight! We haven't even reached Amsterdam yet!"

"What do you mean, Amsterdam?"

"New Amsterdam."

"And what's that?"

"New Amsterdam. That's what Manhattan used to be called. The first European settlement on the island was founded by the Dutch. Then the English pushed them out and renamed the town New York."

"Freaking awesome! Why didn't you tell me sooner that we were flying to Amsterdam? I wouldn't have brought any grass with me."

"Get out of here, you joker! Let's get moving. I can't wait to see the city. We're staying only three blocks away from Broadway and Times Square!"

The friends loaded their suitcases into a yellow cab and stared out the window, each on his side. At first there was nothing special to look at, but in less than half an hour, the glow of the megalopolis appeared up ahead. They had picked up an old taxi, from the times before crime was eradicated – a semi-transparent screen separated passengers from the driver. Bikie was annoyed that he couldn't stretch out his legs, space being too small for his dimensions. But the moment the Empire State Building became visible up ahead he immediately forgot about his discomfort.

"Can we drive over the Brooklyn Bridge?" Isaac asked.

"That will take a bit longer and cost more," the taxi driver replied.

"That's okay. Take us anyway. This is the first time we are in America."

"Done!" smiled the taxi driver.

Everything was happening as if in a fairy tale, it was like the pictures on the Internet. The beautiful Brooklyn Bridge couldn't possibly be confused with anything else in the world. To its right was the Empire State Building, blazing blue. A little further they could see the Chrysler Building with its beautiful, illuminated, frilly yellow design.

The driver turned on to the embankment and the Williamsburg Bridge appeared, connecting the neighborhood of the same name with Manhattan. By now the two friends were so enthralled by the sights of the city that even the enemy headquarters, the UN building towering up along the embankment, provoked only positive feelings. The car turned left, to cross the island and they passed Second Avenue, Park Avenue, Madison Avenue and, finally, the most famous of all, Fifth Avenue. There were so many people in the streets, it looked as if some incredible street fair was under way. The roads were packed with yellow taxicabs, but in general, traffic was moving smoothly.

As soon as Isaac thought about how lucky they were that there was no traffic, they got into a jam.

"Broadway and Times Square are ahead. The traffic's always tricky around here."

"That's OK. We're in no hurry," Bikie replied.

They finally arrived, paid the driver, collected their suitcases and walked into the hotel lobby. They weren't tired any longer and, in any case, had to wait for the professor and Pascal. Bikie decided to go for a stroll and Isaac asked him to buy local cell-phones, while he checked them into their room.

Now that he was alone, he could finally call Michelle in peace. She had to release Commissioner Pellegrini. He had done everything he promised and not tricked them. Isaac sighed with relief.

The first question stubborn Michelle raised was about her coming to join them. Isaac was strongly against. Of course, he would be glad to see her, but the risks were too high.

"You know, Isaac, there's only one person who can tell me where I can and cannot go. And that is me! I'm not a fool, you know that perfectly well…"

"Michelle, please…"

But she did not seem to be listening to him at all.

"I've been talking to Pellegrini here. We had quite a lot of time. He won't let us down. He's a decent guy. He's seen the light and now is dying to get into the fight with us."

"It's not just him, can't you see that?" exclaimed Isaac, trying to make her reasonable, but it was useless.

"Don't interrupt! Let me finish! I'm not going to get in your way or interfere in your business. Do whatever you like I'll simply see my friends."

"Then why are you asking me?" Isaac was beginning to fume. "If you want to see your friends in New York, London or Melbourne, just buy a ticket and fly."

"Oh, Isaac, please," said Michelle, changing her tone. "Why do you keep putting me off all the time? I helped you get to America safely, by the way, so I'm also a member of the team. Besides, I've blown my cover with Pellegrini anyway."

"No you haven't. Tell him that when you realized we had really left, you untied him immediately. He doesn't know that you advised us about Miami."

"I'll go where I want to go!" said Michelle, changing her tone again.

"My God, how stubborn you are! Exactly as Bikie predicted."

Michelle hung up.

Oh, boy! Yes, dealing with her will be pretty tricky.

Isaac had another thing to do that he had been putting off for a long time. He had to contact Wolanski and somehow tell him everything that's been going on. He hadn't yet thought of how to explain that not only did Link live in Peter's bedroom, they'd also held a police commissioner hostage inside the villa. Well, there was nothing to be done about it, he had to call. Isaac reluctantly tapped in Peter's number.

"Hi, Isaac." Peter's voice was as vibrant as always. "How are you getting on? How's the work going?"

"Everything's fine. Things are good. Your house is all safe and sound. Where are you right now?"

"In Dubai."

"Sorry Peter, just a second…" Isaac looked at his phone and then added: "I hope I didn't wake you up? We've got an eight-hour time difference."

"Whoa?" said Peter, calculating something rapidly. "Good for you, guys! I get it! That's great!"

"We solved the puzzle. So we went."

"You did?" There was more joy than surprise in Peter's voice. "I never had any doubt!"

"Listen. There were some problems too. I was called in by the police. They asked about the details of the terrorist attack in Monaco. I told them, you are my employer, just in case."

"Anything serious?"

"Well, not quite," Isaac replied mysteriously. "You know I had nothing to do with it. They just latched on to me."

"I see." This time Peter's cheerfulness vanished. "What should I do?"

"Nothing. It's been fixed already. And the good news is that Vicky will be well soon! An old friend gave me the money. Pascal, I told you about him, remember? He turned out to be a really sound guy. ABSOLUTELY sound, in fact," Isaac said emphatically.

"Freaking hell!" Peter grunted. "That means…"

"Yes, Peter, that's exactly what it means!" Isaac interrupted. "Anyway, you relax over there. Get a tan. There's nothing more to be done in Monaco."

"Listen, Isaac. There's something I need to tell you as well. It's very important. You must find a way to contact me. Call from the hotel."

"OK, I'll settle in and call you. Good luck, old buddy!"

"And to you guys! Don't forget to call."

"I won't."

He did not tell Peter everything to be on the safe side, but did get across the most important points. The quick-witted Peter understood where they were, with whom and why. Now he just had to give more details about Pellegrini, but that could be done from his hotel room.

Isaac glanced at the time. Well now, he ought to get a bite before everyone got together.

13

Bikie came back first bringing six disposable phones: one for each member of the team, one for Pellegrini and one in reserve.

Isaac told him that everything was fine with the commissioner, he hadn't tricked them. Tomorrow he was expected to go back to Paris, arrange an official trip for himself and fly over within a couple of days.

Things were fine with Link and Pascal too. No incidents. They were just tired after two long flights.

"You are quite a sight!" Bikie couldn't help commenting on the professor's new appearance. "A genuine villain out of a children's horror movie".

Link's head was shaved smooth and he had a sumptuous ginger moustache protruding from under his nose, upon which there sat a pair of old-fashioned glasses in a thick tortoise-shell rim.

"Shut up, Bikie!" Isaac said sternly. "I swore that none of us would joke about the Professor's looks."

"Got it," Bikie said as seriously as he could, stifling his laughter.

They decided not to stay up late and went to their rooms. It was well after midnight in France.

They woke very early due to the time difference, and went down for breakfast at the hotel restaurant to discuss their plans for the day. It was decided that the visit to the laboratory in the museum building would be put off for the following day; in the meantime, they would take it easy and recover from jet lag.

They decided to meet for lunch, meanwhile splitting up to wander the city each on his own.

Everyone was on time for lunch, only Link arrived late. He entered the wearing the most mysterious of his cunning smiles, and announced that he didn't come empty-handed. It turned out that he bought tickets to a Broadway show.

"Let's relax a bit today. It's not rock-n-roll or underground, but it's a new classic. Since we're in the Big Apple, we can't pass up Broadway. Especially since no one knows when we'll have another chance to see it."

Everyone was delighted; none of them except the professor thought about going to a Broadway show.

The modernistic design of the theater hall was unusual and impressive. Incredibly huge screens, consisting of large numbers of panels joined together, were on the right and left, in the front and on the ceiling. It was as if the audience was seated in a television-capsule. The seats reclined to a half-lying position.

Shows of this kind appeared recently and were directly influenced by the invention of *Collective Mind*. Modern music no longer simply contained melodies that stimulated varying degrees of emotion: grief – joy – laughter – joy – sadness. Just as the Russian avant-garde artists abandoned the object early twentieth century, the COMUNA computer has partially discarded melody.

The composing program created by *Collective Mind* combined all well-known popular melodies with developments in psychiatry and neuroscience. Calculating which sounds influenced which regions of the brain, the program produced something totally mind-blowing!

By adding 4 D light effects, the producers brought the audience to a state of total ecstasy.

The computer controlled human emotions, alternating sounds and images, so everyone simultaneously laughed, wept, guffawed and sobbed, and then laughed and rejoiced again. At the end they looked at the outer cosmos and galaxies and turned utterly happy.

The final chords of the program aimed to induce in the audience the feeling of ultimate joy. As they left the show, the friends kept talking across each other, sharing impressions.

Even the rock'n'roller Bikie lit up like a neon sign, with a smile up to his ears. An hour later, in the hotel, they all felt overwhelmed with fatigue, and decided to go to their rooms to fall into a deep, calm sleep.

In the morning everyone was quiet, nobody felt like talking.

Link explained that during the show the brain had discharged almost all of its reserves of endorphins, adrenalin and serotonin.

"Our pituitary gland, the hypothalamus and the pineal gland are exhausted. An hour and a half after the show there was a discharge of melatonin, to stabilize the organism, and we fell asleep. Because of that, driving isn't allowed after computer operas and shows. The body needs time to recover, so I took the liberty of scheduling a massage for everyone followed by a day of rest," Link summed up, looking very pleased with himself.

Isaac imagined that Link lectured his students with exactly the same intonation, and thought once again what a class act Link was: not just intelligent, but experienced too. And he was obviously very savvy when it came to cool leisure.

Link added that after these tense weeks, it was an important consideration to cleanse their nervous systems and relax; that was why he had taken the team to the show. It was a sort of rebooting.

Everyone was grateful to him. Isaac was so exhausted, he did not even have the strength to tease Bikie about rock'n'roll. If not for Link's influential character, the hard-boiled biker would never have agreed to any experiments of this sort. But he went along with everyone and came away very content. Isaac smiled as he recalled his friend's foolishly happy face last night.

"That's it! We're relaxing!" Link commanded. "After the massage we'll have lunch, and at four you're going to the Guggenheim."

Link still used the old name for the building of the American branch of the Agency, where one of the four *Collective Mind* global servers was located. Previously it was the Solomon R. Guggenheim Museum of Modern Art, which housed a fabulous collection of art of the nineteenth, twentieth and twenty-first centuries.

COMUNA had only moved into the Guggenheim building quite recently, after having constructed and generously donated new premises to the museum. With much more space, this masterpiece of architecture was immediately dubbed the Eighth Wonder of the World and the very best thing that mankind had built in its entire history.

The Agency was one of the bidders in a proposal for the design of a new home for the museum. Of course, all leading architects of the world submitted their proposals, but there was nothing to match the concept presented by COMUNA. It won in all categories and on all criteria.

To develop the design, *Collective Mind* used absolutely all the ideas of architects, artists and everyone else who had donated their creativity, utilizing at the same time the most advanced and bold engineering solutions, including those that had never been used in construction before. Everyone was absolutely astounded when they saw what combined orange energy was capable of.

It was not known what else the computer used in its proposal, but all members of the jury voted for the design, with the result being that a magnificent building was erected in the presently tranquil area of East Harlem, where property prices immediately shot up.

The building turned out superb, unlike any others, and included elements of some of well recognizable styles from various periods. For instance, at the main entrance a classical column seemed to have been frozen in light-blue melted glass, forming a magnificent arch. The astounding mélange of styles enchanted even seasoned specialists, and day and night ordinary people walked round the building, keeping their eyes glued to it. Journalists promptly dubbed the style "neo-eclecticism".

It was quite a sight. The main gimmick was the building's total lack of symmetry, so that if you walked around it, its contour constantly changed. This accomplished an additional important effect – all viewers liked the design, because everyone could find his own preferred perspective. The same building seemed to have three hundred and sixty views, one for each degree of the circle. From one angle there was a hint of Gothic, from another angle a hint of Modernism, and from yet another of Post-Modernism. Every person walking round it could find a point at which he simply couldn't help gasping in admiration, because it fit so perfectly their own ideal of harmony. No matter who you were, you couldn't not be delighted by it. It was a collection of masterpieces correctly assembled together.

The problem came when the Agency tried to use the same volumetric space approach for designing the museum's next building: the operator who was connected to the computer turned out exactly the same design, only slightly smaller. Almost exactly the same – apparently, the addition of creativity from a few new donors had some effect. And no matter how hard they struggled and shuffled the operators around, they still got identical designs.

To be fair, the new buildings were similar in style, all neo-eclectic, but the designs for skyscrapers and small buildings did in fact differ from each other. With buildings of the same size, there were certain differences that the computer allowed – depending on climate, solar irradiation and the surrounding environment.

As an expression of its gratitude, the Guggenheim Foundation gave COMUNA its old premises. Moving the servers from the United Nations tower to the relatively small white building beside Central Park was not really all that necessary, but the Agency saw it as a political PR opportunity.

Americans are practical people – they turn everything into a business, a show, a way of making money. And the place where OE was stored was no exception. After the Agency's American office was moved to the former museum, they set up a huge permanent exhibition of their achievements there, to promote the idea of uploading. Of course, there was no real-life machinery and buildings on display, just models and 3D photographs. You could upload your OE right there on the spot, but COMUNA's main American server was located somewhere underground.

The basic concept of a visit to the Guggenheim had not changed since its early days – one first arrived via the elevator and then walked down along a spiral, examining the exhibits. Only the exhibits were now of a much different kind. Isaac stopped in front of almost every one: they were so fascinating to him. He even momentarily wondered if they were making a big mistake. He decided that they were not – none of these models, videos and pictures, and everything they depicted, would disappear.

A separate section was devoted to prior ideas and discoveries. Long before the discovery of OE, mankind had sensed that it existed. Why was one person more talented than another? It was a matter of genetics, upbringing, education, but something else, as well. A divine spark, charisma, an aura – these and numerous other terms had now been given a precise definition: Orange Energy.

At the end of the exhibition there were amusements and attractions and anyone could take an express test for their OE level. People were lured with challenges: "Find out how much you're worth", "Be one of today's top ten, of this week's top hundred", "Have you got five stars?". Even though he knew his level, Isaac found it hard to resist being measured again.

On all sides they were selling trinkets, little magnets and postcards with images of the museum, including memory sticks shaped as a small big-headed man. There were no connectors to the computer – they working on blue tooth.

There was a download center in the basement of the museum, while its rear section housed an annex, a conference hall and staff offices.

Link spent no more than fifteen minutes in the museum and then asked Isaac to go outside with him

"I don't want to go back into the museum," he explained. "There is a risk that I'll be recognized. There are more of my portraits in there than 'wanted' posters in a police station. But I have spotted something important there. There will be a conference in the museum in two days. I suggest we think about how we can get into it."

Isaac nodded. He also thought about the conference.

"We'll try our best. See you at the hotel."

As they examined the exhibits, the friends took note of important things such as the location of entrances, security guards and cameras.

Isaac approached Bikie and Pascal and shared his thoughts that were bothering him since yesterday.

"Listen, Pascal, are we sure about your amplifier?"

"Yes, of course! Everything will run like clockwork. I don't know what fancy stuff Link has cooked up, but I'm not worried about my part."

"OK. Bikie, I just thought that the professor is probably developing an exit plan. But we aren't. I think Pascal should go back, we can manage here without him."

"I agree, he's no big loss," Bikie said with his usual sarcasm. "There's no point in the whole crowd scurrying about here, with no backup at home."

"Pellegrini's flying in late this evening and he worries me too. Who knows.... What if we were wrong about him, after all?" Isaac continued. "I think Pascal ought to fly back before Pellegrini flies in, just to be on the safe side."

"Makes sense," Bikie said. "What do you say, Pascal?"

"I don't want to leave. But Isaac has a point," Pascal agreed.

"I'm worried that Link isn't thinking about escape routes. Or maybe he is, just not telling us. I also noticed that his assistant, Redbeard, has not come with us, either," Isaac continued sharing his concerns.

"And what if he has thought about us?" asked Bikie.

"That's fine. Pascal will think about him too. And if something happens, we'll have two getaway plans in place. Will you give it some thought?"

"Yes, of course. But how will the Professor fly out without me, Isaac?"

"Don't worry. Leaving America is far easier than getting into it."

So they settled on that. Having left the museum, they went to the hotel, where Pascal packed his things and went to the airport. Isaac remembered to call Wolanski. He didn't feel like it, but he couldn't put it off any longer. The commissioner was due to arrive soon and Isaac had to warn Peter, just in case. The phone they bought for Pascal was perfectly fine for that.

"Peter, sorry to wake you," Isaac said in response to Wolanski's sleepy 'Hello?' "What hotel are you in?"

"The Armani," Peter replied. "Call me."

Isaac quickly found the number on the Internet, called it and asked to be put through to Peter Wolanski's room. The front-desk receptionist hesitated, explaining that it was late night in Dubai.

"Don't worry, he's expecting my call," Isaac assured her.

Two rings and Peter answered the phone.

"Listen, Peter. My old childhood friend, who became a Veggie, is doing just fine, but what came up is that there is sort of a side effect – he doesn't remember a bloody thing, as if he had been sleeping for two years. But the two of us got a certain persnickety individual all steamed up. With shoulder straps, and all. In short, he got too close to us. It would take too long to explain, but the point is, he had to spend a couple of days as our reluctant guest".

"What?" Peter's voice broke down to groaning. "Damn…"

And he hung up. Isaac dialed his number again, but there was no answer.

In fifteen minutes Wolanski called back.

"Isaac, we didn't agree to this! You shouldn't have dragged me into this, guys. And now this…"

"Wait, Peter!" Isaac snapped. "It's all good. Don't shit your pants, man. This guy is on our side now! Moreover, we know now, we are sure, that all donors are like that. It's like a coma. So everything we are doing is right. After speaking with my friend, this pesky guest changed his mind and he is now going to help us…voluntarily. I trust him. However, I'm not entirely sure. I've warned you just in case. I'm sorry, we were working for you and we pulled these messy stunts in your house. You didn't know anything," Isaac added, just to be sure in case someone was listening.

"I, I… sorry guys, but you are fired," said Wolanski in an icy, but still trembling voice. "And there's something else very important! Make sure you call me before… Call me a day before! Don't forget. Now you're sacked, Mr. Leroy." And Peter hung up again.

"Thank you, Mr. Wolanski. Sorry, again," Isaac mumbled automatically and looked at his watch: the second conversation took 57 seconds.

He felt that Peter apparently wanted to say something. "He's probably scared again," he thought, smiling to himself. "Although he's quite a brave man. Brave enough to overcome his blind fear. It's just that he's still very young and has never come across real danger in his life." He wasn't angry with Peter for freaking out; you can't ask too much from people.

Having finally told Peter about Pellegrini, Isaac felt relieved. Peter didn't call back.

That evening Pellegrini arrived and moved into the hotel next door. He might have been their ally, but a certain mutual dislike still lingered after his kidnapping. However, that was a minor detail compared with the fact that he kept his word: he did not betray them and came to help.

Isaac went to see him at the hotel lobby, where the two greeted each other and went down to the bar.

"What are the plans?" the commissioner enquired.

"Tomorrow we are going to the site. The goal is to get into a conference that is taking place there in two days," Isaac replied briefly. "The server's in the basement. We have to get to it."

"OK, I get it. When are we going?"

"At eleven. So there'll be plenty of visitors around."

"I see. Until tomorrow then. At 10.30 here in the lobby."

"And here, take this," said Isaac, handing the commissioner a local phone.

The commissioner nodded and walked to the elevator, stretching his back.

He obviously didn't fly the Concorde, or in business class. "That's a government employee's business trip for you," Isaac thought in sympathy, as he watched the translucent doors close.

14

Tomorrow arrived and the plotters walked into the Guggenheim again.

Pellegrini hung back at the entrance. Once inside, he went straight to the head of house security and introduced himself, saying that he worked in the police department in Paris and collaborated closely with COMUNA.

"I'm on leave here, and I found out this interesting conference was taking place," Pellegrini went straight to the point. "Could you please help me, as a colleague, get into it?"

"Of course," the head of security replied with a beaming white smile. "I'll give you a guest pass. Here you are."

Pellegrini thanked him and examined the pass without giving away disappointment: it was not exactly what he wanted. No chip, no magnetic strip. He obviously could not get into the basement with that.

"Tell me, I have another question," he continued, mangling the words slightly in the French manner. "Can I take a look at the list of speakers?"

"Certainly. Over there," said the American, pointing towards a square table. "Pick up the program. Only don't take it away, it's my last one."

A stroke of luck this time. Double luck! Firstly, the head of security obviously was not curious and did not ask questions why Pellegrini wanted the list. And secondly, all of the sponsors of the conference were listed on the program. One of them was a five-star hotel. For the first time in ages Pellegrini was able to use a detective's most important skill – good memory. He memorized several names and the name of the hotel where these scientists would be staying for the next three days. To be on the safe side, so that the American would understand why he had wanted to look at the list, Pellegrini muttered: "Oh, Dr. Cohen decided to come after all, wonderful! I definitely must listen to his talk. You are really helpful. I am most grateful."

"You can take a photo of the program on your cell phone. So you won't forget anything," the head of security suggested.

"That's even better!" said the commissioner, giving him a broad smile.

When he found Isaac and Bikie, Pellegrini only showed them his pass for the conference. He decided to tell them the rest later.

"Excuse me, you were here yesterday!" a pretty girl in white uniform caught up with Isaac. "Have you decided to get your level measured, after all? The stand is over here on the right, you almost walked past it."

"Good guess," Isaac gasped in relief and smiled. "I decided to get measured, after all."

Isaac sat down in a comfortable chair. They put a disposable cap on his head, asked him to close his eyes and relax.

"Don't worry, it doesn't hurt at all." It looked like the girl was flirting with him a little.

"I'm not worried. I just don't want to appear stupid in your eyes," Isaac said with a wink, joining her game.

Bikie was observing this scene from a short distance and he gave Isaac a thumbs-up.

A soft melody began playing in the helmet and Isaac started feeling drowsy. The melody obviously had some kind of hypnotic effect, because the next thing he saw, or rather, felt, was that he had woken up. Everything was exactly as his first time in Monaco.

They helped Isaac take off the helmet and get up out of the chair.

"Congratulations, you have a very high level of creativity. I'm awed! Here you are, I've printed out your result and potential sum you could get for your OE." The girl was clearly impressed by both his high rating and the six-figure number.

Isaac glanced at the certificate. The rating was five points lower than his previous result. "But even so, that's a margin of error of only 0.01%," he calculated.

"Maybe you'd like to take part in the records competition?"

"No, thank you."

"You don't want to fill out a questionnaire?"

"No thanks, I don't. And to be honest, this isn't the first time. I'm already registered."

"So you were trying to impress me like this?"

"You read my mind," said Isaac, feigning embarrassment. "Can I come back to you later?"

"Of course you can!" said the girl, rewarding Isaac with an expressive smile.

Bikie slapped Isaac on the shoulder and murmured his approval.

"Well done, you're making progress. She could be useful!"

"And just who was my teacher? Mr. Chrome Casanova himself!" Isaac joked.

They looked at a semi-transparent screen. A video sequence started and a voice over informed them about the operating principle of the system.

"In order to use creative energy, the operator puts on the helmet and starts thinking about a problem. Immediately many ideas occur to him. He notes down these ideas. The computer has a faultless memory. Even if the answer given is not complete, it contains at least the most important part of the solution. Like a skeleton, in which some bones may be missing, either large or small. However, most tasks are answered in complete formulae."

Bikie set off resolutely towards the testing chair. He had his OE tested previously too. But unlike Isaac, he did not refuse to take part in the ratings, and he didn't regret it.

"Well now, here's a little gift certificate for you," the girl at the stand twittered. "It says here that you set the record of the day and the record of the week, so congratulations once again."

"You know, I saw you have a conference on OE here. I just can't make up my mind whether I should offload. Maybe I could attend the conference, as the winner of the week?"

"I wouldn't mind going too," Isaac put in.

"You know, there were tickets on sale, but now it's sold out, unfortunately. Although, wait a minute. I'll be right back." And she disappeared through a door with the words 'Staff only'.

Five minutes later she was back, with a colorful leaflet.

"There, take that. It's an invitation. We sent them out to some journalists and scientists, and a few came back because of the wrong address. This one is a spare. My gift to you."

"Why, you're absolutely fantastic!" Bikie exclaimed. "I'm almost in love."

"Go and enjoy. I see you're a nice guy too, maybe you will contribute to the system somehow."

"Superb! I definitely will!"

Isaac and Bikie couldn't believe their luck when they saw that the invitation was for two persons! That really improved their situation.

"Now," murmured Isaac, barely moving his lips, "counting Pellegrini, all three of us are inside already."

"Don't get too overjoyed," Pellegrini remarked when they left the laboratory and museum. "You and I have got guest passes. They don't give access to the basement where the server is. But don't get too downhearted, either," the commissioner continued ironically. "I've got the names of the people who have full-access passes, and their address."

Half an hour later the team assembled in Link's room, studying the faces of the people who would be going to the conference with a full access pass in their pocket.

"This is the plan," Link instructed. "I know the hotel where they are all staying, I've stayed there before. The central hall there is very convenient – you can see everyone coming in or going out. There are sofas and tables in the hall. You will position yourselves there, pretend to be engrossed in a conversation and wait for someone from the list. Follow him to see which room he is in. And gentlemen, I would rather not even pronounce the word 'steal', but that is exactly what you'll have to do with his pass."

Wasting no time, everyone set off to carry out the plan. At the entrance to the hotel Bikie bent down and picked up a little piece of blue plastic.

"Bikie, you're like a kid, picking up all sorts of bright colored garbage."

Bikie grumbled something to himself. If there were such a thing as a translator for grumbling, it would have produced approximately the following: "You are a little kid, you don't realize that I've picked up a room key card from the hotel. I would explain to you how it could be useful, but you wouldn't understand anyway."

They took up position on a sofa in the central hall. Bikie opened his laptop and started sharing his impressions of New York with Isaac. Pellegrini pretended to be listening. About half an hour went by. Isaac noted that the commissioner was poised like a pointing gun dog. Except that he wasn't nuzzling at the wind.

"Our first one," the commissioner whispered.

Isaac looked around at the front desk, where a man with a suitcase was checking in. It was Dr. Burgers, one of the conference participants. From the polite way in which he was spoken too, he seemed to be an important person. Isaac thought, regretfully, that he did not take the trouble to find out about the participants' achievements: to them Dr. Burgers was just someone with a full access pass.

Isaac turned towards Pellegrini, but the commissioner wasn't there: he had set off towards the front desk. No one but Isaac seemed to notice the way he walked past Dr. Burgers at the precise moment when the receptionist was handing him a blue key card and telling him how to get to his room.

Pellegrini came back and said curtly:

"Two, one, zero."

Burgers had taken room two hundred and ten.

"Let's wait for one more person before we leave." The commissioner's voice had a professionally commanding tone. That couldn't be helped. But this time his tone turned out particularly harsh. "This one is an Austrian. So he must be jet lagged. He'll settle into his room and probably won't leave it again until morning catching up on his sleep. Best to drop in for the pass when he's out. Tomorrow morning that is."

Bikie protested.

"One will be enough. I've got a little idea. You go on, I'll come out with Isaac later, so as not to create a crowd at the exit."

318

"Bikie, have you come up with something?" Isaac asked after the commissioner left.

"You bet! Look, the shift is changing. No one from the new staff has seen what the new guest looks like yet. And that's our chance."

"I don't get it."

"Watch and learn."

Bikie walked across to the attractive looking brunette who had just started working at the reception desk. He lowered his eyes shyly and asked with a slight stutter:

"Do you happen to have a charger for a phone like this? I've got an old model, it discharges quickly."

Bikie put his mobile phone, brightly colored in rock'n'roll style, down on the desk.

"Certainly we do. Are you a guest in our hotel?"

"Yes, I am. I'll leave the phone with you to be charged and go and get a coffee at the Starbucks nearby."

"Very well, certainly. Your name?"

"Burgers. Please, I'm so forgetful, can you stick the number of my room, 210, on the phone. If I forget it, just send it to the room."

"Yes, of course, Mr. Burgers."

"Oh, you're most kind!"

The girl smiled, pleased with the good start to her shift.

"Let's go and have a coffee," Bikie said when he came back.

He explained at Starbucks:

"Look Isaac, have you never noticed that the more brazenly you behave, the more timid people around you get? And vice versa, the more modest you are, the more aggressive others get. As if there is a constant amount of cockiness in the air, and if someone breathes in more of it, then others get less. But never mind that, the main thing is, if you act with self-assurance, other people will believe in you too."

"Bikie, why have you suddenly started talking like a business trainer on TV? What are you driving at?"

"Right now I'm not talking about training, you know. But about how I'm going to get the key to the doctor's room."

"And how's that?"

"You'll see. Just watch."

Bikie went back to the hotel, walked up to the same girl and asked for his mobile phone. Then, holding out a key-card, he added:

"You know, there's something wrong with this plastic card. It's probably demagnetized, it doesn't open the door."

"Just a moment, do you have any ID?"

"Not with me. I left it in the room." Bikie ran one hand across his breast pockets to illustrate.

"Hmm, well, not to worry. I'll reprogram it right now. Are you in two hundred and ten?"

"Yes, glad you remember me," Bikie said with a broad smile. "Although it's hard to forget someone who keeps annoying you with stupid requests, isn't it?" the pseudo guest asked, still flirting with the receptionist.

She smiled back.

"Here's your card. Enjoy your evening."

Bikie and Isaac went to the elevator, rode up to the floor where the doctor was staying, came back down and walked out into the street.

"Bikie, you say I'm lucky, but the real lucky dog here is you!" Isaac declared.

"Why is that? Psychology is neither more nor less than a science, Isaac."

"Bikie, just imagine if that girl had asked for some detail about Burgers."

"It was all covered, I have already read everything about that doctor and I know his full name and date of birth."

"You mean you were ready to state his date of birth?"

"Yes."

"Hmm, Bikie, did you realize that the professor you just impersonated is about sixty?"

"Oops…" Bikie laughed.

Later Pellegrini, who was least conspicuous and had most practice, sneaked into the room and collected the sleeping Doctor Burgers' pass.

Everything else was ready for the break-in. They'd have to figure out the test of the details on the spot.

15

Link declared that he had to be present at the moment of the break-in – it was essential in case of a technical problem. But he could be recognized, so this contingency had to be addressed using the art of makeup. Bikie and Isaac went to a little carnival costume shop in the Garment District to buy what was needed.

Isaac loved fantasizing on the subject of the past, and his imagination ran riot yet again.

"Bikie, imagine that the two of us are living in ancient times, I'm a great king, you're my advisor, and we're walking along the market stalls, surrounded by merchants, local people and out-of-towners, silks and yarns."

A big wooden armchair stood on a large stone podium right at the entrance to the shopping mall. A fat elderly gentleman was sitting in it, with a shoeshine man on a low stool in front of him, moving his hands briskly as he worked on the man's black crocodile leather shoes.

Pointing to the chair, Bikie declared solemnly:

"Oh King, there is your throne, it will be free very soon now."

"Oh my servant, look, your stool next to my legs is not occupied, either."

They bantered with each other all the way to the costume shop, where they bought a natural-looking beard, a wig and some makeup putty for altering the shape of the nose and cheekbones. Link would be unrecognizable.

As soon as they got back, Pellegrini told them he had a plan for getting the professor in without an invitation.

Evening started to draw in and Isaac went down to the lobby to call Michelle before it was too late in Monaco. She was glad to get his call. After hanging up the last time they spoke, she really didn't want to call first.

"You are cruel to me, Isaac" Michelle rebuked. "You could have phoned sooner. There's been no news from you for three days and I have been worried."

"Sorry, hon, I've been overwhelmed. These past days have been grueling."

"A call just takes two minutes! You really could have found the time."

"Well, I'm sorry. I'm just very tired. And not quite acclimated yet."

"How are things going?"

"Everything's fine. We're making progress. We're going to a conference tomorrow."

"Will it happen then?"

"Possibly. Depending on the circumstances."

"Good God, and I have to stay here, sick with worry! Isaac, please, can I come?"

"I love you, Michelle. But if you're here, I'll be distracted all the time, thinking about you."

"Well thank you so much for that!"

"Oh please, Michelle!" Isaac added in a pleading voice.

"I want to be there with you! It's my life, you don't need to make decisions for me. Why are you fussing over me like a nanny? I am twenty-five. I am an independent, grownup girl."

"Do whatever you like."

"I always act as I think fit."

"Michelle, I have to go. I love you."

"I love you too."

Isaac walked wearily back to his room. In the morning he had to call Vicky in the hospital. He kept forgetting that he could only do that in the morning because of the time difference.

An hour later there was a knock on his door. Isaac reluctantly got up and opened it. Standing there in the doorway was Michelle!

"Come in. I thought it must be you," chuckled Isaac. He really was very happy but tried not to show it, keeping a strict facial expression.

"I've been in New York since yesterday. But mind you, if you hadn't called first, I would never have come over!"

"And of course, Bikie gave away where we're staying?"

322

"He's not such a tedious dumb head as you are."

"I'm serious."

"I like you especially when you are that serious."

Isaac immediately relaxed, hugged Michelle close and kissed her.

"Thanks for coming." There was nothing else he wanted to say.

A long, tender kiss… How Isaac had missed that! He looked at her, as if trying to make sure he wasn't dreaming, like he did when they didn't yet know each other. There was a mischievous glint in her eyes. Keeping her eyes on him, with a gentle half-smile she started slowly unfastening the top buttons of her coat, under which … there was nothing. Michelle was letting him know very clearly what she wanted, but allowing him make the first move. After that he took over. As he removed his t-shirt, Isaac felt the ground slipping from under his feet. He was overwhelmed by an all-encompassing sense of adoration. Michelle was mind-blowingly sexy! "She is perfection – no, she's even better!" was the last thought that flitted through his mind before he was swept into a different dimension of passion.

Bikie and Link came down to breakfast later than usual. They had already adapted to New York time, no longer feeling like waking up at six in the morning, as they did the first few days.

Isaac ordered breakfast in his room. He didn't want Bikie to see Michelle, or he would torment Isaac with his comments. However, he still didn't manage to avoid Bikie's gibes – it looked like he and Michelle were in collusion from the very beginning.

Going down into the lobby five minutes before they were due to set off, Isaac found the whole team gathered, including Pellegrini.

"You owe me," Bikie whispered in his ear with a smile. "Something in chrome."

Pellegrini gave Link his final instructions, then turned to the others. His special-ops skills showed clearly. "After all," Isaac admitted to himself, "things feel calmer somehow with Pellegrini."

"So, you and Bikie enter here, through the separate entrance for those with invitations. Make sure you haven't forgotten them. Take your ID's. Then Link and I go in together," the commissioner continued in a confident tone.

Professor thought it over for a while and nodded.

"The conference starts at ten. Since this is the opening, there will probably be a delay for about fifteen minutes. There are always organizational glitches. It will be easier for us to blend in while there's a crowd. At 9:50 we all meet by the elevator."

"What about a pass for Link?" Isaac asked.

"I took care of that, don't worry. I made a colored copy of my own."

Isaac had time to call the hospital and talk to the doctor. Vicky was fine, she could regain consciousness at any moment. A promising way to start the day, although Isaac had been hoping to hear her voice before their plan was put in action.

They reached the museum, and leisurely walked inside. Link followed, Pellegrini was right behind him. Link held out his pass. He was asked about something and started explaining. At that moment Pellegrini pretended to stumble and shoved Link so hard that he almost went flying into the hall, and barely kept his balance. Some coins, a pen, a voice-recorder, scattered on the floor. Pellegrini immediately created a commotion, making fussy apologies, helped Link to collect things, accidentally on purpose dropped his invitation and police badge. He picked them up and apologized at great length to the ticket inspector, whom he had also caught with his elbow. Tugging Link's false pass out of the dumbfounded employee's hand, he handed it to Link, apologizing yet again. Spotting the commissioner's police badge, the inspector immediately calmed down. To be on the safe side, he also apologized because there was such a jam at the entrance. The crowd outside was swelling, and the inspector turned to the next visitor, trying to let people through quicker.

The incident was over, and Pellegrini took Link by the arm and offered to show him to the restroom and help him get tidied up. The inspector at the front door carried on checking newcomers.

Ten minutes later they all gathered by the elevator as arranged. They walked into the cabin and pressed the basement button. A little red lamp came on and Link pressed the stolen card against the terminal. The lift smoothly started downwards. Pellegrini was the first to the doors and walked out confidently. Link and Bikie followed him, with Isaac being the last.

They were all in for a disappointment: they saw a glass partition, a lounge with sofas, doors to meeting rooms. Nothing resembling a laboratory or a server room. Isaac ran the full length of the corridor twice before it was finally clear that they had arrived at the wrong place.

Pellegrini stopped a girl walking by, half-opened his jacket to show his badge and asked where the laboratory was.

The frightened staffer explained that they had to go down one more level, and they all darted to the elevator, which was still standing there, with its doors wide-open.

There was another button below "-1", but to press it you had to insert some kind of a key. Pellegrini pressed on the keyhole anyway, but the cabin didn't move.

"This pass doesn't have clearance to go lower. Only this far, to the meeting rooms," Link said disappointedly.

Suddenly the lift started moving, but, alas, upwards - someone had pressed the call button. The lift skipped past the zero, first and second floors and the doors opened at the third. Two elderly men and a security guard were standing on the landing. Isaac's heart sank into his boots.

"I'm sorry, we need to ask you to step out. This is the service elevator. Could you please vacate the cabin?"

They friends hurried out., with Link walking out with his head lowered, as if he was inspecting his shoes. The men got in and the doors closed.

"That was Blake, the UN Deputy Secretary-General," Link explained gloomily. "The one I handed over the technology before I went into hiding."

Meanwhile Pellegrini was counting something, looking down at the spiral walkway and the throng of people down below.

"What are you counting, Pellegrini?"

The commissioner ignored Isaac's question and carried on counting.

"They went down to minus two," was the answer he gave later. "Or rather, minus two and a half. Obviously the ceiling must be one and a half times the normal height. That's where we have to go."

"Right, Link, you stay here," said the commissioner, taking full control. The fact that only recently they didn't trust him had been quickly forgotten. All that was history. "Or better still, get away from here. You could be recognized. Who has the device?"

"I do," Bikie replied.

"I'm coming too," Link put in. "I have to be there."

"OK, you and Bikie go to the café and wait for our signal. "Isaac, go and mingle with the crowd and listen. Listen to everyone who looks like a local, an American. Follow what they're talking about. Look for people who work in the building. We have to find someone who has a card with lower level access. If you find one first, call me, I'll try to pinch one too. Bikie, Link, if anything happens, leave."

Isaac and Pellegrini ran downstairs and separated, getting lost in the crowd. Everyone was speaking English, but it was pretty easy to tell European English from American. Isaac listened intently to the conversations. People were swirling about and there was no way of telling to whom he had already listened and whom he hadn't. Isaac wanted to understand who was part of the museum staff and who wasn't. He tried to stick to those who had bodyguards or were not carrying briefcases. In his opinion, this meant that they could have an office in the building.

Suddenly, he heard a voice and looked round.

"What's going on here? He almost knocked an old man down at the entrance. Now he's run into the security guard!"

There was a commotion in the middle of the hall – it was Pellegrini who was causing it.

"He tried to lift my wallet," a security guard exclaimed indignantly.

Isaac tried to stick close and figure out what was happening. He couldn't tell what trick the commissioner had pulled, apparently an unsuccessful attempt to steal the security guard's key. In any case, everyone's attention was on Pellegrini now. A security official came over and asked the commissioner to go with him to the same elevator that Isaac and his companions were in only five minutes ago.

It was a total catastrophe. Most of the audience and the delegates have already entered the conference hall, the lounge has noticeably thinned out. Isaac saw Link leaving the Guggenheim. Three minutes later Bikie made his way through to the exit. It was pointless to stay any longer. Bikie had gone out, taking the device with him. Pellegrini was gone too, and Isaac was alone. There was nothing else he could do except move towards the exit, especially since, apart from the Guggenheim employees, there were no more than ten people left in the large lounge. He didn't feel like going into the conference hall alone.

16

Link hailed a taxi. Bikie got out halfway and set off on foot. Isaac also decided to walk: he was in no hurry and felt he needed to settle his nerves a bit. After all, at the final moment, luck turned its back on them and the operation failed miserably. Who knew what was happening to Pellegrini now? Isaac tried to reassure himself that they couldn't do anything to him. The security guard could have imagined it all, couldn't he? Ingenious as he was, Pellegrini would wriggle out of it, Isaac was sure. Besides, he was not linked to them in any way.

Only now, when Pellegrini was in danger, did Isaac start worrying about him and finally felt that he was a full-fledged member of the team. Any remaining traces of dislike and distrust were now a thing of the past.

Pondering over what questions the commissioner might be asked, Isaac, who admittedly knew nothing about the police system and how it worked, was probably missing lots of important details. Probably there were heaps of different ways for them to get caught. Starting with any paper trail that might have been left after his interrogations in France, and ending with the fact that Pascal, a Veggie, had flown to America.

Pascal's administrator could have suspected something; Link could have been caught on camera and identified. Or maybe Pellegrini himself had been under suspicion for a long time. It's great luck that the Agency does not even know that they are fighting against it. Surely with all their technology they'd catch them very fast. An hour later, when Isaac reached the hotel, he called Bikie.

"Everything's cool," Bikie told him. "Total calm at the hotel so far. Link and I are in a café on the corner of Madison and Fifty-Second."

"I'll be right there," Isaac said.

A few seconds later they were sitting together at an inconspicuous corner table in a small diner. They had coffee and the waiter brought sandwiches, but no one felt like eating.

"What are we going to do, Isaac?" Bikie asked. "Any ideas?"

At moments of danger and uncertainty like this, Isaac automatically found himself holding the reins again.

"Let's wait for Pellegrini first," said the professor. "Then it will be clear how badly our cover has been blown. Maybe everything is just fine, or maybe we need to flee."

Isaac was aware of Pellegrini's importance for the whole operation and his specific role in the team. Things really did feel a bit calmer with him around, he brought a definite core of strength by rapidly devising a detailed minute-by-minute plans.

"We have to get into level minus two, otherwise nothing is going to work. That's for certain. Today's the opening, the conference will be on two more days and then the museum will be operating as normal. There's no point in leaving New York. We can't get to the Russian and Chinese servers anyway, and the French one is no good. The only server we have any chance of getting to and hacking is here. So we can't despair. When we came here, we weren't counting on any conference and a week ago we didn't have Pellegrini either. Basically nothing has changed. We just have more information," said Isaac, trying to cheer everyone up.

"Have you any ideas about how to get into minus two?" Link enquired.

"No. But we still have time. Plenty of it. We have money. There are three of us, it's too soon to write off the Commissioner, plus there's Pascal in France, your assistant can come if need be. We can look for allies here. There are loads of options, we'll come up with something."

"We'll get overexposed at the Guggenheim very quickly if we go there every day," Bikie remarked. "It would be good to find someone on the inside who would help us. You could try working on that chick, for instance. She liked you."

"No, I'm not going to. She's not likely to have access the level we need, and I'm certainly not prepared to give her any assignment. I didn't spot any particular intelligence in her eyes."

Isaac got a brief text from Pellegrini, who wrote: "Everything's OK. Will be there soon".

"Excellent. The Commissioner's fine," Isaac gasped in relief. "Let's not make any plans until we've heard his news."

But the commissioner only called Isaac two hours later.

"Hello?" Isaac asked in the most casual voice he could manage. He was all set to add: "You have the wrong number".

"Everything's fine," he heard in reply. "Where do I go?"

"Madison and Fifty-Second. Starbucks."

Bikie looked up in surprise.

"There it is. Opposite," Isaac explained. "From here we have a clear view of the entrance. If he doesn't come alone, we leave."

"OK," understood Bikie. This handy and concise abbreviation immediately immersed in their vocabulary, just as they came to stay in an English speaking country.

Fortunately Pellegrini was alone. Bikie ran to Starbucks to fetch him and the commissioner told them what happened.

He had actually visited level minus two. Not for long, only half an hour, but long enough to get some info. He was taken to an office. There were no real problems, they only asked him a few questions and followed the standard procedures.

"Of course, I was outraged by the way security acted and the fact that I would miss the conference presentations," the commissioner told them. "In the end they let me go quickly and showed me to the conference hall. I had to stay there until lunch to avoid rousing suspicion. You know what, I noticed that the Agency greatly increased their security. This is not good. And some of the speakers looked as though they are the kings of the world."

"For the time, let's get back to business," suggested Isaac.

"All the signs say that our server is on level minus two. While they were taking me back, I asked to go to the bathroom. It was at the end of the corridor, so I examined almost half the level. That's definitely where we need to go. They download creativity there too, I saw a notice on the door along with some posters with instructions. That's in the left section of the corridor, looking from the elevator."

"Thanks, Commissioner! That's all very important, thank you, Luca." It was the first time Isaac had called Pellegrini simply by his first name. "Very useful information."

"Let's meet in the lobby this evening," Bikie suggested. "I'm tired, my head's on the blink. Want to take a walk."

Everyone agreed. They all wanted to be alone with their thoughts. Isaac remembered about Vicky. What a pity it was already evening in Monaco and he couldn't phone the hospital. Maybe she has already come round?

That evening Michelle wanted to come to see Isaac again and offer support. He wasn't in the mood.

"Isaac, why don't I book us a 'spa break for two'?" she suggested.

"OK. But not today. How about tomorrow?"

"There's a really good salon. You're bound to like it, you need a bit of rest and relaxation."

"A spa break for two? A good salon? So you've already been there?" asked Isaac, getting worked up.

"Good grief. Yes, I have! With a girlfriend! Don't wind yourself up. Why are you so edgy?"

"I implore you, go back to Monaco. The last thing we need is to fight." But after hearing about the girlfriend, Isaac calmed down and agreed to go to the spa.

The salon and spa really was magnificent, and Michelle in her short little robe was mind-blowing. They spent five hours there, and these were probably the best hours of Isaac's life. He had to hand it to Michelle – despite her shrewd petulance and a habit of doing everything her way, he thought he ought to trust this unwomanly passion of hers for making independent decisions.

17

The team spent a few days thinking about what to do next. The conference had been over for two days now, so that opportunity was completely missed.

Pellegrini's official trip came to an end and he flew back to France, promising to come back immediately as soon as he was needed. Isaac saw him off to the airport.

Pellegrini promised to promptly initiate paternity testing for Happies' children with creativity and they agreed to stay in touch. Isaac had no doubt that now the head of the Orange Energy Department was more concerned with how to defeat new criminals – COMUNA and *Collective Mind*, which meant, the commissioner's steel grip and proficiency have been channeled in the right direction.

Michelle also had to fly back to Europe on some urgent business. Isaac was upset. He missed her, but on the other hand, without a plan he was sullen and too intense, his mood wasn't conducive to a romantic relationship. On the contrary, he could spoil everything, as usual, so he thought it was for the best.

Pascal had already set something up in case there were problems. They decided not to discuss the details on the phone.

With no business at hand, Isaac decided to visit the Guggenheim again. He wanted to take a look at how it was on usual days, see how many people there were, and all the rest of it. The girl who measured orange energy recognized him again and enquired if he came back to download his OE, after all. Isaac replied that he was still considering it, just had a couple of problems to deal with first.

"Go for it, mister, with a fee as large as yours, I wouldn't think for long. It's simpler to offload your energy and forget all your problems. With a huge payout like that!"

Isaac stared at her, but didn't respond, just thanked her for her advice and strode quickly out of the museum. He had been struck by a sudden inspiration.

As soon as Isaac was out of the building, he called Bikie, with trembling fingers that could barely hit the right keys.

"Bikie! I got it! I have a plan! A plan! And it's simple – you won't believe it!" Isaac exclaimed joyfully. "I'll get a taxi and will be there in twenty minutes. Call the Professor."

"I'll upload my creativity!" Isaac declared triumphantly when they were all together.

He saw that they didn't understand anything, so he explained.

"When I go to upload my OE, I'll be right beside the server. I'll take the hacking device with me. We will install a timer on it, to activate it a little bit later. Since I'll be a Veggie, I'm not sure I'll be able to press the button! To keep it short, the device will hack into the server, and the OE I have just uploaded will come back to me. And to all the others."

The professor and Bikie looked at him with their mouths open. In their eyes he saw amazement and perplexity. And admiration too.

"Are you sure you're not putting us on?" Bikie asked.

"No, no spoof. All serious. How do you like the idea?" Isaac's voice sounded full of pep.

"Isaac, you're nuts. It could be very dangerous!" Bikie sounded shocked. "How do you know, maybe the reservoir is screened off somehow? What if the hack doesn't work? What if during the process there's an explosion?"

"No, the hack will work, and there definitely won't be any explosion," Link said calmly. "I guarantee that. It's an excellent plan. And the reservoir isn't screened, that's for sure. Why would they screen it and from whom? I'm not just talking theory. The experiment with Pascal worked, didn't it?"

"Then it's decided, and we start preparing," Isaac summed up. "Link, it's up to you to modify the device and install the timer. We'll register Bikie as my chaperone; I'll fill out the contract."

"Well, okay, let's keep the plan as it is. I agree. Only let's swap," suddenly said Bikie.

"Swap? With you? What for?"

"Well, think about it," Bikie explained. "If you're ready to do it, why shouldn't I be? There's a risk, but I consider it acceptable. I want to upload instead of you."

"But why do you want to, what's the point?"

"Well, you see... Let's put it this way... You know I'm poor. Even if we do finally complete our mission and they don't put us in jail... Pascal has a fortune. You have your anti-rain device; you'll sell it soon and get rich. But I still have nothing, the same as before, you know? Maybe we'll save the world – and then? I don't even have an apartment to live in. I want to earn something at the end of the day. I want money. And I see how to get it. I'll sell my OE. We'll cash the earnings quickly, the moment I sign the donor contract. And I'll be rich! I don't think COMUNA will go broke instantly because we hack in. My OE will come back and I'll still have the money. Like Pascal."

"Well, Bikie, you're certainly no fool," the professor said. "I'm for it."

Isaac thought about it. What Bikie said made sense. After all, in order to put the plan into action, it didn't matter who went to offload, he or Bikie.

"And, even if something goes wrong... I know you, Isaac, you won't stop and you'll never abandon me. Sooner or later you'll hack the system. So maybe I'll spend a year as a Veggie, so what? I'll never earn that kind of money in my life. I'll give you a couple of my contacts, reliable guys among hackers, they'll help out if need be. I'll write into the contract that I want to live near Paris and appoint you as my administrator. We already know how to snatch a single Veggie's OE from there. And if something goes wrong, it will be a lot harder without you to fix it. You're our main man, after all.

"And well, you see, to tell you the truth it's not even money. I want to know for sure what I am capable of. It's the first time in my life I went against the system. Before, I used to criticize, judge, ignore, but I still remained part of the system. Even when you came, I went with the flow, but the flow this time was yours. What I want to know is that I also can call the shots.

"It is easy to stay aside – no one will arrest you, you won't have problems with the police or at work. And you can hope that someone will do it all. But what if this someone just doesn't exist? It's you or no one. No nice guy is coming over to solve your problems. You or no one.

"You say: 'Tomorrow I'll become a revolutioner, liberator, Julian Assange. Tomorrow. I'll fix my computer, make some money, get better...' Always tomorrow. Assange is my hero. But I haven't been able to be like him, I guess, just not enough balls, that's it.

"He paid the full price, never was false, never had any excuses for tomorrow. He just did his stuff, no matter what, wasn't scared to go against the power of the States and their secret services. And I? I guess I would have never made up my mind, but with your help I got a chance. I even like the idea of some risk, it makes it all real, not like conquering summits on helicopters. That's why this victory for me will be not just ours, but mine. My Olympic gold medal.

"What a chance! Lady Luck smiled on me! Remembering my pervious achievements... all I did was getting into a fight twice. That's all! I have never gone to a demonstration, never spat at a drug dealer's face, haven't put a slob into his place, never kicked a sleeping cop. I was the one who created the world where I lived. Doing nothing, ignoring, letting it go, and got what I deserved.

"I never told you that I had gone to work in the bar as a bouncer in order to lighten my conscience from the weight of my own silence. As if there was real risk and drive... But this was a lie, an excuse. I never touched anyone there. Hey, that's Monte Carlo for you – there are no fights there.

"Uploading my OE will be my identification. My life's checkpoint. I want to do that. Even if this risk is not that big, I don't want to share it. It's mine. Well, you remember my dad got downloaded for heroin. I want revenge."

Bike was speaking disconnectedly, brokenly, repeating things again and again, and this made him sound more sincere. Everyone was listening in silence without interrupting.

"That's it. Wanted to tell you this because I respect you a lot. And you too, Professor," he finished.

"All right, Bikie," Isaac agreed. "Have it your way."

However, Isaac felt alarmed and sick at heart. He was prepared to risk himself, all right. But when it came to Bikie, he saw all sorts of dangers looming up. He still felt bad for Pascal and now it was hard for him to risk his other friend. His doubts whether it was rational to destroy the system returned.

"We'll prepare everything thoroughly, Bikie, and I swear I'll never abandon you when you are a Veggie!" Isaac pulled himself together.

The two friends hugged and Link felt slightly envious watching this firm friendship. He was famous and respected, but in more than sixty years of life, he'd never had a friend like this – as solid as a rock, to cover his back.

So now they had the simplest and least criminal version of a hack. Before this their thoughts had circled around different versions of a multi-stage invasion. Isaac had even theoretically considered an armed assault and taking hostages. But getting in to offload OE was a breeze.

They summed up the plan as Link went off to his room to assemble and test the timer. He had to buy an extra couple of small parts.

Isaac consulted with Wolanski on how to cash a check quickly, explaining that Bikie was going to sell his OE. It turned out there was no problem – it took ten minutes at the most and could be done from an ordinary phone. The banking system had updated its technologies following the rise of COMUNA.

Talking to Peter on the phone this time was much easier - they could get by without hints and code words. They planned their operation to take place three days later, so they could prepare for everything without rushing. In the end Isaac hinted to Peter that this time it would all be over. One minute thirty-two seconds – Isaac noticed that Peter didn't hang up as before.

Then Isaac dialed the number of the hospital. At last there was good news for him – Vicky was brought out of her coma!

He was not able to talk to her, she would not regain her speech fully for a couple of days, but they could already text each other. In his happiness, Isaac immediately called Pascal, who promised to deliver flowers and a phone to Vicky within an hour.

And even though it was not her voice but only a text, Isaac finally got the first words from her in six months. "Isaac, my darling brother, thank you. Come back soon, I miss you terribly!"

Isaac had tears in his eyes. It was good that Vicky could not see him. He blubbered like a little child as he sent her text after text with trembling hands, after waiting so long for her to be able to answer. She was alive and she was talking to him! Herself! His beloved little Vicky.

Bikie went out first thing in the morning and was missing almost the entire day. He said he was going to stroll around the city, drop into Central Park, have a beer and maybe pick someone up to round things off.

He felt like he was going in for surgery: he realized that they'd rescued Pascal, so it was all reversible, and even if everything didn't go right, there was still hope for him to return to normal in the future. But getting downloaded was still repulsive. What if his memory was totally erased?

Early in the evening Bikie pulled himself together, called Isaac, and they went to the museum, where they were shown to the familiar minus one level.

"Hello, I've come to fill out a contract," Bikie began briskly.

"Good evening", the manager said with a smile. "Have you already filled out the questionnaire?"

"I've even done the test already," Bikie said and took out the sheet of paper that was printed for him after the measurement in the museum. "Make a note please, that I will be accompanied by my friend, Isaac Leroy. After downloading we'll go back to our hotel, and then fly to Paris."

"Are you French?" the girl asked.

"Uh-huh. We can go back independently?"

"Yes, of course, there is provision for that."

"And can I make an addition to the contract?"

The girl picked up the certificate with Bikie's test results and raised her eyebrows in surprise. 49020. They didn't see that level of OE very often.

"What kind of addition?" she asked.

337

"One little condition. They have to give me the check before downloading. I've never held that kind of money!"

"That's no problem!" The girl smiled. Another weirdo here. Downloaders usually preferred a wire transfer to their bank account. But weirdness was pretty common among people with high levels of OE. You could never guess what eccentric ideas they would come up with.

All the necessary points, including payment of the fee by check were entered in the contract. Bikie signed it and one copy of the agreement went into his breast pocket.

Bikie went back to the hotel in an elated mood and invited everyone to his room.

"I can't allow the world to have one biker less, even for one hour," he began solemnly. "Who knows how all this will end? So I want to initiate Isaac as a biker!"

He took a scuffed, black biker jacket out of a plastic bag, along with a bandana with the words "Harley Davidson" and a bottle of Aniversario Venezuelan rum.

"A biker can't live without a motorbike, so there's a chopper as well. This kind for now!"

Grinning slyly, he took a silver key ring with a motorbike on it out of his pocket. Isaac laughed, but meekly went through with the ceremony.

"Isaac, you are worthy of being a biker. You might never have thought about it before, but you're a right-on guy and the spirit in you is a biker's anyway one, believe me. You've stirred up such a mess of trouble for the sake of freedom, right now I can't even believe it's real! No one would believe it if they were told."

Bikie poured rum for everyone.

"To Isaac and to bikers' traditions!"

"You are still the good old Bikie I know, even now! I am not sure about the traditions, but I'll make them up and stick to them," Isaac said and drained his glass.

Bikie gave Isaac a stern look.

"I meant, I'll learn them."

The rum was totally mind-blowing.

"The best I've ever had," Isaac remarked.

"Venezuelan," Bikie explained. "Discovered using the method of multiple trial and error tests. My favorite."

Isaac looked pretty good in the biker jacket.

"Never thought it would suit me so well... To bikers!" Isaac proposed, and everyone drank again.

Link was lighting up a big cigar on the balcony.

"Maybe I should quit smoking?" said the Professor when exhaling smoke.

"The important thing is not to give up drinking," Bikie put in, pouring the remaining rum into the glasses. "Professor, how come alcoholism wasn't cured?"

"There's a cure. Only nobody wants to use it."

"What a sobering thought!"

When the bottle was finished, Isaac went to his room. Three missed calls and a message from Wolanski on his French phone. Isaac dialed Peter's number.

"I got my inheritance!" Peter told him delightedly. "So I'm ready to hire you back again!"

"Congratulations! We'll have to see about the job. The day after tomorrow Bikie's going to download his OE. Today was his last boozing session. We tried once already, but it didn't work out."

"You already tried? But you promised to tell me when you went for it!"

"Sorry, Peter, I forgot."

"That's important! Okay then. Not a telephone conversation, I want to speak in person. Good luck. Everything will be fine."

"I hope so."

"I think we'll see each other soon."

"God willing."

Wolanski said goodbye and Isaac decided to have a chat with Michelle - alcohol had put him in a romantic mood.

The next day they relaxed and didn't do anything related to the project. Offloading with alcohol in the blood was against the Agency's rules.

Isaac spent all morning texting Michelle and Vicky.

Link brought the hacking device. He wanted to brief both of the guys, just to be on the safe side. During the previous attempt he was planning to do everything himself, this time Isaac and Bikie would have to operate it alone.

Link's hacking device was built into the housing of an old smartphone, which was rather bulky compared with the modern models. Pascal's compact amplifier easily fitted in there as well. The alarm function was used as a timer.

The hack did not beam back creativity itself, but it switched off the server's magnetic field temporarily. Creative energy sensed the magnetic field of its original owner and went back to that person, which only took about ten seconds.

Not knowing if it would be possible to switch on the hack in open view, Link had covered all the keys with tape, except for the "on and off" key. Isaac slipped the smartphone in his pant pocket, felt for the key and pressed it several times. It was simple and worked easily. Then Bikie practiced for a while. They did not know who would actually activate the timer, so both of them practiced how to do it.

Now they were fully prepared. However, Isaac still felt uneasy about Bikie becoming a Veggie, despite his friend's determination and Link's confidence.

It was something he couldn't help.

18

In the morning Bikie was awakened by a knock on his door.

"Who is it?"

"Link."

Bikie opened the door and saw the professor standing there, holding out a voice recorder.

"Here, take this with you. It might come in handy," said Link. "Hide it deep in your pocket."

"A voice recorder? A really cool one too! Like the one in the movie about Commissioner Jackson," Bikie tried to switch it on.

"No, no stop! Don't you press anything on it for now, it's not quite what you think, just your little insurance policy. This is just a mockup. I'll explain later. Better keep it in your jacket, or you'll lose it."

"Okay," said Bikie, shoving the recorder down deep in his pocket.

"Keep in mind that the hacker and this insurance policy both have to be on the minus two level!"

"Don't worry, I got it …"

"The floor and ceiling weaken the signals. So bear in mind that if you can't carry them in, we cancel the operation! Or you'll be stuck as a Veggie!"

"Everything's understood, Professor."

He was in no mood for discussing what kind of insurance policy this was. He felt too nervous about the uploading, because now it was his life that was at stake.

The professor insisted once again that the hacker and the safety-net device had to be on the minus two level. The device could only be activated there.

Link left and Bikie went to the bathroom, took a shower, trimmed his stubble and called Isaac's number.

"Hey! It's time, get ready and let's get going. I don't want to drag it out, it's getting to be too frightening."

Bikie and Isaac walked into the museum through a separate entrance on the left – a special one, meant for those who came to offload. One didn't have to buy a ticket there, just to present a picture ID.

Isaac put the phone aside and walked through the metal frame. Bikie followed. The metal detector started beeping. The security man looked at a monitor.

"Something in your jacket pocket."

"Ah, yes, sorry, a recorder," said Bikie, recollecting.

Isaac gave Bikie a quizzical look.

"The professor told me to bring it," Bikie replied in a low voice. "An insurance policy."

Taking back their things the friends went down a broad stairway and found themselves on the minus one level, at reception.

Bikie was assigned a staff member as an escort and told to go to the elevator. When Isaac set off after him, he was stopped. Bikie immediately stopped too, pulled out his contract and stuck it in the security man's face.

"He's with me. My chaperone. It's all in the contract." Bikie was all ready to blow.

The security man checked and let Isaac through. Once they were in the elevator, Bikie slapped his pockets twice, checking that everything was in place.

The doors opened at the much-anticipated level minus two. How simple! No metal doors or protective r-bar, no sub-machine gunners, no bulletproof vests. Of course, who would ever get the idea of attacking an orange energy server when there were at least three copies in other parts of the world?

Bikie tramped calmly along after the Agency man. They walked into a large, well-lit office, where a man in a beige doctor's gown was sitting with a young woman in white – a nurse or laboratory assistant. They seated Bikie in an armchair, with Isaac facing him on a sofa. The lab assistant quickly checked the donor's pulse and blood pressure and pricked his index finger.

"A trace of residual alcohol, within the normal range, no traces of drugs, all other signs also normal."

"Well then, we can get started. Do you wish to make any changes to the contract?"

"No," Bikie replied curtly.

"Isaac Leroy has been appointed your temporary guardian. Accommodation at the Versailles Fields boarding house in Paris."

"That's right," said Bikie, getting slightly nervous. "Get on with it."

"Here's your check. Congratulations, young man, you are extremely wealthy now."

Bikie glanced at the seven-digit figure on the neat little piece of grey paper. He gave a crooked grin and stuck the check in his pocket.

"Can you leave us alone together for a couple of minutes? To say goodbye."

"All right, take a moment alone," said the man in the beige doctor's gown. "But relax. You're not in any danger, it's absolutely safe and doesn't hurt at all. You'll still be a normal person, only with low creativity. Believe me, there's nothing terrible about that."

Seizing the moment, Bikie slapped his pockets again. The timer on the hacking device was set for thirty minutes, all he had to do was switch it on. Bikie handed the check to Isaac, closed his eyes and pressed the key.

The doctor in beige soon came back, accompanied by another colleague in a gown, who was going to carry out the downloading of Bikie's energy.

"Shall we begin?"

Bikie nodded.

They put a helmet on Bikie's head and connected several sensors to it.

"Let's roll!" Bikie exclaimed with affected gaiety.

Isaac took hold of his hand. His macho friend usually didn't like any signs of weakness, but this time everything was different.

"Start. Engaging the field... three, two, one," the man in beige counted down and pressed a button.

Even through the helmet Isaac recognized that melody. Bikie seemed to be asleep already. The whole downloading procedure took a minute at most.

"That's it. Now he'll sleep for fifteen to twenty minutes," the man in the beige gown said. "You can wait here or upstairs, on the sofas by the elevator. There's a no-charge coffee-machine and a cooler; please, feel free to help yourself."

Isaac thanked him and asked to be shown upstairs. Once he was alone, the first thing he did was cash the check and transfer all the money to Bikie's account. Then he glanced at his watch. Another ten minutes.

The elevator doors opened and out walked a member of the Agency staff and suddenly…..the Professor. Link has used the same makeup and costume as on the first day of the conference.

"There's his chaperone. You can wait here," said the staff member. "You know each other, don't you?"

"Yes, yes, of course. This is Isaac, my nephew's friend."

Isaac nodded.

"Link? How did you get in here? What for?" Isaac asked when the staff member left.

"I couldn't help it. It's all too exciting for me."

"I see. Sit down. Bikie's already been downloaded, they'll bring him here soon. How did you manage to get down to this floor?"

"I just waited for the first member of staff who approached the elevator. I told him I've just come from the railway station and got lost. Said I was the uncle of the donor being processed right now. They explained that there was a different entrance for that and checked that Bikie really was being downloaded. Then they escorted me here, straight from level zero, not driving the venerable old uncle around the street," professor winked.

Soon a lab assistant came to get Isaac and they went down to the downloading room on level minus two. Bikie had already woken up.

"Well, how did it all go?" Isaac asked him.

"Alright," Bikie answered with a feeble smile.

Isaac felt an unpleasant déjà vu of his conversations with Pascal the Veggie. A perfect copy. The lab assistants muttered something about not wanting to keep them.

"Of course, you still have a couple of minutes," one lab assistant said. "But you can wait as long as you like near the elevator next floor up. I'll show you the way."

"Thanks." Isaac glanced at his watch. He had to stretch this out for another seven or eight minutes. "Where's the restroom?"

"Along the corridor on the left."

Leaving Bikie in the room, Isaac went out, counted off eight minutes and came back. The lab assistant looked annoyed, but Isaac couldn't care less.

He slapped his friend on the shoulder and asked:

"Are you all right?"

"Yes, I'm all right," Bikie replied curtly, not showing the slightest sign of interest.

He was clearly still a Veggie...

"Let's go then," said Isaac, thinking about how to play for time. The elevator was already too close, but they couldn't leave level minus two no matter what.

Isaac stopped, retied his shoelaces and went on. Obedient Bikie tramped after him.

"It's all fine for him," Isaac thought nervously. "For him these minutes are simply passing by. But for me every one's like a year." Glancing at his watch, Isaac discovered that he'd gained another thirty seconds. The lab assistant was calling the elevator.

Isaac began creeping along the wall, already prepared to fall on the floor and act out a heart attack, clutching at his chest, but at that moment someone pinched him on the backside! He swung around – Bikie had a stone-face, but it was clear from his eyes and the corners of his mouth that he was struggling to resist laughter!

There hasn't been a power surge, the lights haven't blinked, in fact, there hasn't been any visible results of the hack at all. But by this time it must have happened.

"Did it work? But of course it worked! Why would a Veggie pinch anyone?" Isaac thought anxiously.

"We can manage on our own from here if you like," he suggested out loud to the lab assistant.

"No, I have to escort you up, that's the rule," said the lab assistant, walking into the elevator.

In the elevator cabin Isaac could barely restrain his joy. Could it really have worked? All they had to do now was cut and run.

Getting out on the level above the protected zone, the guys leisurely sat down on a sofa. Bikie pretended he didn't recognize the professor, but Isaac caught on quickly.

"Come on, don't you recognize your own uncle?"

"Yes, I do," Bikie replied in a theatrically feeble voice.

The lab assistant left without waiting for the mock relatives to embrace. He's done his job, the rest was none of his business. As soon as the elevator doors closed, Isaac sighed in relief and the professor sprang at Bikie.

"Well? Did it work?"

Before Bikie could even answer, they suddenly heard someone running down the corridor. Was it the police?

No, it was the girl from reception, and striding rapidly behind her was… Wolanski!

"Peter?" Isaac was astonished. "Is this a special day for surprises?"

"Is this man with you?" asked the girl. "He demanded to be let through to you."

"Yes, he's with us, thank you."

The girl left. Peter walked up to Bikie, ruffled up his hair and asked:

"How's things, old buddy?"

"Thanks, Peter, fine."

"Are you a Veggie?"

"No." Bikie grinned. "But there are cameras here, so be careful."

Peter held his hand out to the professor.

"Peter."

"I know who you are. I saw your photos at the villa," growled Link, reluctantly shaking the hand. He was clearly annoyed by Peter's sudden appearance. "Isaac, I don't understand the point of these unnecessary improvisations!" The professor did not try to conceal that he was angry.

"He didn't know either, Professor," Peter replied calmly. "I was going to arrive last night, before the downloading, but my plane was delayed slightly."

Wolanski intended to continue, but at this point Bikie got up.

"Maybe we should get out of here first?" he asked.

The plotters finally realized that it had all worked! Isaac and Peter exclaimed "Yes!!!" in unison and dashed towards their friend.

After hugging them, Bikie walked over to thank Link.

"Congratulations, Bikie, and please return the voice recorder that I gave you," the professor still looked agitated.

"Hang on, Link, let's get out…"

"Give it to me right now!" The professor's voice was far from friendly.

Bikie frowned.

"Right now? What's the problem, Professor?"

"Hand it over!" Link barked, taking a handgun with a silencer out of his briefcase.

"What are you doing, Link?" asked Isaac, flabbergasted. "Have you lost your mind? Put the gun away!"

"Give me the voice recorder now! There are plenty of cameras here, and I don't have time to stand here chatting with you!" growled the professor.

"No, I won't! What's in it? What kind of 'extra-insurance'?" Bikie's voice was firm.

Link coolly pointed the pistol on Bikie.

"It's merely a little copy of the latest database. Harmless, but it means a lot to me. The latest technologies that have been developed. It is the payment for my invention. And taking a bullet for it is very bad for your health. You can keep the hack as a souvenir. You never know, it might come in useful."

"What a bastard you are, Link! Now I understand why you didn't want to go to the police! You wanted to steal the technologies right from the start, you were just messing with me! We all took risks here for nothing! Bikie risked everything!" Isaac was absolutely furious.

"It's billions of dollars, you dope! And by right they're mine! What I said about the police was perfectly sincere, you idiot! Everyone wants money. Not only you, Bikie!" Link started losing his temper too. "Go running to the police, Isaac, if you're so smart. You have a good thousand living proofs now!" Then he turned to Bikie: "And you give me that copy, you blockhead, or I'll put a bullet through that tattooed noggin!" Link aimed the pistol straight at Bikie's head.

"I don't believe it's about money. What is it, Professor?" Isaac trembled from betrayal.

"It is knowledge, Isaac. A small portable server. Now it's filled with data and will help me continue my research, develop *Collective Mind*, create its advanced version. There is a pool of knowledge, which I lack to move on," the professor looked at Isaac with undisguised contempt. "Did you really believe that I will agree to destroy the great miracle that I've created? You two are narrow-minded idiots, who conveniently turned up on my way to help me achieve my goal. You will never become scientists with these approaches, inventing your little trinkets. And you can't see three steps ahead!"

"We ruined your miracle, grandpa God!" angrily interrupted Bikie.

"Well, well. Let's see," said the professor, moving the gun to Isaac's head. "Maybe I should shoot him first?"

Bikie wanted to turn to the professor, but Wolanski suddenly stepped in between him and Link, turning his back to the professor.

"Please, Bikie, hand it over. He was aiming at Isaac's head, so now he may be aiming at the back of mine. Hand it over for our sake," said Peter. "You're my friend. Give him the damned technologies, let him choke on them."

Bikie reluctantly handed the recorder to Peter.

"An attractive little gismo. Very stylish. But not worth dying for."

Wolanski turned to Link.

"Here, take it. And now clear out!"

"Brat! How dare you? You three are just three dumb heads, blind with hate, three inquisitors of science! Punks, who tried to kick the ass of evolution. Pathetic froggies! I've created the only possible safe artificial intellect, which has already saved millions of lives. You are just regular half-wits, you were nothing but the means at hand, like a taxi driver who brought me here, not more. COMUNA gave the world as many good things as God! Or more! It gave peace and happiness, created heaven on earth, here and now. Releasing the energy of these people you won't get anything – they will all come back, you'll see. Your lousy freedom is nothing but fighting for survival. Do you really believe this kind of freedom is needed? Your freedom results in wars for different spiritual values, material benefits. Order! That's what they need! Freedom is in order! Jerks!"

The professor mumbled something else and backed away into the elevator he called, still pointing the gun at them. When the doors have almost closed, he smiled sneeringly, swung his arm and tossed the gun into the corridor. It fell with a crashing sound, the silencer flying in one direction and the gun in the other. The pistol was not real. It was a plastic fake.

"Ah, you slime ball," exclaimed Bikie, kicking the doors.

"Let him go," said Wolanski. "The Professor is in for a little surprise too."

"What have you done?" Isaac cracked down on Wolanski. "That asshole tricked us."

"Bikie, Isaac, wait, it's all right. Here, take your voice recorder, Bikie. The professor took away a real one," said Peter, emphasizing the last two words. "I even recorded a greeting for him," Wolanski said with a smile. "Now we're definitely clearing out of here, and quickly!"

"Why didn't you say that the gun was a fake right away?" screamed Bikie.

"Shush! You're a Happy, remember? There are cameras everywhere. So I bought us some time until Link figures out that what he has is fake," calmly replied Peter.

Recovered from the shock, the false donors ran along the corridor to the exit. Not completely recovered yet, Bikie stumbled on the stairway and Isaac helped him get up. Outside, a car with a driver were waiting for them. As soon as they all got in, it drove away.

Bikie checked that he was still holding the professor's recorder. It was there, in his pocket.

"Peter, can you explain all this, maybe?" Isaac asked.

"In a moment," Wolanski replied, "Not here. Have you got anything in the hotel worth going back for?"

"Nothing special. The biker jacket that Bikie gave me. I have my passport with me."

"Bikie, how about you?"

"No. I'll buy everything new now. And a jacket for Isaac too."

"That's just great. Then we go straight to my place."

In the elevator Link held the recorder carefully. It was priceless! "That's strange, the keys are not taped over," he thought. And it looked absolutely new. He suddenly felt vague doubt. The screen indicated that there was one recording. "What the hell is this?" the professor swore and pressed the playback key.

"Hi, Professor," the recorder said in Wolanski's voice. "If you're listening to this, it means I was right. I have a piece of advice for you. It is better to be a heroic freedom fighter than a member of a terrorist group. I wish you luck!"

What sort of drivel was that? Link went berserk with rage upon realizing that he got fooled. The elevator doors opened and he saw the hall crowded with people. The professor tried to jostle his way through them to the exit, but suddenly a man standing beside him shouted:

"Look, it's Professor Link!"

Standing a bit farther off than the throng of journalists was the professor's red-bearded assistant. Link had summoned him a few days earlier and they were supposed to meet today. Redbeard watched what was happening helplessly, not knowing what to do. People were exulting, shouting, squealing. He watched red-faced Link, totally bewildered and frightened, being tossed in the air like a champ by the ecstatic crowd. Others were trying to squeeze through the crowd with microphones ready. How did they recognize the disguised professor, and who sent them here?

Having reached the famous Plaza Hotel, the car stopped. Peter asked the driver to wait for an hour and invited the friends upstairs to his room. He poured himself some water and finally explained everything.

"In my bedroom and all over the house, even in the grounds, there are lots of hidden video cameras," Wolanski began. "I wasn't intending to snoop on you. Well, sorry, maybe just to start with. I didn't really know you, it was just in case. After Amsterdam, to be honest, I never looked even once. But then an alert message was triggered, telling me you'd gone into my bedroom after all. I was angry, of course, but when I saw that it was Link himself, that you'd found him after all, I decided not to say anything. But I keep a few personal things in my bedroom, and it would have been unpleasant if Link found out about them. I watched the recordings once in a while to check that he didn't poke around into my chest of drawers. I also noticed that he always locked the door. That seemed strange to me. Anyway, I started spying on him.

"I'm not stupid either, and when I realized that the Professor was locking the door and working on two separate devices, but only showing you one of them, I concluded that he was doing something you might not like. They were connected in some way, he usually switched them on at the same time. Then I saw that he had bought a gun. I thought it was real at first. It really looks like it."

"Dammit, Peter, and I thought you were super-cool, but it turns out you knew the gun wasn't real?" Bikie chortled.

"Of course I did. How do you think he could have gotten a real one past the metal detector? Think about it!"

"Hell knows. He's a smart guy."

"Damn the gun anyway. In a situation like that, no one could tell it was a toy. Anyway, I had no more doubts: he hid the second device too carefully before he left the bedroom. And then he stuck the gadget in the casing of a voice recorder. Sure, I couldn't make out what the device was, but I bought a recorder exactly like his just in case."

Isaac got a kick out of listening to Peter. It was a real pleasure to deal with intelligent people. Yes, Isaac had screwed up a bit and was too trusting. But did he really have any choice?

"So then it was important not to miss the day when you went for the hack. Hanging about with you in New York was too dangerous, given that you had already dragged a policeman, bound hand and foot, into my home.

"I decided not to put you in the picture about that," explained Isaac. "That way, if anything went wrong, you could wriggle out of it. Who knows, they could have used some kind of a lie detector. But that way, you were clean."

"Isaac, you frightened me so badly with your secrecy and your coded telephone conversations that I couldn't even share my thought about Link with you. And you also forgot to warn me about the first attempt. You should be grateful it didn't work out and we have the 'voice recorder' now." He remained silent for a while, then added: "And I actually wanted to do it myself".

"Peter, you are super," Isaac smiled delightedly. "But I must admit that I was more concerned about hacking into the system and giving the Veggies their energy back. If Link happened to steal something from the Agency in the process, I couldn't give a damn. They're no friends of mine. Although, of course, it's a pity the Professor turned out to be such a lowlife. He deserves a good lesson for that!"

"Oh, you still haven't heard the end of my story. I took care of that too. I made a few calls to various editorial offices and told them Link would be at the American branch of the Agency in the former Guggenheim Museum. As proof I even sent them a photo from my web camera. I knew he would be in disguise, but someone would recognize him anyway."

"And what if he hadn't been a traitor?"

"Then he would have gotten away through the side entrance with us," shrugged Peter. Then he glanced at his watch and added: "By the way, it's time we got out of here. Link most likely knows that he took a fake. We're going to the airport. I've already bought tickets for the flight that's leaving in two and a half hours."

"Peter, but how did you know the Professor would leave on the elevator?" Isaac enquired.

"I didn't. But it's quite logical. He's not twenty years old, to go running along corridors. But even if he had, it would make no difference. To hell with him anyway."

In the car, Isaac admired the city again. If everything worked out, he would be back here soon. With Michelle and Vicky. And maybe with Pascal, Bikie and Peter. But right now he wanted to go home.

Epilogue

At the airport the incredible news was showing on all the channels on all the screens. People thronged round the monitors. Everywhere it said "Breaking News", "Professor Link Found", "Scientific Genius is Back", "Rioting Breaks Out in Veggie Colony in Queens", "Happies Make Shocking Claims".

Bikie and Isaac craned their necks and watched the reports along with everyone else, their eyes glued to the screens. "Happies Riot in Brooklyn and Staten Island", "COMUNA Does Not Comment", "Professor Link's Press Conference Set for 5 p.m."

"At the very least we totally liberated New York," Bikie whispered contently.

"That's for sure. Today, we're definitely the world's newsmakers. When we get home we'll celebrate big time!"

"I wonder if Pascal, Michelle and Pellegrini are seeing this."

"You bet they are!"

Bikie turned towards Isaac, lowered his eyes and said in a guilty voice:

"You know, I wanted to tell you something. I hope you'll understand… I'm not flying out with you two, Isaac. I'll come back, but not straight away. Michelle's waiting there for you, and Vicky. You won't have any time for me right now anyway. And I want to breathe the air here for a while. I'm loaded now. Yesterday I went into a Harley Davidson store and there was this real blast of a machine there! I want it. Since I am in the States and I am rich, I'm going to buy that beauty and ride right across America. I can even meet the local boys and ride with them for a while. I'll drop into Chicago and Vegas. I'm sure you understand, little bro. It's an old dream of mine, and I don't want to put it off any longer. The future is unpredictable, you know."

Isaac gave Bikie a hug.

"Good luck, Bikie. I'll tell you honestly, I will miss you. Hanging with you was cool and great fun. Stay here. Of course, I understand. And while you are at it you can hide Link's legacy somewhere good and safe. It's not safe to fly with it." Isaac gave the devices to his friend.

"Good luck to you too, Isaac. Of course, hanging with you was pretty boring, not heavy, but..." Bikie smiled. "Ah, to hell with these wisecracks! It was awesome! I'm even sorry it is over!"

The guys hugged each other again and walked off in different directions.

Isaac looked out the plane window. He most likely changed the world by turning it back to normal. After this, COMUNA would be a matter for the police. Let them now deal with the Agency, and the millions of Veggies all around the world. Isaac's team has produced what was most important – enough evidence to put an end to the whole thing.

He recalled the news reports: the amazement and horror of the newly awoken Happies, the bewildered policemen, Professor Link, the spokesman of the Agency. Many of the former Happies wept, some from happiness and joy, others from grief at losing years of their lives.

Yes, the world will become more dangerous, but it will be itself again. The best minds would now understand the true value of their lives. After their fortunate rescue, they would never again agree to become Happies. It was as if some huge plane crashed and everyone survived. They have all been given a second chance, and they would not blow it.

It was good that Pellegrini was on top of everything. Let them decide what to do now, when and where to summon Isaac, Bikie and the main witnesses – Pascal and Link. How everything would be done – through an urgent session of the UN itself or some other international organization – was none of Isaac's concern. The important thing was that COMUNA and OE downloading would be stopped forever.

Isaac felt unusual pleasant lightness. Vicky would soon be completely well. In a year, at most, he would earn some money from his invention and buy a decent place to live – he couldn't hang about at Wolanski's place forever. Isaac felt different, new somehow. In the last few months he acquired true friends, one of whom he brought back from the past by plucking him out of the quagmire of the "time machine". But the most important thing was that he has won. And his victory made him worthy of a girl he would never even have dared to approach – the beautiful Michelle Blanche.

He was not worried about Link's sinister prophecies – he was just an old man, protecting his creation with his head off. Not a single idiot will come back to COMUNA, that's for sure. Maybe he was right and this type of artificial intellect was the safest. But did people need it? The world had been living without it. True that people died from diseases and in wars, but they have been advancing. Freedom is worth more than a warm bath. You get tired of the warm bath one day. The idea is to have goals and chances to achieve them, so people need to be able to make their own choice. Isaac caught himself still mentally arguing with the professor, which made him feel a little uneasy. "Inquisitors, war" – those words were firmly stuck in his head, like a splinter. No, the person who gives you your choice back can't be considered an inquisitor, by no means. "Wars for different spiritual values" was very well said by the professor. That was what happened between them.

"Well, after all, victors are never judged. People should have the freedom of choice." He recalled the old saying, feeling tired of these thoughts.

Somewhere on the top floor of a Manhattan skyscraper, in the setting of a luxurious penthouse, the artist Andrei Sharov, an ex-Veggie, was sitting on his expensive sofa. He felt like having a drink, but there wasn't anything. He sat there, turning his head stupidly from one wall to another. Hanging on the walls were high-quality reproductions of his pictures, which he remembered having sold to the owner of a little restaurant. Lying on the tables were brightly colored catalogs and magazines with articles extolling his talent.

A woman he didn't know, who said she was there to look after him, explained that it was his apartment, and he has been living here for four years.

The artist simply couldn't believe that he was so rich and famous. He thought he must have gone crazy, or it was all just some beautiful dream.

Original version edited by Maya Azbukina

English language translation by Andrew Bromfield 2015, Sofia Bakhurina, Dina Kunets

Edited by James Gregory

Production by Maya Azbukina

Cover design by Vasily Klyukin

Cover Illustration by Michael Tsaturyan

www.ingramcontent.com/pod-product-compliance
Lightning Source LLC
Chambersburg PA
CBHW072116250626
47159CB00007B/2476